# Channeling

# Morgan

## ALSO BY LEWIS DESIMONE

*Chemistry*

*The Heart's History*

# Channeling

# Morgan

## Lewis DeSimone

*Beautiful Dreamer Press*

Beautiful Dreamer Press
309 Cross St.
Nevada City, CA 95959
U.S.A.
www.BeautifulDreamerPress.com
info@BeautifulDreamerPress.com

Paperback Edition
Printed in the United States of America

ISBN: 978-0-9981262-4-1
Library of Congress Control Number: 2017941388

Cover design by Tom Schmidt
Front and back photography by Dot
Author photo by Dot

*for Gerry*

"It is Fate that I am here," persisted George. "But you can call it Italy if it makes you less unhappy."

—E. M. Forster, *A Room with a View*

# CONTENTS

## Part 1
### Provincetown

## Part 2
### Manhattan

# Channeling

# Morgan

# Part 1

# Provincetown

# CHAPTER 1

## A View of the Room

It all began with the room. Location, they say, is every-thing.

"It's not the same," Chris said, hoisting his overstuffed suitcase off the floor. "Not the same at all." Landing danger-ously close to the foot of the bed, the suitcase sent the mattress into wavelike shimmers. He had picked the bed closest to the window and now stood peering out at the world.

"It's a perfectly nice room," Derick countered. He placed his own bag more delicately onto the remaining bed, unin-terested in a territorial dispute.

"But we're missing all the action," Chris said. From Chris's profile, Derick could see the characteristic squint and pursed lips that signaled refusal to admit defeat. "If we had a room at the academy, we'd be in the thick of things. This is practically the suburbs."

The workshops had more spaces than the academy had dorm rooms, so housing was done on a lottery system, and Chris and Derick had lost. Fortunately, the academy had a connection at the bed-and-breakfast down the street, so they hadn't had trouble getting a reservation, despite the fact it was high season.

Derick opened his bag, its large plastic zippers like the maw of Audrey II. "It's three blocks away, Chris. We won't miss a thing."

"You don't know what these events are like, Derick. It's all about networking—the person you meet on your way to brush your teeth could be the one who makes your career." Chris turned around now, arms folded before his chest.

"Well, I'm going to make the most of it," Derick said. "We should be glad we got into the workshop at all. It's not as if they accept everyone, you know."

Chris rolled his eyes. "Making lemonade already?"

"No," Derick said, unfolding an orange wool sweater and wondering why on earth he had thought it appropriate for Provincetown in August. "I'm just trying to focus on the positive."

"Good for you. Optimism has never gotten *me* anywhere. It's not about how you feel any more than it's about how good you are. It's about who you know and, in this case, who you run into at the sink. Mark my words, at this very moment some untalented so-called poet from Poughkeepsie is lending deodorant to an editor from Knopf, thereby guaranteeing a book deal that makes his career."

Derick laughed. "Who's the last poet you ever heard of who sold more than a hundred and fifty copies?"

"You know what I mean. Novelist, then. I'll bet you ten to one Danielle Steel got her start by lending the right person her lipstick in the ladies' lounge at Le Cirque."

"I'm not here to meet Danielle Steel," he said. "I'm here for the work."

"Idealist," Chris sneered, eyes gleaming.

"Cynic."

Derick decided to concentrate on unpacking. He couldn't help thinking Chris's mood had less to do with their accommodations than with what he'd left behind in New York. It had been barely a month since his breakup with Brian. Not that it was surprising for the breakup to coincide with this trip: Chris's life had a way of conspiring to heighten the drama.

"If we're going to be relegated to the servants' quarters," Chris said, standing guard at the window again, "we should at least be afforded a view. What, I ask you, is that?"

Finished unpacking, Derick flopped his suitcase shut and

joined Chris on the window seat. "I think it's called Cape Cod Bay." He pointed over the roofs of the buildings across the street.

"But it's behind everything," Chris said. "You can barely tell we're in a seaside town." He bit his lip in resignation. "At least we're still on Commercial Street. They could have put us in the hinterlands of the West End."

"I'd prefer the West End, actually," Derick said. "It's so noisy here at night. How are we supposed to get any work done, let alone sleep?"

Beneath the window, Commercial Street was bustling, a parade of people marching in both directions. In the distance, the bay was flat and smooth, a fact he'd been grateful for on the ferry from Boston. Since he'd forgotten to buy Dramamine, those could have been the most agonizing ninety minutes of his life.

It was Chris's turn to unpack. As Chris glided a gauzy shirt onto a hanger, Derick could see the armoire was already bursting, Chris's things squeezing his own into the far corner. "We're only here for a week," Derick said as Chris finished with the armoire and moved on to the dresser. "How much stuff did you bring?"

"You never know," Chris said, smoothing the folds out of a bright red tank top. "I like to have at least two outfits for each day, plus a little extra."

"How should we dress for tonight?"

Workshops began the next day, so everyone was expected to be filtering into town today. Tonight's calendar held only a welcome cocktail party. Having never attended anything like this before, Derick had no idea what to expect. He was frankly glad to be lodged apart from the rest. The potential intimidation factor was high. He might need the sense of escape the inn provided.

"I'm sure it's quite casual. But one does want to be noticed." Chris held a silky shirt against his chest, modeling it like Wayland Flowers doing the tango with Madame. He dropped his head to one side and cast Derick a maternal look.

"You really have to get over this anxiety, my friend. If you want to have any kind of success as a writer, this is what you have to do. And it's fun. Writers are fun people."

"Present company excepted, of course."

"Of course." Chris pulled his shirt off over his head. His dirty blond hair was standing up in every direction now—unintentionally, for once—making him look charmingly boyish. "I'm going to take a quick shower," he added, removing his shorts and heading for the bathroom. "Don't leave without me."

"No danger of that," Derick said as the door closed.

His anxiety about the workshop surprised him. He wasn't a novice. He'd been writing professionally for years now. His byline appeared regularly in local and national magazines, though the uncredited work paid most of the bills. In any event, he spent more time looking for work than doing it. And the unfinished novel he'd toyed with since college sat idly in a box on the top shelf of a bookcase, its adolescent whining unfit for human consumption. Novels were untamed, messy things with lives of their own. Derick wanted to start over, start small, with something he could control. He'd turned one of the chapters into a short story, and, happily, it had been good enough to get him accepted into this program. But still, he had no idea what to expect from his colleagues. For all he knew, he could find himself in a room full of incipient geniuses, and his fiction career would be over before it had begun.

Eagerton Academy was an upstart organization in a town already well known for artist colonies. In business for only a couple of years, it had put itself on the map primarily by throwing money at prestigious teachers. Nobody was hotter this year than Graham Whitcomb, leader of the fiction class.

It was only one workshop—a week of sitting with a group of other writers, chatting about literature all day, maybe making a new friend or two. At least it was a chance to escape New York humidity for a week.

Derick watched the street as the water continued to run in

the bathroom. The sky had just begun to darken, the colors of the scene sharper now without the glare of the sun to bleach them. The crowd seemed to get thicker by the minute, as if the ferry was constantly spilling people into town.

Steam poured into the room as Chris opened the bathroom door. Clad in a white towel, he was cleaning his ear with a Q-tip, head cocked to one side. His abs were taut, his torso surprisingly tan for someone who spent so little time in the sun. It must be the Italian blood, Derick thought. With his own wan English genes, his only choices were white and fricasseed.

When Derick emerged from the shower later, Chris was standing in front of the mirror, adjusting his shirtsleeves. He smoothed the fabric, tucking it firmly into his jeans to keep it tight against his chest. The pressure made his nipples poke through like rivets.

Derick dressed more quickly. He had less to prove. For him, this trip wasn't about conquering the world, literary or otherwise. He was here to learn, to focus for once. His life wasn't about ambition of any kind these days, and that was just fine with him.

When Chris was finished deciding how many buttons to leave undone on his Donna Karan shirt, they headed for the academy.

The inn was silent as they made their way downstairs, the other residents, perhaps, just winding down their visits to the beach or the shops, not quite ready for dinner. They passed through the quaint living room, an epidemic of chintz, and headed out.

Derick pushed against the door, and it opened with an unexpected jolt. Stumbling, he found a man on the stoop, his hand on the knob, in mid-pull. Long dark hair swaying before his face, he smiled awkwardly through a Sonny Bono mustache.

As the man pulled the hair off his brow, Derick caught a familiar glint in his movie-star blue eyes. From a distance, he imagined, the hair would hide the sharp lines of his cheekbones, the perfect proportions of his face, the faintly pink skin. And there was no disguising the muscular chest, the slender hips. Derick felt like he should be embracing an old friend, but something about this guy wasn't quite right.

"Pardon me," Derick said. He stood aside and let the man pass.

They joined the flow of foot traffic just as twilight was settling in, the air cool and welcoming. They made their way slowly to the West End, where the kitschy shops gave way to art galleries and quiet residences, classic Cape Cod houses with worn shingles and faded white trim.

The academy was housed in a surprisingly squat building on a side street, far from the hurly-burly of Commercial. Derick's stomach did a cartwheel as they approached. He flashed back to the art gallery openings his sister routinely dragged him to—opportunities to stare at indecipherable splashes of color on a wall and pretend to say something intelligent about them, if only because the artist herself might be standing behind you. He had survived such evenings thanks only to the free wine, so tonight he intended to head directly to the bar.

But first he had to get through registration.

"Welcome!" cried an overweight woman behind the table as soon as they entered the lobby. "Welcome to Eagerton. Are you in one of our workshops?"

"Yes," Chris said, affecting his party smile. He marched toward the table. "Graham Whitcomb's fiction workshop."

"Of course," said the woman. "Name?" She positioned her fingers over a cardboard box full of envelopes on the table in front of her, ready to riffle through it.

"Prince. Christopher."

The woman nodded solemnly and reached toward the end of the box. "Here we are." She handed Chris an envelope, then turned her smile expectantly toward Derick.

"Sweetwater," he said. "Derick." Saying his name backward made him feel like he was in the military or MI6.

She skimmed through the envelopes and suddenly

stopped, flummoxed. "I don't have a Derick," she said, scowling. She paused. "Frederick?"

He frowned. "That'll do."

As he opened the envelope, the woman said quickly, "There's a lot of useful information, including the location of your workshop and a general schedule of events. But the most important thing right now is the lanyard." She arched her back and raised her eyebrows, as if to see inside the open envelope. "It's in there somewhere," she added with a laugh.

Derick pulled it out. He hadn't been counting on a name tag. There it was for all the literary world to see: Frederick Sweetwater. He felt his face reddening already.

Chris draped the lanyard around his neck and led Derick into the next room. The space was more cramped than he had expected, no bigger than a large living room, with a few dozen people milling about mostly solo, trying to discreetly read other people's names off their chests. A few were gathered in small groups around high tables, talking loudly over plastic cups of wine.

"He's not here yet," Chris said, scanning the room.

"Who?"

"Whitcomb."

"Any other familiar faces?"

For a moment, it seemed Chris hadn't heard the question. "Vaguely," he said at last. "You see people here and there, but sometimes you just don't know."

Derick laughed. "The literary equivalent of gay bars. 'Pardon me, have I bought you a drink before?'"

A shockingly young, shockingly thin man sauntered toward them, his posture an apparently deliberate effort to hide a natural slouch. One hand grasping a white wine, he extended the other toward them.

"Ashton Bainer," he said, in answer to a question that hadn't been asked. "I'm in Vanessa Haverstock's poetry workshop."

"Chris Prince." And the bright smile flashed. Whenever Chris did that, Derick found himself wondering just how many teeth he had.

"And Frederick?" Ashton said, releasing Chris's hand and reaching for Derick's.

"Derick, actually."

Ashton's hand was soft, the fingers bone-thin and bending immediately with the pressure of Derick's palm.

"I really should get a Sharpie or something," he said, "and X out the first few letters."

Ashton laughed politely. "So who are you working with?"

"We're in Graham Whitcomb's workshop," Chris offered.

"Really?" Ashton said. "I worked with him at Dayton."

"Did you? And yet you've switched to poetry?"

"It's not a switch, really. I've always done both. They feed off each other, of course."

"So what was it like," Derick said, "working with Whitcomb?" He still felt woefully unprepared to be scrutinized by a prize-winning novelist.

"It was amazing. I learned so much. Amazing people. Lindsay Poole was in our class."

"Really," Chris said, deadpan. He was clearly as unfamiliar with Lindsay Poole as Derick was.

"What are you working on?" Ashton asked.

"I'm putting the finishing touches on a collection of stories," Chris said. "My agent is anxious to get it out there, but she says it needs just a few more pieces. So I thought I'd try one out here."

"Oh, you have an agent! That's great. Have you published any of the stories?"

"A couple," Chris said. "Literary journals mostly."

Derick found himself staring at Ashton's wine. "Where did you get that?"

Ashton pivoted his head. "Back there," he said, pointing vaguely.

"Thanks," Derick said. "I'm parched."

"Hold on," Chris said, "I'll join you." He turned back to Ashton. "Very nice to meet you."

Ashton glided softly past them, as if he'd been intending to all along.

"Liar," Derick said with a laugh.

"What?"

Derick sneered. "The agent. The brilliant story collection."

"What? I should tell him I'm writing a mystery novel and have never published a thing in my life?"

"But you *are* writing a mystery novel, Blanche, and you *have* never published a thing in your life."

"Well . . ."

"And Dayton? Really?"

"What's wrong with Dayton? It's the most famous MFA program in the country."

"And they produce pretentious twits like Ashton."

"Oh, Derick, I thought you were a professional."

"I'm a professional journalist. This is another world."

"If you want to be a serious writer, you go to Dayton. Everyone went to Dayton."

Everyone might have gone there, Derick thought, but it seemed that only one person ever emerged, a single voice that they all shared. The Dayton voice was humorless, adjectiveless, actionless, emotionless. He knew he was supposed to like it. The *New York Times* liked it, the *New Yorker* liked it. But after reading the twelfth novel from the twelfth author in which a working-class protagonist from a nondescript Midwest city did and learned nothing for two hundred pages, he had had to stop.

"I want life to be my teacher," he told Chris, "not some factory."

"Life can take you only so far," Chris retorted, looking around the room. "Then you need connections."

Chris opened his eyes wide, as if he'd just spotted an old friend, or someone he wanted to turn into a friend. "Speaking of which," he added and dashed away.

He was probably expecting Derick to follow, but Derick needed sustenance first.

The crowd grew thicker as he approached the bar. He squeezed past Vanessa Haverstock. He didn't follow contemporary poetry, but she was hard to miss. Thanks as much to her luxurious chestnut hair and runway model face as to her art, she had become a media darling in recent years. Even in person, she was striking, green eyes suggesting a fierce intelligence, lasers cutting to the core of whatever she saw in the room.

Most of the others were clearly students—the eager, the anxious, the distinctly insecure. They ranged in age from early twenties to well past retirement, the older ones in sport coats or sensible dresses, the younger uniformly in black from head to toe, with scowls to match.

When he finally made it to the bar, he had exactly two choices: white and red.

"Red wine, please," he said to the bartender. "Unless you have some Scotch hidden back there."

The bartender chuckled, sharp dimples carving a mid-point in his cheeks. He was around Derick's age, maybe a tad younger. No doubt, this was merely a gig to see him through a Provincetown summer. At a New York party, the bartenders were all frustrated actors, never knowing which guest might be the one to discover them and pull them out of Lana Turner hell. But the chances this delicately handsome guy was a writer, Derick thought, were quite slim. No wonder he seemed so relaxed beneath that tuxedo shirt.

"Unfortunately not," he said. "On the other hand, this town is full of places that can accommodate." He winked. "And the party shuts down at nine."

"Thanks," Derick replied. "I needed that." He didn't feel obliged to point out he was referring to the reality check as much as the drink.

The bartender broke into a toothy smile that softened his square jaw. Derick couldn't tell if he was flirting or just amused by the ambience. As the crowd closed in against the table, the bartender quickly turned to the next customer, one hand on a white bottle, the other on a red.

Derick headed for the safety of the far corner but was waylaid as he passed a couple hovering beside a table. "Good evening," said the man, white hair belying smooth skin. "How are you?"

"Fine, thanks."

He was about to pass when the woman, voice arching over the crowd, asked, "Which group are you in?" Her smile was pinched, as if her lips were glued shut, able to open only to let words out. "Whose workshop?"

"Graham Whitcomb."

"Oh," said the woman with a sigh, "I love him! I wanted to work with him, but apparently his workshop was full up by the time I applied."

Derick matched her tight-lipped smile. Placement was competitive, not just time-sensitive. But whatever floats your boat. Something about being with all these writers was bringing on an addiction to cliché. Or maybe it was just the size of the drink, which he had already half finished on his way across the room.

"What do you write?" the man said.

"I'm sorry?"

"Mystery?" prompted the woman. "Romance? Thriller?"

"Umm, I don't know," Derick said. "I don't think in those terms."

"Oh," the woman said with a dip of her head to the side. "You must be one of the 'literary' ones." She pronounced the term with something more than air quotes. More like rubber gloves, Derick thought, as if it were a virus she most assuredly did not want to catch. "I write romance myself. Proud of it. You'd be surprised how big the market is for a well-written romance."

Derick wondered if she knew what an oxymoron was.

"Well," he said, gesturing with his glass, "I really should get back to my friend."

"Of course," said the woman. Her companion nodded with a scrunched chin and a somewhat dazed look as Derick backed away.

On his way toward obscurity, he spotted a buffet table at the side of the room, beneath a purple banner reading, "Welcome Writers!" The *W*s intertwined, highlighting the unfortunate lack of alliteration.

In any event, there was cheese.

He was stacking a slice of Gouda onto a Triscuit when someone jostled him. A feminine hand appeared before him, reaching for the crudité.

"First time?" the woman asked, scooping a baby carrot into the dip. She was a head or so shorter than Derick, her hair a black bob that swayed in front of her eyes as she leaned forward.

"Pardon me?"

She swirled the carrot in her raised hand to keep the dip from dripping onto the floor. "You're wearing that look that says, 'What am I doing here, and who the hell are these people?'"

Derick laughed. "Are you a writer or a mind reader?"

"Is there a difference?" She bit into the carrot with a loud snap. "I've just been to my share of events like this. Everyone trying to wear their bona fides on their sleeve so the rest of the crowd knows they belong. It can be a little intimidating at first."

"That's one word for it."

She loaded up a small paper plate with a few more vegetables and spooned a puddle of dip beside them. "We'd better get out of the way," she warned. "Writers are hungry people. It's that starving-in-a-garret myth. This table will be cleared in five minutes."

Derick loaded up on cheese and followed her out of the crush.

"Don't worry," she said, "it gets better once the actual work begins. Right now, it's all just posturing. Tomorrow, the truth comes out."

"Along with the claws?"

She pursed her lips cynically. "You'll be fine," she said. "I can tell."

"Really? Do I look like a brilliant writer?"

"Excessively," she said, shaking her head with a William F. Buckley swagger. "I'm already envisioning you cradling a Pulitzer."

"Isn't it just a piece of paper?"

"You can cradle a piece of paper. And still rehearse your acceptance speech with a hairbrush." She bit into a broccoli floret. "I'm Sera," she said. "Sera Mathison."

"Good to meet you. Derick Sweetwater."

She pointed her chin toward his chest. "Says Frederick."

"I'm working on that."

Her eyes crinkled slightly when she smiled, gold flecks emerging from the mahogany. "So shall we get the formalities over with? Prose or poetry?"

"Prose. Fiction."

"I'm nonfiction."

"Memoir?"

She let out a grunt. "God, no. Nobody wants to read about my life. More like personal essays. My opinions are far more interesting than my experiences."

Sera wore a green dress with a pleated skirt, completely inappropriate for the occasion, yet that was why he liked it and why, he expected, she had put it on. "And whose workshop are you in?"

Derick found himself leaning forward, less because of her height than a desire not to be overheard. "Graham Whitcomb." He was beginning to think he had uttered that name more times tonight than his own.

"Lucky you!" Sera said. "I hear he's a trip."

"How so?"

"I'll leave it up to you to tell me after you meet him."

"He should be here any minute, shouldn't he?" Derick scoped the room. He knew Graham only from the photos on book covers.

"No," Sera said, "I heard he's not coming tonight. Meeting with the Hollywood crowd who are apparently turning his award-winning novel into a dumbed-down movie. He's flying in tomorrow to make the grand entrance. He likes grand entrances."

"Who are you working with this week?"

"Martin Firbank," she said.

15

"From *Vanity Fair?*"

"Yep. I want to learn how to write scandalous profiles of mob wives and dirty politicians."

"That's where the money is." He laughed but mostly on the inside.

"Tell me about it." She wagged a carrot at the crowd. "Look at these people," she said. "Look at the ambition, the drive. It's like Churchill Downs, everyone thinking they're going to be the one to hit the trifecta. Like there's a trifecta to be hit."

Derick followed the carrot toward the gaggle currently clustered around Vanessa Haverstock. They seemed rapt.

Sera's voice was softer now but even more exasperated. "Why is everyone so anxious to make it in a profession where nobody actually makes it? The most successful writer I know holds down three part-time teaching jobs and is happy to find ten hours a week to actually sit at his desk to do anything besides grade papers. And his best-selling book, by the way, earned him about five grand in royalties."

"I take it that's not Graham Whitcomb you're talking about."

She rolled her eyes. They stood side by side like a couple on a banquette in a fancy French restaurant, he thought, the kind who are more concerned with being seen than being together.

"Would you like to play a game?" Sera asked, sidling in again.

"Sure," said Derick. "I don't have anything else to do."

"It's an easy one," she said. "You'll love it. I call it Spot the Poet."

Derick had to restrain his laughter, lest the wine go down the wrong pipe. "There's one," he said, gesturing with his glass.

Sera looked toward where he was pointing. "Not Vanessa," she chided. "That's cheating. There are all of three poets in this country that nonliterary people have ever heard of, and she's one of them. Try harder."

"What does a poet look like?"

Sera turned to him, head cocked to the side. "Just find the ones who look like they'd rather be absolutely anywhere else but in a room full of people. And mismatched clothing is a dead giveaway."

As if on cue, a lanky young man passed by—pale skin, ill-fitting jacket, frozen expression.

"Like that," Sera said. "Poor baby looks like a good meal or a piece of ass would kill him."

"Really? I hear poets are animals in the sack."

"Well," she admitted with a shrug, "they do have rhythm."

They continued the game for a bit, and finally Sera put her empty plate down on a side table. "Can I say something that's going to make you and everyone else in this room hate me?"

"I hope you do."

"Come outside with me. I need a cigarette."

"And then you'll tell me the hateful thing?"

She smirked. "No," she said, "that *is* the hateful thing. I smoke. It's the twenty-first century. I'm a leper."

"You're also a writer. Aren't writers supposed to smoke?"

"No," she said, jiggling her cup before him, "now we just drink ourselves into oblivion."

"At least some traditions remain intact."

They got outside just as the sunset was fading into dark. When they reached the parking lot, Sera dug into her purse. "And please note," she said, "no cloves. I'm a real smoker, not one of those fancy-pants people. Cancer should smell like cancer, you know what I mean?"

"So how long have you been coming to these things?" Derick said as they walked.

"Ages now," she said. "Since my divorce, actually. I have always written, but it wasn't until I got rid of my husband that I really did anything about it. I just decided that I'd re-strained myself for long enough, in a lot of ways. Once Abe was out of the picture, the time came to let loose. I traveled, I learned ballroom dancing, and I started to send my work out. And I got published. Here and there, small things mostly.

Then I started doing workshops. I met people. I hate to say it," she added, gesturing with the smoldering cigarette, "but it works if you work it."

"How appropriate. It feels like a twelve-step group in there."

"True," Sera said. "Only instead of trying to help you stop your addiction, they just encourage you to keep it up. It's more unhealthy than these things, actually." She took a long drag, and a moment later, she arched her neck and expelled a cloud of smoke toward the stars.

"So where have you been published?" he said. "Am I likely to have read your stuff?"

She chuckled. "I write for entertainment magazines. *People, Entertainment Weekly, Us*, that sort of thing. You've probably read my work on the toilet."

"Charming."

"I just stumbled into it," she continued. "I met an editor at a party once. We were making small talk, and I told him I was going to LA on vacation. Next thing I know, he has me doing a piece about Rodeo Drive, 'where the celebrities shop.' One thing led to another, and soon enough I'm a semi-regular contributor."

"In the right place at the right time."

"For what it's worth. But I'm tired of doing puff pieces. I need something to sink my teeth into. So here I am."

They walked past rows of quaint houses, the sort of places that seemed tailor-made for artists. And they were. This town had more writers than fishermen now.

"And what's your excuse?" Sera said. Her cigarette was now just a short stub of orange light in the hand that swayed at her side.

"Graham Whitcomb, of course. He's one of my favorite writers."

"That's your excuse for being at the conference. What's your excuse for writing?"

"Does one need an excuse?"

She laughed. "Most people would think so. But there's

something about you," she added, "something that makes me think you take it seriously. Like you actually have something to say."

At the next corner, they turned down a side street, toward the bay.

"Most of those people," Sera went on, waving a hand behind her, "have absolutely nothing to say. At least nothing that hasn't already been said, and much more eloquently. To be honest, I've stopped reading fiction. If I read one more story about the meaninglessness of life, I'll shoot myself. Not because it's depressing. But because it's not true."

"Not true?"

"Of course not. If your life is meaningless and boring, you're just not doing it right. But according to most 'serious' writers, if you drain all the life out of life, you get art. It's like alchemy in reverse. Life is gold, art is shit."

He laughed.

"So what do you write about, Derick?"

"I suppose if I said nihilism you'd burn me with that cigarette."

"I probably would."

"The truth," he said, "is that I'm what the people in that room might call one of the lucky ones."

"Really?" Sera expelled a plume of smoke like a missile into the air.

"I actually make a living as a writer. Of sorts."

"And what sort would you be?"

He chuckled nervously. "Can you keep a secret?"

"Depends on how juicy it is." She winked.

The street was empty, but still he looked around once more. "I'm a ghost."

Sera tilted her head sharply, like a deaf pigeon. "Beg pardon?"

"Ghostwriter."

"Fascinating!" Her eyes widened. "So whose ghost are you?"

Derick laughed. "That's confidential. I'd have to kill you."

"It's better than being bored to death with my crap."

"I do a variety of stuff," Derick said. "Mostly people who are experts in their field but couldn't write a grocery list on their own. Businessmen, lower-level politicians, the occasional actress."

"That sounds intriguing."

"It's not glamorous, believe me. Sometimes it's like grading papers. Elementary school papers."

"I thought ghosts wrote from scratch."

"Usually," he said. "But some clients fancy themselves wordsmiths, so they'll often give me a few pages to get things rolling. Those are the most difficult cases, persuading them to just talk and leave the writing to a professional."

"Sadly," Sera said, "everyone learns to put a sentence together in third grade, so they all assume they can write." She laughed sharply but turned her attention quickly back to Derick.

"Mostly," he said, "I interview them, try to cobble together something that makes sense. The hardest part is making sure it's all in their voice. It can't sound like me. I'm supposed to be undetectable."

"You're a ghost."

He smiled. "Like Casper."

They walked in silence for half a block or so. "But you're not here for that," she said. "What do you really want to write?"

"I can't say," he admitted. "I've played with some ideas but haven't quite figured it out yet. I'm afraid I have more questions than answers."

"Good," Sera said sharply. "Questions are far more interesting. Questions are possibilities."

Derick laughed again.

"What?" she said.

"You're a character."

"Oh god," she replied, shaking her head, "I hope it's not Anna Karenina. I have to take the train back to Philly from Boston."

# CHAPTER 2

## Bed and Breakfast

In the morning, they arrived downstairs to a large platter of homemade muffins, fresh coffee, and an assortment of cereals and juices. "Wow," Chris said, "nice spread."

"I bet you say that to all the girls," said Dwayne, the owner, emerging from the kitchen with a pitcher of milk. He danced around the table, his moves belying his sixty years, and settled the pitcher beside a box of granola.

"Did you sleep well?" Dwayne asked, rearranging the tall display of yellow and white daisies at the center of the table.

"Yes," Chris said. "The room is very comfortable."

"I hope you don't mind being at the front of the house. It can be a little noisy at night."

"Not a problem," Derick chimed in. "At least not last night." As he poured himself a cup of coffee, he spotted a couple of forty-something men seated at a small table in the corner of the room. "Good morning," he said, nodding.

They were both balding, with trimmed beards flecked in gray. They could have passed for twins. From this distance, their wrinkles even seemed to be in the same places. They smiled broadly and echoed Derick's words in chorus.

Dwayne, shaking his head in self-deprecation, hurried over. "Pardon me," he said. "Bill, Bob, this is Chris and . . ."

"Derick," Derick said, picking out a muffin.

"Derick," Dwayne repeated. "They're from New York."

"Nice to meet you," said the one on the left, presumably Bill.

"Where are you guys from?" Derick said. He tore open a

packet of Equal and spilled it into his coffee. He spotted Dwayne disappearing back into the kitchen, his hosting duties fulfilled now that he'd introduced his guests.

"Indiana," said the other one, the probable Bob. He gestured to the seat beside him, and Chris dutifully settled his breakfast there.

"That's a long ways off," Chris said.

Bill nodded. "I know, but we wanted some place special for the wedding."

"You're getting married?" Derick carried his things over and sat beside Bill. "How exciting!"

"Yep," Bill said, "on Sunday. You should come. We're doing it at the beach. Very casual."

"A few of our friends are coming from back home," Bob added. "But it'll be small."

"That sounds lovely," Derick said. "I haven't been to a gay wedding yet."

"No," Chris piped in, "most of the weddings I've been to are rather dreary."

Bill cast a sympathetic look across the table. "So what part of New York are you guys from?"

"Upper West Side," Derick said. But the looks on their faces revealed that the specificity was lost on them. "Manhattan," he added.

Chris took a long sip of coffee, hiding behind the mug.

"I'd love to live in New York," Bill said. "My company's headquartered there, but I don't think I could ever persuade Bob to move."

"Really?" Derick said. "Why not?"

Bob's neck seemed to sink into his shoulders. "I don't know," he said. "Just too intense for me. Too much noise, too many people, too much . . . everything."

Chris let his mug rattle back onto the table. "Have you ever been there?" he said, somehow managing to sound curious rather than threatening. Derick was impressed by his restraint.

"No, but I've heard."

"About what? The nightly stabbings on every street corner?"

"No!" Bob laughed nervously. Derick imagined the wheels spinning, the effort to be polite mingling with the sudden fear that Chris was a serial killer. "I just meant the crowds and all. I need open space."

Chris snapped a chunk off his muffin and popped it into his mouth. "That's why God created Central Park."

Bill and Bob were hardly opposites, but neither were they clones. Instead, Derick thought, they complemented each other rather nicely. He liked the way Bill smiled through Bob's awkward statements, the tenderness with which Bob sidled up against his lover as he poured milk into his cup. Their interactions, down to the simplest gesture, seemed to come naturally, as if they had always belonged together. Derick had grown so used to drama, the endless task of negotiating difference. By contrast, the ease he sensed between these two was positively exotic.

"So how long have you been together?" Bob said, eyes wide. He suddenly reminded Derick of a character in a puppet Christmas special, the gold prospector who saves Rudolph from the Abominable Snowman.

Chris grabbed Derick's hand delicately and nudged him under the table. "Six years," he said quickly, before Derick had a chance to speak. "Six glorious years."

"Aw, that's wonderful. And they say people can't stay together in the big city."

"Is that what they say?" Chris's eyes narrowed in puzzlement. "I don't know about that. For Derick and me, it was love at first sight. Wasn't it, honey?" He squeezed Derick's hand tight enough to cut off circulation.

"Absolutely," Derick gasped. "And it just keeps getting better." He stepped hard on Chris's toes until Chris let go of his hand.

"Better and better," Chris echoed.

"So what are you boys doing today?" Bill spread marmalade on his toast.

Derick burst in, fearing Chris was about to come up with another lie. "We're going to a writers' workshop, actually. At the Eagerton Academy. It's an all-week event."

"After which we're free to just lie around and bask in the glow of each other," Chris said languidly.

Derick wanted to stomp on his foot again.

"So," Bill said, "you're writers?" He cast them a dubious look. Apparently, Derick and Chris made credible lovers, but thinking of them as writers required a leap of faith.

"Can't say I've ever met a writer before," said Bob. "What do you write about?"

Chris squeezed Derick's arm. "Derick is working on a period piece. A wildly romantic story about Edwardian England, but with lots of man-sex. Think of it as an erotic *Downton Abbey*."

"Isn't that interesting!" Bob said, the gentle shaking of his head adding a new significance to his name.

A creak on the stairs announced the arrival of more guests. A fiftyish woman with curly auburn hair emerged from the landing, a practiced smile carved into her face. Behind her was the handsome man they'd seen last night, the one with the odd mustache.

"Good morning," said the woman cheerfully, loudly addressing the room.

The boys' table greeted the newcomers en masse, smiles all around and more than a little curiosity. Derick still couldn't place the man but was now even more convinced he knew him.

"Another beautiful day in Provincetown, no?" said the woman, carefully plucking a stem of grapes from the fruit plate. Her sharp voice battled against a half-obscured accent Derick couldn't place, the hybrid sound foreigners who have been in the country for a long time gradually develop.

"Yes, Greta," said Bill. "Another day at the beach for you two?"

"I don't know," she replied, evaluating the muffins. "What do you think, Harold?" She leaned a shoulder against her companion. "Just a quiet stroll through town, maybe to explore the galleries?"

"That would be lovely," said the man softly. Even his voice sounded familiar, piquing Derick's curiosity even more. He found himself staring, imagining the man without the mustache.

There was no room left at their small table, so Greta and her companion took the next table over. "Hello," she said, stretching a hand out across the gap, "I am Greta."

"Nice to meet you," Derick said.

She shook hands with Derick and Chris in turn, her smile lifting and falling mechanically as she made eye contact with each of them. "And this is Harold," she said.

Harold smiled sheepishly and extended a hand. Derick took advantage of the moment to study his face more closely.

"Don't tell me you guys are on a honeymoon, too," Chris said.

"No, no," Greta replied. She shook her head, but her hair refused to move. "We've just come to get away. It's so relaxing here, and so beautiful."

"Where do you live?" Derick asked.

"New York."

"Another one!" cried Bill. "See?" he said to his lover. "Everyone's there. We have to at least visit!"

"Yes," Greta said, "by all means. You would love it." She turned her attention to Derick suddenly. "You are from New York, as well?"

"Yes," he said. "I live on the Upper West Side." He felt another kick from Chris. He should have said *we*, but the game was already old.

"What a charming neighborhood." She patted Harold's hand, inadvertently stopping it on the way to reach for a spoon. "We have a place on the East Side," she said. Her tone suggested that *place* meant "palace."

Across the table, Harold slipped his hand free to stir his coffee. As he took a sip, his eyes met Derick's. His mustache hidden behind the mug, his eyes were able to stand out. And

Derick remembered in a flash: Clive Morgan's eyes, gazing at some ingénue with the same intensity on a large screen, in close-up. But he had lived in New York long enough to know not to fawn over a celebrity. If Clive Morgan told you over breakfast that his name was Harold Whatever, the polite thing to do was nod and keep the conversation rolling.

"Have you been whale watching yet?" Greta said abruptly. She spoke every sentence with the same flatness of tone, no interrogative lift to her words.

"That sounds wonderful!" said Bob. "I'd love to go."

"Perhaps," Greta said, her smile returning, "we could all make an outing of it. How long will you boys be in town?"

"'Til next Monday," Chris replied.

"Lovely," Greta said. "Then we'll have plenty of time to get to know each other."

Derick caught Morgan's eye once again. His expression seemed a cross between terror and relief. Clearly, he knew his secret was out.

"You're incorrigible," Derick whispered to Chris as they made their way back upstairs while the others lingered over coffee. "Now for the rest of the trip, we have to pretend to be a couple."

"It'll be fun," Chris shot back, unlocking the door to their room. "Think of it as regional theater."

"Speaking of theater," Derick said once they'd gotten inside, "you do know who that was, don't you?"

"Who *who* was?" Chris stood in the bathroom doorway, squeezing toothpaste onto his brush.

"Harold."

"Friend of yours?"

Derick laughed. "I can't believe you didn't recognize him. It's Clive Morgan."

Chris pulled the brush out of his mouth, the toothpaste foaming up around his teeth. "Clive Morgan?" he mumbled. "The actor?"

"One and the same."

Chris finished quickly and spat out the toothpaste. "That's wild," he said. "Why the bad dye job?"

"I guess he's afraid of paparazzi. You know, P'town's crawling with them."

Chris pondered. "It may not be a TMZ hot zone, but I can understand why he wouldn't want the world to know he's here." He smirked, tilting his head against the doorframe.

Derick slid past him so he could brush his teeth. "There *have* been a lot of rumors about him," Derick said, hovering over the sink.

"As much as any of those pretty boys in Hollywood, I guess."

"What about Greta?"

"Not the best choice in beards," Chris said. "She's a little scary. And way too old for him."

"Well, if he needs a guard dog, she'll certainly do the trick. The boys of P'town will keep their distance from her."

"Ah, the price of celebrity!" Chris said, grabbing his sunglasses from the dresser. "I can hardly wait."

"If we don't hurry up, we're going to miss our chance." Derick flashed his watch in Chris's direction. "The workshop starts in ten minutes."

Derick hadn't taken a writing class since sophomore year of college, when he'd found himself in a cold, tiny room full of undergraduates, a single window looking out upon a quad full of Connecticut snow. The snow hardly had a chance to melt that winter before more wafted in to blanket the place. The workshop started late in the afternoon, and by the time they left, darkness had settled on the campus. The temperature dropped precipitously while they all sat inside ripping each other to shreds, so the snow crunched underfoot as he later trudged through it to the dining hall. There was a metaphor in there somewhere, he was sure.

Eagerton Academy couldn't have been more different, at least on the surface. Their workshop met on the second floor, in a large room bursting with sunshine. The room was dominated by a long table, like the setting for dinner in a BBC miniseries, missing only the candelabras and crystal goblets.

A couple of people already occupied opposite corners of the table. Derick and Chris took seats in the middle. Derick pulled a notebook from his backpack and placed it on the table, which was dark and pockmarked with age. Next to one triangular gouge, he found a doodled daisy etched into the wood like an arboreal tattoo.

People filtered in one by one, filling in the empty spaces around the table in an orderly fashion that might have been choreographed by Busby Berkeley. At most they smiled at one another, softly dipping their heads in acknowledgment of human presence. It was a motley crew, Derick thought. He remembered some of them from the night before—the gangly middle-aged woman whose face was all teeth and glasses; the brooding young man now in a loose T-shirt almost as black as the loose jersey he'd worn at the party. They all sat patiently, gazing down at the table or studying their fingernails, one man anxiously tapping the edge of his pen against a notebook. Derick had forgotten that odd feeling of incompleteness that overtakes a classroom in the absence of a teacher. If a student sits in a classroom and a teacher isn't there to see it, does he really exist? The consensus in this room was a resounding *no*.

Suddenly, outside, they heard the slapping sound of flip-flops against linoleum. All eyes turned toward the doorway, where a tall, slender man appeared. His face burst into a huge smile as soon as he spotted the twelve pairs of eyes taking him in.

"Good morning, everyone," he said loudly.

Except for the thin file folder he plopped onto the table, Graham Whitcomb looked more like he was on his way to the beach than a classroom. Flip-flops hung loosely at the end of hairy legs bare to the knee, under a pair of chocolate-brown cargo shorts from which he pulled a fountain pen and small pad of paper before settling into his chair at the head of the table. His yellow T-shirt clung tightly to a surprisingly muscular torso, the arms clearly hungry for a tan. Except for the wide and heavy-rimmed glasses, the bridge grazed slightly by a long swath of salt-and-pepper hair swooping down across his forehead, he was virtually unrecognizable from the photos gracing the dust jackets of his books.

"How is everyone on this lovely day?"

There were titters down the length of the table as everyone's eyes focused directly, sycophantically, upon Graham. The teeth-and-glasses lady was beaming, her smile exposing all thirty-two of the pearly whites.

Graham immediately asked for introductions. He nodded first to the young girl at his side, a pretty redhead whose voice shook as she spoke. "I'm Emily," she said softly, "and I'm from just outside Pittsburgh."

The introductions continued around the room, revealing a cross-section of accents and backgrounds. The brooding boy revealed a Southern drawl, which he tried to harness with shortened vowels. The result was a garbled response that might have been "I'm Scott from Birmingham" or "I shat on a broom."

Teeth-and-glasses turned out to be British, her enunciation somehow balancing out Scott's and explaining her forced posture. At that moment, Derick decided to call her Mrs. Thatcher.

He was so distracted coming up with mnemonics to remember names, he was actually taken by surprise when his own turn came. "I'm Derick," he said, surprised by his nervousness.

Graham made a show of interest in everyone, eyes aglow with welcome. When the circle came back to him, he didn't bother to introduce himself. He didn't need to. Graham Whitcomb was the reason they were all here.

Derick had followed Graham's career from the beginning. His first novel, *An Open Book*, had been just that, a confessional story about a young gay man struggling to be open about his sexuality while still insisting on his place in the larger world. Derick read it not long after his own coming-out, and related profoundly with the protagonist. He felt validated by its relatively happy ending, so different from the majority of gay novels he read in those days, whose protagonists most often ended up alone and miserable, if not dead.

Graham wasn't an especially prolific author, and his next couple of books were largely retreads of the same territory. Nevertheless, Derick had watched for them and quickly absorbed each as it appeared. The fifth, *Charity*, was Graham's breakthrough. It had come out a year ago to wide acclaim. Graham's first book with one of the big six publishers, it was also the first to focus on straight characters. The protagonist this time was a woman, Charity Sharpe, who feels driven to save the world and ends up being destroyed by it. The novel received universal acclaim and, a few months ago, had won the National Book Award. And Graham Whitcomb became a star.

"Why are we here?" he asked now. It was hard to tell from his expression whether the question was merely rhetorical. "Why do we do what we do?"

Mrs. Thatcher cautiously lifted a hand into the air. "Self-expression?" she ventured.

"Yes, certainly," Graham said. "But why do we bother? When the odds are completely stacked against success, why do we bother? Why do we spill our own blood onto the page when we know we'll be lucky to reach a few thousand people and will never be able to quit our day jobs? Why do we sacrifice our nights and weekends, not to mention our relationships, for something with such a low return on investment?"

Chris perked up. "Speaking for myself, it's not really a conscious question. I don't have a choice."

"So it's a compulsion?" Graham pursued. "An addiction?"

Chris smiled. "You could call it that."

"No," Graham said, leaning back in his chair, "that's too

easy. That's what writers always say. It's the romantic notion that we're just scribes, slaves being manipulated by this abstract thing called *Art*, which uses us to get its own point across. That's *Amadeus*. And let's face the facts. Most of us are not Mozart. We're Salieri. Why does Salieri do it?"

"Fame?" A thirtyish man with wire-framed glasses and an intense expression.

"Unlikely." Graham waved a hand as if swatting a gnat.

"Masochism?"

Graham smiled. "Possibly."

"Hubris?" Derick said at last.

Graham's eyebrows lifted, disappearing briefly into his bangs. "Now I think we're getting somewhere. Say more."

"Well, we all know the statistics. The chances of winning the lottery are a billion to one, but millions of people keep buying the tickets. They all think they're the one who's going to make it. As if the numbers don't matter."

"Do you think you're going to make it?" Graham said. His eyes were magnified by the glasses. There was no escaping them.

"Yes," Derick said, "I do."

He had no idea where it came from, that confidence, the audacity to make such a statement. But Graham seemed to want it. He had pulled it out of him.

"Good," he said, smiling.

And so began the lecture. Graham talked about his own idols—Hemingway, Miller, Whitman. "They dared to reveal themselves, to take risks. It never occurred to them that they might fail. Failure to Hemingway was using the wrong verb. It wasn't about anyone else's opinion. The only opinion that mattered was his own."

There were perplexed looks around the room. They had come here for encouragement, not dissuasion.

"It's hard work," Graham said, "isn't it? And only a few make it. You have to know that going in. But if you're to have any hope of being one of those few, you have to not care about the odds. You have to ignore them altogether." He paused dramatically and turned his eyes directly to Mrs. Thatcher. "Can you do that, Agnes? Can you have that hubris?"

The deer blinked in the headlights, and the Sister Wendy teeth parted in a smile. "Yes," she said, slurping the sibilant thirstily. "Yes, I can."

Graham leaned back and cradled his head in his hands, elbows out. "Good for you, Agnes. Good for you." His eyes brightened suddenly, and he leaned forward once again. "Now," he said, opening the file folder in front of him, "shall we dig in?"

A month or so earlier, copies of all contributions had been sent to each participant in a thick envelope. And just last week, they'd received an email from Graham telling them which ones they'd be reading on the first day. With only a week of workshops, there was no time to waste.

As luck would have it, first up was Agnes. They dug in.

# CHAPTER 3

## Aspects of the Familiar

Workshops at Eagerton Academy lasted three hours a day. Derick's attention started to flag after two. Clearly, he wasn't alone. Class participation had definitely decreased by the time the third story came on the docket. The author, a petite girl named Cindy, smiled hazily through the session, as if she assumed the lack of criticism from her peers was a sign of approval rather than sheer exhaustion.

When Graham finally adjourned the class, the sound of chairs squeaking back from the table was almost drowned out by simultaneous yawns. Standing at last, Derick stretched his arms above his head until he heard a crack somewhere in his neck. He gathered his things and stuffed them quickly into his backpack.

Back at the inn, they showered and changed, then headed out to wander Commercial Street before dinner. There was a strut in Chris's movement, a gentle swaying of the hips, a swagger in the shoulders. He had used more product than usual in his hair, which now rose in a peak that added an inch or two to his height.

He was on the prowl, in revenge mode. Despite overwhelming evidence to the contrary, Chris still believed in romance. That was why he'd been so devastated when Brian left. The present ritual of rolling up his sleeves and heading out to do battle was really a form of therapy, Chris's way of healing his heart, his way of saying "fuck you" to Brian once and for all.

That, of course, was how Derick saw it. But Derick had a way of projecting.

They had dinner at the Lobster Pot—a long wait, but worth it to have a table by the window, looking out on the beach at last.

Over dinner and a bottle of Chardonnay, they talked about the other workshop participants. They invented back stories for each of them, imagining a life of crime to explain Vincent's mysterious air, a chip in Cindy's neck implanted during a visit to Stepford.

"Scott's the one I'm intrigued by," Chris said. "I've always had a thing for rednecks."

Derick took advantage of the topic to ask for the skinny on Brian. So far Chris had offered few details, had in fact actively avoided the subject. On the train to Boston, he had spent the entire time with his nose in Whitcomb's *Charity,* which he had already read twice. Whenever Derick had turned to check on him, he'd been confronted by Graham's self-satisfied grin on the back cover.

"Where is Brian staying?" Derick asked now, fishing through his bouillabaisse.

"What?" Chris was busy peering around Derick's shoulder at a loud table across the room.

"Brian," he repeated. "Where's he staying?"

Chris pursed his lips again and gazed into his wine. "He's trying to make partner." He lifted the glass. "By *making* a partner."

"He's sleeping with one of the partners in the firm?"

"I sure hope so," Chris said. "Otherwise, living with him would be a big mistake. As a roommate, Brian's only talents are in the bedroom."

"But he's been with the firm for less than a year. Isn't that a little risky?"

Chris's face grew suavely dramatic. "Oh, but he's *in love!*" he said in something very close to an Anne Baxter impression. "It's real this time, you know. It's not just glorified friendship." He spoke the words as if they had quotation marks around them.

"Is that what he called it?"

"That's what it had *become* between us, he said. He wasn't denying there used to be something more. But all good things come to an end, don't they? And time wounds all heels. I hope." He took a quick swallow of wine and placed the bottle back in its chilled holder with a flourish that attracted the waiter, who promptly refilled both glasses.

They'd been through this all before, of course. Derick could no longer count the times they'd been through this. Chris and Brian's relationship was the stuff soap operas are made of. Anger, recrimination, jealousy, subterfuge, revenge—it was all there, from the petty to the deadly serious. And in the end, the drama served mainly as prelude to saccharine sentimentality. Or was it, Derick wondered, the other way 'round? The two were forever testing each other as if no protestation of love could ever be trusted, as if each knew a secret, horrible truth and refused to relent until the other spoke it first.

Usually, Derick didn't say much. After three years of this, he had learned not to say much. No matter how strongly Chris vowed to get out, he would inevitably go home to find flowers on the table, or Brian making his favorite dinner, or just really good sex, and his resolution would crumble like day-old coffee cake. Expressing disapproval would only turn Derick into the object of resentment. Friends, he had decided, were like therapists. They shouldn't give advice, only lead you toward your own answer.

Derick had to tread carefully. "Maybe you were just too different," he ventured.

Chris placed his glass down gently and looked up at Derick. "Have you ever been in love?"

"Sure. You know that. You know about Garrett."

Chris laughed. "You were in love with Garrett for about five minutes, until you found out he'd voted for Ralph Nader."

"Ralph Nader cost us that election."

Chris rolled his eyes. "And Kelly. What was his problem? Oh yeah, he made that weird face when he came in for a kiss."

"He looked like a kissing gourami. All lips."

"And let's see, Burt. Yeah, Burt. He was the one who put salt on his food before tasting it."

"Making decisions without evidence."

Chris made a phone gesture with his hand. "Hello, Pot? This is Kettle . . ."

Derick focused on the wine. "I thought we were talking about you."

"Oh, honey, we're always talking about me. This is fun for a change." He smiled mischievously. "Besides, I'm single now, and I'm going to make the most of it. You're the one who needs a little romance."

"I don't *need* anything."

"Come on, don't you want to be in love?"

Derick laughed. "After seeing what it's done to you? No thanks."

"Here's your chance," Chris said. "If you can't find love in P'town, you can't find it anywhere." He stuck a lobster fork into the end of a claw and expertly drew out the meat.

"I don't expect to find it here," Derick said. "I'm not interested."

"Good." Chris sliced off a piece of the lobster and dipped it in butter. "They say it always happens when you're not looking."

Derick laughed. "So do car accidents."

Chris sat back, grinning. He had taken the seat in the corner, affording himself a view of the room and all the other men in it, while Derick had no option but to watch Chris or the darkening sky.

"My God, I don't believe it," Chris said slowly, peering over Derick's shoulder. "It's BB!"

Derick turned to see. "Who?"

Chris stood and leaned over the table, waving. "Bradley Beane. What on earth is he doing here?"

Derick watched as a tall man in a black linen sweater entered the dining room.

The first thing one noticed about Bradley Beane was his height. It was impossible to miss, in fact. At six-two, he towered over nearly everyone he met. The second thing you noticed was that he dressed like an undertaker—always in black, usually in high collars that sealed tightly around his wide neck. But his most striking feature was his gaze, coming from piercing dark eyes that seemed to be his secret weapon as a psychologist. Derick imagined they allowed him to actually read his patients' thoughts.

When he'd first met Brad, seeing only his imposing demeanor, Derick had prepared himself for an endlessly dull evening full of only the most intellectual conversation: existential philosophy, the stock market, Michel Foucault, that sort of thing. Shaking Brad's large, firm hand, black hair carpeting its knuckles, Derick had felt his whole body quiver in dread. He nearly fell to the floor with surprise when Brad proceeded to note his resemblance to Jeff Colby on *Dynasty*.

"But you're probably too young for that, aren't you, dear? I know we all want to forget the Reagan years, but there were some redeeming qualities about the eighties, don't you think?"

The comment was so out of line with the image he projected, it was as if Meryl Streep had opened her mouth to reveal the voice of Jennifer Tilly. Derick had been in platonic love with him ever since.

Brad whispered to the friends he had come in with, gesturing for them to follow the host to their table and that he would catch up later. As they took their seats, Brad broke away to come toward Chris and Derick.

"What on earth are you doing here?" Chris repeated as Brad reached the table.

"Just taking a little vacation," Brad said, coming in for an awkward hug, careful not to topple the tiny vase in the center of the table. "It's August, after all, when all good therapists are expected to leave New York. You can't imagine what I'll come home to after this. Without me, they go completely bonkers."

"How are you?" Derick said. "I don't think I've seen you since Chris's last birthday party."

Brad laughed. "The one where he cried when we lit *all those candles*? I'm sure we didn't have much time to chat there. Chris's birthdays are always such traumatic events. He doesn't let you notice anything else. Or any*one*."

"But, honey," Chris protested, "you know as well as anyone, it's all about me."

Brad rolled his eyes. "You know, Chris, the strangest thing is that you actually think that's funny. As a professional, let me assure you that narcissistic personality disorder is no laughing matter."

But Chris laughed all the more. Even when he was the subject of criticism, at least he was the center of attention. He was in his element, his eyes suddenly alive. He was clearly relieved to be freed from serious conversation and lifted onto the higher plane of small talk.

Brad was Chris's oldest friend, in both senses of the word. He was the first person Chris had met when he moved to New York, and remained his only real acquaintance over forty. "Way over forty," as Chris was fond of teasing him, though Brad never admitted how far he stood on the other side of that imaginary line defining middle age. "You'll be there soon enough," he would tease right back. "You may never catch up, god willing, but I'll get my revenge when the crow's feet start sprouting on that alabaster skin."

"And what are you guys doing here?" Brad asked now. "Why didn't you tell me you were coming to P'town?"

"I did," Chris said. "The workshop, remember?"

"Oh, right. Working on the Great American Novel." He pivoted toward Derick. "And you?"

"O ye of deaf ears," Chris said. "Derick's at the workshop with me."

"Are you working on the Great American Novel, too?"

"I'm not sure how great it is," Derick replied.

Chris was sadly shaking his head. "Honestly, Brad, you never seem to hear a word I say. I would assume a psychologist would need to acquire listening skills."

"What?" Brad turned to him, eyes glinting. When Chris emitted a predictable groan, Brad said, "If you had to spend your entire day listening to people whine about their problems, you'd be tempted to tune out the world by five o'clock too, I assure you. Besides, I always listen to the important things."

"Like what? What could be more important than *moi*?"

Brad laughed. "You mean aside from shopping, booze, and sex?"

"You're incorrigible."

"You heard it from the horse's mouth," Brad said, turning back to Derick. "I'm incorrigible."

"The best people always are," Derick said.

"So where's Brian?" Brad asked curiously.

"Brian's busy," Chris announced, returning to his wine.

"Busy," Brad echoed. "Yes, lawyers are always 'busy.' As long as there are ambulances to chase, vacations will go untaken."

"Not that kind of busy." Chris carefully adjusted the napkin in his lap. "Busy with his new boyfriend."

Brad's thick eyebrows arched sharply, as if the McDonald's logo had grown hair. "When were you planning to break the news?"

"It just happened."

Brad sneered comically, nodding. "So what did the little bastard do this time?"

"It's not all his fault, Brad."

"Not his fault. You supported him through law school, listened to him piss and moan for months while studying for the bar, sat home alone every night ever since because he preferred marriage to his job over marriage to you, and then he dumped you for another man. And it's not all his fault?" Brad was the only person Derick knew who could express rage and contempt with complete calm. His performances were a marvel to behold.

"Don't hold back, BB," Chris said, reaching for his wine. "Tell us how you really feel."

"Lawyers," he said with a dismissive sigh. "Every person I

know who was involved with someone in law school was summarily dumped as soon as the little shyster got a job. In addition to torts and contracts and all that other mumbo jumbo, they take a required course in arrogance. They receive official training in looking down their noses at anyone who's not their kind. So who'd he dump you for?"

Chris sheepishly met Brad's stern gaze. "A partner."

"Domestic or imported?"

They all burst out laughing. Derick was grateful for the release in tension.

"I'm sorry, Chris," Brad said. "I know it must smart."

"No, not really," Chris replied, looking up. The redness that had swelled his cheeks a moment ago was gone. "That's the amazing thing. I invested more in this relationship than any other, and yet it's been remarkably easy to get past."

"That's because you had plenty of time to prepare," Brad said.

"Plenty of time? It came as a complete shock. He just came home and announced that he was moving out."

"That's not what I mean," Brad said. "You've been complaining about this relationship for at least a year now. I think you got all the mourning out of the way well before the official breakup."

Derick wasn't surprised Chris had kept the news from Brad. When you were living with fear and uncertainty, Brad was the last person you would talk to, unless you were paying for his services. He cultivated the image of the wise old man, never mincing words, never hesitating to express an opinion as directly as possible. It went with the black wardrobe, the costume of a priest, Derick thought, keeper of some sacred truth he shared only in well-chosen, well-timed aphorisms.

"Well," he said, "now that I've spoiled your evening, I must get back to my own. There's more damage to be done before the night is through."

"Where are you staying?" Derick said.

"I'm at the Boatslip."

"Now there's a place with a view," Chris said, nodding to Derick.

"A view?" Brad repeated. "I guess it depends on what you're looking for. Personally, all those prepubescent, hairless things lounging by the pool aren't my type. But tea dance can be fun. You should stop by tomorrow. Just a few more days in paradise before I have to return to my neurotic minions. Give me a call on my cell."

Brad made his way back across the room. "You see," Chris said, "you can't escape New York. It'll follow you anywhere."

Toward the front of the room, Brad settled in with his friends—probably, Derick thought, using more or less the same line on them.

Chris insisted on having coffee with dessert, if only to keep Derick awake for the rest of the evening. Though he sipped at his own cappuccino, he didn't really need the caffeine. He had a wiry energy, an alertness in the eyes that scanned the room.

Derick had seen Chris through several transformations, back and forth from bachelorhood to serious boyfriends. He had learned to identify the signs of comfort with any given role: the lightness in his expression when he finally let his resistance go and allowed himself to revel in the joy of a new love; the hard edge that crept in as he prepared himself to be alone again. And tonight, less than a month and several hundred miles from Brian, he had already passed to the next stage, a delicate balance of the carefree and the intense, a self-assurance that lit up his eyes and added a fluidity to his movement. He was completely in the moment, not worrying about the past, not planning for the future. He was just here, in this half-real, half-fairy-tale town, being himself. Derick almost envied him.

Brad was embroiled in conversation with his friends as Derick and Chris were leaving, so they simply waved on their way out the door.

The breeze had picked up since they'd been inside. As they made their way to the center of town, Derick imagined for a moment that Chris was literally going where the wind took him. It carried them together down the street, like Dorothy and Toto, to the familiar alley where a dozen or so bikes were already parked, music booming through the walls of the A-House.

Outside, Derick hesitated. He checked his watch. "It's already eleven," he said.

Chris turned, arm outstretched. "One drink," he said. "You'll sleep better and wake refreshed."

"Good thing you're a novelist and not a doctor," he said.

"The best writers are lushes, you know that. Come on, Hemingway!"

Derick followed him inside. An hour or so wouldn't hurt anything.

He had always appreciated the ambience at the A-House. The wood everywhere and the antique look of the furnishings gave it a homey, masculine quality he seldom found in Chelsea or Hell's Kitchen. He could imagine being a regular at a place like this. He could imagine fitting in.

What he loved most about gay bars wasn't the conversation, the potential for flirtation. What he enjoyed was simply observing. Derick studied mating rituals, and bars were the ideal environment. On the rare occasion when a straight friend had dragged him to one of their pickup bars, he had stood quietly in a corner, just watching like Jane Goodall in the jungle, he thought. Observing a foreign species.

Straight women, he'd decided, were too self-conscious; the men, not self-conscious enough. The excessively pretty women wore their femininity like a fashion accessory, the limp wrist or exaggerated wiggle a perfect match for the beaded purse or the pearl-studded clip that pulled their hair together. And the men they teased shamelessly, who ensured interest by always seeming to rise above it: gum-chewing blocks of granite who strode obliviously through the world as if it had been created just for them (which, of course, having been created *by* them, it was). Derick understood why the women exaggerated themselves with lipstick and eye shadow in colors unknown to nature or towering high heels that accentuated their curves at the risk of sending them crashing to the ground with one false move. They underwent these machinations simply to get through. The men they sought were blind to subtlety. Lost in their own solipsistic worlds, they had to be hit over the head to notice anything. These modern women were simply reversing the caveman paradigm. Now they were the ones carrying the clubs.

The process was more complex in the gay world, lacking the easy dichotomy of gender. And here, the men were completely self-conscious, even if that didn't stop them from acting like stereotypical men. If butchness in the American heterosexual is simply the absence of affectation, in the gay world it is its epitome. The standoffishness that dominates a gay bar is based not on obliviousness, but pure calculation. The beautiful boys, Derick thought, knew precisely who was cruising them. They made a science of avoiding eye contact while peripherally registering every pair of eyes that glanced their way. Tonight, in this bar, the men in muscle shirts were enacting a role as deliberately chosen as the one they would later play on Halloween, in bugle beads and two-inch nails.

Beside him, Chris affected the stance mirrored throughout the room—butt against the wall, one leg rigid, the other bent slightly at the knee. The fingers of one hand were curled outside a jeans pocket, the thumb hooked on a belt loop, while the other hand clutched the neck of a beer bottle. The stance, repeated along the wall as in a chorus line, recalled the uniform yet funky choreography of a Fosse number. All they needed were bowlers.

And yet, Derick couldn't imagine that anyone in this room could possibly be more self-conscious than he was himself. He felt aware of each square inch of exposed flesh, and even the hidden ones. He worried that the looseness of his shirt could be misinterpreted as the mask for a spare tire, and sucked in his gut with each breath. He checked himself from tapping a foot in time to the music, or staring too long at someone too beautiful to respond. He was convinced this was why bars were always so crowded, the open-shirted bartenders never able to take a moment's rest: everyone had to drink steadily just to loosen up, continuously pouring alcohol into their systems to keep the terror at bay.

"The men are different here, don't you think?" Chris said, sidling in close but still gazing out at the room. "Less attitude, less bitchiness."

"I thought you liked attitude," Derick replied.

Chris lifted his beer bottle to emphasize nonchalance. "My own, dear. Not anyone else's."

On a cynical day, that could easily have explained Brian. Throughout most of their time together, Brian had been finishing law school and studying for the bar, while Chris taught by day and worked on his novel at night. His nose in a book, his energy spent worrying about his future, Brian didn't have time for attitude. He didn't have much time for the relationship, either, but that didn't seem to bother Chris when he was dedicating all of his spare time to his book and cultivating the contacts to get it published.

They'd opened their relationship up quite a while ago, at least implicitly. Cruising gave Chris something to do when Brian was working late. And as long as it was only sex, there was no threat.

Chris seldom spoke to him in bars, partly because of the loud music but mostly, Derick suspected, so no one would assume they we*f*re a couple. In fact, Chris barely acknowledged him most of the time—an occasional darting of the eyebrows to indicate that he'd spotted a "live" one, a half-hearted smile if the pickings were slim. Cruising brought out the serious side of Chris. Derick wondered if anything else in his life garnered as much life-or-death attention.

For Chris, cruising was a shortcut to mental health; instead of spending months and thousands of dollars on therapy, he had a few beers and picked up a stranger. And for one night, they could convince each other that everything was all right. For one night, sex could mean everything and nothing at once.

As a rule, Chris found a spot and stuck to it. He didn't pursue; he waited. Tonight he stood at the edge of the dance floor, his face half in shadow. The less patient men wandered in circles through the room, searching. Chris gazed nonchalantly at the constant stream, occasionally resting a longer glance on a shoulder, a slim waist, a biceps bulging through a tight sleeve. Even, as the evening wore on, another pair of eyes.

Tonight's winner, with dark, wavy hair and a long, pointed nose, showed up just before midnight. He was a couple of inches taller than Chris, and when he sidled in beside him, Chris's shoulder reached the top of the stranger's chest, the crown of his head level with dark eyes. Chris must have seen him coming from yards distant, while Derick was looking elsewhere, because they began talking almost immediately. Derick couldn't hear, though he stood only a few feet away. When people want to be overheard in a bar, they yell. The man laughed at something Chris said, and a large hand came up to lean upon Chris's shoulder. Chris rocked slightly with the pressure and continued with his story. By then their eyes were locked.

And that was all it took. It was like fishing, Derick decided. Carefully baiting the hook, casting the reel in the right time-tested spot, and waiting. Hours of waiting. But when you get that first, sudden, half-unexpected nibble, it's all over. And the hours of sitting in a cramped boat, the hunger, the cold that has seeped into your skin, all fade from memory, leaving only the sudden taste of victory.

This was Chris's natural element. He could stalk and capture prey with the best of them, as if the object of desire were merely something to be overcome, used up, its naked skeleton tossed aside when the appetite was satisfied.

Derick took a last swig of beer and laid the empty bottle on a shelf behind him. He flashed raised eyebrows toward Chris, but the gesture went unobserved. He turned around and made his way along the edge of the dance floor and out the door well before closing time, a salmon upstream.

# CHAPTER 4

## Who's Afraid of E. M. Forster?

O n the second day, they had removed the table so they could interact more intimately. In the new configuration, the chairs were arranged in an ellipse, with Graham at one of the narrow ends.

Graham Whitcomb was a lanky figure, all arms and legs. Derick suspected he really wanted to get rid of the table so he'd have more room to stretch out. His body was constantly in motion, arms gesticulating, legs crossing and uncrossing. When he was listening, his limbs would calm down for a while and he'd slouch, legs splayed in an echoing angle, one arm draped over the arm of his chair, one over the back, so that his body took on the unnerving shape of a swastika.

Graham used each story in the workshop as an opportunity to teach a particular concept. Agnes was the poster child for character problems. Jonathan needed a remedial lesson on the yawn-worthy standby of show-vs-tell. And Jessica suffered the season's supreme backhanded compliment: "This is beautifully written," Graham said, shaking his head over the pages. "The problem is, I just don't care about these people."

But caring about people wasn't Graham's forte. His primary concern was voice. In fact, one could say that Graham Whitcomb was obsessed with voice. Especially his own.

"Voice," he told the class on the third day, when they were about to read Derick's piece, "is the quality that separates gifted writers from merely capable ones. Thousands of people are capable of constructing eloquent sentences. But it takes a voice to make those sentences sing."

Graham certainly had a voice. It bellowed over the classroom. His round, precisely enunciated syllables resounded across the ellipse, bouncing off the far wall like so many perfectly aimed squash balls. Graham Whitcomb had a voice, and he loved its sound.

Derick was second up that day. He had had trouble concentrating on the first workshop, a discussion of Kirk's story, which he had much enjoyed when he'd read it on the train. As the first hour drew to a close, his breath became steadily shorter.

"Any last thoughts?" Graham asked, rolling Kirk's manuscript up in his hand like a makeshift telescope.

Cindy raised her hand into a crooked shape, elbow higher than wrist. "I think it's funny and all," she said, "but I don't get the title."

Graham unrolled the manuscript and looked at the first page, squinting as if seeing it for the first time. "*The Chrysler as Big as a Whale,*" he said. "Interesting."

"But what does it mean?" persisted Cindy, her arm still hanging as though suspended by marionette strings.

"It's the B-52s," said Maryann. "What's the song? 'Love Shack,' I think."

Heads nodded, accompanied by relieved sighs.

"Is that all?" said Graham.

Agnes stared blankly ahead. She had an excuse, Derick thought. It was a cultural thing. Meanwhile, amid the silence in the room, Kirk squirmed.

"Not just that," Derick said at last, drily. "It's a joke. It's also an allusion to Fitzgerald." He paused. Seeing no reaction, he added, "*The Diamond as Big as the Ritz?*"

Now Agnes's wasn't the only blank face. Only Graham looked on knowingly. "Why the reference to Fitzgerald?" he said.

Thankfully, Vincent helped. "The themes are similar. Fitzgerald was all about the hollowness of the American dream. I think Kirk—um, the *story*—is saying something along the same lines."

Graham leaned his lankiness toward Kirk. "Is Fitzgerald a particular favorite of yours?"

Kirk looked up, startled to be included in the conversation after nearly an hour of enforced muteness. "Yes," he replied.

"Good choice," Graham said. "It's important to have literary role models. What about the rest of you? Whose work most influences your own?"

Agnes was the first to volunteer. "Barbara Pym," she said. As if there could be any question.

The others named their favorites in turn, with little comment other than a knowing nod. Updike was popular, with a couple of votes each for Cheever and Ann Beattie. Aside from Kirk's choice, none of them predated World War II.

"And yours?" Graham said, finally gazing at Derick.

"Forster."

"Really?" Graham said. His voice took on an almost British accent, as if he were inadvertently channeling the master, or making fun of him.

Derick nodded.

"Don't you find him a bit . . . well, precious?"

"No," Derick replied. "Quite the opposite, actually."

A writing workshop is no place to share your literary preferences or your personal past. From that point on, everything you write is viewed through a single lens. Instantly, Derick could feel that. Either his work would be reduced to an imitation of Forster, or he would be criticized for not living up to his role model. In a crowd whose sense of literary history went no further back than Eisenhower, he was doomed.

Graham always began by asking the writer to read a couple of paragraphs aloud. It struck Derick as an appropriate way to begin, reminding everyone that the author was in the room, that these words had come out of an actual human being.

When his turn came, he chose the opening of his story, which he considered one of the strongest parts of the piece.

"They met in the summer of 1967. On the other side of the

country, people were wearing flowers in their hair and singing folk music. In New York, Roger was finishing business school and shopping for neckties. Gwendolyn was very good at picking out neckties."

He looked up from the page and caught Graham's eye. Graham cast a perfunctory smile and quickly turned away. And with that, for the next fifty minutes it was as if Derick were not present at all. He might have been a ghost on the margin, a subtle reminder, but he couldn't speak, and tried not to reveal any emotion. He tried his best to completely detach from the experience. He was a stenographer, taking notes on how a diverse group of people responded to a text. He couldn't take it personally. When an artist started taking criticism personally, he was as good as dead.

"The writing is lovely," said Cindy. She pointed a bright red fingernail at the page before her and read: "She gazed at him nervously, tentatively, squinting as at an oasis in the desert, wondering if it might really be a mirage."

"Oh yes," said Agnes, leaning back with a smile, "I rather liked that bit."

"The problem," Vincent said, twisting his lips in hesitation, "is that nothing really happens. The story doesn't really go anywhere."

"Neither does a Virginia Woolf novel," said Cindy. "Or Henry James, for that matter."

"Let's avoid comparisons," Graham said. "They don't really help anyone."

Cindy squinted. "I wasn't really comparing. I mean, this is nothing like Virginia Woolf. I was just pointing out that there's always an exception to any so-called rule."

"True," Graham said. He sat back with a long, ponderous pause. "But before one can start breaking the rules, one needs to master them."

Derick stared at his notebook. He wanted to bore a hole into it with his eyes, a wormhole he could sink into and disappear through the chair, through the floorboards, through to China if need be.

The discussion continued around him, but it was so much white noise. Only Graham's words got through the static.

"What's really missing here is voice," Graham said. "We get beautiful language and very interesting insights into the characters, but the story struggles for a sense of unity, something to tie it all together."

"A point of view," Chris offered. His familiar voice broke through.

"Exactly," Graham said. "Who is this narrator? What's his stance? Even a third-person narrator has something at stake in the story. Even when he claims impartiality. Perhaps most of all when he claims impartiality."

The rest was a blur and over soon enough. Everyone passed their marked-up manuscripts to Derick. He bundled them up, sight unseen, with a modest *thank-you,* and stuffed them into his bag.

He ran to the bathroom and met Chris in the doorway on his way back in.

"Okay," Chris said, "that went well."

"Did it?"

Chris looked puzzled. "Don't you think? I thought it was very constructive. Now you know exactly what to do to fix it."

Exactly what to do. Yes, Derick thought. He should change it to first person to satisfy Vincent; leave it in third to please Agnes; cut out the love scene for Jessica's sake; add graphic sex to give it the edge Jonathan recommended. Of course, he knew exactly what to do now. Piece of cake.

When the next victim was wriggling on the wall and the workshop finally ended for the day, Derick begged off getting a drink with Chris. He walked quickly back to the inn and dropped his bag onto the bed. With thirteen manuscripts inside, it made a deadly thud. He dug through the pile for Graham's copy and planted himself on the window seat.

In his attempt to give Derick a voice, Graham began by taking away his adjectives. Derick's manuscript was now a symphony in red, every descriptive modifier erased by a bloody scar that left the story wounded and, in Derick's view, hollow. Graham had taken away his style and given the story Hemingway's.

After the initial shock of seeing scores of red gashes across the pages, Derick turned back to the beginning and read the story through without the fleshy adjectives, just the bare bones that Graham had left on the page. The skeletal plot free of lyrical asides, characters free of shorthand psychological clues, was lifeless. Graham had killed the story, Derick thought. Ripped the flesh off and left nothing but a dead husk.

But then he looked more closely. If the flesh of verbiage had given the story life, it was a life no more organic than the one a bolt of electricity had given to Frankenstein's monster. The pieces were all there, but there was no synthesis. Graham wasn't trying to improve the story by taking away the descriptive language; he was trying to show Derick he had no story to begin with. It was a fiction based on fiction— resurrected movie plots, an unconstrained homage to the melodrama of Victorian novels. To breathe, fiction had to be based on life. That's what Graham was telling him. He was telling him to find a voice or remain speechless.

Derick turned his eyes from the manuscript to the window, where life blundered past in all its chaotic aliveness. A woman carrying a large and toppling ice-cream cone licked at it furiously while her friend laughed. Across the street, two men stood rigidly in the shade of an awning, gazing angrily at each other, clearly in the midst of a quiet, vicious argument. Somewhere else a bicyclist wobbled unsteadily around a crowd, hesitant to go at a more comfortable pace for fear of running into someone.

Stories were down there, Derick thought. Everywhere. And there were voices. The woman with the ice cream had a unique perspective on the world. The arguing couple was a story in motion, love turned into momentary hate, betrayal and disappointment pushing everything else aside. Together, their voices, whatever they sounded like, made a discordant song, cacophony where there had once been harmony.

Or so he imagined. He could imagine whatever he wanted

from the safety of the window. He could hear what he wanted to hear. But he himself was silenced. He had no idea what his own voice sounded like, what his take on the world was. He was just along for the ride.

There was a knock at the door. Startled, Derick rose abruptly. The manuscript slipped from his lap, the pages fanning out onto the floor. He stepped over them, caught the corner of one on his foot and kicked it spitefully under the chair.

He pulled open the door to find Bill and Bob hovering in the hall. "Hi!" Bob said brightly. "So you *are* here. We thought you might be out and about. It's a gorgeous day."

"We don't want to disturb you," Bill said, "if you're writing."

"No, I'm not writing."

"Well then, we were just about to go to the Boatslip for tea dance." Bob's gaze was hopeful, innocent.

Bill smiled mischievously. "Which, I told him, has nothing to do with tea."

"I knew that, silly!" Bob gave his lover a playful pat on the shoulder. "Anyway," he said, turning back to Derick, "would you like to join us?"

Derick smiled. "I'd love to," he said. "I could use a stiff drink. Or three."

"So where's your other half?" Bob said as Derick bent to put on his sandals.

"My what?" As he raised his head, he noticed Bob gazing with concern at the two unmade beds.

Derick laughed. "Look, I'm sorry, guys, Chris was just pulling your leg. We're not a couple. The truth is that he's just my annoying best friend." The truth felt surprisingly refreshing. He couldn't stop smiling.

"I don't get it," Bob said. "Why did he pretend you were . . . ?"

"That's just Chris," Derick said. "Always making shit up." He popped to his feet, glad to leave the manuscript behind. "Now," he said, "let's go have some fun."

He wanted to get drunk. He believed in getting drunk. Alcohol had never disappointed him.

The place was already crowded when they arrived, though the dancing was still limited to a side room off the bar. They got drinks and headed to the deck to check out the crowd. A couple of people still frolicked in the pool, but most lingered in pockets around the deck, everyone animatedly engaged in conversation. It was nothing like the posing of last night. Here, it seemed, no one was alone. Even the ones who walked in by themselves soon ended up chatting with total strangers. Expectations and suspicion seemed to dissipate in the sea air, leaving interaction safe.

"Isn't that Chris up there?" Bob pointed to the building behind the pool.

Chris and Brad stood on a balcony, gazing down at the crowd like the Perons. Spotting Derick, Brad began waving and gestured that they were on their way down.

"Who's that?" Bill said.

"That's Brad, a friend of ours from New York. He's a psychologist."

Bill laughed. "He must be having a field day here."

In a couple of minutes, the party was complete. Chris cheerfully introduced Brad to the Billy-Bobs, as they had come to refer to them behind their backs. "So how was your day, hon?" he asked, kissing Derick on the cheek.

"The jig is up," Bill said, smiling into the fading sun.

As Chris pulled away, Derick said, "I told them about us. How you broke my heart and we're through."

They all laughed, and Bob said, "I don't know how you could have gotten along, anyway. Both writers, you'd probably end up killing each other."

"Or worse," Chris said, "using each other in our books."

"The ultimate revenge," Derick said, toasting. His mood was already starting to lift, thanks in no small part to a Long Island iced tea.

"Actually," Chris added when the laughter had died down, "my book has a murder in it."

"Oh?" Bill said. "So who'd you kill?"

"The victim is based on one of my exes, of course." Chris

pulled the cherry out of his drink and plucked the fruit off the stem with his teeth. "A disco ball falls on his head at a nightclub."

"I thought you said it was murder," Bob said.

Chris smiled mysteriously. "Those things don't just fall by themselves, you know."

"Speaking of mysteries," Derick said, leaning in, "what do you make of our fellow guest at the B&B?"

"Clive?" Bill smiled mischievously.

"You noticed?" Chris said. "Why am I the only one who didn't recognize him?"

Derick smirked. The drink was making him cocky. "There was a mirror in the room, hon. You were distracted."

"We spotted him right away," Bill said. "The night before you guys arrived. He came down to the hot tub."

"You were in the hot tub with him?" Chris cried.

"Yeah, but of course Greta never left his side," Bob said disconsolately.

"Women in a hot tub," Chris said, shaking his head. "There ought to be a law."

Brad interrupted, his eyes stern. "Wait wait wait," he said. "What are you guys talking about?"

"Clive Morgan," Chris said.

"Clive Morgan the movie star? Clive Morgan the closet case?"

"Yes," Derick said, "he's staying in our B&B. We had breakfast with him. And his pit bull, Greta."

"She's not so bad," Bill said. "I chatted with her a bit. She's just looking out for him."

"Does she think anyone really believes they're a couple?" Chris said.

"I don't think that's what it's about. I think she works for him, like his assistant or something."

"Keeping the paparazzi away," Derick said.

"Not to mention the stray hands of the P'town boys." Chris leaned against the railing to get a better view of the deck.

Brad scoped the crowd, too. "It sounds to me like he wants to get caught."

"Why would he want to get caught?"

"So he can stop hiding. It takes a lot of energy to keep that closet door closed."

"What's he afraid of, anyway?" Chris said. "He's worth millions. His career could crash and burn tomorrow and he'd still be set for life."

"Ah," Brad sneered, "but the humiliation."

"It's not easy for everyone," Bill said. "That's what you New Yorkers fail to recognize."

"*Au contraire*, we know it all too well," Brad replied. "I'm from Winnetka, Illinois. I moved to New York specifically because it was harder where I came from. I moved there so I could be myself and not have to deal with . . . cultural limitations."

Bill's brow crinkled, but he went on. "All I'm saying is, I can understand why he'd hesitate. When you're brought up to believe that what you are is wrong, it's hard enough to admit it to yourself, let alone let the whole damn world find out. None of us is in his position. We're not famous. When we come out of the closet, only twenty or thirty people find out. He's talking millions."

Brad smiled. "All the more reason."

Bob decided to change the subject. "I'd like to read your book," he said to Chris. "I like a good mystery."

"Thanks," Chris replied. "I'll let you know if I ever find a publisher."

"So what's it about besides killing your ex?"

"It's about a child custody battle. The abusive husband manipulates the system to get custody of the kid, and then he winds up dead."

"Sounds good. Did the wife do it?"

"You'll have to read it to find out."

"That would be too obvious," Bob said. "Never go for the obvious."

"Unless," Brad said, "that's exactly what he wants you to think. He throws you off by making it so obvious that it never occurs to you that she really did it. But perhaps she did."

"Jeez," Chris said, "no one's even read it yet, and you're already speculating. Talk about buzz!"

"So where are the gay characters?" Bob said.

"It's not a gay book."

"He didn't ask you that," Brad pointed out. "He asked if there were gay characters."

"Maybe. I don't provide intimate details about all the characters' sex lives."

"I'll bet the detective's gay," Bob said. "That would be hot."

"I need another drink," Chris said, pulling himself away from the railing. "Anyone else?"

Derick turned to look out at the beach. The white sand was broken here and there by driftwood and jagged strips of seaweed, charred by the sun. A cool breeze blew off the ocean, rippling the collar of his shirt.

"He's a handful, isn't he?" Brad said, sidling up beside him.

"Yes, he is." Derick took a long sip of his drink, refreshing his buzz.

"If he weren't so much fun to be around, I'd have dumped him long ago."

Derick laughed. "I know how you feel."

"So why the workshop, aside from the fact that it's in glorious Provincetown?"

"It was supposed to be a chance to focus on my fiction, which I never give enough attention to," Derick said. "I do a lot of freelance work, subjects that other people choose for me. *Styles* that other people choose for me."

"So, you came all the way up here to find yourself."

Derick laughed. "Partly. But the scenery doesn't hurt." He gestured toward the waves, cresting more rapidly now as the tide began to come in. "And Chris convinced me that I needed 'connections.'"

"Why am I having such trouble reading enjoyment in your tone?" Brad had a suspicious glint in his eye.

"Because you're a psychologist, I suppose. Aren't you people trained to know when someone's lying?"

"What are you lying about?"

Derick took a deep breath. "I'm over it," he said. "I came here to see what it would be like to take my work more seriously. And to see if anybody else would take it seriously."

"And?"

"And I just don't feel it, you know?" He held his cup by the mouth and dangled it over the railing. "I just don't think I have what it takes—the drive, I mean. I could become a better writer. But I'd have to really want it. And I don't really know what the hell I want anymore."

Suddenly Bob was standing between them, leaning back conspiratorially. "Movie star alert," he whispered.

They turned to find Clive and Greta emerging onto the deck. Clive had pulled his hair into a short ponytail, making his face somewhat more recognizable. Now only the sunglasses and the mustache protected him.

Clive moved smoothly through the crowd, garnering the occasional cruise but, as far as Derick could tell, not a single double-take of recognition. Even in New York, at least tourists would stare and whisper about celebrities. But at the Boatslip, fame didn't matter. All that mattered was whether you were hot. And on that score, Clive Morgan had a lot of competition.

He whispered something to Greta, who nodded severely and pointed toward Derick and the others. Clive smiled and headed over as Greta vanished under the tent housing the bar.

"Hello, gentlemen," Clive said. He was wearing a dark T-shirt that hugged his chest and showed off the flatness of his stomach.

"Hi there," Derick said, suddenly feeling nervous.

"We haven't met." Clive stretched a hand out to Brad.

"Nice to meet you," Brad said. "I'm Brad. I'm a big fan."

Derick's mouth fell open. He'd forgotten to tell Brad that Clive was incognito.

Seeing Derick's reaction, Clive laughed. "That's okay," he said to the group. "It's silly, really, but Greta insists I try. If I introduce myself as Clive, it's a slam-dunk, but tell someone

57

your name is Harold, and they might think twice. Of course, I've always hated Harold. That's why I changed it in the first place."

"Clive is a stage name, then?" Bill said.

"Of course. Outside of England, I don't think anyone names their child Clive. My manager says it adds a touch of the exotic."

"Are you enjoying P'town?" Brad said.

"Very much. I love the Cape, and I get up here far too seldom. If only the film industry could move to Cape Cod, I'd be in heaven."

"You spend most of your time in LA, then."

"LA and New York. I have homes on both coasts."

"Which do you prefer?"

"I hate to choose," Clive said. He gazed briefly out at the deck. "My life isn't about either/or. It's about both/and." Derick vaguely remembered hearing him say the same thing in one of his movies.

Chris and Greta appeared together, each carrying a couple of drinks. "Look who I ran into," Chris said as they entered the circle. He passed a cup to Derick, who stared at him suspiciously.

"You read my mind," Derick said.

"No," Chris replied, "I looked into your cup."

Derick spilled the ice from his first cup over the railing and slid the new one into it.

"So, Harold," Chris said, "how has your day been?"

Clive laughed. "The charade's over. You can call me Clive."

Chris sighed melodramatically. "What a relief."

Greta's brow crinkled, eyes narrowed in the setting sun. She looked older now, as if a few hours of sunlight had managed to coarsen her skin, drive the creases deeper. Abruptly, sensing Derick's gaze, she smiled a painful smile, limited to her lips, unmatched by her eyes. Derick was reminded of a childhood board game, mixing and matching pieces from different faces—a woman's eyes with a man's coarse lips, a strong square chin with a delicate pointed nose. As the conversation bounced back and forth before her, she turned the same smile to each speaker, as if she were watching a tennis match and not rooting for either player.

"What's your next movie?" Bill said.

Clive murmured, hesitant to speak.

Bob's eyes suddenly lit up. "Wouldn't it be funny," he said, gently punching Chris's arm, "if they made a movie of your book and Clive starred in it?"

Brad tapped Derick's foot gently with his sandal. Derick caught a mischievous gleam in his eye.

"So," Clive asked facetiously, "is there a part in it for me?"

Chris laughed. "I don't know. Maybe."

Bob was the only one who seemed truly excited. "I think he should play the gay detective."

Chris rolled his eyes. "There is no gay detective."

"I'm sure it'll be a great success," Clive said. "What's it called?"

"*Disco Murder*," Chris replied.

"Well, that's evocative," Greta said, jumping in.

"*Disco Murder?*" Brad said. "And it's not gay? Tell me again, is it about a murder *at* a disco, or the murder *of* disco? Because I'd love to read about *that!*"

Chris stared daggers and turned back to Clive. "Anyway," he said, "it's all a bit premature, I think."

"Perhaps," Clive said. "You never know."

"Actually, they're both writers," Bob said.

"Who?"

"Chris and Derick. They're both doing that . . . what's it called again?" He turned absently to Derick.

"Workshop," Derick said. Strangely, he felt himself blushing.

"Then you must know Graham," Clive said.

"Whitcomb. Yes," Chris replied, "we're working with him."

"What a coincidence. So am I."

"Really?"

"Yes, we just met last night. That's why I'm in Province-town, actually. The studio wanted me to talk to him, get his take on the character before filming starts."

"Wow," Chris said, "I'd assumed they were going to make a film of *Charity*, but I hadn't heard anything yet."

"Take it from me. It's happening. I'm quite excited, actually."

"You must be," Chris said. "It's a great book. But . . ."

"I know," Clive said with a smirk. "The lead is a woman. I play the feckless husband. I'm looking forward to not being the hero for once. The character is so complex, it'll be really fun to play."

Greta broke in, her speech high-pitched and fast. "Of course, Clive has another major film starting soon. *Charity* is just, what do you call it? A prestige project."

"In other words," Clive said, "it doesn't pay as much as the brainless movies where I get to blow shit up." He scrunched his chin.

Everyone laughed. Everyone except Greta.

"That's really exciting," Derick said. "I can't wait to see it."

"We start filming next month in New York. If you remember the book, you know how important the city is to the story."

"It's practically another character," Chris said.

"Isn't it always?"

"So what do *you* write about?" Clive asked. Derick wondered if he was simply eager to change the subject. "More blood and Donna Summer music?"

"No," Derick said. "I'm working on a love story, I guess you'd say."

"Tragic, I hope," Brad said, winking at Derick. "The best ones are always tragic."

"Not sure yet," Derick said. "I haven't decided how it turns out."

"Who wants to dance?" Chris asked abruptly. Derick was suddenly aware that the music had grown louder.

"I don't know," Bill said, "I'm a little nervous. Is there a disco ball in there?"

"We can dance on the deck," Chris said. He was already half turned away, flicking his head toward the dance area.

"Later," Derick said as Bill and Bob followed Chris.

Derick watched from the railing as his new friends started dancing, each using a style completely his own, Bill not even in sync with the music. He flailed his arms jerkily while Bob fluttered around him, both of them smiling broadly. They had no idea what they were doing, but they were loving every minute of it.

"How long are you staying in town?" Brad asked Clive, pulling Derick back to the conversation.

"We leave on Monday," Greta said. "Clive is appearing at a fundraiser in New York."

"You must get asked to do a lot of those," Brad said.

Clive parted his lips, but it was Greta's words they heard. "It's for an organization we belong to. We are trying to raise consciousness about important issues. Clive has been active in the organization for quite some time."

"Really." Brad's expression fell at the sound of the word *consciousness*. Derick prepared himself. "What is it?"

"The Vyse Foundation," Greta said. She enunciated each syllable carefully, as though hyper-correcting for having stumbled over it before.

"I'm sorry," Derick said, "but I've never heard of it."

Greta chuckled. "That's not surprising. We don't advertise as blatantly as other groups," she said.

"It's unique," Clive added. "Somewhat spiritual, but mostly focused on personal empowerment."

"We seek to integrate all people and all aspects of the individual."

Brad nodded slowly. "Interesting," he said.

"It's still relatively small," she went on, "but growing. We have quite a following in Hollywood. Jimmy Teasdale, Lauren King, Felipe de Vega."

"A real movie star parish," Brad said.

"You could say that." Clive's lips curled up. His eyes were still hidden behind the dark glasses, which gave his smile an air of mystery.

"Good luck with the fundraiser." Brad turned to Derick. "Now *I* feel like dancing," he said. "Anyone?"

"Sure," Derick said, following him out toward the pool.

"They're Moonies," Brad whispered, dragging him through the crowd. "Manson children, those wackos who put on purple shrouds and waited for the Hale-Bopp comet."

"I don't know," Derick said, trying to calm him. "Everyone's entitled to their religion."

"Tell me that the next time some idiot straps dynamite to his chest and blows up a bus."

Once they were several yards away, Brad turned and began to dance. He kept his eye on the railing, as if expecting Clive and Greta to follow them, dynamite and all. "I've heard of these freaks," he said. "They're completely bonkers. It's all about mind control."

"You're kidding. These aren't Okies we're talking about. They're educated, accomplished people."

"Exactly. That's where the money is."

"You sound paranoid," Derick said. His head was starting to pound. He'd drained that second Long Island too quickly.

Brad raised his hands above his head and waved them around. "Believe what you want," he said, "but I'm staying the hell away from those people."

Derick threw his head back to feel the sun on his face. He wanted to escape into the heat and the music. He did a three-sixty, swirling slowly away from Brad.

"Hey, you decided to join us after all!" He was suddenly nose-to-nose with Bob, whose arms were extended to his sides, fingers snapping in counterpoint.

"Yes," Derick said, "we're here."

Bob's lips moved silently over the music.

"What?" Derick asked, leaning forward.

"Great music, isn't it?" Bob yelled directly into his ear now.

Derick threw his head back too quickly and suddenly lost track of his feet. He was tripping over someone—Bob, Brad, someone to the side, he couldn't tell. And all at once he was stumbling back, falling.

Just as quickly, he felt strong arms beneath him, holding him up, and he saw a smiling face leaning toward his. "Hey,

watch it there," said the man as he helped Derick to a standing position. "You okay?"

"Yeah, I'm fine, thank you," Derick said, "just extremely
embarrassed." He laughed nervously. "I have no idea what
happened."

"I think you were distracted by my beauty," said the man,
thick eyelashes fluttering around bright blue eyes. His blond
hair was trimmed short, sticking to his head in sweaty
patches. He looked familiar, but Derick couldn't place him.

"That must have been it."

"Hey there," Bob said, "you all right?" He had stopped
dancing, but his arms were still flailing.

"Yes," Derick said crisply, "I'm fine."

"I think you need a drink," said the blond savior, his arm
still warm on Derick's back. The bartender, that was it. The
bartender from the Eagerton reception.

"I think that's a good idea," Derick said. "My treat."

"That's an even better idea."

His name was Jared, and he drank cosmos. "You're really
light on your feet, aren't you?" Jared asked as they drew away
from the bar, drinks in hand.

"I'm usually a little more Fred Astaire than that." Derick
followed him to the deck railing.

"No worries," Jared said, "I love a man who falls for me."

"I love a man who catches."

Jared laughed. "Don't get your hopes up."

"I didn't mean it that way!" Derick said, cringing. "Just—
you know . . ."

"I know," Jared said. He laid a hand gently against Derick's
chest, fingers splayed. "I'm just yanking your chain."

Derick was content to leave the party noisily behind, to
leave the entire day behind. After a while, as the crowd
thickened, he could no longer make out his dancing friends
or the mysterious Clive and Greta. For a moment at least, he
was free of them. Jared kept the conversation lively but easy,
asking no probing questions, offering no complicated answers. They spoke mostly about Provincetown—the beauty

of the beach, the ease of the summer lifestyle. When they discovered they were both from New York, it was as if that were the side story. The real story was right here, with the fading sun behind Jared's head, glowing around his blond hair.

## CHAPTER 5

## At Herring Cove Beach without a Parasol

D erick Sweetwater was not the romantic type. He'd been in love once or twice, or what he considered in love: a lightheadedness when the person in question entered the room, a sexual urge that refused to be quenched. The rest of us might label those sensations symptoms of youthful infatuation, but to Derick they were love, and he did not cherish the feeling. It was upsetting to his routine, distracting. Most important, it was risky. It would be one thing to suffer through all that and come out the other side happily married, but to go through the same turmoil only to break up in the third month seemed cosmically cruel at worst, and at best, a waste of valuable time.

The solution, he learned, was to be stingy with his heart without denying his body. More than once he had seduced someone on the first date by whispering in his ear: "The only way to get rid of temptation is to yield to it." Some guys had succumbed to the wit. Others were simply impressed by his ability to quote Oscar Wilde.

He had needed neither for Jared. So, when he woke up in the morning in a strange bed, with a pale naked arm draped over his chest, he knew he had slipped. He hadn't used a clever line to distance himself, to turn the joining of bodies into something purely physical. Staring at the light blond hairs on Jared's forearm, downy but erect in the cool air, he remembered that the seduction had been wordless. It hadn't really been seduction, at all. They had stepped into it together, like a dance routine they instinctively knew and didn't need to rehearse. He could have blamed it on the Long Islands, but he knew better. It had, in fact, felt perfectly natural. There had been no hesitation, no need for questioning or drawing precautionary boundaries. He had done it all willingly, gladly, openly.

He was absolutely terrified.

"There you are," Jared said then in a surprisingly husky voice. Derick didn't remember his voice sounding so deep last night. "You were sleeping like a rock."

"Was I?" He turned his head to meet Jared's eyes. "I hope I wasn't snoring."

"Not really. Just a little heavy breathing."

Derick laughed. Somehow, Jared's eyes made him feel safe. The panic ebbed. "Wasn't that *before* we fell asleep?"

Jared bent his free arm against the mattress, rested the side of his head against an open hand. "It isn't every day a man literally falls into my arms, you know."

"Sorry about that. Again." His mouth felt dry. He could only imagine his breath. "What time is it?"

"Nine thirty."

"Shit. Already?" He sat up. The room was bright, cluttered, small. "I have to be at the workshop by ten."

"You can use my shower."

"No thanks. I should get back to my place, get a change of clothes. Can't do the walk of shame directly into that den of vipers."

"Den of vipers?"

His bare feet on the cold hardwood floor, he looked around for his jeans. "The workshop," he said. "Those people can be vicious."

"I hope they weren't mean about your story."

"No worries. They tore it apart with the politest of smiles on their faces." He pulled up his zipper with a hard tug and bent down to grab his shirt off the floor.

"They're probably just fools."

As he popped his head through the neck of the shirt, he saw Jared watching him, sitting up in bed, hands folded in his lap. The lower half of his body was covered discreetly by the ivory sheet, the upper half emerging from it like one of the unfinished Michelangelo statues he'd seen in Florence.

"You haven't read a word of my work," Derick said, "and you know they're fools not to like it."

"Of course," Jared said. "Call it intuition."

Derick plopped down in the armchair to put on his socks and shoes. It had been dark last night when they got back, and he'd had too many other things on his mind to notice the décor. The place looked lived in. A pile of books sat atop the desk, beside a photograph of Jared with an older couple who must have been his parents.

"Are you here for the whole summer?" he asked, holding the back of a shoe with one finger while he jammed his foot in.

"Yes," Jared replied. "I'm between jobs at the moment, so I thought it would be more fun to wait tables here than in New York."

"Are you a waiter in New York?"

"Not full-time. I kind of cobble things together. A little of this, a little of that." He drew a hand through his hair. His eyes were blue. So blue.

Derick spotted a familiar image on the wall—a framed album cover, a drawing of a young Bette Midler with too much hair and too much makeup. *The Divine Miss M,* he read.

Jared turned to look at it. His eyes softened, as if he were gazing up at an altar. "A classic," he said. "And aptly named."

Shoes all tied, Derick stood up and slapped out the wrinkles in his jeans. "I never really got into her," he said.

Jared gasped. "Sacrilege. What kind of homosexual are you?"

Derick sighed. "Not much for diva worship, I'm afraid."

"You're not one of those gaybros I hear tell about, are you? The kind who go to sports bars and drink Budweiser."

Derick chuckled. "No. But you won't catch me at a Liza Minnelli concert, either."

"I did catch you on the dance floor, though."

Derick leaned over the bed and kissed him.

"What are you doing later?" Jared asked.

"I don't know."

"We'll see about that."

If inspiration were predictable or subject to will, it would cease to be inspiring. When Derick forced himself to write, he was almost guaranteed to fail. The keys remained immovable, the pen only hovered above the page. He couldn't make the muse appear, just as he couldn't choose when she would leave. It was all a crapshoot.

As with art, so with life. He had learned long ago that he couldn't make himself give a damn when circumstances weren't right.

He sat now, in the shadowed half of the room, head down to signal concentration on the text, while voices murmured around him. All he saw was words on a page.

He looked up into the sunlight cascading through the row of windows on the far side of the room. Graham's graying hair gleamed. It seemed to have lightened over the past few days, bleached by the sun. Or perhaps his face had just grown more tan.

They were discussing Vincent's piece, a self-contained story that hit every note in Graham's symphony of writing tips. Finally, a session where they didn't have to watch the writer squirm. Vincent's story followed all the rules, with just enough quirkiness to make you almost not notice the fact that it followed all the rules. Instead of critiquing anything, everyone simply took turns quoting their favorite excerpts while Vincent blushed in the corner.

And at that moment, watching him awkwardly absorb the adulation, Derick knew that Vincent would be a star. As if writing well weren't enough, he was also adorable: no more than twenty-five, with perfect skin and perfect bone structure and dark eyes that seemed designed for gazing off into space from the back of a book jacket.

From a chat they'd had after class the other day, Derick had surmised the story was completely autobiographical. Perhaps that was partly what kept people from saying anything negative. To criticize the central character would be tantamount to criticizing Vincent himself. He had already revealed enough vulnerability on the page with the brother who'd died in infancy and the mother who'd run away and never looked back.

Only Graham was willing to go there. Graham, in fact, went right for the most vulnerable part of all—the last-page revelation that the teenage narrator was in the midst of an incestuous relationship with his aunt.

"This is wonderfully bold," Graham said. He was visibly excited for the first time all week, his voice quick and pitched to a major chord.

Vincent's story was the antithesis of anything Graham himself had ever written. It had a direct language that laid emotion bare on the page, a sexual explicitness, and an unabashed gaze at the ugliness of life. Graham loved it, but he wouldn't be caught dead writing it. The more Derick thought about it, in his dark corner of the room, Graham's work was actually more like his own, and Jessica's, even Agnes's, the three people who had suffered the most under his sharp tongue and even sharper pen.

Derick gently pinched the tip of his nose and inhaled. He could still smell Jared, as if particles of him were imbedded in Derick's fingers, or perhaps lodged somewhere in his nostrils. He closed his eyes for a moment and was back in Jared's bed, legs entwined, an unseen hand swirling softly along his spine.

He needed a fling. Chris had been begging him all week to get laid. He would have been happy with that, happy to see Jared again, every night for the rest of the trip, if not for the pesky fact that Jared, too, lived in New York, and that made this the opposite of a fling. If he might run into Jared at any moment shopping at Zabar's or ducking into the Duplex for a cocktail, then anything they did now would only lead to awkwardness and complication. And Derick didn't need complication.

He couldn't wait to get back to the routine of New York, to turn into a ghost again. Hiding behind someone else's life in a self-indulgent memoir was easier than exposing his own through fiction.

"What do you think, Derick?"

When Graham's voice broke through, it sounded tired, as if he'd already asked the question once or twice before. Derick turned toward him and affected a smile. "It's lovely," he said. "I'm speechless."

He'd learned that one years ago. It was his go-to remark to cover up for not paying attention.

"Well," Graham said, "on that note, let's take a break."

People started passing the marked-up manuscripts around. Derick looked down at his and discovered he'd been drawing little heart shapes in the corner. He bore his pen down ferociously to cast them into a dark oblivion. Vincent might think he was making a pass. He didn't want to be thought a dirty old man.

"What's wrong with you?" Chris asked, suddenly at his side as he continued to scribble.

"What do you mean?"

"Did you get any sleep last night?"

Derick looked up. All he needed was for Chris to grill him with questions. But this time it was unavoidable. "Not really," he said. He flipped the pages back over and passed the manuscript along.

"That sounds promising. I want to hear all about it."

"I'm sure you do."

Brad insisted on bringing an umbrella to the beach. He attached it to his bike with a bungee cord. The rainbow fabric stuck out a few feet behind him, the weight throwing him off balance. Derick lagged behind just to watch out for him as they made their way down the street and crossed the highway. After parking their bikes at the wooden fence on the side of the road, they hiked across tide pools toward the dunes, Brad carrying the rolled-up umbrella like a flag in a parade. When they'd trudged over the dunes and selected their spot on the sand, he planted it proudly.

"One small step for man," he said, pushing the latch and opening it, "one giant parasol for mankind."

Herring Cove Beach had a linear progression of neighborhoods, starting with a tiny straight portion, near the parking lot. Entering through the dunes, they had come into the somewhat larger lesbian spot, where bikini tops were rarer and the chance of seeing children only slightly less likely. They had moved through slowly, the sand burning their feet until their skin numbed to its warmth, toward the gay section, which dwarfed the others in both size and density. It was like moving from the suburbs to the city, all the private enclaves that much closer together, so that finding one's place became far more than an arbitrary choice.

There was one more neighborhood beyond this, behind a heavy series of dunes, where the nude sun worshipers lay, enacting their own distinct rituals.

They arranged their towels around the umbrella, Brad commanding the middle spot, completely in the shade. "I haven't had a sunburn in twenty years," he said, lathering on sunscreen, "and I'm not about to start now."

Chris, on the other hand, laid his towel slightly out of the shade and immediately positioned himself directly toward the sun. "I plan to tan as much as possible this week. It's my last chance, and it has to last all winter."

"Good luck with that," Brad said. "Better luck to your dermatologist." He reached for the cooler and twisted the cap off a beer bottle. He held it out to Derick, who hesitated for a moment. "You're on vacation," Brad said. "Live a little."

They clinked bottles and sipped.

71

"Do I hear alcohol?" Chris said, eyes still closed against the sun. "Save one for me. I'll have it when I'm ready to roll over."

"Like a rotisserie chicken," Brad said. "With melanoma." He turned his attention to Derick. "So tell us more about this guy."

"What guy?"

"*What guy*," Brad repeated, mocking. "The one who literally swept you off your feet. Your knight in shining armor."

"He's very sweet," Derick said, reaching for the *Vanity Fair* in his knapsack. He started flipping through the ads, but Brad quickly stamped his hand onto the pages, in the middle of an Abercrombie model's pecs.

"Darling, you vanished into the crowd and refused to answer your cell phone all night. I suspect he was more than sweet."

"If it was one of *your* escapades, Brad," Chris said from the distant towel, "he'd be bittersweet."

"No comments from the peanut gallery." Brad pointed his bottle like a bazooka.

"We just talked," Derick said. "He's interesting, and very nice."

"You just talked." Brad leaned back to direct his words to Chris. "Is he always this evasive about his sex life?"

"What sex life?" Chris said.

"Hmmm," Brad said. "What's that all about?"

"I don't tend to broadcast my 'escapades' as loudly as Chris does."

"Oh, you'd need a bullhorn to be louder than that, my friend." Brad arched his neck and took a long sip of beer. "So, are you going to see this guy again?"

"It's a small town," Derick said. "I'm sure we'll run into each other."

"So you *did* fuck him."

"No," Derick said, laughing. He paused. "We made out for a while, that's all."

Brad was staring.

"And we took a little walk."

Chris cleared his throat, the sound echoing across the sand.

"And then we fucked."

"That's more like it," Brad said, scratching his arm.

"You know," Chris called from the towel, "maybe you should have a double wedding ceremony with the Billy-Bobs."

"Thanks," said Derick. "I'll be sure to make you the flower girl." He leaned back on his elbows and watched the water. A few people were body surfing, riding the waves awkwardly back to shore, sputtering when they emerged in the shallows.

A few feet away, a woman in a one-piece black suit slid gracefully out of the water and began walking up the sand. She made the transition from water to land seamlessly, as though barely noticing a change. As she moved closer, her features coalesced.

"Hey," Derick said, "isn't that what's-her-name?"

"Eva Braun?" Brad said.

"Greta."

She swung her arms rigidly but methodically and suddenly turned her eyes toward their umbrella, as if summoned. She was still several yards away, just far enough to credibly not recognize them. But instead of taking advantage of the distance to turn away and pretend not to see them, she stared openly, lips sealed, features hard. She made no attempt at a smile as she had yesterday. She might as well have been walking on her private beach, silently willing the interlopers to get off her property.

She turned then and headed to the right, her stride now even more calmly determined. Halfway up the beach, she stopped at a green-striped umbrella and settled down next to a figure in a straw hat. From this distance, Derick could just make out a wisp of Clive's hair.

"If I were a sensitive soul," Brad said, "I'd venture to say she doesn't like us."

"I never knew the beach could be so chilly," Derick said.

"What's the big deal?" Brad said. "Does she think we're going to go tell the world that Clive Morgan is a screaming queen? It's hardly news. I can't tell you how many people have claimed to spot him at every gay bar in West Hollywood."

"And why does she care, anyway?" Chris said. "I mean, she's not his publicist or something, is she?"

"Still," insisted Derick, "do you have any idea what it would do to his career?" He lay back and closed his eyes against the sun.

"No," Brad said, "I don't. And neither does he. No male star at his level has done it yet. All these queens are ceding the movement to the lesbians. Ellen DeGeneres is the hero of this crowd, not Clive Morgan."

"Lesbians are apparently easier for America to swallow," said Chris.

"Interesting choice of words," Brad said, "but the sentiment may be right. If straight men are the audience you're worried about, then yes, lesbians appeal to their sexual fantasies, and a gay action hero is an oxymoron. But are we really talking about men? Who actually lines up to see Clive Morgan films? Women. The men only go to his stupid action pictures. The women see everything."

"And do women want to know that their idol is gay?" Derick said.

"Please," Chris said, "women love gay men! Who do you think buys gay romance novels? Women."

"Maybe that's because only women believe in romance."

The twist of another bottle cap echoed across the sand. "We need some entertainment," Brad announced. "Let's go to a drag show."

"Fabulous idea!" Chris screeched. "Which one?"

Derick chuckled. "How many are there?"

"Oh, dozens! Drag in P'town is like . . . oh, I don't know . . ."

"Cheese in France?"

"Something like that, yes."

Derick sighed. "Count me out. I'm not interested in seeing some guy flounce around in a sequined evening gown."

"Seriously?" Brad said. "You don't like drag?"

"I've never understood it," Derick said.

"Then I guess it's safe to say you've never done it."

Derick laughed loudly.

"Not even on Halloween?"

"Never."

Chris decided to pipe in. "It's not butch enough for him," he said. "It's hard to flex your biceps in a ball gown."

"Whereas you don't know where *your* biceps are."

Chris's voice took on a slightly distant quality; Derick guessed he was now facing Brad head-on. "It's internalized homophobia, if you ask me."

"It is *not* internalized homophobia!" Derick shouted. "I've never been the least bit uncomfortable with my sexuality. I've never been in the closet. But if I don't follow all your rules, I'm not gay enough."

"What rules?" Brad said.

"Liking the right music, the right clothes. Diva worship. And, now it would seem, drag."

"Drag queens are our people," Chris argued. "Stonewall, anyone?"

Derick shook his head. "I'm grateful for that. But really, we come in all shapes and sizes. You don't have to like drag or wear gold lamé Speedos in the Pride parade or frequent the Dick Dock to be gay. The only thing we really have in common is that we sleep with other men. It's just sex. That's it."

Silence. Another beer bottle.

Finally, Brad said softly, "What you're describing isn't gay. It's homosexual."

"And what's the Kinsey number for that?"

A breeze blew off the water, tossing sand onto their towels. Derick stood in the sunlight and wiped the sweat from his brow. "I'm going in," he said.

"I'll join you." Brad slid out from under the umbrella, but Chris didn't budge.

"Give me a minute," he said, pushing a cap down over his eyes. "I'm not done with this side yet."

"If he's asleep when we get back," Brad whispered, "we'll have to turn him over so he's even."

As they made their way over the sand, Brad moved in closer. "Are you all right?"

"I'm fine. Sorry I got so worked up. Chris really knows how to push my buttons."

Brad laughed. "That's what friends are for."

Near the water, they spotted a woman with a dark helmet of hair stretching slowly in the sun. One arm bent, then stretched forward as the other moved behind, echoed by the lifting of a foot.

The first touch of the waves was a stinging cold on Derick's feet, which got easier the deeper he ventured in. At any given moment, it was only the line where the surface of the water met his skin that remained cool. The solution, he knew, was to dive in, but he put it off, slowly moving forward, taking the water inch by inch. Beside him, Brad had no patience. When the water was barely up to his hips, he spread out his arms and fell backward, splashing into an oncoming wave that washed over him. He jumped up, laughing, sputtering.

Finally, Derick threw himself in and swam parallel to the shore. The salt water supported him with ease, and after a few strokes, he lingered, floating on the undulations, waiting for the next big wave to carry him in.

Up on the beach, the sand was dotted with umbrellas and towels laid out in a multicolored patchwork. He had strayed far enough down shore that he could no longer easily pick out their own spot or, farther still, Clive and Greta's. Nearby, a young redhead grasping a boogie board marched deeper into the water, seeking a wave like an explorer, or a sailor awaiting battle.

The sound was muffled, yards from shore. On the beach, every whisper was magnified, snatches of various conversations knitting together from far and wide. But here, with the water to absorb the noise and the wind to carry it away, there was a soothing quiet.

He swam, arms smoothly alternating strokes even as the waves spilled over him. In the predictable rhythm of the water, he finally felt the peace he'd been craving all week. Buoyed by the ocean, he turned on his back and floated, ears in the water, eyes closed against the sun.

When he dropped his legs and stood back up, toes digging into the sand, he was a dozen or so yards from where he'd started. The density of umbrellas on the beach had given way to a sparser population—mostly single towels, no coolers, no conversations ringing across the sand. Derick let the next wave carry him to shore. His foot caught a rock as he landed, the waves pummeling as he struggled to stand. He felt like Robinson Crusoe, dumped onto a foreign shore. A few heads turned as he made his way onto the dry sand, inspecting the invader in the swim trunks. Everywhere he looked were fully naked men. One obsessively applied sunscreen to parts that seldom saw the light of day; several others were lying on their bellies, smooth asses round in the air. The braver ones lay flat on their backs, legs slightly spread, brazenly welcoming the sun's rays.

There was no assumption of privacy. Everyone at a nude beach, Derick thought, wants to be looked at. But still he relegated the surrounding bodies to his peripheral vision as he made his way up the sand. He could find a private place in the dunes to pee before heading back. He was glad to have swum so far. It would make the walk back that much longer and more leisurely. He'd have time to clear his head before the onslaught of wit and sarcasm, the expectation to keep up.

The sand swam down around his feet as he pushed on. At one point, he had to grab onto a tall reed to pull himself up the steepest part of the slope. At the crest of the dune, he looked out at the beach and saw the white sand rolling, the tufts of beach grass fighting their way through. This was what he loved most about the Cape, a shoreline unlike any other he'd known. Most beaches were just flat stretches of sand, white dividing lines between water and cold civilization. Here, with the rough dunes going on for miles, oases of grass carving up the white, the beach itself was the destination, a refuge from both land and sea.

It was late summer, and the grass was high, waving in the breeze like a wheat field in some old movie. He descended the other side of the dune and found a spot to pee. It felt good to release himself fully to the air, and he understood the freedom the men on the other side of the dune cultivated.

He walked along through the dunes, the rippling grass. It felt cooler there, higher up, where the wind could whip more freely.

Off to his right, a naked man had staked out territory on a sandy plateau. Sitting up against a piece of driftwood, he surveyed the horizon as though looking for something or someone. Similar outposts were planted here and there throughout the dunes, men eagerly watching, waiting.

He no longer felt like an invader. No one was hiding their intentions here. They had no shame or modesty, and therefore Derick had no need to feel he was intruding. This was just the way of life in this particular spot of the beach. At the shore, crabs scurried back and forth, fighting to get back to the water that had deposited them upon unfamiliar dry sand. That was the habitat there, the world he walked through on his way for a swim. This was another.

The path scooped down and then back up, climbing the dunes like the back of a dinosaur. When Derick reached the top of the next one, he was confronted by a surprisingly thick and tall patch of grass. He pushed through, hoping to find the path cleared ahead. The grass opened onto a small space, a circle of white sand in the vegetation, like a mysterious crop circle.

Something rustled ahead of him, and there, suddenly, were two men, locked in an embrace, hands investigating each other's naked backs as they kissed. Derick stopped, afraid to make noise by moving back too quickly, unsure which way to turn.

Their skin gleamed in the sunlight, clumps of sand stuck in sweaty patches. Their bodies were open to the sun, the sky, the breeze that ruffled their hair, but they seemed oblivious to it all, locked in a silent passion, the adventure of a new, unknown body—hands, skin, lips, an uncharted territory, a frontier.

The sand grew warm under his feet, and Derick shifted in place, his foot crunching onto a brittle stick and interrupting the silence. The man facing him, dark hair spilling over his companion's neck, looked up suddenly and gazed directly at Derick with an expression that was half shock, half relieved smile. Clive Morgan's eyes were laughing.

"Where have you been?" Brad asked suspiciously as Derick approached the umbrella a few minutes later.

"I had to pee," Derick said.

"Really." Brad gestured toward the distant dunes. "I hear there are a lot of distractions over there."

Chris laughed. He was on his belly now, profile resting on folded arms. "Especially when you take your dick out."

Derick settled back onto his towel. He was tempted to share what he'd seen, but somehow gossip felt like more of an invasion than the moment itself. Nothing was to be gained by confirming their suspicions about Clive. It would only prolong a conversation he had already grown tired of.

"Think whatever you want," he said. "You will, anyway."

He lay back down, arms angled out from his sides, and let the heat spill through his pores. When he gave into it like this, the heat drained all his energy, drawing his attention away from thought and into the tingle of his skin, the drop of sweat that slid down his chest, the red and orange light that danced behind his eyelids. When he surrendered, the beach—that postmodern symphony of waves and murmuring voices all bitten by the wind—was a form of meditation, the very physicality of the world heightened and ironically blocking out his everyday perceptions, shutting off judgment and memories and plans.

They lingered for an hour or so longer, mostly in silence. Finally, Brad could no longer stand it. "I don't know about you boys," he said, stuffing his book into a bag, "but I need a shower and a cocktail."

"In no particular order," Chris said.

They packed up and made their way back to the highway. Derick could no longer see Clive's umbrella. He and Greta had left, or had blended somehow into the crowd. That was exactly what Clive probably wanted most of all, at least here.

Derick relished the bike ride back, the cool air rushing past as he pedaled down the highway toward Commercial Street. Once on the main drag, they had to slow down significantly, but the hubbub gave him back some of the energy the sun had stolen. His senses rejuvenated as he maneuvered his way through the crowd, constantly shifting course to avoid running into someone.

Chris stopped in the middle of the road and waited for him to catch up. "Brad invited us over for a drink," he said, gesturing toward Brad, who was already a block ahead. "I'm going to go straight there. You want to come now or later?"

"Later," Derick said. "I need to shower first."

"See you there," Chris said and pushed the pedal to continue riding. Derick followed until the crowd grew too thick, then began walking the bike.

He locked the bike on the rack in the alley beside the inn and immediately pulled his backpack off his shoulders. His shirt was stuck to his back in a pool of sweat.

A chair screeched across the floor as he climbed onto the front porch. Jared was standing there, clutching a magazine in his hand.

"What are you doing here?" Derick said.

Jared smiled. "Waiting for you, of course."

"Don't," Derick said, sensing he was about to be brought into a bear hug. "I'm all sweaty. It's disgusting."

"That's your opinion." Jared pursed his lips theatrically. He was taller than Derick remembered, or perhaps the ride from the beach had just gotten Derick used to hunching over.

He felt aware of how he must look: sweat everywhere, sand in his hair, eyes bleary from the sun. Jared seemed perfectly put together, nothing out of place.

"How did you find me?"

"You told me where you were staying, remember?"

"How long have you been here?" Derick pulled the front door open, and Jared caught it behind him.

"Half an hour or so. I had time to kill."

Inside the room, Derick tossed his backpack on the bed and kicked off his shoes.

"I know what you're thinking," Jared said. "You think I'm a stalker. We just met yesterday, and here I am, already lying in wait."

Derick laughed. "I wasn't thinking that."

"No," Jared said, "I know your type. You're the type who thinks things should move very slowly, and that anyone who jumps the gun must be seriously deranged."

"Sounds like the voice of experience. Do you often get accused of stalking?" Derick draped himself onto the seat and opened the window wide. He slapped his sneakers together outside the window and watched the sand fall.

Jared sat on the foot of the bed and crossed his legs. "Let's just say that most men I meet have a hard time getting in touch with their feelings."

"But you don't."

"Nope," Jared said, lips curling. "I'm quite comfortable with my emotions."

Derick picked at the front of his shirt, pulling the fabric away from his chest. "Listen," he said, "I feel grubby as hell. Do you mind if I take a shower? You're welcome to stay."

"Sure," Jared said. "You go right ahead. I'll just snoop through your things."

Derick laughed and strolled into the bathroom. "I'll leave the door open so I can keep an eye on you."

"That goes both ways," Jared said, peering flirtatiously as Derick pulled off his shirt.

The shower was luxuriating, lukewarm water spilling onto

his back. He turned into it and closed his eyes against the spray as he lathered. He could feel the pores that the heat had opened closing against the water. His skin was flexible and alive.

When he was done, he stayed inside the shower and yanked a towel off the wall to dry himself. The yellow towel was draped around his waist when he finally stepped out onto the bath rug and met Jared's eyes across the room. He hadn't moved. He was still sitting there, legs crossed, still wearing the same curious smile.

"I love a hairy chest," Jared said.

Derick patted his chest self-consciously. "Umm, thanks." He went to the dresser to find a clean shirt. "So, to what do I owe the honor of your visit?"

"I thought you might like to have a drink with me," Jared said. "Or a bite to eat."

"Isn't it a little early for that?"

"Well," Jared said as Derick turned around, "we could come up with something else." He stood and took the shirt from Derick's hand. He draped it carefully over a chair. Turning back, he grabbed the nape of Derick's neck and pulled him into a long kiss.

"I don't even know you, mister," Derick breathed as their lips parted for a moment.

"What's to know?" Jared whispered into Derick's ear. "Don't you love mystery?"

Jared's skin was smooth and surprisingly white. He might have spent the summer in Finland rather than Provincetown, his body unsullied by the sun. As they stood naked together beside the bed, the breeze wafting around them, Derick stroked Jared's muscles, his arms hard and rounded, sharp stubble rising over his pecs. He hadn't noticed it last night.

"You shave," he whispered. "A man who loves chest hair, and you shave your own?"

Jared smiled mysteriously. "I have my reasons," he said.

"It shows off your pecs better, I suppose."

"Yes," Jared said. "I've always believed that a man has to have either a gorgeous chest or gorgeous hair to cover it up."

Derick peered at him suspiciously.

"Don't worry," Jared said, "you have both."

All through their lovemaking, Derick found himself listening for footsteps, watching the door. He hadn't shared a room with anyone since college. He wondered if he should have hung a necktie from the doorknob.

Jared settled back onto the pillow. "I guess last night wasn't a dream, after all."

Derick laughed and sat up against the headboard. "My friends are waiting for me at the Boatslip," he said. "Do you want to go over there and officially meet them? They're still curious about you from last night."

Jared sighed and pulled himself up to a sitting position. "No thanks," he said, "I have a lot to do. Maybe later."

Derick laughed. "What do you have to do? It's P'town, for heaven's sake."

"Some of us have obligations," Jared said.

"More bartending?"

Jared slid off the bed and started getting dressed. "How about a moonlight stroll on the beach later?" he asked. "Around midnight?"

Derick put the towel away and came back into the room. Jared was already dressed, everything but the sandals. "I don't know," Derick said. "Sounds awfully romantic."

"You can handle it," Jared said, patting his shoulder. "You're a big boy." He pulled his cell phone from a pocket. "What's your number?"

He entered the number into the phone and tucked it away with a dramatic flourish. "Midnight," he said. "Stay awake, now." He kissed Derick hard on the lips before dashing out of the room.

"Who was that masked man?" Derick mumbled to himself, slipping his underwear on at last.

A moment later, the door clicked behind him. "Who was that?" It might have been the echo of his own voice.

He turned around to find Chris standing by the door. "Who?" he asked, fumbling with his shirt.

Chris laughed. "That guy I just passed on the stairs. You little minx!"

"It was Jared," Derick said. "He was lying in wait when I arrived."

"What did you do to him last night?" Chris peeled off his shirt and tossed it into the corner.

"Nothing," Derick said. "That's just it, I guess. I left him wanting more."

Chris, on his way into the shower, peered over his shoulder with a smile. "Ah, still waters do run deep," he said.

"Why did you abandon Brad?"

"I didn't. I just decided I needed a change of clothes. And there's nothing in Brad's closet I would dare put on. Everything's black, for Christ's sake. Doesn't he know it's summertime?" He turned on the water, which reverberated against the tile and swallowed his words.

"So what do you think?" Chris said a few minutes later, drying himself in the bathroom doorway.

"What do I think about what?"

"Didn't you hear what I just said?"

"No," Derick said, slipping on his canvas shoes. "The shower was too loud."

"Brad got us tickets for a show tonight."

Derick frowned. "Don't tell me. Drag."

"You don't have to come if you don't want to. But this one's supposed to be the best in town."

Derick had to laugh at Chris's persistence. "Drag is so tired," he said languidly, giving in.

"Oh, honey," Chris replied, "you have got to lighten up." He draped the towel over the shower rod and stepped naked into the room. "Get in touch with your feminine side," he said, opening the armoire doors.

## CHAPTER 6

## Bustiers and Freudian Slips

The line outside the Crown & Anchor snaked through the parking lot. "I thought gay people were always late for stuff," Brad said, checking his watch. "It's fifteen minutes before curtain, and half of P'town is already here."

"But the doors aren't open yet," Chris said. "Now *that's* gay time."

While Provincetown dispersed during the day, its people variously strolling the streets, biking in the dunes, or lying on the beach, at night it all coalesced. Nearly every face was familiar, and the ones you casually passed in the afternoon suddenly seemed like old friends. Directly before them in line, a beautiful young couple they'd spotted on the beach were holding hands, whispering in each other's ear and smiling at everyone around them, all Abercrombie aloofness gone for the evening.

Chris had teased Derick mercilessly over drinks, describing to Brad how timely his return to the room had been. "One minute earlier, and god knows what I would have stumbled upon!"

"So who are we seeing tonight?" Derick said as the line began to move.

"A number of people," Brad said. "It's a drag revue."

"Ooh," Derick said flatly, "how exciting."

Chris sneered. "Derick, *watch* the drag. Don't *be* one. Try to get over your issues."

Derick laughed and punched his shoulder. "What issues?" he asked in a gruff baritone. "Fuckin' A."

"There comes a time," Brad said, "when you have to leave your issues behind and go with the flow. When in Rome, you go to the Colosseum. In P'town, you go to a drag show."

Inside, the seating was cabaret style, straight-back chairs clumped around tiny drinks tables, all facing the stage. They ended up a third of the way from the front, on the aisle.

"This way," Brad said, scooting his chair under the table, "we're close enough to see everything but spared being dragged into the show."

"No pun intended," Chris said.

"In my profession, we call it a Freudian slip."

The room filled up quickly, and waiters began racing around to take drink orders before the show began. Derick had had enough hard liquor this week, so he ordered a beer.

"Wuss," Brad said before asking for yet another Long Island.

"I have a feeling I'm going to need my wits about me," Derick explained.

By the time the lights went down, he was halfway through the beer. The crowd began to murmur excitedly, and with the arrival of the hostess, general chaos ensued.

She was at least six feet tall to begin with, so the heels and teased blonde wig brought her into NBA territory. Squinting at the audience under sparkling eye shadow, she proceeded to berate the fashion choices of the front row.

"And where are you visiting from, hon," she said, leaning forward and affecting a country accent, "Appalachia? And is this your boyfriend or your brother? Oh, stupid question— one and the same!" She reassumed her towering height and pursed her lips. "That's one of the unsung benefits of being gay," she said. "You can fuck your relatives and not worry about disturbing the gene pool."

She introduced herself as Missy Sissy ("men have used me to count the distance from a lightning strike—one Missy Sissy, two Missy Sissy"), and most of the audience seemed to know her well. In fact, the ones up front, whom she picked on relentlessly between introducing the acts, hooted the loudest, as if they had sat there specifically to be insulted. S&M without the welts. Derick cringed and slouched in his seat.

The musical numbers were easier to take. A series of drag queens in increasingly bizarre outfits appeared on stage to lip-synch and awkwardly dance their way through a series of cheesy, incongruous songs. After the first couple of acts, Derick's resistance melted, and he found himself laughing as loudly as anyone else.

At one point, when a tall redhead appeared on stage, her short dress revealing surprisingly meaty legs, Chris leaned in and said, "I'd like to see *her* naked!"

"Don't you mean *him*?"

"Whatever."

The sound of a big band began to spill loudly through the speakers as the performer stood as demurely as a man in stilettos can, in the middle of the stage. Ass back and tits forward, she pouted like Betty Boop. And as she slowly began to move, the voice of Bernadette Peters appeared to emerge haltingly from her mouth. *"I'm just a Broadway baby,"* she intoned, body swaying to the lilt of the music.

She turned the song into a striptease, slowly peeling off white elbow-length gloves and slapping them to the floor. Her lips moved impeccably, less lip-synching than ventriloquism. Aside from the curly wig, no single part of her really resembled Bernadette, but somehow it all came together authentically. More than any of the previous acts, she seemed like a Broadway star slumming at a drag show in Provincetown.

As the music began to swell, Bernadette strutted forward and off the stage, and the audience roared. She slinked down the aisle, rustling someone's hair, lifting someone else's chin. And then her eyes landed on Derick.

Brad had been wrong. They were not seated far enough back to be safe.

Bernadette marched toward him, her face reading huffy desire. As the song reached its crescendo, she slunk into his lap, her head thrown back over his shoulder. She stared into his eyes as she rose back up, her own a deep, powerful blue. And she winked.

"Oh my god," Derick said, watching her ass wiggle its way back up to the stage.

"Lucky you," Chris said. "When's the last time you had a drag queen sit on your lap?"

Derick sighed. "About three hours ago," he said. "That's Jared."

❖

With a final round of insults, Missy Sissy closed the show and the lights came up as the rows quickly emptied out. Except row J, where Derick was being grilled for dirt.

"How could you not know he was a drag queen?!" Chris cried.

"It's not the sort of thing you think to ask on a first date."

Brad pulled his chair out of line to make a triangle with them. "Good thing he's not a *famous* drag queen. It would be embarrassing not to recognize him."

"Recognize him?" Derick asked. "Who knows what RuPaul looks like without makeup?"

"I do," said the others in concert.

Derick rolled his eyes. "You win," he said. "You're just gayer than I am, I suppose."

Brad patted his shoulder. "No, honey, believe me, you're a lot gayer than this one will ever be." He shot a wagging thumb toward Chris.

"What's wrong with my gayness?" Chris said.

A chair screeched across the aisle, announcing the sudden appearance of Jared, still in full drag. "There's something wrong with your anus?"

"My *gayness*," Chris quickly corrected.

"Oh, that's much worse. When something's off with people's gayness, my whole career is shot to hell."

"You were fabulous, by the way," Brad said. "And unique. Who thinks to do Bernadette?"

"A serious Sondheim queen, that's who." And Bernadette's enormous hand, made even longer by two-inch ruby-red nails, landed gently on Derick's shoulder. "Are you okay, hon? I thought you were going to have a heart attack when I landed in your lap."

Derick tried to smile. "It was just the shock," he said.

"Good. Because from the look on your face, I was afraid I needed to lose a few pounds."

"Don't even think about it," Brad said.

Bernadette was still focused on Derick. "It was as much of a shock to me to see *you* here. But once I did, well, I couldn't resist that lap."

"I thought you were a bartender."

"I told you, I have a lot of jobs. Do you have any idea how expensive this mascara is?" Bernadette—Derick could not yet think of her as Jared, not with the wig and the eyelashes—arched her back, the dress growing even tighter against her breasts. "So," she said, gazing at him now, "still up for that moonlight stroll?"

Derick just stared.

"Don't worry," she said, laughing, "not in these heels. I'll change."

"Let's all have drinks," Chris said excitedly.

Bernadette cocked her head with a sigh. "Great. But I have to change out of this *shmatte*. It could take a while."

"We're in no hurry," Brad said.

She smiled and sought out Derick's eyes. He nodded, smiling dutifully.

"Okay. I'll be as quick as I can. If Missy hasn't already stolen all the cold cream." She marched back up to the stage and through the curtains. Despite the heels, her walk was decidedly more masculine now.

"Marry him," Brad said without missing a beat.

"What?"

"I always wanted to have a drag queen in the family. Can you imagine the parties?"

Derick dropped his head into his hands.

"What's wrong?" Brad said. "She—he's fabulous."

"You haven't met him yet."

"Well, if *he's* half as charming as *she* is, you're the luckiest man in town."

They waited outside, where the air had grown brisk, the sky nearly black above the lights of the hotel. When Jared emerged several minutes later, it was as if the past hour hadn't happened, as if Bernadette had never existed. He was dressed in pale streaked jeans and a plaid shirt that hung baggily on his flat chest. He pulled Derick in for a hug and pecked him on the cheek.

"Who are you?" Chris said, laughing.

"Jared," he said with a smile and an extended hand. "Nice to meet you."

Derick introduced them all, and they headed off to the A-House. Jared took his hand as they emerged onto Commercial Street. His grip was firm, the long fingers, sans nails, closing assuredly over Derick's.

The dance floor was packed when they arrived, but there was no line at the bar. Brad ordered drinks all around and passed them out one by one as they appeared at the bartender's station. The four of them walked in procession toward the back of the room and out to the patio.

"So how long have you been doing your act?" asked Brad. He seemed to be studying Jared's face for traces of makeup.

Jared pursed his lips in thought. "I first did drag a little in college, just for fun. And I've performed here and there ever since. But I started taking it seriously only about a couple of years ago. My so-called normal job was beginning to drive me nuts. For me, wearing a necktie and pretending to give a shit about stock portfolios took a lot more acting than putting on a dress and singing a few songs. I feel more authentic up there, even when I'm pretending to be someone else."

"Why Bernadette?"

"Are you kidding? I adore her. And nobody else does her." He sighed. "But I want to do so much more. I mean, look at Missy. She is, as they say, *fierce*. I'm not quite there yet. I don't have a drag persona, really. What I do is more like female impersonation."

"Well," Brad said, "if imitation really is the sincerest form of flattery, Ms. Peters would be proud."

Jared laughed. "Maybe her, but not my mother."

"Your family doesn't approve?" Derick asked.

"My family doesn't *know*." He turned again to Brad. "But enough about me. What do you guys do?"

"*Moi?*" Brad said. "I shrink heads."

"Fascinating!"

"Yes," Chris said, nodding furiously. "He has an amazing collection of them on narrow shelves all around the house. Little shriveled-up things all wearing the same expression." He put on a look of horror, mouth softly open, eyes wide with fear.

Jared's laugh was resonant, deep. But still Derick kept seeing the red curls framing his face.

"Seriously," Jared said, "do you deal with schizophrenics or what?"

"I should be so lucky," Brad said. "No, my clientele is pretty much the walking wounded. Or the whiny little bastards, as I like to call them. Mostly well-off people who get terribly upset when things don't go their way."

"It sounds like you really love your work."

"Oh yes," Brad said. "It offers hours of entertainment. I could tell you stories . . . if only I *could* tell you stories." He leaned in for a whisper. "That pesky confidentiality thing, you know."

"In a way," Jared said, his features suddenly animated, "I suppose that's why I've been drawn to performing. I mean, I think I see things in people that they may not see in themselves. And being up there on stage, I can reflect it back to them."

"So you're really playing *to* Bernadette Peters?" Brad said.

"No." Jared relaxed against the wall. "If anything, I'm giving the audience back their vision of the feminine. It's becoming more and more acceptable to be gay in this country, but to be feminine even for a night? Well, that's still a problem."

Derick gazed across the room, suddenly aware of how mixed the crowd was. Ordinarily, the wispy boys were invisible, his focus always drawn to the muscles, the beards, the cool indifference of the masculine pose.

"Do you think of yourself as feminine?" he asked, pulling his eyes away from a furry chest in the distance.

"You mean when I'm not on stage."

Derick nodded.

"Off stage I just think of myself as human. We're all a little of this and a little of that, aren't we?"

Derick's eyes wandered again. "Are we?"

Brad shook his head pitifully. "Oh honey, take it from a shrink."

"Now that the PBS portion of the evening is over with," Chris said, "I need to dance."

"Yes," Brad said, "you do. Something to flush away the toxins." He grabbed Chris's hand and pulled him into the crowd. Derick and Jared followed but kept a careful distance.

As they swayed gently to the music, Derick studied Jared's body—meaty thighs straining against his jeans, forearms thick with blond hair leading down to veiny hands. This was not the body that had preened on that stage. He couldn't reconcile the two.

The other dancers crowded around, each one carving out his own space. The music pounded, the vibration moving up through his legs, into his belly.

As he turned, his hand grazed Jared's, and he looked up, into the eyes. Even in this light, his eyes were hypnotic. This time he let himself focus on them. His feet did what they would, unregulated, unchecked. His feet could take care of themselves for the moment. He was dancing with his eyes.

The colored lights flickered on Jared's face, his pale skin transforming by the second. Even as the music transitioned, the DJ sliding, sometimes jarringly, from one song to another,

Jared's eyes stayed riveted on his. Derick wanted to look away, toward the safety of invisibility, but he couldn't.

Chris crashed into Derick's side and broke the spell. "Refill?" he asked. Brad was hovering behind him.

"Sure," Derick said. "We'll be there in a minute." As Chris and Brad slid out of the crowd and toward the bar at the front of the room, he reached out for Jared.

Jared smiled more brightly now. The moment was over— the moment of silent communication couldn't last forever. Epiphanies come on an installment plan.

"Your friends are a trip," Jared said. The moonlight glinted off his hair, the tide a backbeat to his words.

They were walking along the beach, the compacted sand by the water hard and smooth beneath their feet. They had removed their shoes, which now dangled by the laces in their hands.

"I shocked you tonight, didn't I?" Jared asked. He was looking toward the curve of the beach, their path illuminated by lights on a house deck just ahead.

Derick laughed nervously. "I can't say I was expecting to see you there. In a dress."

Jared's voice was soft, almost swallowed by the waves. "I wasn't expecting to see you, either. I should have known better."

"Better?" Derick asked.

"I've dated guys who couldn't handle it. Or they assumed that just because I wore a skirt from time to time, they were necessarily the ones who wore the pants." He laughed and stopped suddenly, turning to face Derick.

"You look good in pants," Derick said.

"Thanks. So do you."

Derick playfully punched his shoulder and resumed walking. Jared caught up quickly and took his hand, interlacing their fingers. They didn't speak again, just let the sea underscore their thoughts.

The beach at night was painted in shades of gray, drained of the day's vibrant color. And yet, in the darkness, it was still alive in the crash of the waves, the smell of the sea, the gritty sand creeping between his toes. In the darkness, in the quiet, the beach felt still more real, pared down to some essential core, an energy from which everything else sprang. If the tourists came there every summer for the culture of the town, it was that primal energy of the beach that had created the town in the first place. When you got down deep enough, this was the source: the ocean, the sand, the cool breeze that ruffled his hair.

They walked along slowly, letting the sand grip their feet with each step. Their hands slackened, so that the pressure was no longer there and the twining of their fingers became the natural state of things. They zigzagged up the beach when a wave washed toward them, the water bubbling frothily as it was absorbed by the sand. They continued in silence until a break came between the buildings, a path leading back to the street, the other reality.

They emerged into the glow of a streetlight just across from the inn. People were still milling about, but fewer of them, with less intensity, less purpose in their stride. Now that the bars were closed, they had fewer options, but these hardy souls seemed unwilling to surrender the night without a fight.

Jared stopped on the narrow sidewalk and swung his arm so their clasped hands flowed back and forth playfully. In the cone of orange light, his features were sharper—the angular nose slightly flared, the eyes wide, tiny remnants of glitter still clinging to the lids. His expression was at once exhausted and energized, as if his body, like Derick's, was craving sleep but wishing it weren't.

"Tomorrow?" Jared said.

"It's a busy day. The last workshop, and then there's a reading in the evening, kind of a closing ceremony."

"You don't sound particularly enthusiastic."

"Sorry. I'm just anxious to get it over with. The weekend should be good. I can finally relax."

"So I'll see you then."

"Sure," Derick said. "We're doing a whale watch on Saturday, though. Maybe after that?"

"Sure. We'll figure something out."

A bicycle sped by on the street, its bell jingling tinnily. Only a few hours before, they had made love, caressing every inch of each other's body, but now Derick found himself hesitating for a simple goodnight kiss. It was always like that, after the initial blush of infatuation, once consummation carried them below the surface, where the fantasy lover becomes merely a man. But this time a man who had recently wiped lipstick off his mouth.

Jared didn't notice the hesitation. He swooped toward Derick's face. Derick closed his eyes and felt again the pressure of Jared's kiss, the softness of his lips, the gentle way he parted them, just enough.

"Good night," Jared said, and he smiled. He turned on his heel and vanished down the street.

Derick stood silently for a moment, watching the darkness far down the street shrink and swallow his form.

He turned again and crossed the street, and another figure, an almost formless shadow, appeared before him on the porch. "Beautiful evening, isn't it?" the voice said. He recognized the German accent.

"Yes," Derick said, climbing the stone stairs to the porch.

Greta was sitting in the corner, feet squarely on the floor, hands cupped softly on the arms of the wicker chair. "You were walking along the beach," she said. He assumed she intended it to be a question, but you could never tell with Greta. He wondered for a moment if she had been spying on him.

"Yes," he said. "It's beautiful out there at night. So quiet."

He could see her silhouette more clearly now, but her face remained in darkness, her expression impossible to read.

"You enjoy the beach in daylight, as well, of course," she said.

She knew, he thought. She knew what he had seen.

"But it is so busy during the day," she went on. "So many people, so many things happening, one can hardly be sure what's real and what's not." Her head didn't move as she spoke. He could barely note the flutter of her jaw.

"Pardon me," he said, "but I'm really exhausted." He reached for the doorknob, relieved when it gave way so easily, "I'll see you at breakfast, then."

"Sleep well, Mr. Sweetwater."

He nodded and went inside. Only when he'd closed the door behind him did he realize his hand was shaking.

# CHAPTER 7

## The Pottery Barn of Literature

C hris survived unscathed, disco ball and all. His selection for the workshop was the first chapter of his novel, which, Derick knew, had already gone through at least a dozen drafts. It was as fine-tuned as any 20 pages Chris had ever written. Even Derick had edited it for him once already. It wasn't a literary piece; Chris made no pretense of any motive other than to entertain. And in that, all these drafts later, he had clearly succeeded. At one point, the workshop became a round robin of favorite humorous passages read aloud, prompting gales of laughter from everyone, even Graham.

The last workshop of the week, it was also the briefest. In the end, they hadn't much to say about a fun romp involving murder by disco ball. That was how Derick framed it to Sera when he ran into her outside the building that evening.

"Well," Sera said, deadpan, "clearly that's a story that's just dying to be told."

They were early for the reading, the final event on the week's agenda. There had been shorter readings every night all week, with various people from the program, including the teachers, presenting excerpts from their work, but Derick had skipped most of them and had politely declined when asked to participate. Sharing his work on paper was one thing. The prospect of performing it live was terrifying.

Tonight's event was part reading, part celebration. He hoped it would end the week on a higher note, perhaps bring him out of the literary funk he'd felt for the past couple of days.

"I love Chris," he told Sera, cupping his hands before her lighter to protect the flame for her cigarette. "We've been friends for years. But his work is just so different from mine. It doesn't seem fair to compare it, but . . ."

"I know," Sera said. "You don't want to badmouth your friend. But we're talking about his work here, not his value as a human being. It's okay." She exhaled a swirling column of smoke. "It comes down to a simple question: would you rather succeed at something easy and, in the end, insignificant, or set an ambitious goal and marginally miss?"

"That depends on what you really want."

"Precisely. Do you want to make money, or do you want to do something meaningful with your life? Because, let's face it, Derick, this country is illiterate. They call us 'starving artists' for a reason."

A cool breeze made its way off the water and ruffled Derick's hair. "I guess I just wanted more positive feedback. I got criticism of my piece, but not really anything particularly useful. I mean, I knew it needed work, but I was hoping for advice on how to make it better."

"What?" Sera said. She held the cigarette to her side, hand splayed perpendicular to her skirt. "You brought something that needs work?"

She was squinting at him painfully, the way she might stare at a child who'd just willfully touched a hot stove. "That was your first mistake," she said. "Don't pay attention to the brochure. Workshops aren't about working on your work, despite the name. They're about impressing people. Silly boy. Everyone else brings stuff that's practically perfect. They've probably brought the same damn piece to every workshop they've ever attended, revising it ad nauseam until they finally strike gold. Gold is what they're looking for. The only 'help' they want is a book contract."

He sighed. "I totally fucked up, didn't I?"

"I don't know." She flashed him a lopsided, mischievous grin. "What did you learn?"

"That I don't want to do this again."

She laughed. "That's something."

Her laugh was infectious. He had to make a conscious effort to speak. "No, seriously," he said at last. "It's not just that Graham tore my story to shreds. It was looking at the stuff he *did* like—the stuff that got consensus in the room. With one or two exceptions, it was all perfectly predictable stuff, the sort of thing you can find on any bookstore shelf with your eyes closed."

"The Pottery Barn of literature," she said. "Everything matches."

"Exactly!"

"Gee, hon, I had no idea you were so naïve. How old are you again?"

"I'm thirty-six."

She rolled her eyes. "And finally popped your artistic cherry."

"Don't get me wrong." People were walking past them now in larger clumps, heading inside. Derick glided toward the sidewalk and lowered his voice. "I never had illusions of being a best-selling author. But now, well, I just don't feel like bothering with it anymore."

Sera found a trash can and stubbed her cigarette out on the side before tossing it in. "Okay," she said, "the thing to remember is that we're talking about two very different things: writing and sales." Her eyes were wide, focused. "There are no two ways about it, literary success is a complete crapshoot. Emphasis on the crap."

"Then what's the point?"

"Let me finish," she said. "The only way to get anywhere is to separate the two in your mind. You don't write to sell books. Leave that mercenary path to Jackie Collins and Graham Whitcomb. You write to write."

"Are you giving me that whole 'I write because I have no choice' pep talk?"

"Not quite. But have you ever sat at your computer all alone, and written a perfect sentence?"

"I wouldn't say perfect."

"Say perfect."

"Okay, perfect. I've written a perfect sentence."

"And how did it feel?"

Derick bit his lip, remembering. "It felt pretty damn good," he said with a laugh.

"A literary tree fell in the forest, and nobody was there to hear it. Nobody but you. And it still sounded fabulous." She turned around and led him back up the path to the academy. "We don't write for these schmucks, Derick. And we don't write for some imaginary audience. If you don't do it for yourself, there's no reason to bother. And if you *don't* do it for yourself, it's going to be the same sort of shit that *they* write. You want to be on the best-seller list? Really?"

Yes, he wanted to say, I do. But for my own stuff, not some celebrity memoir like every other celebrity memoir.

But soon enough, they entered a clamorous room. Most of the seats were already taken, so they gladly sat in the last row, as close to the door as possible. "Always have a good exit strategy," Sera whispered as they settled in.

The program director, an earnest woman named Alma Kittredge, introduced the readers one by one, beaming each time as if she were in the presence of Austen and Fitzgerald themselves. She was one of the believers, Derick thought. She had faith that the next Hemingway really was in this room. Derick wasn't so sure.

First up was Agnes. Derick recognized the passage from the story she'd workshopped, but she had clearly revised it significantly in the past few days. Unfortunately, it was mostly dialogue, and she made no distinction between the voices. That, combined with the nervous speed with which she read, made it impossible to tell the difference between the characters.

"Ah well," Sera whispered over the applause, "at least she has that British accent. I'm not sure what else could save that twaddle."

"You're incorrigible," he said.

"I know. Isn't it delicious?"

While the prose writers read just a few pages of a single work, most completely out of context, the poets had time to read several pieces. Ashton Bainer managed to squeeze in four poems, but Derick had trouble telling them apart.

Ashton's voice rose with each stressed syllable, and each line ended with the interrogative inflection Derick had come to see as *de rigeur* for poetry readings. And, just in case the audience couldn't hear the rhythm, exaggerated as it was, Ashton rocked back and forth over the page, as though propelled by the stress marks.

*When the SUNset GLITtered?*
*On the broken SHARDS of my SOUL?*
*A ciCAda CHIRPED?*
*In the PASture?*

The words coasted over Derick's head. His mind was wandering back to yesterday, to the pattern of freckles on Jared's neck, a pixilated map of Greece.

Sera's head drooped over Derick's shoulder, her lips open beside his ear. "GET me? OUT of here?" she grunt-whispered.

Alma took to the podium again with a portentous expression. "Our final reader," she said, "requires no introduction from me."

Sera couldn't help herself. "Why is it that immediately after saying that, they always go on to introduce someone?"

Derick stifled a laugh and turned his attention back to Alma.

"Graham Whitcomb has been a literary idol of mine for quite some time and now, I'm happy to say, a friend. His newest novel, *Charity,* received the National Book Award, and he's offered to read a passage from it for us tonight. Ladies and gentlemen, Graham Whitcomb."

Emerging from a corner of the room, Graham made his way to the podium through a loud ovation. "Thank you, thank you," he said, scowling in faux humility.

Derick wondered what he'd been like before the award, when he was just another writer struggling for attention. He wondered if Graham had been as much in love with himself then as he seemed to be now.

Graham placed his copy of the book upon the podium, several pink post-its sticking out from the side. He held one and flipped the book open. Then, lifting it dramatically into the air, he began to read.

His voice was suddenly deeper, the cadence slow, syrupy—pauses coming at odd points, phrases lilting like waves. "The only misfortune in Charity Sharpe's life," he read, "was the size of her ambition. Since childhood she had imagined herself a successful novelist, her name filling shelves in the library, her photograph in the windows of bookshops, literary hordes begging for her autograph, prizes bestowed, the pantheon open to another figure. She worked hard. She wrote her first short story at the age of seven, her first novel in her teens. She was always writing, always reading the great authors for inspiration and tips on style. She took creative writing classes in college, got an M.F.A. at a small Midwestern university known more for its agriculture programs than its art. She tried on the style of other successful writers, for practice, seeking the elusive voice her teachers always spoke about: the laconic Hemingway, the circular Woolf, the bellowing Bellow. Charity had the diligence, the sensitivity, even the imagination of a great writer. What she didn't have—and what none of her teachers and role models could give her—was talent."

Sera stifled a laugh, which came out as a quiet snort, and quickly turned it into a deliberate cough as cover, the sound enhanced by the dramatic gesture of a hand against her chest.

Of course, Derick had read the book before, but then it had just been a story. Now, in this environment, he understood it had come from this world so familiar to Graham and so new to him. The room was full of Charity Sharpes. Perhaps, he thought, Graham had chosen this passage as a passive-aggressive message, or perhaps just a warning. He wondered, indeed, if Graham had chosen it specifically for him.

Graham shifted his gaze around the room as he read, as though he were checking that the whole group was still with him, or perhaps he was looking for the reassurance of the occasional nodding head.

The language remained stiff, whether in description or dialogue, but Graham's voice climbed and fell dramatically. He periodically peered over his glasses to heighten the effect. The book had sounded completely different in Derick's head as he'd read it casually in his armchair, on the subway, on a park bench. Now, in Graham's voice, the tragedy of the story was immediately apparent.

The sudden silence when Graham closed the book was jarring. In just a few minutes, Derick had fallen into another world. He realized now, in a way that had escaped him before, that *Charity* was indeed a radical departure. Graham's previous work had been good, but it was all of a piece. This book seemed to have sprung of its own accord, as if its energy had been swirling through the world looking for a channel, and had finally found one in Graham Whitcomb.

Sera nudged him in the midst of the applause. "Can we go now?" she whispered.

"Yes, please." Derick squeezed past the people to his left and led her out of the room.

They waited to talk until they were safely outside. "Thank God," Sera said, "if I had to listen to one more poet, I would have lost my mind."

"Ashton's kind of sweet," Derick said, "in a tragic way. He read each poem as if he'd never seen it before."

"Method acting." Sera led him toward the sidewalk. "But I have to SAY? No WONder? So many PEOple? Hate POetry? When it ALL? Sounds exACTly like THIS?"

"You forgot the hand gestures," Derick said. He spread his arms out like wings and skipped along the street, swooping under the trees.

Sera caught up, laughing loudly, and fell against him.

It took several blocks before their laughter trickled out. Finally, Sera asked, her tone strangely serious, "So what are you going to do, now that this extravaganza is over?"

They were just emerging from the quiet side of town. At

this point, people were sauntering in both directions along the street. "We're staying in town for a few more days," he said. "Whale watching, if you're interested."

"No thanks," she said. "I've had enough of creatures blowing hot air for one week." She paused. "No, I was asking about your career. Are you going to go home now and write the Great American Novel?"

That was an easy one. "Umm, no," he said crisply. "I think we can rest assured of that."

"Don't give up, Derick."

The moon was surprisingly low and huge in the sky. "I wouldn't say I'm giving up," he said. "But I am rethinking what I want."

"You know what the Buddhists say, Derick. Detach from the outcome. Just do it."

"I thought that was Yoda."

"Him, too."

He walked Sera home. She had rented a furnished apartment a few blocks away from the beach. "The sound of waves crashing would only keep me up," she said. "I prefer city sounds, like sirens. The force of nature is way too scary."

"Stay in touch," Derick said. "Tell me when you're in *Vanity Fair*."

They hugged, and she went inside. Standing by himself on the sidewalk, he listened for the ocean. Sera was right. From this distance, you'd never know you were in a seaside town. In the silence, he became profoundly aware of solitude and was momentarily terrified. The week had been intense enough for him to actually feel a connection with virtual strangers, people who would in all likelihood remain strangers. He had no faith he and Sera would stay in touch, any more than that he'd hear from Agnes or Vincent now that everyone was returning to their real lives. It had been only a week, but suddenly it felt like a chapter of his life was ending.

He turned on his heel and headed toward the safety of Commercial Street, where the rumbling of the ocean competed for attention with footsteps and voices and laughter.

In a few days, he would return to normal. He'd call his agent, Larry, as soon as he got back and let him know he was ready for the next assignment. Surely some business tycoon or third-rate singer needed a flunky to put his superficial story into words. He needed to get back to what he was good at: making sense of other people's lives.

He wandered around for a long while, meandering slowly past the busy world. A line outside the Crown & Anchor waited for the next show. Derick strode past quickly, even though he knew Jared was probably deep inside the building, putting on his makeup, squeezing into that sequined gown, rehearsing his pout. That was a whole other thing he didn't want to deal with right then.

The most important thing he'd ever learned about writing was the value of pushing through the stuff you don't want to look at. He had written a story with tears in his eyes, reliving a childhood pain in the guise of fiction. The memory tore at him, but he pushed through, disguised the truth with made-up names and unfamiliar faces. And when it was done, he never wanted to do it again. But then he read over what he had written. The words on the computer screen were so poetic, he could barely believe they were his.

He knew that. He knew the stuff you don't want to look at is the stuff that makes you grow, the truth that sets you free. But still he could choose not to look. And tonight, he was choosing not to look.

He found another bar, nowhere he'd been with his friends. He didn't want to be with anyone familiar tonight.

The bar was quiet, nondescript, the sort of place where the absence of décor is precisely the point, the sort of place where the only thing that matters is that nothing should seem to matter. He ordered a martini, the next best thing to Valium for settling his nerves. The bartender nodded, mixed the drink, and brought it back to him, raising five fingers to silently signal the price. A bargain, Derick thought. Now he had an excuse for three.

As he slid an olive off the toothpick with his teeth, he caught a familiar face on the far side of the bar. Graham smiled wanly and gestured him over.

Maybe he wanted to twist the knife, Derick thought. But he couldn't turn back at this point. He made his way through the thinning crowd and slid in beside Graham.

"Lovely reading," he said softly.

"Thanks." Graham lifted his glass with a lopsided grin. "Nice to see you, Derick. Out celebrating the end of a successful week?"

"Well," Derick said, "I don't know how successful it was. Clearly, I have a lot of work to do."

"Don't we all," Graham said, but his relaxed demeanor shifted abruptly as he scoped Derick's expression more closely. "You'll do fine," he added. "I know you will."

Derick took a sip of his drink. "It was a great workshop," he said. He figured now was as good a time as any to practice his skills at fiction. "What are you working on at the moment?"

"Nothing," Graham said. "I haven't written a word in months." He swayed his glass delicately an inch above the bar. "Just interviews and readings."

"How exciting."

Graham laughed a bitter laugh, not at all like the welcoming chuckle he'd routinely let out during the workshop. "Not really," he said. "I didn't become a writer in order to attend promotional events. I did it to write."

He took a long draft of his drink and settled the glass down hard. "I know that sounds ridiculous," he said, "ungrateful. But I spend so much time talking about my last book that I don't have a minute to think about the next one." He leaned in even closer now, and Derick could see the bags under his eyes. This was not the first bar of the night. "In fact," Graham said, "I have no idea what the next book is about. *No idea.* That's never happened to me before, this long after finishing something. Usually, my head is spinning with new ideas before I even turn in the previous manuscript. Normally, I can't wait to finish a book just so I can move on to the next one. But not this time." He signaled to the bartender with a wagging finger over his empty glass. "This time I have no fucking idea what to do next."

"Well," Derick said, "there's no rush. *Charity* is wonderful. You might as well take your time and just enjoy this."

"True," Graham said, lifting his now-full glass in a toast, "for this moment may never come again." He paused, savoring the whiskey.

The drink, or perhaps just Graham's apparent drunkenness, or the fact that he had unexpectedly encouraged Derick's work, emboldened him. "It was quite a departure," Derick ventured, "from your earlier work."

"How so?"

"The characters," he said hesitantly. "Before this, you always had a man at the center of each book."

Graham nodded with a sly smile. "A gay man," he said.

"Well, yes."

"Let me tell you a secret." Graham's eyebrows squeezed into a dramatic *V*. "Sometimes a little sublimation is good for the soul, channeling your energies in an unexpected direction. At least it's good for art. Subtext is more important than text. It resonates."

"I'm not sure I follow."

Graham sat up straighter, more sober all of a sudden, energized back into lecture mode. "Gay people have written about straights forever. Take your favorite, Forster. He was as gay as they come, but his best novels are all about straight people—straight romance, even. He channeled his own feelings into a straight story, and created one masterpiece after another."

"In those days, he didn't have much choice."

"That's not my point. Just consider what that sublimation did for the quality of the work. Maybe the challenge of making it palatable for the mainstream was actually good for the art."

"*Palatable?*" Derick repeated. "That makes gay life sound like cod liver oil."

"That's not what I'm saying," Graham countered. "I'm just suggesting it's good for an artist to write about people who are different from him."

"Updike seemed to do pretty well for himself writing about straight WASPs."

"I don't really think it applies to ..."

"Non-minorities?"

"Who wants to limit their audience when they don't have to?" Graham asked. Energy apparently spent, Graham slumped his shoulders and returned his gaze to his drink. "They're making *Charity* into a film, by the way. It's official."

"Congratulations. Are you going to write the screenplay?"

"God help me, no. I think catering to Hollywood's expectations would push me completely over the edge."

Apparently, Derick thought, Graham was willing to compromise only so far. The energy that had illuminated his expression as he expounded his theory had now dimmed. He lifted the glass once more and drained the whiskey. The oracle had spoken and now craved only oblivion.

# CHAPTER 8

## Shamu and Her Pod Go for a Swim;
## Tourists Watch Them

H e had remembered the Dramamine this time. As the
boat pulled away from the harbor and picked up speed,
Derick looked out at the dwindling Provincetown skyline and
cherished the calm in his belly. His biggest concern at the
moment was sheer exhaustion. He hadn't slept well, and this
was the earliest he'd gotten up all week. A quick continental
breakfast at the inn, and here they were, huddled on the boat
at eight in the morning, practically the crack of dawn when
you're on vacation.

"Whose brilliant idea was this?" Brad said, yelling over the
engine and the pounding spray. His dark hair was whipping
wildly in the wind.

"Have you ever seen whales up close?" Chris said.

Brad gave him what Derick had come to think of as the Dr.
Beane look, chin tucked, eyes squinting slits, lips a horizontal
line of derision. "I've been to my share of tourist traps in
Times Square," he said, deadpan.

The door to the cabin slammed, and the Billy-Bobs
emerged. Bob was leaning over, clutching his stomach.

"Already?" Brad said. "We've barely left the dock."

"He's really not used to the water," Bill said, one arm
around Bob's shoulders.

Bob forced himself to straighten up and make eye contact.
"I'll be fine," he said. His face was the color of celery.

"I thought you were country boys," Chris said. "Aren't we
the ones who are supposed to be ill equipped for nature?"

Derick pulled the package of Dramamine from his pocket. "This is our equipment," he said, holding the box out to Bob, "but I think it's too late. You're supposed to take it half an hour before coming aboard."

"He'd probably just throw it up now," Bill said. "But thanks."

"I hope you're better by tomorrow," Brad said. "Wouldn't want you vomiting at your own wedding."

Bob laughed and instantly bent over again. "Better go back inside and sit down," Bill said.

The boat kept moving for another twenty minutes or so, carving a frothy wake into the ocean that sealed up as soon as they'd passed, eaten by the waves as if it had never existed.

"Jared was pretty great the other night," Chris said as the three of them stood at the rail—on the shady side of the boat, avoiding the rising sun. "He seems like a really nice girl."

"Shut up," Derick said, nudging him.

"I think he's wonderful," Brad said. "A very wise man. You could learn something," he added, turning his eyes to Chris.

"So what do *you* think about him, Derick?" Chris ignored Brad's look. "You're the only one who hasn't expressed an opinion. Ironic, isn't it?"

Derick studied the sea. No sign of land now. They were at the mercy of the ocean and whatever swam beneath it. "I like him," he said simply.

"Damning with faint praise."

"No," Derick said, turning back. "I just don't know him well enough to make a definitive statement."

"You were pretty hot for him before you saw him in a dress," Brad said.

"That's got nothing to do with it."

Now they both were giving him the Dr. Beane look.

"Okay," he admitted, "it makes me a little uncomfortable."

"It's not as if he dresses like that all the time," Brad said. "It's just his work clothes. I dated a surgeon once. I swear, he never wore scrubs on a date." He paused. "Unless I asked him to."

"You're right," Derick said. "It was just the shock. Freaked me out a little."

Chris laughed. "The look on your face when he landed in your lap!"

"It just never occurred to me. I mean, Jared doesn't—"

"Look like a drag queen?"

"Well, yes."

"What do drag queens look like," Brad said, "when they're not in drag?"

"I don't know," Derick said. "More feminine, maybe?"

Brad laughed. "Does Meryl Streep look like Julia Child? It's called acting, my dear."

"Are you going to see him again?" Chris said.

"We're leaving in a couple of days."

"Non sequitur," Brad said.

Derick paused. "We're having dinner tonight," he said. "Before the show."

Brad nodded. "So, what do you think it is?" he asked. "What makes you uncomfortable?"

"This doesn't feel like the time or the place for a therapy session, Brad."

Suddenly, Chris, pointing into the distance, called out, "What's that?"

"What's what?"

"I think I saw one." His arm was still extended. "Out there."

Brad's voice fell. "I should hope out there. There's no room for any on the boat."

The engines suddenly cut, and a voice over the loud-speaker proclaimed, "Here we are, folks. We're going to sit here for a while and see what comes by. A lot of whales have been spotted right here in the past few days."

For a moment everyone was quiet, as if they feared a noise from above would scare away the whales. Free of its powerful engine, the boat began to bob on the waves.

Derick pictured the whales big as the boat or bigger swimming through the clear water beneath them. "What's to stop them from turning us over?"

"Who?" Chris said.

"The whales," he said. Suddenly he thought this was a very bad idea. "I mean, what if they perceive us as an enemy?"

"You've seen *Jaws* too many times."

"That was a shark."

"Same difference." Chris leaned on the railing and watched the waves. "Don't worry about it. They do this every day."

And suddenly, a huge gray back arched out of the water, dorsal fin pointing toward the sun. A communal gasp echoed across the boat as the tail emerged in the air and, almost instantly, slipped back under the waves.

"That was amazing!" Bob cried, rushing to the railing. "Did you see that?"

Derick turned to see the color back in Bob's face, his eyes almost sparkling. And he realized that his own fear of a whale lifting the boat on its back was gone, as well. They had entered another space for a moment. No sickness, no fear. Just awe.

The guide narrated from the loudspeaker like a sportscaster, leading everyone to the various spots around the boat where the whales began to emerge. The boat rocked as people moved from one side to the other, and their astonished cries became the dominant sound.

A mother and two calves, each the size of an SUV, were putting on a show. They knew they were being watched, the guide said. They liked to entertain.

For the most part, the whales stayed a few dozen yards in the distance, gracefully coming up for air every now and then, their backs catching the sunlight as the occasional plume spouted from their blowholes. But once or twice, one of them could be seen much closer, swimming more gently, no showing off, no saber rattling, just trying to get a closer look, a feel for who she was dealing with. Almost as soon as someone spotted her, she would vanish, plunging deeper into the water, reemerging a minute later beside the rest of the family.

As the others shifted toward the front of the boat to get a better view, Derick lingered behind and concentrated on the calm of the sea. The sun was high in the sky now, and he had to squint despite the sunglasses. Sunlight fractured along the waves, like the shattered glass of a mirror ball.

"They're incredible creatures, aren't they?"

Pale hands grasped the rail beside him. Derick followed them up to Clive's face, smiling beneath a straw hat, his eyes invisible behind Ray Bans. "It gives you some perspective," Clive continued. "We may rule the world, but they still dwarf us."

"We're just compensating," Derick said, nodding, "like a race of Napoleons."

Clive laughed, a sound that started out forced, but soon morphed into something uncontrollable, genuine. "Are you enjoying your time away?"

"Yes," Derick said. "It's been an interesting week."

"How's the book coming?"

Now it was Derick's turn to laugh. "Not very well."

"Isn't it going to be more difficult to work on it when you get home?"

"Yes," he said. "I have to spend half my time doing my freelance work and the other half looking for more."

Clive gazed out at the ocean. "What you need is a patron."

"Yes." In the distance, he could just make out the wharf, the buildings that lined the water like tiny colored boxes in a cubist painting.

"I've been approached by a publisher myself," Clive said. "Or my manager has. They want a memoir." He sighed dramatically. "I don't know what that says about my career, that it's already time to look back."

"Just phase one, I'm sure," Derick said, meeting his eye. Or the dark glasses, at least.

"Well" Clive said, "I have packed a lot of life into thirty-five years." He pursed his lips. "It would be interesting to tell the whole story."

"The whole story?"

"I've been thinking about it." He removed the glasses and tucked them into his shirt pocket. "By the way," he said, "I really appreciate your discretion."

"My discretion?"

Clive moved closer, though no one else was around. "The other day," he said. "At the beach."

Derick nodded silently.

"Discretion is in short supply," Clive went on. "Sometimes I wish it were the old studio days. They had a gentleman's agreement with the press then."

A cry went up at the front of the boat. More ballet from the whales.

"Anyway," Clive said, "I was thinking this book would be a great opportunity to set the record straight, so to speak."

"That's a big step."

The boat began to rock more violently. Derick grabbed the railing.

"There's only one problem," Clive said. "I can't write."

"Of course you can."

"No," Clive said, shaking his head, "believe me. It would be dull, dull, dull. I'd need some help."

"I'm sure they have great editors."

"No," Clive said. He dropped his hand onto Derick's, pressing it against the cold of the railing. "I need to work it out with someone I can trust first. I can't just present this story, messy as it is, to some arbitrary editor."

The waves steadied again, the boat calm.

"Would you do it? Would you work on it with me?"

Derick took in the idea. "Why me?"

Clive smiled knowingly. "You've done it before, haven't you? Turned other people's lives into stories?"

"How did you know?" His name had never appeared on a title page. The role of the ghostwriter was to be unseen. That's why they called them ghosts.

"I have my sources," Clive said. "And you're good. Your work on Debbie Kirkendall's book was excellent."

Derick chuckled. "My clients are a secret," he said. "I can neither confirm nor deny." He turned toward the water just as a splash of sunlight glinted off the waves.

"They're offering me a lot of money," Clive persisted. "I'm sure we could arrange something quite beneficial for you."

"I don't know." Derick tried to imagine it, feel Clive out. Could he work with this man? How could he not?

"It would probably take only a few months. And you wouldn't have to work again for a long while. You could just focus on that novel."

"It's tempting," Derick said.

Clive dipped his head, a smile curling onto his lips.

"I'll think about it."

"When do you get back to New York? We could meet next week and iron out the details."

"Sure." His stomach felt lighter suddenly, a feeling the Dramamine could not have helped. "I'll think about it over the next few days, and we'll talk in New York."

"How can I reach you?"

Derick dug into his back pocket for a card. He smiled, passing it to Clive. "Freelancers," he explained. "We can't leave home without these."

Clive took the card and dropped it into his pocket behind the sunglasses. A huge communal cry went up, and the crowd started returning from the front of the boat.

"Remember," Clive said, his voice growing even quieter despite the noise that threatened to overwhelm it, "discretion. We can't tell anyone just yet."

"Absolutely."

The crowd was surrounding them suddenly. Chris nudged up behind Derick. "Aren't you watching?" he asked. "Look at that!" He pointed off to the side, directing Derick's attention back to what they had come here to see.

The adrenaline rush subsided almost as soon as the engine revved back up for the return journey. The passengers scattered to the various corners of the boat, many inside to avoid the spray and the sun. Greta, who had reappeared as mysteriously as always, dragged Clive toward the bow, which was now virtually deserted. From his spot against the side rail,

Derick could see them deeply engaged in conversation, or some simulation of it—Greta lecturing, Clive listening with his head down, glasses once again blocking out the world.

"What's that all about?" Brad said.

"Lovers' quarrel, probably," Chris said.

"I think not." Brad turned to Derick. "You two were pretty embroiled there for a while, though, weren't you?"

"What?"

"Honey, I may have been up there with the whales, but it's really humans who fascinate me. And you two were . . . well, one wonders."

Derick sighed. "Don't worry, Dr. Phil. Nothing's going on that would interest you."

"*Au contraire*," Brad said, "everything interests me."

Chris sidled between them. "Don't tell me you're cheating on the drag queen with the movie star."

"What is this, *Gilligan's Island*?" Derick broke free from the crush.

"Which one's Ginger?" Chris asked, in all seriousness.

"Look out," Brad said, "here come the Howells."

Bill and Bob approached, arm in arm to steady themselves against the rocking of the boat. "Wow," Bill said, "that was really amazing, wasn't it?"

"We don't have anything like that in Indiana, I'll tell you that," Bob said. His face was now pink from the sun, a much more flattering color.

"There are a lot of things we don't have in Indiana," Bill added.

Behind him, the argument continued between Greta and Clive. Her tight curls barely moved in the wind, while Clive struggled to keep his hat from blowing off into the sea. He was speaking now, his expression calm, lips moving methodically. Derick imagined the even, deliberate tone. They seemed like sparring politicians in a debate—she raging for emotional impact, he undercutting her with reasoned argument.

He was tired of being a ghost, the invisible hand behind

the story. Not that Clive had specified that. He could have been envisioning an "as told to" attribution, or even co-authorship. It was probably a negotiable point. Derick wasn't sure which would serve him best: to make a name for himself on the cover of the book, or to simply take the money and run, blessed with continued obscurity. The fame might help him sell his novel, but it might also predispose the critics not to take it seriously. Unless he was able to lift Clive's memoir above the tabloid level of most celebrity books, most of the brainless twaddle he'd been involved in before. The book was sure to get attention no matter how it was done. But if it were done sensitively, if it were less a tell-all than a political, cultural statement, there would be no drawbacks at all.

The shoreline was drawing quickly closer, the outline of the buildings clearer, the figures of people now emerging from the specks dotting the wharf. Just at the edge of the dock, he spotted a burst of blond hair. An arm waved broadly through the air, too far away to be recognized, as if the person were waving to the boat as a whole rather than any particular passenger.

Still the tall, sturdy figure was familiar and attractive. As the boat drew closer, the length and firmness of Jared's tanned legs became clearer, the hair peeking out the end of his T-shirt sleeve as he waved, and finally the round face, the broad smile, the gentle cleft in his chin.

Derick held on tightly as the boat slowed down, and the waves gained more and more power over its sway. He felt a sudden jolt when they pulled up to the dock, and his sneakered foot slipped across the slick floor. He righted himself quickly, but Brad's hand was already under his arm. "Careful there, Professor," he said. "This is supposed to be the easy part."

They disembarked wordlessly, the only sound the clatter of feet against the aluminum gangplank. He lost sight of Greta and Clive in the crowd.

The sun felt instantly hotter without the cool wind off the

water to counteract it. Derick followed Brad and Chris, who hopped onto the wharf with surprising agility. His legs felt almost weightless, too light for dry land.

"How was it?" Jared said, beaming at the end of the gang-plank. "Did you bring me back any caviar?" He put an arm around Derick and led him along the wharf. Brad and Chris had halted up ahead, their curiosity far too evident.

"It was great," Derick said. His head was still reeling, more from Clive's offer than the excitement of the whales. He was bursting to talk about it, to get someone's advice, but he would have to sit with it on his own.

They reached the end of the wharf and entered the chaos of Commercial Street. "Where are you two headed?" Brad said as they all stopped before an ice-cream shop.

"An idle stroll through town," Jared said. "I thought we'd climb the Pilgrim Monument and work up an appetite."

"I haven't been there in ages!" Chris said.

Brad grabbed Chris's hand and drew him in. "Have a great time," he said pointedly. He squeezed Chris's arm as if he were trying to hold a squirming cat. They took a sharp turn on Commercial and merged into the crowd.

In the middle of the hubbub, Derick was again struck by the magical Provincetown light, a yellow-white sheen on the world, like the finishing glaze on pottery. A man in a top hat rode past the wharf on a red bicycle, and Derick watched him pedal down Commercial Street. The bicycle flowed elegantly through the crowd, making S curves around the pedestrians, the reds and blues and yellows as vivid as the squares of a Mondrian, but rounded, unmediated, alive.

An electric vibration shuddered through his fingers as Jared clasped his hand. He turned his gaze back, and saw Jared's smile, leaning toward him, and they kissed.

"Come on," Jared said. "I want to show you something."

In all the years of coming to Provincetown, Derick had never before visited the monument. He had never thought of Provincetown as a place for sightseeing. To him, it was just a people-watcher's town. The most interesting thing wasn't the town itself, but what the tourists turned it into. He had thought that, at least.

"Obviously," Jared said, leading him up the stairs, "you've never been here in winter. That's when Provincetown is at its most beautiful."

Derick couldn't picture the boisterous streets paralyzed by snow, the wind freezing the world. "What is there to do in the winter?"

A few steps above, Jared stopped and turned back to look at him. "Nothing," he said. "Absolutely nothing. That's the point." He smiled and resumed the climb. "You should consider it sometime," he said. "If you want to get some writing done, come here when there are no distractions. It worked for Eugene O'Neill."

Derick ran his fingers along the wall, the names of various Massachusetts cities etched into the stone. It was the quietest spot in town, he decided. He might have been miles away from Commercial Street rather than just a few yards.

When they emerged onto the platform at the top of the monument, the wind was whipping fiercely. Jared stood at the edge, and Derick came up behind him, peering over his shoulder at the town, the ocean in the distance.

"Beautiful, isn't it?" Jared said.

"Yes." A sudden wave of vertigo swam through him. He had been afraid of heights since childhood. Someone had once told him that acrophobia was less a fear of falling than a fear of jumping. Like all emotions, it was impervious to logic.

"I like the rest of it," Jared said, "the beach, the street, the clubs. But this is my favorite place in town."

"Why?" Derick continued to look, holding on to Jared, and the feeling passed. Holding on helped stabilize the world. "What do you love so much about it?"

"This is as far away from New York as I can get," Jared said. "It's so peaceful." His hair was soft against Derick's cheek. "Sometimes," he said, "I need to stop running around, thinking, and just look at it all."

"What's so bad about thinking?"

Jared laughed. "Thinking leads to worrying," he said. "And sometimes it separates you from what's in front of your eyes." He leaned back against Derick's chest.

Derick draped an arm around him. "What do you worry about?"

"Making a living. Growing old."

"You could always transition from Bernadette Peters to Elaine Stritch."

"Very funny. What about you?" Jared whispered. "Why do you worry?"

Derick bit his lip. Jared might as well have asked why he breathed.

He tried not to think. He tried to just let the answer come out. "I worry that I don't know what I want," he said.

"You're a writer."

"Am I?" Derick asked. "Wouldn't it be easier to just live?"

"What do you mean?"

"I don't know," Derick said with a laugh. "I don't know."

They stood silently as the sun climbed the sky and the colors before them grew sharper, shimmering. Derick leaned forward, nestled his chin upon Jared's shoulder, and watched the world.

## CHAPTER 9

## The Flat and the Round

T he Billy-Bobs had no shortage of friends. They arrived in stages throughout the week, an eclectic assortment of current neighbors from Indiana, college classmates from Iowa, and scattered acquaintances from throughout the Midwest, all wide-eyed and enthusiastic as children the first time Barnum & Bailey comes to town.

"You have to understand," Bill explained. "Where we come from gay weddings don't happen every day. This is an event, and nobody minds traveling a thousand miles for an event."

They were at breakfast on Sunday morning, and Dwayne had made cinnamon buns—Bob's favorite—in honor of the occasion. Bob now sat before the window, gleefully licking white icing off his fingers.

The breakfast room was more crowded than it had been all week. Dwayne ran back and forth to keep the coffee carafes and creamers filled, checking the next batch of pastry in the oven. Derick and Chris sat over their coffee, quietly stunned by the activity.

June and Betty, the boys' best friends and next-door neighbors, were all smiles, beaming at the wedding couple. "We live on the gayest street in town," June said, adjusting Bill's collar, which had turned up in the back.

"Really?" Chris asked. "How many gay people are there on the street?"

"Just us," Betty said with a laugh. "But that makes it pretty gay for Radford."

Betty's hair was a halo of tight salt-and-pepper curls, her

eyes bright blue and energetic, belying her age. She watched June from her seat beside Bob. June was an inch or so taller than Bill. She hovered over him, brushing his hair with the back of a hand, checking his shoulders for dandruff.

"June's a stylist," Betty said, as her partner moved toward her side of the table. Standing behind Betty now, she bent down and kissed her forehead. Betty, arms folded on the table, smiled matter-of-factly.

"How long have you been together?" Derick said.

"Forever," June said, squeezing Betty's shoulder.

"Twelve years," Betty said. "It just *seems* like forever."

A chorus of groans rippled through the room. "Nice thing to say on my wedding day," said Bill as he topped off his coffee.

"What's your secret?"

"No secret," June said. "We just fit together, I guess."

Betty nodded in affected seriousness. "Don't tell anyone," she said, "but it's the herbal tea."

They all laughed.

"But we're not the only ones," Betty continued, turning to Bill. "What's it been, five years already for you guys?"

"Six." Bill stirred sweetener into the cup. "But you know what they say, that piece of paper changes things."

"No," Betty said, "what changes things is the joint tax return."

Over the course of breakfast, the couple's other friends made appearances, each wrenching center stage from the last for a moment or two but always in jest, a sense of irony that Derick wouldn't have expected. Each subset of guests—the Indiana gang, the Iowa gang—had their own coded language, but it didn't stop them from communicating across lines, even to Chris and Derick, the newcomers from the big city. The mere fact that they were friends of Bob and Bill earned them instant acceptance into the club.

Frank, the truck driver, sauntered over to their table, all shoulders and chest, and gave Bill a firm pat on the back. "I hope you don't have any jitters about the wedding night," he said, laughing loudly at his own joke. "'Cause I could give you a few pointers."

Chris took advantage of the moment to gather his breakfast dishes and slip away from the table. Derick followed closely behind. Frank soon had the happy couple deep in conversation, but all that could be heard from the far side of the room was Frank's laughter.

The wedding was scheduled for sunset, so the excitement and anxiety were destined to overwhelm the atmosphere all day. Chris suggested they escape by spending the day at the beach.

"I already made plans with Jared," Derick said.

"Great!" Chris replied, leading him upstairs. "The more, the merrier!"

Derick's mouth fell open, but nothing came out.

"I really need more sun," Chris was saying as he unlocked the door to their room. "I can't go back to New York looking pasty."

"Why not? It's healthier."

"Not for your reputation," Chris said. "Frankly, when I see Brian, I want to look my best."

"Why do you care what Brian thinks?" Derick asked, heading into the bathroom to brush his teeth.

"It's all about what people think, Derick." Chris pulled his red Speedo out of the top drawer of the dresser. "Especially ex-boyfriends."

Once Derick had given in to Chris, Brad would inevitably tag along as well. His intimate day at the beach with Jared quickly became a group outing. Almost before he knew it, they were riding their bikes in a caravan back to Herring Cove.

Jared seemed to fit perfectly at the beach. His dirty blond hair revealing highlights in the bright sun, his lean body seemed planted in the white sand like a half-naked Lawrence of Arabia. He slathered his body with sunscreen from head to toe.

"The sun is terrible for anyone," he said by way of explanation as he worked a slab of white goo into his arm, "but it would be murder for my career."

"I don't know," Brad said. "With a little color, you could just move from Bernadette Peters to Rita Moreno."

"Unfortunately," Jared replied, "I couldn't do a cha-cha if you paid me, so that's out." He sat on his towel well within the shade of the umbrella and passed the sunscreen to Derick. "Please," he said, turning his back. He turned on an unexpected Garbo accent: "And don't be stingy, baby."

Derick squeezed a huge dollop into his palm and rubbed it between his hands before working it into Jared's back. Jared's skin was soft, giving willingly to the pressure. It was hard now to imagine those wide shoulders cramped into a dress, the strong neck emerging from a rhinestone collar.

When he was finished, he closed the sunscreen container and dangled it over Jared's shoulder. Pivoting, Jared grabbed it and leaned forward to kiss him. "Thanks," he said with a measured nonchalance. "Your turn?"

The sunscreen felt shockingly cold on Derick's back, but Jared's fingers moved quickly. It was less an application than a massage, his muscles coming to life under Jared's hands.

"I wonder if we'll see Clive and Eva Braun today," Chris said, gazing out at the ocean.

"Can we please not talk about them for once?" Derick said. He dropped his head forward as Jared worked his shoulders.

Brad sighed. "All I'll say is, that girl has got to loosen up someday. Hell, both of them. And that's a professional opinion, by the way."

"Enough already," Chris announced. "I need a swim."

"I'll join you." Brad rose from his towel and followed Chris down to the shore.

Jared laughed as they scampered away. "I think we made them a little uncomfortable," he said.

"What did I say?"

Jared laughed. "I don't think it was the conversation. You should have seen the look on my face when your hands were all over my back."

Derick laughed. "You should see *my* face now."

Jared's hands worked their way quickly down toward

Derick's chest, and suddenly he was pulling him down against the towel. The sun was no longer in his eyes, everything blocked by Jared's face. And now the heat rose within him as well, as Jared came in for a kiss, soft lips opening slightly, one hand gently cradling Derick's head.

He wanted to resist. The situation was so public. Even in the middle of the kiss, he could sense the presence of others around them, voices vaulting over the sand. Derick had always been cautious about public displays of affection, particularly with men he barely knew. When bar pickups reached for his hand on the way out the door, he would draw it away quickly, to scratch a non-existent itch, to feel for the wallet that never shifted in his pocket.

But it was only a kiss, he told himself. And after the way he'd discovered Clive the other day, a kiss seemed completely innocent.

By the time the others got back, they were both lying quietly on their towels, Jared still in the shade, Derick daring his face into the sun.

He sensed their presence as a shadow on his skin, a sudden shift in the atmosphere. "Nice swim?"

"It was great," Chris said. Derick could hear him laying out a towel on the sunny side and settling down upon it. Derick's eyelids went swiftly from black to orange. "Lots of hot boys down there."

Derick heard the lid yanked off their tiny cooler, something being removed. Brad's voice arched over the popping of a can. "You two look so comfortable," he said. "I feel like I should be sitting behind you with a notepad."

"Do you want to hear all about my relationship with my mother, Dr. Beane?" Jared asked. "It's not the most exciting story."

"That's what *you* think," Brad said. "Boring stories are precisely the ones that reveal the most." He sighed, his voice fading as he seemed to settle down on his towel. Derick pictured them all lying in a row, four supine bodies saluting the sun.

"I'm looking forward to the wedding," Jared said into the silence.

"Good," Chris said, "I was hoping Derick would invite you."

"You know what they say about weddings," Brad said with a lascivious tone. "You either bring your future husband with you, or you meet him there."

Chris laughed. "And seeing as all the other guests just escaped from the farm, Derick, you'd better hope Jared's the one."

"They're not that bad," Derick said. "Some of the boys' friends are pretty nice."

"Hey!" Jared cried, slapping Derick's wrist playfully.

"I didn't mean that," he said. "I just meant that they're not all hicks. Chris really has to watch his stereotyping."

"Oh please," Chris said dismissively. "Stereotypes exist for a reason. You don't think they were made up out of the blue, do you?"

"I'm just asking you to be open to the possibility that there's a world outside of Manhattan."

Brad gasped. "Say it isn't so!"

"Whatever," Chris sneered. "Sweet as they may be, the Billy-Bobs are hardly breaking stereotypes. Except to prove that gay men can be just as boring as straight people."

"Well," Brad said, "that's something."

"And they're just so . . . mushy," Chris said.

"Chris is very down on romance these days," Brad intoned.

Chris sighed loudly. "Think whatever you want. This is not about Brian."

"I happen to like them," Derick added. "They're made for each other."

Chris sighed. "They're the same person."

Maybe, Derick thought, that was the secret. Maybe *soul mate* was just another way of saying *mirror*. The drama of Chris's relationship with Brian had everything to do with how different they were. Chris lived for drama. And Derick was scared to death of it.

A breeze washed over his face, and he felt Jared's hand squeeze his.

"Well," Brad said, "now that that's settled, let's all promise to behave at the wedding. No cold water along with the rice."

"Yes, Dr. Beane," Chris whined.

"Great." Brad's towel rustled, his voice growing muffled. "Now who wants to do *my* back?"

There are flat characters and round, as has been elsewhere reported. For our purposes, despite her ample bosom, June Lawson was decidedly flat. She stood in her Birkenstocks at the edge of the beach, directing people toward the spot where the wedding was to take place. There were only twenty or so guests, but for June, the event seemed to require a major choreographic effort. Once everyone was arrayed on the sand waiting for the grooms to make their appearance, she marched through the crowd, spreading them out evenly, relieving a clump here, filling an empty space there.

"Was she a drill sergeant in a previous life?" Brad asked into Derick's ear.

"Or maybe this one," Derick replied. With the short hair, the round figure, the plaid shirt and ill-fitting cargo shorts, June struck him as a walking stereotype. He wondered if she even realized it, if it mattered at all to her. Even a positive stereotype is still a stereotype, and he had been vigilant most of his life for any sign of one in his own behavior. But none of that seemed to faze June. She was who she was, and if who she was fit into a type, then so be it.

What Derick failed to consider was what might lie beneath the stereotype. There are flat characters in books, but there are no flat people in life. He would learn that soon enough. But today was about Bill and Bob. June, at least, knew that much.

Under her expert direction, within minutes the entire crowd was assembled into a uniform fan shape opening up from the shore. By the time Bill and Bob took their places on the sand, the sky was a pink and orange Rothko canvas. The justice of the peace, a lanky man in his sixties, welcomed everyone and cast a professional smile around the crowd. It was clear that he had done this hundreds of times already— probably in this precise spot on the beach—marrying a couple who didn't even live in his jurisdiction. The weariness in his tone turned the perfect setting into just another postcard.

Derick was standing fairly far back in the crowd, his hand lightly grazing Jared's. He couldn't hear what was going on. The substance of the vows was swallowed by the gentle waves and the breeze. It was like a stunningly colorful silent movie, Bill and Bob's lips moving in turn, but all the communication coming through their eyes.

At one point, as Bob murmured something into the wind, Jared grabbed Derick's hand and squeezed it, the warmth of his long fingers comforting in the cool breeze. And suddenly, the justice smiled broadly, his voice finally strong enough to arch over the crowd as he pronounced Bill and Bob "spouses for life." If they'd been in a church, that would be when the organ started, but Mendelssohn had no place on the beach.

Rather than marching through the crowd, the grooms stood in place as everyone swarmed around them. Just then, Jared squeezed Derick's hand again and, smiling enchantedly, pointed toward a shadowy form in the distance, a stick figure moving gracefully at the edge of the shore.

"Tai Chita Rivera," he whispered with a stifled laugh, as they both watched her dance in tribute to the setting sun.

# Part 2

# Manhattan

# CHAPTER 10

## The Picture of Clive Morgan

G raham Whitcomb eschewed flashbacks. "If a scene is interesting enough to be in your story," he preached, "then it should be interesting enough to be in chronological order." Graham thought flashbacks were a form of cheating, a cheap device to manipulate the reader's emotions.

He had elucidated this theory over the corpse of Maryann Dunster's story on the second day of the workshop. After listening to the rest of the class discuss the pros and cons of Maryann's piece, Graham held up his own copy, revealing huge passages crossed out in red ink, sometimes leaving only a single sentence on the page. These, he pointed out, were passages of plot summary rather than scene, or the protagonist's reflection on her life rather than her experience of it.

He flipped through the story quickly until he got to page six, where the flashback began. "And here," he announced, "is the root of the problem." If Maryann would simply reconstruct the story and put the scenes in chronological order, he went on, she wouldn't need all that reflection and summary. A simple cut and paste, and all was right with the world. Everything except Maryann Dunster's face, which was still chalk-white at the far end of the table.

She barely spoke for the rest of the week. Derick saw her now and then in the lounge downstairs, a pen suspended over her yellow pad, or fingers hovering lifelessly over her laptop's keyboard. The words wouldn't come. Maryann knew how to interpret life. She was just clueless about describing it. She was probably clueless, Derick thought, about living it.

He could relate. Since his own vivisection at Graham's hands, every time he sat down to write, he felt extremely self-conscious about what he was doing. He kept correcting himself, rearranging pieces to put them into an order Graham would approve of, pulling out the reflective passages that he would hate.

The problem, he realized after a while, was that there *was* no beginning. It was something scientists and priests had been arguing over for centuries. Does this story, for example, begin when Derick arrived in Provincetown for his week at Eagerton Academy? Or does it start further back—with Chris's breakup from Brian, or with Derick's own broken heart over the stream of imperfect men New York had thrown his way? Or perhaps still further, at that moment in a hospital on Long Island when he first drew breath through a cry that nearly deafened his shocked yet relieved mother?

Ultimately, the beginning is little more than an arbitrary choice. The docking of the ferry at Macmillan Wharf that August day is as good a place as any to start. But you still want to know how they got there, don't you?

Derick hated to admit it, but in the end Chris was right. It was all about connections. He'd gotten his first job in New York through an alumnus of his college newspaper. He was a lowly copy editor at a vaguely literary magazine published out of a tiny office in the Village, but once he'd persuaded the editor to let him start writing, one thing led to another. And as his network expanded, so did the job offers.

He'd met Chris at a party held by an editor who couldn't stop talking about the budding novelist he had just started dating. Their relationship fizzled out within weeks, but Derick soon felt he'd met his best friend.

He'd gotten his first ghost commission a year later, when Chris took him to a holiday party at the private high school where he worked. One of his students was the daughter of a former Broadway actress, now soap star, whose career needed a boost. Derick had idolized her during her days in the theater, and told her so over champagne. "You should write a book," he innocently said. And so a career was launched.

Derick hated the term *ghost writer*. He preferred to think of himself as a coach, prodding his clients with questions, drawing out their most interesting experiences and ideas. He was just the word guy, the one who put it all together. He might not have been successful at making up his own stories, but he was an expert at constructing theirs. And no one was better at putting a sentence together; on more than one occasion, he had been lavishly praised for his expert use of the semicolon.

But despite his talents, his byline appeared only on journalistic pieces, never a book. Even the longed-for "as told to" eluded his grasp. When he was ghostwriting, Derick didn't need a voice of his own. He was Edgar Bergen, putting words in otherwise wooden mouths.

And so he headed across town to Clive Morgan's house with trepidation but no illusions. He was used to celebrities by now, if always on his guard. His agent had once set him up with an aging cabaret star from Paris, a tiny, languorous woman who had greeted him while draped along a silver divan. She never rose during the course of the entire interview and barely glanced in Derick's direction while prattling on about her life. Within five minutes, Derick had the distinct impression that, in her view, the whole of human history had been quite consciously constructed merely to facilitate her presence on the planet. There was no reason to write the book, Derick decided. The only person in the world who truly mattered was sitting before him, and she already knew the whole story.

As he made his way across town, he wondered if Clive would greet him the same way. He had been perfectly friendly in Provincetown, but here on his own turf, there was no telling what might happen. He had made an effort to avoid flaunting his fame and wealth in Provincetown. But the rules were different in New York. In New York, fame and wealth were precious commodities. And the fact that Clive had made his money on his own, without the silver spoon that fed most of the mouths on the Upper East Side, was no guarantee he would be any less pompous. Derick knew one doesn't have to be born with money in order to lord it over others. Those who have money thrust upon them are often the most pretentious of the lot.

The long walk through Central Park gave him ample time to get his bearings before the meeting. Although he had yet to find a spot where a building wasn't visible somewhere beyond the trees, it was still possible to imagine that the world really was made of green grass and lush vegetation rather than concrete and glass.

Emerging from the park onto Fifth Avenue, Derick always felt as if he were stepping into perennial summer. A sudden eruption of sky and open spaces freely let in light that other parts of the city vampirically fended off. And it was almost antiseptically clean here. Unlike the mishmash of styles on the West Side, the buildings here all wore the slate-gray uniforms that seemed written into some code. Fitting in was everything. If the green awnings above the entrances weren't numbered, Derick was sure residents might easily find themselves entering the wrong building. That, apparently, was what doormen were for.

"May I help you, sir?"

Standing at the threshold, Derick found himself fumbling for words. He was struck by the doorman's sense of ease, despite being buttoned into a stiff uniform on such a warm day. Observing his impeccable state, Derick suddenly realized what the walk through the park must have done to his own appearance. He wiped a hovering lake of sweat from above his lip and took a deep breath.

As though blind to Derick's condition, the doorman smiled brightly. Derick half-expected him to click his heels.

"Yes," he mumbled. "I have an appointment with Mr. Morgan."

"Ah." The doorman led him inside, where he checked a clipboard at his desk. "Your name, sir?"

"Sweetwater. Derick Sweetwater."

The man smiled again, and Derick felt pleased with himself for getting the right answer. "One moment."

Derick strolled across the lobby toward a mirror in an ornate gilded frame. He mopped his brow with a handkerchief and checked his white shirt for creases. His hair was unkempt, but that made him look more the intellectual writer. With a final pat to calm a particularly unruly wave, he pronounced himself suitable.

He turned at the sound of the doorman putting down his phone. "Seventh floor, sir," he said, gesturing toward an open elevator.

"Thank you." Derick stood still for a moment, suddenly wondering whether the doorman expected a tip. But the man merely smiled, his hand pointing, not palm up. Derick decided to smile back and simply follow the pointing finger.

The elevator was just wide enough to fit three or four people comfortably. He imagined Clive's party guests forming a line in the lobby, going up two pairs at a time. The few minutes between arrivals would offer time to greet each one properly, while the continual ringing of the bell would give Clive a convenient excuse to duck out of any conversations that went on too long.

Derick pressed 7 and the door shuddered closed after him. He checked his hair once again in the mirrored wall and practiced his celebrity smile. He had discovered it long ago. A certain turn of the lips, just the hint of teeth, the softest crinkling around the eyes, and he produced a smile that conveyed deference with just the right touch of professionalism.

With a sudden jolt, the elevator doors opened upon a long hallway. The doorman hadn't told him which way to turn and, of course, there were no names posted anywhere. He thought of going back downstairs to ask the doorman. He thought of pulling out his phone and calling Clive. Instead, he began to rummage through his bag, searching for his note-

book. Maybe he had written down the apartment number
and just forgotten it.

He was still scouring through the bag, separating pens
from headphones and a very old packet of gum, when he
heard a door open at one end of the hall.

"Mr. Sweetwater." That voice again. It was even more disturbing now, winding its Germanic tone around his name, the
*w*s a tad harder if not quite *v*s, the *a* held a nanosecond too
long.

He put on the smile and lifted his head. Zipping his bag
closed, he marched swiftly down the hall. Somehow he knew
it was best not to keep Greta waiting.

"It is so nice to see you again," she said. In the dim light of
the hallway, the harshness of her look had smoothed out, but
she still stared with that familiar penetrating gaze.

"You, too," he said. Greta gave him the full force of her
palm, shaking his hand with a single efficient pump and pulling away as if she had exerted the precise amount of energy
required and was now ready to move on to the next social
nicety.

"Do come in," she said, standing back beside the open
door.

He stepped delicately into the marble-tiled vestibule,
framed by enormous gold vases with palm fronds emerging
to scrape the delicate wallpaper. It wasn't quite the décor
Derick had expected—a bit old-school, a bit feminine. He
spotted a Picassoesque painting on the far wall, a disjointed
figure sketched in primary colors reclining on what appeared
to be an elephant carcass. That was more like it.

Greta led him through an archway and into a surprisingly
intimate living room. As they entered, Clive rose from a sea-
foam sofa in the middle of the room. "Derick," he said, "welcome." He held out his hand, and Derick, still stinging from
Greta's grip, was suddenly stunned by its softness.

"Have a seat," Clive said, gesturing toward the sofa. He
looked up at Greta with a surprising firmness.

Startled, Greta turned toward Derick. "Tea, Mr. Sweetwater?"

"That would be lovely."

Greta backed her way out of the room.

"So," Clive said, "did you enjoy the rest of your stay in Provincetown?"

"I did."

Clive's hair was lighter and much shorter now. Finally clean-shaven, he looked more like the familiar face Derick had seen on movie screens, roughly handsome, a strong chin. He was clearly more in his element here, surrounded by his own things, a safe world of his own creation.

An uncomfortable silence reigned until Greta returned with a tray she put on the table between them—a white teapot, cups, a plate of sandwiches. Derick took the opportunity to scan the artwork on the walls. The widest wall was like an eclectic mini-gallery: Lichtenstein, Diebenkorn, Warhol.

"Thank you, Greta." Clive smiled up at her expectantly, and Derick noticed her eyes darken. He imagined that she wanted to say something, to warn him about Clive, perhaps. But instead she recovered her plastic smile and once again backed out of the room.

"Beautiful paintings," Derick said, gesturing toward the wall.

"Thank you."

"Who's that last one, over the piano?" It was a bold canvas, arch colors almost assaulting the room, highlighting the gentility of the others by contrast.

Clive turned, one hand on the arm of the sofa. "That's a new artist I recently discovered. Nicoletti. I love his work." Clive leaned in to pick up the pot. "Shall I play mother?"

Clive poured the tea carefully, angling the pot with a delicate gesture that prevented a drop from spilling. "I really got into high tea when I was making a movie in England a few years ago. Every day we'd break at about three for tea and cakes. It seemed so civilized." He settled the pot back down and poured a dollop of milk into each cup. "Sugar?" he said, lifting the lid off a bowl of white and brown cubes.

"One."

When Clive passed him the finished cup, it felt like the climax of a ritual, as if he were receiving a piece of art or a communion wafer.

"So," Clive said, settling back with his own cup, "tell me all about yourself, Derick."

The later interviews would focus on Clive, of course. But this one, apparently, was to confirm Derick's bona fides, to determine whether he was trustworthy enough to be the first to hear Clive's secrets.

He related his résumé translated into complete sentences: college, the path of his writing career, various credentials. He never revealed to a new client who his previous clients had been. Though the titles would lend flesh to his résumé, it was a breach of trust to reveal the open secret that these people hadn't written their own books. Aside from the sense of obligation he had to them, however, his reticence now would impress the new client that he would accord him the same degree of confidentiality. Besides, usually his agent handled the arrangements, and he could testify to Derick's professionalism. He still hadn't told Larry about Clive, though. He wanted Clive's permission first.

"It must be a very interesting line of work," Clive commented.

"It has its moments."

"You're like a therapist, aren't you? You sit there with your notepad, and your clients tell you all about their lives. And then you try to make sense of it."

He had never thought of it quite that way, but Clive was right. He turned the chaos of real life into a credible story with an arc and a series of conflicts and resolutions. His purpose was to take the coincidences that defined people's lives and make each one look preordained. As he had already decided to do with Clive: write into his origins, however humble, the inevitability of this present moment—a handsome, accomplished man sitting on a sofa in front of a poster of himself in last year's box office champ, surrounded by wealth that would make a Rockefeller take notice.

"What sense do you think you will make of me?" Clive said, as though reading his mind.

"I don't know yet," he lied. "If I already knew everything there is to know about you, we wouldn't need to write this book."

"Touché." Clive's lips widened into a larger smile.

Now that the subject had been broached, Derick plunged in. It was usually best to get the big questions over with at the start. "What would you like to accomplish with the book?"

Clive held a tiny cucumber sandwich in his hand, a perfect square of white bread, crusts neatly trimmed, a hint of watercress peeking between the slices. His manicured nails enclosed the sandwich like the gentlest of armed guards.

"That's simple. I want to tell the truth."

The cup and saucer rattled in Derick's hand. Clive's coyness on the subject in Provincetown had been unconvincing. In the intervening weeks, Derick had prepared himself to find that he had changed his mind.

"Don't act so surprised," Clive said. "You know what I mean."

Derick nodded. He searched Clive's face for a smirk, a glimmer in the eye, some indication he was joking. This could simply be another test. Perhaps he was supposed to laugh.

"Good," Derick said at last. "I think that's wonderful. This could be a very important book."

"Oh, it will be," Clive said. "It may destroy my career, but it will be an important book."

It was just what Derick had been hoping for, but he had not expected it to be this easy. So this wouldn't end up being just another puff piece about a pampered star. This one, in fact, could change things. It could mean something.

They discussed the details for a few minutes—meeting times, what to expect. He asked if Clive minded him recording their sessions, assuring him he would keep the recordings securely locked in a drawer at home.

"I trust you implicitly, Derick," Clive said. "Whatever you need to do for the sake of the book."

Derick took another sip of tea and gazed at Clive's smile across the rim of the cup. He couldn't wait to begin.

"Just one thing," Clive added. He wore a suddenly nonchalant expression, the same look his character in *Espionage* had worn when lying to his girlfriend. "This is just between us for the time being. No one can know we're working on this."

"Of course," Derick said. "But we'll need some sort of agreement. Usually, my agent handles the contract directly with the publisher."

"Ah, but we have no publisher yet. I don't want to make a deal with one until we have a manuscript. Don't want to let the cat out of the bag ahead of time."

"I thought you said you had a publisher."

Clive sighed. "Someone has expressed interest, but I'm not about to put anything in writing. Not yet, anyway."

"Of course."

"Tell you what," Clive said. His eyes brightened, and the spy from *Espionage* was suddenly replaced by the stockbroker in *Bull Market*. "I'll have my lawyers write something up. In the meantime, I'll pay you ahead of time—say, half your usual fee, as a retainer." He paused and pursed his lips. "No," he said. "Double it. Something tells me you're worth it."

Clive bit into the sandwich. A sliver of watercress hovered for a second before disappearing between his lips like a forked tongue.

## CHAPTER 11

## Climaxes, Anti- and Otherwise

He was working—or trying to work, when Jared called. At this point it was mostly research: surfing the Web for old stories about Clive, fetching a complete filmography from IMDb. If he was going to tell the true story, he first had to understand the false one.

"Are you hungry?" Jared said.

"You're back."

"Yes, a few days ago. I would have called sooner, but . . . well, you can imagine."

"I know," Derick said. "It's hard enough catching up after only a week away. A whole summer must be a real shock to the system."

"It's pretty crazy," Jared said with a laugh. "So, are you hungry?"

"Sure." At this point, he would take any distraction he could find. Jared could as easily have invited him bungee jumping.

"How about Chinese? Do you know the place on Columbus, just down from the movie theater?"

"What's it called?"

"I have no idea. It's something Chinese."

"What's the matter, you don't speak Mandarin?"

"I speak Pot Stickers and Orange-flavored Beef. And I'm fluent with chopsticks."

"I'm game," Derick said.

"Great. See you there in half an hour. Text me if you can't find it."

"How many Chinese restaurants could there be on the Upper West Side?"

"Yeah, right."

Before logging off his computer, Derick ran a quick search on yelp. "Hmm," he murmured, scrolling, "at last count, thirty-nine."

❖

He seldom went to new restaurants. After so many years in Manhattan, routine had become his defense mechanism. When you found the most efficient route to somewhere, he thought, you used it every time. When you found the friends who got you, you didn't bother looking for anyone else. There simply wasn't time.

China Cabinet wasn't part of his routine. He couldn't remember the last time he'd been there. Probably on another date with someone he'd already forgotten, someone who hadn't lasted more than a few weeks. They seldom lasted more than a few weeks these days. Derick was getting picky. Set in his ways at the ripe age of thirty-six.

The hostess seated him at a table near the window. The dark paneled walls were draped here and there in red velvet, which matched the tablecloths pressed under squares of glass to prevent stains. Derick leafed through the oversized menu, but it was just for show, something to do while he waited.

A waiter appeared and stood attentively beside the table. He beamed down at Derick as only someone not fluent in English would dare to do, hoping the smile itself could compensate for a lack of shared words.

"I'm still waiting for my date," Derick said. "But I'd love a drink." He flipped to the back of the menu, in search of specialty cocktails. He needed something sweet.

"Mai Tai?" the waiter asked, nodding enthusiastically.

Derick pursed his lips, anticipating the flavor of all that fruit masking all that alcohol. "Yes," he said at last. "That's exactly what I want."

He gave up on the menu. He would let Jared decide. As long as it didn't involve tofu, he'd be fine with anything. Instead, he sipped his drink and gazed out at Columbus Avenue. A couple passed slowly by, the woman's arm snugly captured by her lover's, her head leaning against his shoulder. A few singles moved swiftly around them, as though impatient with the pace of their stroll.

He loved the anonymity of New York. He could often go through an entire day walking the streets, riding the subway, and never see a familiar face. He loved the comfort in being surrounded only by strangers.

He had barely started the Mai Tai when his phone rang. "Hello?"

"Whatcha doing, handsome?" Unless Jared was in character, the voice was much too high.

"Lucy. How are you?"

"Fine. Except that I'm beginning to think my little brother's ignoring me."

"Never." Derick turned in his chair to directly face the window for privacy. "I've just been really busy lately."

"I haven't seen you since you got back from the Cape. You must be in love. This is always what happens when you're in love."

"What happens?"

She sighed. No one could sigh quite like Lucy. "You become completely inaccessible and secretive."

"Secretive?"

"I know how it is," she said. "I'm superstitious myself. When I meet someone new, I deliberately don't tell anyone for at least two months, just so I don't jinx it. It's kind of like keeping a pregnancy quiet until the first trimester is over."

A blond man dashed across the street and approached the restaurant. He had Jared's build, but as he got closer, Derick noticed the long nose, the deep-set eyes. The man passed directly by and turned the corner.

"So are you seeing someone?"

"Me?"

"Yes, honey, you. This isn't a party line."

A boisterous quartet of women who had already had their fair share of alcohol entered the restaurant. The hostess seated them toward the back.

"Sort of," Derick said. "I met someone in Provincetown, actually."

"Oh god, long-distance never works."

"No, he lives here. As a matter of fact, I'm expecting him any minute."

"Yikes, I'm interrupting a date?"

"No, he's not here yet. I'm at a restaurant."

"So, while you're waiting . . ."

One of the women in the back hooted out a high-pitched cry. Derick turned with a start to find them all huddling around their table. Several colorful shopping bags sat on the floor between their chairs. It must have been someone's birthday. Or, god forbid, a bachelorette party.

"What do you need, Lucy?"

"It's not me. It's Mom."

The phone grew warm against his ear. "What now?"

"I worry about her," Lucy said. "Rattling around in that house by herself. You know, she refuses to rent out the downstairs apartment. She's doesn't want 'riffraff' moving in. Can you believe that? She actually said 'riffraff.'"

"Mom always did have a colorful, if meaningless, vocabulary. I think that's how I became a writer."

"Don't laugh," Lucy scolded. "This is serious."

"Why, Lucy? Why is it serious? She's not worried about it. It sounds to me like it's more your problem than hers. It's not as if she *needs* to rent out the apartment. The building's paid for. She doesn't need the money." The townhouse had constituted the bulk of her settlement in the divorce. Any realtor in New York would say she'd gotten the better end of the deal.

"She's isolated," Lucy said. "You should invite her to dinner or something."

"So, that's what this is about. Did she ask you to call me?"

"No. No, of course not."

"You're just being a busybody."

"Yes, if that's how you want to put it. I'm a worrier."

"Oh, Lucy. Don't you have your own life to worry about?"

"No," she said quickly. "My life is just fine."

"That's why you're calling me on a Friday night to talk about our mother."

The sigh again.

"I'm sorry," he said. "I didn't mean to—"

But he did mean to. That was the hardest part. He meant every word he said. He just wasn't allowed to say it. That's what family was about—the things you weren't allowed to say.

He turned at the sound of a chair wobbling beside him. Jared, clearly out of breath, was standing at the table, one hand on the back of the empty chair. He leaned over to kiss Derick on the cheek. And suddenly both sides of his face were equally warm.

"Look, Lucy, I'm sorry, but I have to go. My date just arrived."

"I understand." He could imagine her pout. She had always won their mother over with the pout. "Have fun."

"I'll call you tomorrow."

"Good night, Freddy." And she was gone. He silenced the phone and tucked it back into his pocket.

"I'm sorry," Jared said, dropping the dark napkin into his lap. "I had the hardest time getting a cab."

"You should show them some leg," Derick said with a wink. He pulled a long sip of his drink through the straw, until he heard the hollow scraping at the bottom of the glass.

"Have you been waiting long? You finished a whole drink."

"No," he lied, "not that long. I was just talking to my sister. If I talked to her more often, I'd be a complete lush."

Jared laughed. "It's karma," he said. "We get the family we deserve. You must have been a real pain in the ass in your previous life."

Derick waved at the waiter with the empty glass, the other hand making a Victory sign. Reinforcements were on the way.

"So what's the deal with your sister?"

"Codependent," Derick said. "She decided long ago other people's lives were more interesting than her own."

"What does she do?"

"She worries."

"Professionally?"

"If she could get paid for it, she'd be set for life. No, she does something on Wall Street."

"Something?"

The waiter reappeared so quickly, Derick wondered if his sense of time was completely off, as if he had had cannabis in his cocktail. "Thank you," Jared said with a dash of surprise as he lifted his Mai Tai.

"I don't know," Derick said. "Something with stocks. She never talks about it. I think she secretly hates it, but she'd never say so. The important thing is that she's the responsible one in the family. She takes care of our mother."

"Does your mother need taking care of?"

Derick laughed. "Did Medea?"

"Wow, I picked the wrong time to show up for dinner."

*Yes*, Derick thought, *I was a lot nicer thirty minutes ago.* "Sorry," he said. "I'm exaggerating. It's a long story. You really don't want to hear it."

"So tell me about Provincetown," Derick said after they'd ordered dinner. "How was it after I left?"

Jared dropped his chin into his palm with a melodramatic sigh. "Oh . . . lonely."

Derick laughed. "Yeah, the quiet of that place is unbearable."

"Seriously," Jared said, "it was fine. Labor Day can be a little crazy, with everyone trying to get in their last bit of summer debauchery. But I'm used to it." He turned his head, and the candlelight caught his eyes. Derick remembered the beach, how the sun had brought out the blue in his eyes.

"It's good to be home, though," Jared added.

"I missed you."

"I missed you, too." Jared sat back. "So how's Chris?"

Derick took a sip of his drink. "I haven't seen much of him since we got back. Detoxing."

Jared laughed. "He *is* a handful. But very amusing."

"He has his moments." Derick nudged the chopsticks away from his plate. "What about you? Are you working?"

"I will be. Next week. I got a temp job. The agency loves me, so they usually have something lined up by the time I get back."

"That's good. I guess this means I don't have to treat you to dinner. What kind of work is it?"

"Accounting. After three months of squeezing into that dress every night, it's very comforting to just stare at a spreadsheet for eight hours a day."

"So Bernadette gets some time off?"

Jared smiled and waved a hand dismissively toward the window. "Oh, she had a great run in Provincetown. But it's time to expand the act."

"Oh?"

"I have a whole repertoire, you know. You should see my Liza."

Derick flashed him a blank look.

"Minnelli," Jared said, leaning in.

Derick laughed. "I know. I was just teasing you."

"Never tease me like that," Jared said, fingers splayed against his neck.

"Seriously," Derick said, looking around the restaurant, "what now? Do you have other shows lined up?"

Jared sighed. "There are a lot of opportunities in the city. But there's also a lot of competition. At this point I'm just getting my feet wet, so I have to take whatever comes up, just to get known."

"You're really into it, aren't you?"

A delicate smile flickered on Jared's face, his eyes softened by what appeared to be surprise. "Yeah," he said. "I love it. It's empowering and fun and . . . I like dressing up." He laughed. "Don't look so shocked."

Derick shook his head, too dramatically. "Oh no," he said, "I'm not shocked. I guess I just thought it was . . . a hobby."

"Well, if a hobby is something you enjoy that doesn't pay

much, then yes, it's a hobby. But it's also the work that means the most to me, so the stuff I cobble together to pay the bills has to work its way around that." He pulled a lock of hair behind his ear. "Besides," he said, "I won't be able to do this much longer. There aren't a lot of middle-aged drag queens out there, and I got a late start to begin with."

"So what will you do when it's over?"

"Oh, back to the accounting, I guess. Full-time, permanent, and bored to tears. But at least I'll have some nostalgia. At least I'll know that I spent some time pursuing a dream, having fun."

"That's nice," Derick said. "To dreams."

They toasted, glasses aloft.

"I have a surprise for you," Jared said as the pot stickers arrived.

Derick poured a pool of soy sauce onto his plate as Jared dug into his bag to retrieve something. He held the DVD in one palm, supporting it by the other the way shop girls display perfume bottles. *Dawn Comes Early*, starring Clive Morgan.

"I thought we could watch it tonight. It'll be so much more interesting now that we've met him. Well, now that *you've* met him. I just saw him across the dance floor."

Derick smiled. He had already placed an order with Netflix for the entire Clive Morgan canon. Research.

"I wonder what he's up to," Jared said. His eyebrows took on a sharp arch when he pursed his lips. "I mean, what's his life like when he's not in some gay mecca like Provincetown?"

"He lives in New York and LA," Derick said. "They're not exactly the hinterlands."

"No, but still, he must have to be so careful."

Derick shrugged. He affected a lack of interest to see if that would kill this strand of the conversation. Thankfully, the arrival of their entrees finally put an end to the Clive Morgan portion of the meal. Sort of.

"So how's the book coming along?"

"The book?" Derick said. "How did you—what book?"

Jared scooped a clump of rice onto his plate and cast a concerned look across the table. "Your novel, silly."

"Oh." Derick sighed heavily, suddenly aware his neck had gone completely tense. "Fine. It's slow, though. I'm not quite sure where it's going."

"Have you invented a character for me yet? 'Cause I could give you stories."

Derick laughed. "I'm sure you could. But no thanks. Somehow, the plot will just reveal itself. They always do."

At least he'd remembered to clean the house. A place for everything and everything in its place, as his mother was fond of saying. He was amazed sometimes by the amount of stuff one could cram into a one-bedroom apartment. There were two basic solutions for New York living. People like Chris favored a minimalist aesthetic, as if the purpose of a home were to contain space rather than things. Derick's place was more maximalist—neat and organized, but with every square inch taken up by something. Mostly books. The shelves had been filled long ago, his annual weeding out of the ones he knew he'd never read not quite keeping up with the constant stream of new purchases. Short towers of books were stacked against a wall here and there, haphazard piles of paperbacks leaning eagerly toward the bed as if in hope he'd grab one some sleepless night so that the pages could finally speak.

Derick hung their coats in the hall closet and pressed the door tightly closed.

"Come," Jared said, patting the sofa cushion beside him. He pulled the DVD out of his bag again. "Let's see what our friend is up to."

"I'm kind of exhausted," Derick said, kicking off his shoes.

"Oh come on. I've never seen this one." Jared waved the package before him, so that Clive's image seemed to be dancing in air.

149

Reluctantly, Derick reached for the DVD and put it into the player.

It wasn't one of Clive's better films. Derick hated most action pictures, no matter who starred in them, but Clive was particularly unbelievable as the suave international spy. His acting was plainly visible in those roles. It was the Clive Morgan persona up there on the screen, not a particular character. Derick preferred his quieter films, the domestic dramas or better still, the self-effacing comedies, when that perfectly chiseled face wore a puzzled expression, and the modulated baritone turned into a high-pitched squeak of confusion. Derick had always preferred real people to heroes. Heroes were one-dimensional. The flaws of real people made them so much more interesting—the insecurities they hid behind fragile veneers, the sadness at the core of arrogance.

He opened a bottle of pinot noir and settled in beside Jared on the couch. The pre-credit sequence of the film had Clive, mustachioed under a fedora, pressed against the outer wall of a government building in a fictitious Eastern European nation. As security guards milled about, he dashed from one hiding place to another, the music building to suggest danger. A glamorous woman appeared in a doorway and spotted him, beckoning him forth with a mysterious smile. As he moved toward her, she drew a pistol from behind her, but Clive was too fast for her. Deftly, he lifted his own gun, silencer attached, and shot her in the center of the forehead, a perfect red circle appearing against her skin as she slumped to the ground. He ran through the doorway and began a shoot-out that soon left bodies strewn all over the place. Finally, he broke into a glass case and found the apparent object of his quest—a small wooden box—and dropped it into the inner pocket of his trench coat before running back into the night.

"Love the mustache," Jared said, snuggling against Derick's shoulder.

They both laughed at the irony as Clive peeled the mustache off and tossed it on the ground as he made his way over the fence, and the opening credits began to roll.

"He's a master of disguise," Derick deadpanned.

"So we've learned."

Following the formula, the impenetrable plot moved from one country to another, the movie more a travelogue than anything else. Along the way, Clive changed appearance every fifteen minutes or so: the dapper businessman in London, a stooped butcher in Burgundy, a rickshaw driver in Cambodia. He got into life-threatening situations with unfortunate regularity.

Once he had dispensed with the requisite number of bad guys on the streets of Athens, Clive headed for the beach. As Clive peeled off his shirt, Derick marveled at the disconnect. The well-rounded pecs and six-pack abs had been virtually nonexistent on the naked figure he'd seen in the dunes of Provincetown. He picked up the DVD box and saw that the film was three years old. It was Clive's most recent action movie. Ironically, he tended to keep his clothes on in the romantic comedies.

Jared made circles on Derick's chest, moving slowly down with each revolution. He nibbled gently at Derick's earlobe. Pulling away, he whispered, "Man, Clive looks pretty hot in this, doesn't he?"

Derick stroked Jared's shoulder and pulled him closer. He kept his eyes open during the kiss, peering over Jared's ear as Clive dashed down a crowded street in pursuit of the latest nefarious character. Even when he paid attention to such movies, the plots were extremely hard to follow. But in this case, with Jared's hands all over him, Jared's breath in his ear, he didn't stand a chance. He sat back against the couch and watched the film through glazed eyes.

The climax occurred, predictably enough, in New York, where Clive found himself face-to-face with another femme fatale who looked an awful lot like the one he'd killed in the beginning.

"Isn't that the same actress?" Derick said.

Jared looked up at the screen for the first time in ten minutes. "I think so. Maybe they're supposed to be sisters."

"Or maybe they just couldn't afford another actress."

This one had a vaguely Russian accent. Clive was tied up on a chair in a room at the Plaza, Central Park visible in the background. The woman leaned over him seductively, her lips close to his as she hissed an insult and reached for the gun still sitting in his holster. Standing back up before him, she stroked the gun reverently, admiring its heft. "Vat a shame," she whispered. "Ve can't let zis go to vaste."

Jared's hands were warm, soft, surprisingly strong. Derick took in a sudden gulp of air and arched his back slightly.

Clive's face was wet with perspiration, his hair matted to his forehead. The close-up was intended to show thinking behind the pale eyes. He had a plan. Off-screen, he was probably untying the knots of the rope. The close-up was a distraction, like a magician's business keeping the audience's eyes on one thing while the trick happened somewhere else.

The Russian lady held the gun against Clive's temple and gazed into his eyes as the music, a romantic variation of the theme that had run endlessly for the past two hours, built to a crescendo. And suddenly, as she pulled the trigger, Clive jerked his head aside and the gun slipped on his sweat, the shot veering off, cracking the window behind him, opening onto the world of Central Park. He kicked the woman and knocked her to the floor. And, of course having untied himself (as Derick suspected), he jumped out of the chair and grabbed the gun from her.

Now the film's moral dilemma: Should he kill her or bring her to justice? Which was the most effective way to guarantee a sequel?

Derick threw his head back against the sofa, eyes closed. In the darkness, a gun went off. Derick's breathing gradually slowed down as Jared lifted his own head and kissed him softly on the lips.

The credits rolled.

# CHAPTER 12

## Spy vs. Spy

They began with the basics.

"My mother wasn't exactly Mama Rose," Clive said, "but she was very supportive from the beginning."

"What was the beginning?"

Clive lowered his eyes. "Modeling," he said after a pause. "You know those department store ads that everyone tosses away when sorting the Sunday paper? Well, that was me. I was the boy's section—ugly polo shirts, Wrangler jeans, that sort of thing. But I liked it, and I was good at it. I liked the attention. I remember being at dinner once with my family when the waitress kept staring at me. I didn't say anything, but I knew she'd recognized me from the ads. I consider her my first fan." He laughed and reached for his tea.

Derick held a notebook on his knee, but he'd barely written down a thing yet. The recorder, on the round table between them, was doing most of the work.

While Clive had been quite comfortable talking about the details of their agreement, his demeanor noticeably changed when they started discussing his life story. For the first few minutes, his voice trembled, and he struggled for words.

"Is this all right?" he asked now, recrossing his legs and leaning forward. "Am I making any sense?"

"Yes, of course. Just relax. We're only having a conversation."

Clive emitted a nervous laugh. "Just a quiet conversation. You, me, and a few million readers."

Derick tilted his head with a bright smile. "Fingers crossed."

The book-lined study felt more like a college library than a movie star's home. All the glitter was outside, in the living room and the foyer. Derick hadn't seen the rest of the apartment, except for a single trip to the guest bathroom, which was all pink marble and gold fixtures. He would have to get a tour at some point. He could only glean so much from discussion. The objects people surround themselves with often say more about them than words.

"We don't have to go in any particular order," he said, gilding his voice with his practiced reassuring tone. "Sometimes a more impressionistic approach helps. We can just see where the conversation leads. If we jump around in time, that's fine. We may see themes emerge. Once you relax into it, you may even remember things you wouldn't if we were going chronologically."

"Like cocktail party chatter, then?"

"Exactly." Derick gestured to the table. "Just imagine these are champagne flutes instead of teacups."

"I can fix that, you know." Clive pressed his hands against the arms of the chair as though to get up.

"Maybe later," Derick said, reaching out to stop him. "Let's see how far we get on Earl Grey."

Clive relaxed back into the chair. "I never liked tea as a child. My mother, of course, was from England, so she insisted on it. My poor father practically had to sneak his coffee. Instant, of course. My mother couldn't stand the smell of coffee brewing."

"Wow," Derick said. "I love it."

"So do I, but I didn't drink a drop of it until my twenties. My first movie set, actually. It got me going for those five a.m. shoots."

"And yet we're drinking tea now."

"Greta insisted. I guess she thought tea was more literary or something."

"She must read a lot of Victorian novels."

Clive laughed. "I doubt it. She didn't even learn English until her thirties."

"How did you meet Greta again?" Derick threw out the *again* as a ploy. He had no memory of Clive ever answering this question before, but if he believed he had, he'd be more willing to answer it now.

"At Vyse," Clive said. "She was already a long-standing member when I arrived."

"And now she works for you. Connections. I have a friend who keeps telling me it's all about who you know."

"He's right. In my business, at least. For every person who succeeds, there are hundreds with the same amount of talent. Luck and connections. Unfortunately, that's what it usually comes down to."

Derick wanted to get back to Greta and this mysterious Foundation that took so much of Clive's time, energy, and finances. Already he had an urge to prove Brad wrong about it. Clive didn't seem brainwashed. He sat there like a perfectly reasonable man, a perfectly normal man with a highly improbable life. Maybe Vyse was his way of keeping in touch with the world he'd left behind when fame dragged him into another realm.

But that could wait. If Vyse was really as important to him as the gossipmongers said, they would get to it soon enough. For now, they were just developing trust, so it was best to keep to the safe stuff.

As Derick had expected, the conversation jumped around, despite the list of questions he'd prepared. They went from childhood to his first movie set, back to his first acting gig on a small Denver stage, and on to world travels. As soon as he'd finished high school, Clive became a full-time actor, and he'd barely taken more than a few months off since. "You never know when the roller coaster's going to come to a screeching halt," he said. "So you just keep riding it, wherever it takes you."

"But there must be some goals," Derick said. "Things you want to work on, parts you want to play."

"Sure. I do fight for roles now and then, things I hear about through the grapevine that my agent makes sure I get considered for."

"Awards? Any ambition for the Oscar?"

Clive sighed. "I'd be lying if I said I'd never rehearsed the speech. But I don't choose roles hoping they're Oscar bait. The one nomination was great. We'll see." He laughed. "Who knows? Maybe *Charity* will do the trick. They say all it takes is getting cast against type."

"Has it started filming yet?"

"Next week. You should drop by the set. I think that would give you a great perspective."

"I'd love that," Derick said.

When they emerged from the study, Greta hovered nearby, as if she had been lying in wait. Derick imagined her holding a glass between her ear and the wall, listening, trying to make sense of the murmuring voices inside.

His hand was on the knob when the door suddenly fell open. All three of them backed away as if a house of cards were about to fall.

"Excuse me," said an unfamiliar voice. A tall, lanky man poured into the room, keys still in one hand, while the other clutched two or three shopping bags. He laid the bags down under the side table and turned a startled expression to the group gathered as if to greet him.

"Jeremy," Clive said quickly, almost stuttering.

Jeremy moved closer, as though to kiss him, but Greta interposed. "You've been shopping," she said, gesturing redundantly toward the bags.

"Yes," he said. "I needed a few things." He was responding to her, but gazing directly at Clive.

"Jeremy," she said, "have you met Mr. Sweetwater?"

Derick extended a hand and introduced himself.

"Jeremy is Mr. Morgan's assistant," Greta said. "Well, one of them." She laughed. An industry joke, no doubt, as if a single assistant could ever handle all the affairs of a major star.

"I see."

Derick had no opportunity for small talk as Greta's first objective was clearly to hustle him out the door. "Very nice of you to stop by, Mr. Sweetwater," she said.

Derick blinked at her. "Thank you." He turned on the threshold to face Jeremy once again. "Nice meeting you," he said.

Jeremy nodded, and the door closed quietly between them.

Nothing in his research had prepared him for Jeremy. His face didn't look familiar, and Derick hadn't found any references to his name anywhere. Needless to say, Clive had said nothing about having another assistant, let alone one who shopped at Barney's and was accustomed to kissing his boss.

On the elevator ride downstairs, Derick kept one hand in his pocket, clutching the tiny digital recorder. He felt like a character in one of Clive's spy movies, smuggling a stolen treasure right under the nose of the villain. When he had first pulled out the recorder, Clive's lips had curled into a dubious smile, his eyes angling toward the closed door.

"As long as it's just between you and me," he'd said.

The meaning was clear. It was okay for Clive to tell Derick things, if Derick wrote it all down in his own handwriting. But Clive's voice saying the same things on a machine constituted evidence. For a moment, Derick hesitated. If the recording actually inhibited Clive from talking, it would defeat the purpose. Perhaps it would be better to learn shorthand, if that would ease Clive's mind. But his experience with other clients had already proven that people are more likely to clam up when their interviewer spends half the session bent over a notepad. It was rather like theater, the notepad a fourth wall that kept the feelings in check. With the recorder doing its job on the table between them, they were able to make eye contact, to pretend they were simply two friends having a conversation, that every word Clive spoke wasn't a potential quote.

Besides, they had already agreed Clive would have the right to veto anything in the manuscript. So even if he spilled a secret, it needn't go any farther. Like the existence of the recordings themselves, it would be their little secret.

With a jolt, the elevator spilled him out. Hand still in his pocket, Derick nodded politely at the doorman and made his way through the lobby and into the sunshine. Fifth Avenue was sparkling, the shadows of the trees along the park stretching onto the sidewalk and the first story of the slate gray buildings lining the street.

He decided to wander through the park for a while, to enjoy the sunlight. He wasn't due to meet Chris for an hour, which gave him plenty of time to get downtown. Not that it really mattered; Chris was seldom less than thirty minutes late. There was no rush.

He hadn't told anyone about the book or his meetings with Clive. Not even Larry knew about it. Larry would be thrilled with this one, when the time came. In their five years working together, Larry hadn't landed as big a fish as Clive Morgan. He would be flabbergasted Derick had managed it on his own and grateful that he could still get his commission even when half the work was already done.

The tea at Clive's had dehydrated him, and the air outside was surprisingly warm for September. He found his way to a bench under a willow tree and sat, just to catch his breath.

He opened his eyes at the sound of a dog barking not far away. He couldn't afford to let his attention slack and wake up being mauled by a Rottweiler.

But it was hardly a beast. The dog, large but coated in shaggy white fur that made him look like an oversized angora cat, stood about six feet away, straining at its master's leash.

"I'm so sorry. She's never like this."

The dog was glaring at Derick playfully, without a trace of threat. What startled Derick more was the identity of the owner. "Jeremy," he said softly.

"Yes." He smiled cautiously, then rolled his eyes in self-deprecation. "Forgive me. I have a terrible short-term memory. Now if I'd met you an hour ago instead of just five minutes, this awkward situation would never have happened."

Derick smiled back, but even more cautiously. "Derick," he said. This was too much of a coincidence. Greta wasn't the only spy in that house. "Beautiful dog," he added.

"Haven't you met?" he asked. "This is Precious." He

yanked at the leash, but to no avail. "But I call her Greta when she misbehaves. And today she's a real bitch."

Derick laughed, instantly wondering if this was a test. "Well, she's beautiful," he said.

They gazed at each other for a moment, the dog triangulating the configuration like a referee in a ring. Derick had no idea what to say. Clive hadn't given him a script for this scene.

"So how's the book going?" Jeremy said, breaking the silence at last.

"We're just talking so far. I haven't written more than notes."

"Well, I'm sure it will be wonderful."

Derick smiled. It was the only trick he had left in his repertoire.

"Listen," Jeremy said, "I just ask you to be understanding with Clive. He's going through something right now. I don't know, a midlife crisis or something. Don't be surprised if he doesn't finish the book."

"Really?" Derick rose from the bench, and the dog instantly began to wag her tail.

"Yes, he's a Gemini, you know. He just flits from one thing to another. Every two months he has a new obsession. Right now, it's the book. But he may not go through with it. I don't want you to be disappointed." With his leash-less hand, Jeremy delicately brushed back his strawberry blond hair.

"I think he's pretty serious about the book," Derick said. He bent down and offered his hand to Precious for inspection. The dog sniffed it with the enthusiasm of a forty-niner panning for gold.

"Maybe he is," Jeremy said. "I'm not saying he gives up on everything. Lord knows, he'd better not!" He tossed a laugh toward the sky, as if it were a prayer. "Just don't get your hopes up."

Derick didn't know how to respond. He rose to his full height, but the effort was lost on Jeremy, who stood almost a head taller. "Nice meeting you," he said.

A few steps beyond, he sensed that the two of them—dog

and master—were still occupying the same position. He looked back and confirmed it. He hurried out of the park, wishing more than ever that he could tell Chris everything.

❖

"Don't *you* look like something the cat dragged in!"

Chris was in his usual spot in the back corner of the bar, presiding over a red modular sofa. He had explained to Derick once that where one sat was essential to good Feng Shui, and nothing was better than a red chair facing the door. From here, he could see every entrance and exit. He knew everything going on in the room.

"It's been a long day," Derick said, dropping onto a seat perpendicular to Chris's. "And the weather out there can't make up its mind. It was hot uptown, but freezing by the time I got here."

"Autumn in New York, darling," Chris said. "They write songs about it. Stop complaining."

Soft jazz played in the background, so much more soothing than the cacophony of late-night bars. Derick sank slowly into the chair.

"So what time does your beau get here?"

"Around six thirty."

"Fabulous," Chris said, "then we have plenty of time to dish."

"I don't want to dish about Jared," Derick said. "Certainly not with you."

"Then how about me?"

Derick looked up at the sound of the feminine lilt. Lucy, smiling mischievously, stood behind Chris, leaning with one hand against the back of the sofa.

"Hi, sis!" He rose from his seat as she came around the sofa, and they hugged. She felt firmer, as if she'd put on weight, but when they pulled apart, he couldn't see much of a difference. "You look great," he said.

"I've been working out." She arched her eyebrows.

"Really? You?"

"Yes, Freddy, girls have muscles, too, you know."

"I just meant—"

"I know." She scooted him back toward his seat. "You just don't think of me that way. Well, big sisters are supposed to be able to protect their little rug-rat brothers. Muscles might come in handy one day."

"Oh god," Chris moaned, "not anytime soon, I hope. I hate the sight of blood."

Lucy was inexplicably devoted to the Lower East Side, so they didn't see much of each other. She couldn't have been farther away without, god forbid, leaving Manhattan altogether. Distance mattered in New York. Distance got exaggerated in New York. What would seem like a lovely stroll in a small town, was equivalent to the Bataan Death March here.

But they were in her neighborhood now, or closer to it, at least. He should have thought of inviting her himself, he supposed. It would have been nice if Chris had told him.

"I wish you'd told me Lucy was coming," he said now, afraid his scolding look was invisible in the dim light.

"We wanted it to be a surprise," Chris said. "You love surprises, don't you?"

"I hate surprises," Derick said. "And where's my drink?"

"Sorry, your highness, I didn't want it to get warm so I didn't order it ahead of time."

Derick harrumphed facetiously and made his way toward the bar.

He had introduced Chris and Lucy years ago. It had been an accident, really. He was out shopping with Lucy for family Christmas presents, and they ran into Chris scoping out neckties at Saks. It was just a casual introduction, but before he knew it, they were laughing with each other about things Derick didn't even get. In the course of a few sentences, they'd discovered a common sense of humor that fueled them for hours. The three of them ended up having lunch together, then strolling up and down Fifth Avenue to window-shop, stopping at the end of the day for hot chocolate at the Plaza.

And now they were bosom buddies. How could he have forgotten that? Why hadn't it occurred to him that Chris might invite her tonight, as if she was *his* sister instead?

Derick took a deep breath as he waited for the bartender's attention. He had wanted to decide when Lucy met Jared. They had only just started dating. Anything could happen. The last thing he wanted was for Lucy to fall in love with him the way she'd fallen in love with Chris, and then hound Derick mercilessly if it didn't work out.

He ordered a martini and, laying the money on the bar, corrected himself. No, the worst thing would be if she told their mother about Jared, and he had to field questions from *her* ad nauseam—good *or* bad.

He hadn't even taken a sip of his drink when it all hit the fan. Just as he turned around, he spotted Jared in the corner, bussing Chris on both cheeks and shaking hands with Lucy. Derick stopped in his tracks and swirled the olives out of the way so he could take a long swallow. Even with well gin, no drink was more effective than a martini. One more, and he'd be able to handle anything.

"Where have you been?" Chris cried as Derick finally returned to the table.

Jared rose from his place beside Lucy to give him a kiss. As he touched Derick's arm, the drink wobbled, and Derick turned to right it, Jared's lips slipping onto his cheek.

"I think you'd better sit down, old man," Chris said, "before you break something."

"I don't get it," Lucy said. "He was perfectly normal a few minutes ago. Now he's walking like Foster Brooks." And she and Chris burst into a chorus of laughter.

"How was your day?" Jared whispered, settling Derick down beside him.

"Fine," he said.

"Derick's a mystery man these days," Chris said. "He won't tell us what he's up to. Maybe you can worm it out of him, Lucy."

She turned toward Derick now, long chestnut curls bobbing. "Tickling used to work." She reached for him threateningly.

"No!" he cried. "The martini."

Lucy settled back with a laugh. "So what's up, Freddy?"

"Nothing," he said. "I'm just working on something."

"A top-secret something," Chris said. "I think it's the new Manhattan Project."

"Chris, you think the Manhattan Project is an a cappella group."

Derick concentrated on his olives. "Who says I'm working on anything, anyway?"

"I know how you get when you're working," Chris said. "You go into hiding like Eva Braun in the bunker."

"You do?" Jared leaned in with a smile.

"Get yourself a drink, Jared," Chris said. "You'll need it."

When Jared was out of earshot, it was Lucy's turn to lean in. "He's cute!" she said. "Why have you been hiding him from me?"

"I have not been hiding him."

She turned toward Chris. "He never introduces me to his boyfriends," she said. "I think he's ashamed of me."

"Don't feel bad," Chris replied. "I've only met a couple."

"Really?"

"Yeah, Derick's possessive that way."

Derick placed his drink on the table. "Guys, I'm right here."

"We know, hon. But you're not talking, remember?"

"I'm not talking about my book project," he corrected.

"Ah, so it *is* a book!"

Derick sighed. "Yes, it's a book. But I've been sworn to secrecy myself."

"Who is it, Howard Hughes?"

"Howard Hughes is dead. And no."

Jared returned with a cosmo, nearly overflowing. "What about Howard Hughes?" he asked.

Chris rolled his eyes. "Derick was just informing us that Howard Hughes is *not* the subject of his new book."

"New book?" Jared said, dropping a hand gently on Derick's shoulder. "Is this the novel you were working on in P'town?"

"No," Derick said, shrugging. "I hit a wall with the novel. This is something else."

"What is it?"

Derick laughed nervously. "I can't really say."

"Can you give us a hint? Is it juicy?"

"It has potential," Derick said, slyly arching his eyebrows.

"Oh yeah," Jared said, "it's juicy." He lifted his drink up to his lips, and Derick spotted something blue on his fingernail. "What is that, ink?"

Jared put the drink down and inspected his hand. He laughed. "No," he said, "it's polish. Guess I missed a spot last night."

"Polish?" Lucy leaned forward, a rubbernecker craning for an accident on the highway.

"I had a show," Jared said. He scraped at the polish, one hand curled under the other.

"It can wait," Derick said to Lucy, lounging against his seat. He threw his head back, closed his eyes, and let the conversation bounce over him. He had completely lost control of the evening.

Derick's head throbbed, and he went to bed without even brushing his teeth. Jared had to bring him some aspirin. "And drink this," he said, handing him a huge glass of water.

"I can't. I'll throw up."

"If you *don't*, you'll throw up. Now drink it."

Satisfied, Jared turned out the light and climbed into bed beside Derick, who lay curled on his side. Jared's arm fell over his belly, Jared's legs curled behind his, toes touching.

Derick fell asleep almost instantly but woke several times during the night. And always, Jared's arm was somewhere on him—his belly, his chest, leg, shoulder, gently massaging the back of his neck.

# CHAPTER 13

## The Spelling Habits of Baristas

I t started with an innocent email.

> Dear Derick,
>
> I bet you never thought you'd be hearing from us again, but our dream is coming true (or mine, at least). I've just been offered a transfer to New York City, if you can believe that, and we'll be moving to your neck of the woods in a few months. Would love to chat and get your thoughts on the lay of the land—where to live, etc. My company has offered to put us up temporarily in a corporate hotel, but I'm sure it won't be in a particularly fashionable neighborhood. I've heard how hard it is to find an apartment in New York, so if you have any leads we'd certainly appreciate it.
>
> How are things with that wonderful boy you met in Provincetown? Can't wait to see you again. Bob sends his regards.
>
> Cheers,
>
> Bill Keaton

Rushing across town, Derick read the email on his phone as he walked, so he had barely enough time to avoid getting jostled by oncoming pedestrians, let alone process the message.

He finally came to a sudden stop at West 14th, where a line of trailers strangled the already congested neighborhood. A tangle of black cables led beyond, all the way into the shadowy overhang of the High Line, where officious-looking people milled about in fleece jackets and wool caps.

A security guard stopped him at the edge of the yellow tape. "I'm expected," Derick said. "I'm with Mr. Morgan."

The guard flipped over a page on his clipboard. "Name?" he asked doubtfully. Derick imagined he had already had to fend off dozens of wily fans.

"Derick!" Just behind the guard, Jeremy, an identity badge on a lanyard around his neck, came striding toward them. "So glad you could make it." He sidled up to the guard. "It's okay, Anthony. He's with me."

Jeremy shook his hand and handed him a lanyard of his own, with the word *PRESS* printed in bold letters on the badge. No name. Today, Derick was just *Press*.

Jeremy led him across the heavy cobblestones, past the trailers. "Clive's still in makeup," he said. "This scene is all of two pages in the script and two minutes in the film, if it doesn't get cut, yet it takes all day. This industry can be the biggest time suck on earth."

It seemed like chaos on the surface, but as Jeremy showed him around, he could see the order beneath the madness. The director and cameramen were above them, setting up the shots on the High Line itself. He could just make out a camera pointing north. Down on street level, various other people jockeyed for attention, one young woman in faded jeans scurrying frantically about, calling out names and being largely ignored.

They might have been organizing a street fair or a small parade rather than something that would appear on an enormous screen someday and cost millions of dollars. It all seemed so small and ordinary, just busy people going about their business. Derick was afraid his illusions would be shattered. Maybe it was best to pay no attention to the people behind the curtain.

"Progress on the book?" Jeremy said.

It had been weeks since that first day, when they'd met, enough time for autumn to take a firm hold on the city.

Derick hadn't even seen Jeremy on any of his subsequent visits to the apartment. Clive said he spent most of his time looking after things in LA.

"It's fine," Derick said. He was distracted by an argument across the way. The young woman had evidently found the person she'd been looking for, and he was none too happy with whatever she had come to tell him. "I think we're getting somewhere."

"Am I in it yet?"

Instinctively, Derick turned his head with a jolt. Jeremy winked and let out a sharp laugh. "Just kidding," he said.

"I really shouldn't . . ."

"Oh no, I expect you can't say anything. Even to me."

"I'm sure there's nothing I could add, anyway. Clive must tell you all about it."

Jeremy laughed again. "Oh, right," he said with a cynical raise of the eyebrow. "Clive keeps me extremely well informed!"

Jeremy left it at that and continued the tour, pointing out the trucks storing various pieces of equipment, identifying who was who by their job function. It was all a bit of a muddle after a while. Derick preferred focusing on the gestalt of the experience. He tried to fix the images in his memory, so that when he saw the final film he could imagine all of this, like gazing at a painting and seeing the *pentimento* underneath.

The craft service area was at the end of the block, a large white tent positioned over a few tables—drinks on one side, food on the other. At the moment, it was largely doughnuts and croissants. Lunch would come in later, Jeremy said. Something warm in chafing dishes.

"Would you like some coffee?"

"Sure."

Jeremy leaned in for a whisper. "Truth be told, the coffee sucks. And it's awfully chilly out here. I know a Starbucks around the corner. Shall we try that instead?"

Derick looked askance. "There's a Starbucks around the corner? Wow, who'd have thought?"

"A sarcastic wit," Jeremy said. "I think I like you." He slipped past the tent, looking over his shoulder to make sure Derick was following. For once, Derick chuckled at the air of espionage that seemed to surround all things Clive.

They found the Starbucks on 9th Avenue just as a strong wind was coming up behind them. The door closed with a loud thump.

Jeremy gazed at the menu behind the baristas. "I feel so naughty," he said.

"Running away from the set?"

"No. I'm going to get a peppermint mocha. Clive would kill me."

Derick laughed. He was beginning to think that he liked Jeremy, too. "You're a bad influence," he said, ordering the same.

They stood at the end of the counter and waited for their drinks. "At last!" Jeremy said when the barista called out their names. He grabbed his own cup and passed Derick the other.

Derick frowned. Over the red holiday motif on the cup, he read the too-familiar *Derek* in an almost indecipherable Sharpie scrawl.

"What's wrong?" Jeremy asked.

"My own fault," Derick said, "they misspelled my name."

"Well, how *do* you spell it?"

"D-e-r-i-c-k. It's short for Frederick, actually."

"Hmm, that's interesting."

"No worries, at least this version makes sense. I've had it spelled with a *y*, an *o*. God help me, one barista in the Village even thought I'd said Perick."

"Thank god for the *e*."

The balding man beside them shifted the bag on his shoulder and laughed. "Sorry," he said, "I couldn't help overhearing. It's an occupational hazard here. That's why I don't tell them my real name anymore. It always comes out in some weird concoction. You have to have a Starbucks name. Mine is James." He turned his cup so they could see it. "Easy, nobody misspells that." He winked and headed out into the wind.

"And people say New Yorkers aren't friendly," Jeremy said coyly. "Shall we?" He motioned toward a table in the back.

"By all means."

Jeremy dropped dramatically onto the banquette. "It feels so good to get off my feet for a bit."

"Are you on the set often?"

"Now and then," he replied. "But today it was largely because of you. Clive wanted to make sure you were well taken care of."

"I appreciate that." Derick studied the snowflakes on his cup.

"But he likes you. I think talking to you is good for him."

"You make me sound like a therapist."

"No, it's just—"

"No, that's okay. In a way, I suppose I am. Like a therapist."

Jeremy smiled. "He seems a little more upbeat these days. It's either you or the movie, and I know it can't be that."

"What's wrong with the movie?"

"Nothing in particular. But work always stresses him out. He's a bit of a Method actor, and this character he's playing is kind of a creep."

"Oh dear. It can't be good when a Method actor brings his work home."

Jeremy laughed. "Let's just say I'm glad he didn't get that Jeffrey Dahmer part he was so gung-ho about."

They lingered, chatting mostly about the movie business. Jeremy spent most of his time as a go-between, fielding calls and requests for Clive's attention. "It can be challenging," he said. "Most of these people are awfully demanding. And they have no idea who they're talking to. I may be the one who answers the phone, but I'm basically invisible. In their eyes,

I'm certainly not the one he has dinner with every night, or who holds him until he falls asleep."

He said it all with a surprising flatness, and Derick imagined he'd spoken the lines many times before, if only in his own head.

Derick sensed his own features soften, as if it was his job to express the feelings Jeremy's words painted. "That must be difficult."

Jeremy threw himself back against the chair. "Are you kidding? I get to be his *assistant*." He gestured with one open hand, like a magician revealing that a coin had miraculously disappeared. "When we go to premiers, I get to sit in the limo. I even get out first, so I can hold the door for him and his date."

Derick sipped his drink. The peppermint was too sweet. It disguised the coffee. He might as well have been drinking a milk shake.

"You know," Jeremy went on, quieter now, "I see all these people getting married these days, even friends of ours. And I wonder. I mean, I have plenty of money. It's not like I have any strong financial incentive for marriage. And god knows we'll never have children. But there's also just the public acknowledgment, you know—standing up there, taking vows. Introducing him as your husband. That might be nice."

Derick remembered the Billy-Bobs on the beach. They had faced each other, holding hands with the setting sun behind them. And the sand was crowded with their friends, with invited guests and strangers just wandering by, all witnessing. He had spotted a tear rolling gently down Bob's cheek, but they were both smiling. Beaming. He'd never seen two happier people in his life.

Jeremy cocked his head to one side. "I don't want to always be walking a few steps behind, holding the dog's leash."

"You never know," Derick said. "That could all change."

"How?"

"The book."

"He's going to come out in the book?"

He was going too far. He really shouldn't say it, but Jeremy's expression was so genuine. He needed to hear it. "Maybe. He's suggested it."

Jeremy wrapped both hands around his cup and gazed out the window. "Really," he said. "I'll believe that when I see it."

❖

They usually went in together. There was strength in numbers. Lucy brought the wine.

"Okay," she said, stopping at the top of the stairs. "Deep breath."

He watched her, matched her inhale and the gently prolonged letting go.

"Perfect," she said, "now we're ready for anything." Firmly, she pressed the doorbell.

Belowstairs, the entryway to the basement apartment was littered with fallen leaves, mostly still orange and yellow, only a few crusted over in dingy brown.

The door slowly opened. He could smell the turkey before even a sliver of the room was in full view. "Happy Thanksgiving!" his mother belted out when the door was fully open. She threw her arms out and welcomed Lucy into a brief hug. She led them inside and then grabbed Derick into her orbit in turn.

"Happy Thanksgiving, Mother." As he rested his chin on her shoulder, her dark hair tickled the side of his face. She'd been wearing the same cologne for thirty years. His nostrils were suddenly full of the familiar floral, powdery scent.

"All the preparation is done," she said, leading them both down the long hallway toward the kitchen. "I was just about to start whipping the potatoes."

The kitchen faced the back of the house, looking out on a tiny yard and the grim wall of the expansive apartment building on the other side of the block. When he was a boy, Derick had stationed himself here for hours at a time, in the dark of night, gazing out at the signs of life across the way. It was like watching a play. He'd search out a light in a distant window and wait for someone to pass by. Most of the time it would just be someone fixing a meal or sweeping a floor, but once he'd spotted a couple arguing, their faces just inches from each other, the raised voices pushing through the window and across the backyard like hand grenades. Mostly, though, Derick kept his eye on the third window on the second floor. Its only occupant was a thirtyish man who routinely strode brazenly by in white briefs, occasionally stopping to look out the window, as if he were spying, too.

"He won't tell me what it is," Lucy was saying, digging through a drawer for a corkscrew.

"What what is?" Derick said. Her voice woke him from a sudden trance, and he caught himself gazing out the window, his eyes instinctively going toward the second floor. The man would be in his sixties by now. Derick certainly didn't want to see that.

"Your new project."

"Oh, Lucy, do we have to talk about that?" He pulled three wine glasses out of the hutch and placed them on the wooden island.

"I want to know," said his mother, her voice nearly drowned out by the immersion blender she stirred in vicious circles through the potatoes.

"I'm sorry," he said, "both of you, but I can't discuss it." He watched as Lucy struggled with the cork. "You know how confidential my work is."

"And you never even get your name on the books. Derick, it's like you don't even exist to these people, like you're—"

The cork finally popped. "A ghost?" Derick said.

"Well." Done stirring now, Mrs. Sweetwater pulled out the blender and tapped it against the rim of the bowl. She scooped out a fingerful and tasted it. "Delicious," she pronounced. "Your old mother still has the touch, kids."

Lucy looked up from pouring the wine and caught his eye. They'd already discussed the possibility of a trip to Shake Shack on the way home.

"Okay," their mother said, lifting the lid off a sauté pan, "if we can't talk about Mr. Boswell over here, then we'll just have to give you the floor, Lucy. What's going on in your life?"

Lucy took a gulp of Merlot and leaned against the counter. "Work is pretty good."

"Really? You people still haven't cleaned up that mess you made, have you?"

"What mess?"

"Lucy, the economy is in a shambles. Don't you watch the news?"

"That's not my fault."

Mrs. Sweetwater froze in place, slotted spoon hanging limply from her hand. "Darling, you work for an investment bank. Now, really."

"Don't blame me," Lucy said defensively. "I didn't sell any bad mortgages. And I didn't buy a house worth more than I could afford. Blame those poor idiots."

"The poor idiots who got suckered into the American dream?" Mrs. Sweetwater lowered the heat on the sauté pan. Over her shoulder, Derick spotted her candied carrots. He decided to keep an eye on them. More than once, she had let them go one second too long and they had burned to a crisp.

"The American dream was a lie to begin with, Mother. Really."

"It worked for your father. He came from virtually nothing, and look what we have." She gestured around the room. They had bought the brownstone in the 1970s "for a song," their father was fond of saying. It was the best investment of his life.

"That's just it, Mother. It works for some people. If it worked for everyone, well . . . it wouldn't work."

"I suppose you know best. You learned it all from the master."

Lucy sighed. "Why don't we talk about something we agree on?" she said. "Like my pathetic love life."

"This is Thanksgiving, Lucy. I don't want to get depressed."

"Well then, talk to Derick. He has a fabulous new boy-friend. Maybe they'll give you the grandchildren you're so eager to spoil."

"What's this?" His mother gave him the same pursed-lip look she'd been tossing his way for years, ever since she first caught him eating Santa Claus's cookies.

Derick sighed and spoke to his wine glass. "It's nothing, just someone I've started dating."

"More than three months ago."

"I don't know where it's going. I don't know if I *want* it to go anywhere."

His mother shook her head wearily. "Derick, really. When I was your age, I already had two children in grade school."

"What does that have to do with it?"

"I want you to be happy, settled down. Marriage would be good for you."

"Like it was so good for you?" Lucy piped in, studying the legs of her Merlot.

"We had circumstances, your father and I."

"I'll say."

Mrs. Sweetwater focused her gaze on Derick. "So tell me about him. What's his name?"

"Jared," Lucy said.

"Would you let me talk for myself?"

"Somebody's got to wear the pants in this family."

"Never mind her," his mother said, turning to wall off Lucy. "I want to know."

Derick sighed. "Why can't you be one of those horrible Christian mothers who are appalled by homosexuality?"

"Would that make it easier?" she said with a laugh. "If I just talked fire and brimstone and didn't want to hear a word about your life?"

"What time is dinner?"

"Let me just take out the turkey. We'll let it rest and can eat in half an hour."

"Great," he said. "Lucy, you did bring *two* bottles, right?"

She smiled and waved her glass his way. "I never travel light, little brother."

The table was already set, so it was just a matter of moving the platters into the dining room. In the old days, they would often entertain friends at Thanksgiving, so the room was full. Now, with just the three of them hunkered at one end of the long table, Derick felt dwarfed by the emptiness. If it hadn't been a holiday, they would have eaten in the kitchen.

Last year, after his father moved out, Derick had been promoted to turkey carver. So now, even though his mother insisted on sitting at the head of the table, he stood to do the honors.

"White for me," his mother announced. It was tantamount to the Pope saying he'd prefer a Catholic mass rather than a seder.

"What about you, Lucy?" she said as Derick handed her a plate full of breast meat. "You haven't gone all vegan on us yet, have you?"

"Why would I go vegan?" Lucy finished the first bottle of wine, evenly dividing it between her glass and Derick's.

"I don't know," Mrs. Sweetwater said. "I hear a lot of crazy stories about the Lower East Side."

"You should get out more, Mother."

"And you should visit more," she said as Derick passed Lucy a plate with a drumstick hanging over the edge. "Both of you."

With work, love, and any mention whatsoever of the person who had so recently carved the turkey off the table, their only choice was to talk about the food. Which, of course, meant more lying.

"Great stuffing," Lucy said, smothering hers in an extra dollop of gravy.

"Thank you, dear."

They had had exactly the same meal for the past thirty Thanksgivings, which was only as far back as Derick could remember. Their father, however, had been in charge of dessert, so this year Derick had bought an apple pie at the bakery near his apartment.

Watching his father bake had been the most incongruous thing about the holiday. For one day of the year, Joseph Sweetwater donned an apron and rolled out dough on the kitchen counter. He had taught himself, piecing together tips from various cookbooks and a few Julia Child episodes. Derick would often help him, the men of the house alone in the kitchen, usually while Lucy and his mother were out shopping.

"What did you bring?" his mother said abruptly. Her plate was nearly empty. She ate so ravenously when they were together, he had to wonder how she stayed so slim.

"Apple pie," he said.

"My favorite." She pushed her chair away from the table and began to clear. Lucy, whose plate still contained mounds of vegetables, picked it up and followed her.

"Coffee?" his mother called from the kitchen.

"No thanks," Derick said, "I'll just have another glass of wine."

The dishes cleared, they settled around the living room with plates of pie. For ten minutes, the only sound was the clinking of fork against china.

"Yum," Lucy said, spearing the last chunk of apple on her plate, "I've been dreaming about this pie."

Derick laughed. "Good, because I sweated over a hot credit card to get it."

"I don't dream much at all," Mrs. Sweetwater announced. "Never have."

They both stared incredulously at the literalness of the non sequitur.

"You mean you don't remember," said Lucy. "Everybody dreams. Otherwise we'd all go bonkers. The subconscious has to process its crap somehow."

"No," her mother insisted, eyeing Lucy's wine glass with suspicion. "I don't dream at all. The moment my head hits the pillow, I'm out until the sun is shining on my face. And I feel like no time has gone by at all."

"Okay, that's just weird." Derick got up and scoured the sideboard for port.

Lucy wouldn't let it go. That was the thing about Lucy: she let nothing go. "Really? Never? I can't believe it."

"Believe it, darling. Your mother doesn't lie."

"Ah," Lucy said, sitting back, "now it makes sense."

"What?"

"That's the one sentence that can't be proven. 'I never lie.' If you're a liar, then you're basically confessing it. If you're not, well, no one would ever know."

"I don't follow you, Lucy. All I'm saying is that I never dream."

Derick found an old bottle of tawny and poured out two servings. "Here, Luce," he said, "distract yourself."

They could go on like this for hours. They often had, Lucy running rings of logic around their mother's head without making a dent in her defenses. In order to convince someone of anything, he'd admonished her more than once, you have to get them to listen. Stella Sweetwater was not a listener.

He stood before the bay window and gazed out. A gust of wind dove down the stairs and brought back up a small tornado of dead leaves.

"Mom," Derick said, turning around cautiously, "I have some friends who are looking for a place to live."

"That's nice, dear," Mrs. Sweetwater said, carving into her pie with the edge of her fork. "I hope they're wealthy. I hear rents are exorbitant these days."

This had to be handled delicately, he knew, but the idea was spontaneous, so he was winging it. "I think they'd really love this neighborhood."

She laughed. "This neighborhood? Well, good luck, I never see any vacancy signs. Every square inch is taken."

He paused. "Well, not *every* square inch."

He stared at her for a few seconds, until her head finally rose and her eyes met his warily. "What do you mean?"

Suddenly Lucy broke the spell. Lucy was an expert at

breaking spells. She had no patience for them. "Downstairs!" she cried.

"What?" Their mother looked genuinely puzzled, but Lucy was on her own agenda.

"Who are these people?" she asked.

Derick reluctantly turned to his sister. "A lovely couple I met in Provincetown," he said. "I think I told you about them. They got married on the beach."

Lucy sighed, her face opening up in a romantic gesture, as though she were picturing sunsets.

"On the beach?" Mrs. Sweetwater said, scowling. She was no doubt picturing sandy feet stomping on her Orientals.

"It would be perfect for them," Derick said. "And I'm sure they could pay market rate."

"That's a lot, Mother," Lucy said, eyes even wider. "It's a no-brainer." Finally, she was coming in handy.

But Stella Sweetwater had never been accused of an over-reliance on rational thought. "I can't rent out the apartment," she said, scratching the back of her head and inadvertently pulling her hair from its carefully arranged chignon. "What if I need the space?"

"For what, Mother?" Derick moved closer, feigning curiosity rather than mere incredulity.

"I have things, you know that."

That was certainly true. His mother had a lot of things. The living room was so crowded with "things" he wouldn't be able to fall down without breaking several of them—knee-high vases sitting empty on the floor, tchotchkes covering every surface, an indefinable sculpture in the corner that looked like a cross between Rodin and Walt Disney.

"I could spread them out more," she said.

"By putting them downstairs?" Lucy said. "You'll never see them."

"That's not the point. I could visit them."

"Your house isn't a museum, Mother."

"Perhaps not, but it is *mine*."

"It would just be so convenient," Derick said. "Bill and Bob don't have much time to look for a place. Who knows, maybe it would just be temporary. If it doesn't work out, they'll go somewhere else."

"I don't know these friends of yours," she said. Now she was pulling at her hair, having discovered the collapse of the chignon and trying desperately to fix it.

"They couldn't be nicer," Derick said.

"I'm sure, honey, if they're friends of yours. But still, I just don't see the point."

Derick sighed. "Mother, that apartment has lain empty for ages now."

"Exactly," she said. "So what's the rush?"

"It's a waste," Lucy argued. "Do you have any idea of the demand for real estate in Manhattan?"

"I've never had tenants," she continued, staring out the window. "From the day we moved in, the downstairs was your father's office. That's why we bought this building in the first place, so we could have the whole place to ourselves and not worry about neighbors."

"Well," Derick said, "things have changed, haven't they?" He reached down for his wine and finished it. "Just think about it, okay?"

She had already returned to her pie, apparently done with thinking. Derick rolled his eyes at Lucy and slipped out of the room. The stairs creaked beneath him, so he increased his pace to call less attention to himself.

His old room was upstairs on the right, the walls still the same cobalt blue he'd picked out when he was ten. His mother had feared the color was too dark, so she'd insisted on bright furnishings. The white bedspread was still here, and the rug that covered most of the hardwood floor. A few of his old books lined the shelves, and the occasional toy—keepsakes he didn't have room for in his own apartment, but that his mother refused to throw away.

"What are you doing up here?"

"Traipsing down Memory Lane," he said before turning to face his sister.

"And leaving me alone on Crazy Street."

"Sorry."

"No worries. She just retreated to the kitchen to pack our doggie bags, so I decided to sneak upstairs."

"Oh boy, leftovers." He snickered and turned back to his old desk, sharpened pencils still in a mug on the corner.

"Are you okay, Freddy?"

"I'm fine. Why wouldn't I be?"

She paced across the room, her head now framed by a Wesleyan banner. "I don't know. Is it Jared?"

"You're just not going to let up on that, are you? Jared is fine. But no wedding bells, okay?"

"Mom's not the only one who worries about you, you know."

"I appreciate that, Lucy, I really do. But honestly, I'm fine." He leaned against the desk. He felt a subtle carving in the wood behind him, and tried to read it with his finger, like Braille. He wondered if it were the initials of some boyhood crush.

He felt a sudden prick as a splinter entered his fingertip. He pulled his hand up to his face and checked. "So," he said, probing the injury, "how's *your* love life, sis? Really." He put the finger in his mouth and squeezed it between his teeth to drive out the splinter. It emerged surprisingly easily.

She sighed. "I date. Now and then. There aren't a lot of men who are champing at the bit to marry a financial VP with a tattoo on her shoulder and a nostalgic love for punk rock. They don't know what to make of me."

"Tattoo? You got a tattoo?"

She gestured toward her shoulder. "Just a little one. It's not visible unless I'm . . . well, not very professionally attired."

"Let me see!" He charged at her. She rolled her eyes and dutifully pulled at the collar of her blouse.

There, just under the bra strap, was a three-inch image of a naked man with a hand resting on his own shoulder. "Is that David?"

"Uh-hunh. When I went to Florence last year, I just couldn't stop staring at him. I must have hung around that gallery for an hour, just to catch every angle. So powerful, so . . . ideal."

Derick smiled. "I love it. It's very you."

"Thank you."

"You are, after all, a slayer of giants."

Lucy led him to the doorway. "Speaking of which, we'd better get back downstairs, before she starts cooking again."

Mrs. Sweetwater was sitting by the bay window in the front room. The street seemed incongruous behind her. It looked like any other street in this neighborhood, like his own, barely ten blocks away, but somehow it didn't seem to fit her. It was if they lived miles apart. His world was an entire city, hers this hermetic paneled space.

If she'd left the house more often, they might have run into each other doing daily errands. But Stella Sweetwater preferred to stay put. She had her groceries delivered, even though the store was directly around the corner from her building. Her only regular foray out was a monthly hair appointment. She was terrified of the color gray.

As they were getting ready to leave, Lucy tried to persuade her. "For Pete's sake, Mother, just go out and get some air once in a while."

"There's plenty of air right here," replied her mother, opening a window as evidence.

The November wind flowed in like a frigid tsunami, and Derick ran around her to pull down the sash. "What are you doing?" he scolded. "It's arctic out there today."

"And you want me to go outside, Lucy. What are you trying to do, kill me?"

She hadn't always been quite so bad. The general timidity that had long been part of her character, however, seemed to have turned into full-blown agoraphobia after their father left. Derick couldn't tell whether she was afraid something in the outside world would hurt her, or that she would come home to find another piece of her inside world missing.

# CHAPTER 14

## Once More, with Drag Queens

So far, there had been no surprises in the tales Clive rattled off every afternoon. He had already told Derick in excruciating detail about his rise to stardom, which was surprisingly short. His second play in Denver was a low-budget production of *Brighton Beach Memoirs*. One night he was discovered by a Hollywood producer who happened to be in town for the Denver Film Festival. The producer, Bobby Stark, hated everything at the festival and had gone to the theater under duress for lack of anything better to do in what he freely termed a "godforsaken hell-hole," when he was suddenly confronted by a far too handsome and far too goyish Eugene Jerome. And, in a story worthy of Eve Harrington herself, he went backstage after the performance and told the eighteen-year-old Harold Fitzpatrick that he would make him a star.

Right off the bat, Derick could tell it was all bullshit. Clive was telling him the story as if it were already a Hollywood script. Every show business cliché he could come up with ended up on disk, and Derick smiled politely through them all. This was part of the process—the game he always had to play with his subjects. They were all so caught up in their own images, Derick had to coax them back to their real lives, remind them that they had been human beings before they became the products of some mad press agent.

Ironically, despite their promising start, Clive seemed to grow less open as they went on. His created persona was a little farther away from the real one than most of Derick's previous clients. Derick had no choice but to smile his way through every interview and clutch the illicit recorder on the way home, knowing he wouldn't bother to listen to these early sessions at all. The heart of the matter wouldn't come out for weeks yet. They were still in the courtship phase, building trust.

"Jeremy was very helpful when I visited the set," Derick said, hoping to coax something more substantial out of the conversation.

"I hope it didn't completely disillusion you. Most people are shocked to find out how excruciatingly boring filmmaking really is."

"How long has Jeremy worked with you?" It was a polite way of asking which came first, work or love.

"Several years," Clive said. "I'm not really sure." He glanced up at the antique clock on the wall. "It looks like we're out of time for today. I have to get ready for a dinner meeting. And tomorrow's another early day on set."

"Of course." Derick shut off the machine and tucked it into his pocket as he stood up.

Their sessions had become like dance moves—two steps forward, one step back, pivot. From time to time, Clive would tease him with the prospect of talking about his love life, but just as quickly, he would back away and change the subject. Derick was learning patience. And he was not a patient man.

He was tired of the mystery of Clive, the need to fill in a story on the basis of the paltry nuggets thrown his way. So far Clive had said nothing significant, other than casual reference to his failed marriage and the women he'd publicly dated—the red-carpet dates, he called them. He'd introduced Derick to Jeremy, of course, and hinted that there had been other men, but no details had yet emerged. There was still no story, no arc Derick could lay over the book, no way yet to make sense of Clive's life.

That was his job, to make sense of it. That was what writers did.

❖

Lucy had always had trouble hiding her enthusiasm.

"I am so excited!" she screeched, leading Derick into the club. "I mean, I've seen my share of drag shows, but none of them featuring my future brother-in-law."

Derick felt like he was the one being dragged. With Lucy's sharp fingernails dangerously close to his jugular, he was being dragged into a new world where everything was upside down, and that in itself was enough to keep everyone else amused. He still didn't get the basic joke.

The pre-show music, blaring through the speakers suspended from the ceiling, was a medley of show tunes interrupted by the occasional thumpa thumpa he was used to hearing in other gay clubs. But at least, unlike most of them, this time the music was subdued, a background rather than a distraction. He could still hear Lucy's every word. For what that was worth.

"This is fabulous!" she said, scoring a table near the front. Derick felt a shiver of panic, wondering if Jared would dare sit on his lap again. The dramatic effect couldn't quite be repeated, except that this time it was actually on his mind, so the cardiac reaction might be a bit more severe. He looked quickly around for a waiter.

"So what's his act?" Lucy said, her chair screaming against the hard floor as she shifted it into position for a full view of the tiny stage.

"I can't say for sure." Derick avoided her gaze. There were too many other things to watch out for, too many wide bustles waddling through the room with little concern for boundaries. "He said to be prepared for a surprise. I just hope it doesn't involve lap dancing."

"Ooh, that would be fun."

He turned her a deadpan expression. "Are you sure I can't get you a Xanax?"

Finally the room began to settle down. There was no longer an evening gown or A-line skirt in sight. All the drag queens seemed to have disappeared backstage, as if they'd been wandering around as a mere teaser, or to reassure the audience they were in the right theater. *Death of a Salesman* was down the street.

Derick was halfway through his first cocktail and searching out the waiter's eyes by the time the lights dimmed. The familiar screeching sound of Sweeney Todd's motif rent the darkness. Derick sat up straight, envisioning sharp knives hovering at his throat.

The lights came up abruptly on a drag version of Mrs. Lovett, a rolling pin in one hand, a rather unappealing meat pie in the other. She took in a gulp of air, eyes bugging out, and cried, "A customer!" in a rather sloppy attempt at Cockney. "Rather a lot of customers tonight, I'd say. Lots of tasty meat out there." She worked her way into the audience, leering, the rolling pin tapping a jagged rhythm against her side.

She broke into song, a patter that replaced Sondheim's wit with made-up lyrics about pounding meat and rolling sausages.

Beside him, Lucy was eating it all up. She peered at the singer, and Derick imagined that she was trying to determine if Jared lay somewhere beneath all that clown makeup. He didn't. For one thing, Mrs. Lovett was too short. Drag can change a lot of things about a person, but it can't lop a foot off his height.

The show was billed as a Broadway night. "No Britney! No Whitney!" proclaimed the poster out front, over a classic photo of Patty Duke ripping off Susan Hayward's wig.

He'd like to think he knew what he was getting into.

Lucy's laugh was infectious. It always had been. Her sense of humor had often saved him when they were kids. Lucy had a way of laughing off the absurdities of the world. Her laughter was a message to stop taking things seriously. Her laughter was permission.

He caught her eye as Mrs. Lovett punctuated a high note by smashing a meat pie against the floor, and they both burst out. He watched the rest of the act through Lucy's eyes, and it began to make sense in its inherent nonsense. This was just life he saw before him, as Lucy pressed her shoulder against his. It was now.

He was still laughing when a spotlight opened at a corner of the stage, reflecting off six feet of sequins. Bernadette came slowly forward, singing a different song now, something he wasn't familiar with, something about trumpets. As before, she started out gently, but when she got to center stage, just in front of Derick, she was belting.

Derick realized suddenly that only music was coming through the speakers. The voice wasn't a recording. It was Jared. And it was beautiful. He was beautiful. Derick could see Jared's eyes gleaming out from the long lashes, Jared's cheekbones lifted by the makeup, Jared's mannish torso cinched in at the waist, one strong leg peeking out from a slit in the gown.

"Yes! Yes!" Lucy cheered, standing up as Bernadette made her graceful exit toward the back of the stage. Finally settling back down, she sidled against Derick. "That was incredible," she said. "He's so talented. What's he going to do next?"

"I have no idea," Derick said.

The four performers took turns on stage. Derick imagined the costume changes weren't easy, so the extra time between scenes must have come in pretty handy. They got through a pedestrian Liza Minnelli and an Idina Menzel who seemed able to burst eardrums all across town.

Derick was on his second martini when a strangely familiar figure appeared in a narrow shaft of light at center stage. She was dressed in black from head to toe—short pants and a tight jacket—and a severe black bob framed her face. The unmistakable opening bars of "All That Jazz" permeated the theater, and an announcer's voice proclaimed, "Ladies and gentlemen, a special treat for you this evening. A little Broadway to get your heart racing, a little Eastern medicine to slow it down. I give you the one, the only, Tai Chita Rivera!!"

Jared stepped slowly forward, not dancing so much as punctuating each beat with a thrust of an arm or a leg, a dramatic arching of his back that set his dark Mao jacket quivering but kept the incongruous bowler hat firm on his head. The exercise was so discordant with the lascivious content of the song, the room was quickly in a hilarious uproar. He had painstakingly choreographed every move, from the sudden jab of an arm into the air to the elegant twirl as his body shifted direction.

His face was pale and still, just enough rouge to pull up his cheekbones. He didn't make eye contact with the audience, as if he were really in a trance, focused on his chi.

Derick stopped searching for Jared beneath the makeup and the costume. He even forgot about the glitter that had earlier defined Bernadette. Now he was focused solely on this woman on stage, this woman who seemed to transcend both her namesake and the man underneath it all. This was Jared, too. And that tall imposing Bernadette, encased in sequins. And whatever else they were yet to see as the show went on. It was all Jared. And it was beautiful.

"So what did you think?" A makeup-free Jared came up to them outside the theater.

"It was fantastic!" Lucy cried, her excitement undiminished by the loss of illusion. She draped her arms around Jared's neck and, standing on her toes, kissed his cheek.

"Well," Jared said with a laugh, helping her safely back down to earth, "thank you. I'm glad you enjoyed it."

"Me?" she said. "Everyone enjoyed it! Did you see that ovation, or were the lights too bright in your eyes? The whole place stood up at the end of your Chita Rivera number."

Jared smiled. "That was nice."

"Nice? It was brilliant. How on earth did you come up with the idea?"

Jared met Derick's eye and cracked a smile. "Something we saw in Provincetown," he whispered.

"You stole someone else's act?"

"No!" Jared looked around, apparently afraid to spill trade secrets. "More like an inspiration."

"Well, you can take that inspiration to the bank, mark my words."

"I will," Jared said. He moved to the curb to hail a cab. "Now, who wants a drink?"

"Why don't we hang out here?" Lucy said, gesturing back to the club.

"Actually, I made plans with my friend Xander. I told him we'd meet him in Hell's Kitchen."

"I'm game."

Derick sighed. "My sister loves gay bars."

When the cab dropped them off across town, Jared draped arms with both Derick and Lucy. "Forewarned is forearmed," he said, leading them toward the bar. "Xander can be a little challenging."

Derick laughed, squeezing Jared's arm against his side. "He can't be any more challenging than my friends, and you've survived them."

"Yes," Jared persisted, "but Xander's challenging in a different way."

Derick stopped at the door and turned dramatically. "Wait, he's not horribly deformed, is he? Are we about to meet the Elephant Man? Dick Cheney? What?"

Jared laughed and pushed past him. "Just don't say I didn't warn you."

"I've handled challenging people before, you know. Hell, I worked with Monica Montgomery."

Jared turned around, still holding the door open. "I knew it!" he said. "I knew you were her ghost."

Derick felt his ears turning red. He shook his head, but it was too late. Jared's excitement was palpable.

"Tell him that," he said. "Tell Xander all about Monica Montgomery. There's nothing he loves more than gossip about people he hates."

"I will not!" Derick said, laughing. "And why does he hate her? Clearly, he hasn't read the book. I made her look quite charming."

Inside, he took gentle hold of Jared's shoulders and looked

him in the eye. "Seriously, hon," he said, instantly realizing it was the first time he'd used the word, "there's nothing to worry about. Everything will be fine. Xander will love me."

Jared smiled. "Xander *will* love you," he repeated. He took in Lucy. "And you."

"Of course," Derick said with a laugh. "Men always like Lucy more than me."

They found Xander near the back of the bar, in a little clump of very handsome, very sober-faced young men. He had a drink in his right hand, so he held out his left when Jared introduced them—palm down, as if he were expecting it to be kissed rather than shaken.

"So nice to meet you," he said with a flat smile. He was tall, his dark hair parted on the side and held in perfect waves that gleamed in the overhead light. "Did you enjoy our little star here? I saw the show last night. Spectacular, didn't you think?"

"Absolutely." Lucy was eyeing Xander's glass.

"We need to get you drinks," Xander said. "We need to get everyone drinks."

As if by magic, a waiter appeared, tray in hand. "What would you like?" Xander asked Lucy, one finger pointing toward the waiter as though to freeze him in place.

"A cosmo," she said.

Xander blinked pointedly and turned to the waiter. "A cosmopolitan for the lady," he said. "And . . . ?"

"Whisky sour," Derick said quickly.

"Two." Jared put an arm around his waist.

Xander nodded, and the waiter vanished into the crowd.

"Ordinarily," Xander said, "I don't go in for drag, but I'm always willing to make exceptions for my friends. Particularly when they're as talented as our little RuJared here." His dark sleeves were rolled up midway to the elbow, revealing a delicate gold bracelet on one arm. "His originality is the key. I mean, could you believe that Tai Chi thing? Now that's theater. Most drag is so predictable. If you've seen one Barbra Streisand, you've seen them all as far as I'm concerned."

"And even then," said the boy at his side, "I'd go for the real thing."

Xander smiled. "So spake Sasha. Everyone, this is Sasha. Sasha, everyone."

"Well," Lucy said, "I think drag is fabulous. Even when it's Barbra. Or Bernadette."

"Thank you," Jared said. "I love when people are entertained by it. But for me, it's got to be more than just..."

"Eyeliner?"

"Yes!" Jared laughed. "Among other things. It just feels freeing somehow. Not that there's anything trans about it. It's not that I feel like a woman exactly. I just feel in touch with the womanly part of myself, if that makes any sense."

"Of course it does," Lucy said. "I work in a very male-dominated world. I completely get it."

"Well, I don't," Xander said. "I love you, darling, and you're brilliant at what you do, but why anyone would deal with mascara and pantyhose when you don't have to is beyond me."

The drinks finally arrived, and Derick grabbed his, half-expecting it to vanish in his hand like a mirage. Jared made a toast, and Xander reluctantly pressed his glass into the circle. "And what do you do, Derick?" he said. "Whatever it is, presumably you stick to menswear."

"Derick is a writer," Jared said. "I told you that."

"Oh yes," Xander said. "The workshop in Provincetown."

"He's a very good writer, actually." Jared nudged Derick's shoulder and smiled.

"And what do you do for a living?" Xander said.

Derick turned back and met Xander's eye.

"I mean, writers have to do something for a living, don't they?"

"Well, as a matter of fact... I write."

"What a relief," Xander said. "I was afraid you were going to say you work at Starbucks or something. This town is full of so-called artists who work at Starbucks."

Jared gallantly changed the subject and started telling anecdotes from his shared past with Xander. They had met a few years ago, when both were new in town, when Xander was just an intern at his PR firm and Jared hadn't yet put on a dress. Xander relaxed a bit, reliving old stories. Derick used the occasion to breathe. He smiled politely, but he wasn't following the conversation. Beside him, Lucy was staring across the room.

"What are you looking at?" he whispered.

"Nothing."

"Well, it can't be worse than what you're not looking at."

They chuckled, faces close together as though to capture the sound.

Xander made his excuses a few minutes later. "Sorry," he said, "I have to get up at the crack of dawn tomorrow. Otherwise known as nine a.m." He set his glass down on a table. "It was lovely to meet you both," he said. And in a moment, he was gone, his entourage dispersing in his wake.

"Well," Jared said when they were all out of earshot, "he was on his best behavior."

"He was?" Lucy barked. "Then what's his worst look like?"

Jared laughed. "You don't want to know. Let's just say, I like to keep on his good side." He let out a deep breath. "He liked you, though."

"How on earth could you tell?" Derick said. "He didn't ask a single question."

"No, no, he asked about your writing."

Derick squinted. "He asked where my money comes from."

"Well, I'm afraid that's how Xander sees the world. With price tags attached."

Lucy laughed.

"What?"

"I was just imagining a character for your next act. Minnie Pearl."

They all toasted to that.

❖

He woke with a jolt at four thirty, a dream still vivid in his mind. He was in his mother's house, and Lucy burst into the room, wielding a butcher knife. She came at him fiercely, but smiling the way she smiled with Chris over their private jokes. And she stabbed him, again and again—in the chest, the arm, the hand that reached up to block her. Blood was everywhere, great pools of blood seeping into the floor-boards, rippling across the room. Derick fell to the floor, watching his life drip away in red puddles.

And suddenly Lucy was gone, and another figure came into the room. Their father approached slowly, wielding a mop, dragging a bucket behind him. He slapped the mop against the floor, soaking up the blood, spreading it around. He rinsed the mop in the bucket and started over. But there was too much blood. So much blood, he would be cleaning it all night.

# CHAPTER 15

## The Gypsy's Curse

If he couldn't push, maybe a nudge would do.

"Do you remember Bill and Bob," Derick said, "the gentlemen we met in Provincetown?"

Clive turned his head to one side and pursed his lips for a moment, his profile framed by the dark bookshelves that lined the study. "The ones who got married on the beach. Of course."

"They're from Indiana. Some small town whose name I can't remember. As I'm sure you know, that's not the friendliest environment for a gay couple. We made fun of them, Chris and I, for being naïve, unsophisticated, a little too earnest. But I don't see it that way anymore. Now I think of them as incredibly brave."

Clive's lips were sealed, his eyes focused, as if he were listening to an academic lecture.

"They had everything to lose by living their truth: their livelihood, the respect of friends and neighbors. But they never thought twice about *telling* the truth. They never pretended to be anything other than who they are."

Clive nodded gently. "Well, good for them."

"What are we doing here, Clive? What do you really want this book to be?"

"We'll get there, Derick. I just need you to be patient."

"Have I said too much?"

"No," Clive replied. "I needed to hear it. That's why I hired you." He smiled and lifted his glass. Whiskey had won its war with afternoon tea. There was a long pause, and then, suddenly: "I haven't told you much about Alison yet, have I?"

Alison Prentiss, according to the tabloids at the time, was the love of Clive's life. A glamorous up-and-coming actress when they met, she married him after a whirlwind romance, and they became Hollywood's "it" couple for a while.

"She was supposed to be the one," he continued. He got up from the chair and looked out the window. "Until then," he said, "I'd dated a lot of women, but none very seriously. I didn't take any relationship seriously. I was married to my career. And yes, there were more than my share of men, but that was just sex. I thought Alison could fix all that. She was beautiful, smart, accomplished. If I couldn't love Alison Prentiss, then . . ."

Derick leaned toward Clive to capture every word.

"It's silly, I know," Clive said. "At some level, I suppose, I was hoping Alison would cure me. At that point, I thought it was something that needed curing. And I tried. I did love her. But when push came to shove, it wasn't enough."

"Did she know why?"

Clive was gazing out toward the park, eyes wide, as if he'd just spotted something familiar. "Eventually," he replied, "I told her. And I had to let her go."

He paused, and Derick whispered, "You had to let yourself go."

"Yes," Clive said. "That was the wake-up call. I was willing to continue the charade, but only to fool the rest of the world. I couldn't fool myself any longer."

Clive turned away from the window and met his eye.

Derick smiled. He had the story at last.

Opera usually left Derick speechless. After the curtain fell on each act, he liked to sit quietly for a moment, just to absorb it all. So he especially appreciated the Met's practice of taking curtain calls between acts rather than saving them all up for

the end. And it seemed the kindest thing to do for those sing-
ers whose characters died early on. Why should Scarpia have
to stick around the theater for another hour after Tosca
plunged in the knife?

But tonight, they were seeing *Carmen.* Everyone survived,
at least until the last act.

"What a ballsy little tramp!" Brad said as they rose from
their seats after the first act. "A girl after my own heart."

Chris rolled up his program and slipped it into a jacket
pocket. "Forget it, BB, you'd hate her. She smokes."

"True," Brad admitted, sidling out of the row and onto the
red-carpeted stairs.

On the balcony level, Derick waited by the railing while
Chris and Brad fetched drinks from the bar. A couple of
flights below, the grand tier patrons ate at white-draped tables beneath the oversized Chagalls. Most of them seemed to
be barely picking at their food. Opera to this set, he supposed, was less an art form than a social event, where
overdressed women dragged their indifferent husbands
away from their stock portfolios in order to show off a new
gown or diamond necklace.

Someone tapped him on the shoulder, and he turned
around to find a whiskey and soda staring him in the face.
Brad smiled devilishly behind it.

"So, what do you think of the performance?" Derick said.

"I don't know," Brad said with a sigh. "There are those
moments when something stupendous happens. But they're
only moments, here and there. I can't tell whether opera's
getting worse or I'm just getting jaded."

Derick nodded. "It's all still fairly new to me," he admitted.
"I've seen only a handful of operas."

"You're lucky," Brad said. "You're still exploring."

Chris poked the lime in his drink as though hoping to
drown it beneath an ice cube. Looking around, he murmured,
"They sure could stand to expand the demographic here.
Like, lower the average age."

"You never know," Brad said, "maybe they'll attract the

millennials with a hip-hop opera. The whole world's going to hell, anyway." His eyes suddenly brightened. Controversy, Derick had learned, was Brad's lifeblood. "You remember our old pal, Clive Morgan?" he asked abruptly.

Derick looked away. A tall woman was posing by the bar in an elegant dress, oversized black-and-white polka dots trailing down to her ankles.

"Well," Brad went on, "did you see his most recent film, *Grace*? It was exquisite."

"I must have missed that one," Chris said.

"So did nearly everyone else," Brad said. "Nothing blows up."

"I watched it recently, on DVD," Derick said. More research. "You're right: it's kind of wonderful."

"So," Chris said, "tell me about it."

"It's about a long-married couple—Clive and Brigitte Damboise, my god why can't Americans be that good?—who don't communicate anymore. They live together, they do things together, but their psychological lives are completely separate. In the course of the film, very little actually happens. It's all about image and suggestion—the way he stares at the salt shaker when she places it on the far side of the table. He doesn't want the salt, but he resents that she's put it so far away that he would have to ask if he did want it."

"You're kidding," Chris said. "The big moment in the film is an argument over a table setting?"

"Believe me," Brad said, "there is more life in that salt shaker than you'll see in anything else out of Hollywood this year."

"What on earth is your point?" Chris said. His glass was nearly empty. He swung it gently in the air, rocking the ice.

"My point," Brad said pointedly. "It's just sad. Clive has real talent. And he wastes it on crap."

Derick felt himself blushing. "Maybe you can't make a living and a statement at the same time," he said.

"Precisely. And before you know it, they'll be performing *Cats* in this building."

Still surveying the room, Chris managed to deadpan, "And we all know how much you love cats." He took a long swallow from his drink and finally came alive, turning back to face them. "Does anyone need a refill?"

"No," Brad said. "But there's hardly time for another drink, anyway, Chris. Carmen will go back to torturing poor Don José any minute now."

"I drink fast," Chris said, pulling away from them.

"You make it sound too easy," Derick persisted. "I'm sure Clive wants to make art. But he also wants a good life, and money."

"He has plenty of money already. I think you give him too much credit. It's not like he's some starving artist doing what he has to to make ends meet."

"Someone like me," Derick said with a laugh. "Penning celebrity memoirs while my novel grows dust."

Brad's face fell. "I'm sorry," he said, "but yes, that's a completely different story. Speaking of which, what are you working on these days?"

The crowd started to move toward the auditorium. "Let's get back," Derick said and led Brad inside.

Chris was late getting to his seat and had to squeeze past everyone else just as the curtain was rising. Derick tried to catch his eye as he sat down between them, but Chris kept his focus on the stage. He looked flushed, perhaps from rushing to get to his seat, perhaps from the alcohol, perhaps from some other source of excitement. On his left, Brad met Derick's gaze with a cynical sneer. At the next intermission, Chris was sure to meet an inquisition.

An hour later, Don José completely under the gypsy's spell, they made their way back to the bar. Chris insisted on fetching the drinks and sent Brad and Derick off to find a spot by the rail overlooking the atrium. Through the crowd, they could see Chris conversing with the bartender, ignoring the drinks laid out before him.

"What is he doing?" Derick said.

Brad laughed. "Check out the bartender. That explains everything."

All he could make out at first was a shock of dark hair, a tight-fitting white shirt, impressively broad shoulders.

A moment later, Chris dragged himself away, whether because of the press of impatient customers or guilt over his thirsty friends, it was impossible to tell.

"Okay," Brad said, accepting his drink from Chris's hand, "who is he?"

"Who?" Chris said, holding a glass out to Derick.

"The bartender, Chris. You know, the hunk you've been flirting with for the past five minutes." The jig was up.

"Angelo Cucina," he replied. "Italian."

"The real thing?"

"Accent and all."

"How *is* your Italian these days?"

Chris laughed. "I'll let you know in the morning."

"My God, you have a date already?"

"He said he'd meet me at Barrage after the show. Unless I decide to skip the last act."

"And miss Don José's revenge?" Brad said. "I wouldn't think of it. Even if the tenor can't hold a note." He cradled his drink, staring back at the bar. "Angel of the kitchen," he murmured. "Does he cook?"

"You sure ask a lot of questions, you know that?"

"Maybe you should ask more yourself."

"Hey, I'm just trying to have a good time. If you're going to interrogate someone, try loverboy over here." He tipped his glass toward Derick.

"What did I do?" Derick said in a faux huff. "I'm just standing here, perfectly innocent."

Brad smirked. "Even I don't buy that one."

"How *is* Bernadette?" Chris asked.

"Jared," Derick corrected. "And he's fine."

"Just fine?" Brad said.

"He's a really sweet guy, but we're taking it slowly."

"Are you in love?"

"After four months? Please." Derick took a long sip of his drink. It was stronger this time, the whiskey burning the back of his throat, tickling his nose.

"What? It should take longer?"

"If it's real, yes. You have to be careful with romance. It's all hormones. It's not love."

Brad smiled, lips sealed. "Don't you think hormones have anything to do with love?"

"No. In the beginning, it's all about lust—nature's way of tricking you into reproducing."

Brad laughed. "How on earth does that apply to us?"

"The principle's the same. Gay or straight, it's all about spreading your seed." He turned to glance out the huge windows at the dramatically lit fountain that anchored the plaza. "At the moment, I'm more interested in tending the garden."

"Which garden?" Chris said.

"My own."

"What do you mean?"

They were squeezed together against the railing, surrounded by the well-dressed hordes.

Derick hunched his shoulders and leaned over the rail for air. "I'm not going to rush into anything. I don't *need* to be in love."

"Oh, reason not the need, sister," Chris proclaimed dramatically. "Why are you being such a drama queen about it? You like the guy. Just see where it goes."

"I'm not sure it's going anywhere."

"How on earth can you know that at this point?"

"It's just physical right now. We have very little in common."

"Commonalities are irrelevant," Chris said. "If Mother Nature tells you that you fit together, you listen to her. The hormones are the only thing you really can trust. They may not last very long, but they're true."

199

"I don't believe truth is temporary, Chris."

"Everything's temporary," Chris said, draining his glass.

Brad drew closer. For once he was speaking softly. When people have something important to say, Derick had always noticed, they say it softly. "My first lover and I," Brad began, "came from very different worlds. And he said something to me I've never forgotten: *Differences are gifts.*"

In the distance, bells tolled gently, warning about the end of intermission.

"Speaking of love," Derick said, desperate to change the subject, "I don't think I ever told you. Bill Keaton's been emailing me."

"Who's that?" Chris said.

Derick sighed. "The Billy-Bobs!"

"Oh, those old queens. What does he want?"

"They're moving to New York."

"You're kidding."

"I love those two," Brad said.

Chris was having none of it. "Good god. It's like the Beverly Hillbillies, only in the wrong direction."

"They want help finding an apartment."

"Queens is nice," Chris said flatly.

"I suspect they were thinking more like *your* neighborhood."

Now Chris was definitely awake. "The Clampetts in Chelsea? They'd be eaten alive."

"I admit," Derick said, "they will be fish out of water in this town. But they're lovely people. I'd like to do *something.*"

"You just let me know when the housewarming is, and I'll be sure to dress in gingham and bring over a nice tray of hot-cross buns."

"I think it'll be fun to have them here. It'll be nice to have friends who aren't so jaded about everything."

Brad, who had been gazing for the past few minutes into the middle distance between them, suddenly lifted his head, features as relaxed as a Buddha's. "They'll be a breath of fresh air in this town, the Billy-Bobs." He gestured around the room. "At least they're open to adventure. They don't pretend to have it all figured out already."

"Do you have it all figured out?" Derick said.

"Of course not. I'm hoping the answer doesn't come to me until I'm on my deathbed, breathing my last. To know it any sooner would make all the rest anticlimactic."

The bells were ringing louder now, and the crowd began to move toward the auditorium. "In the meantime," Brad said in a softer voice, leaning toward Derick, "all we have are those tiny epiphanies when it all *seems* clear. Even though a minute later it may be a complete muddle again, it makes perfect sense for that one moment. That's what we live for."

With that, they returned to their seats and waited for Carmen to die.

# CHAPTER 16

## Assassins

He had to knock several times. On every other visit, his knuckles had barely struck the door before it opened, revealing Greta's plastic smile. But now, his rapping went unanswered for a full minute, echoing in the long, dark hallway. The doorman had buzzed him in, had called upstairs, as usual, to alert them that he was coming. Yet he was left standing here, self-consciously adrift. He imagined another door opening down the hall, a suspicious neighbor poking a head out to accuse him of trespassing.

Finally, the door jerked open, and Clive himself was standing in the foyer, tumbler in hand, whiskey sloshing around against a couple of ice cubes. "Come in," he said gruffly.

The apartment was eerily quiet. "Where's Greta?"

"Greta's away," Clive said, his attention on the deadbolt. He flipped it with a strange urgency, an action hero hiding out from the bad guys.

Clive led him into the living room and dropped into one of the facing sofas. The pastel pillows were disheveled, an afghan tossed over one arm. With a touch of trepidation, Derick settled himself on the other side of the table. They hadn't met in here since his first visit. With Greta out, perhaps he no longer needed the cloak-and-dagger theatrics.

"It's just you and me," Clive said, taking a long sip from his drink. His eyes were bloodshot, his speech mildly slurred.

"What happened?" Derick scanned the room, searching for signs of other things out of order, some way to determine just how long Clive had been alone and why.

"*This* happened." Clive bent over the coffee table and plucked a magazine from beneath an orange ceramic bowl. He tossed it toward Derick.

It was the *National Talker*, a glossy tabloid he was used to seeing at grocery store checkout lines, not on Fifth Avenue coffee tables. LOVE ON THE BEACH screamed a headline in red, beside a grainy photo of two nude figures embracing on the sand, one naked butt covered by a gray box, the ocean itself an afterthought in the distance. Beneath the headline, in slightly smaller font: *Clive Morgan's summer fling?*

"Oh my god," Derick said shakily. He recognized the image. It was the same scene he had stumbled upon in Provincetown, albeit from a different angle. On the beach, he had seen Clive's face clearly, but the photo had been taken from the opposite direction, so only the other man's face was distinguishable.

"I'm sorry, Clive."

"You were there," Clive said flatly.

"Yes. But I didn't tell anyone. And you saw me yourself. I didn't have a camera. I had just gotten out of the water."

Clive smiled halfheartedly. "I know. I wasn't accusing you. God knows who did it. It's a telephoto lens—look how grainy the image is. That's the saving grace. It proves nothing."

"How can they even claim it's you?"

Clive laughed. "They don't," he said. "That little question mark is their defense. They're not saying it's me. They're *asking* if it's me."

Carefully, Derick opened the magazine, afraid of what else he might see. As he turned the pages, Clive continued to speak. "Greta is meeting with my lawyers right now. This sort of thing has happened before, of course, and we usually just let it go. Sometimes the publicity is worse if you engage. But this time it's a little too egregious. I mean, I can't deny it, Derick. That is, after all, me."

"But no one else knows that," Derick said, finally finding the article. It was accompanied by a snap of Clive walking beside an unidentified Greta on Commercial Street, and a close-up of Clive clearly taken in Hollywood.

> Provincetown, Massachusetts, once a quiet fishing village, is now a well-established gay mecca, a vacation retreat for gays and lesbians from around the world. It's usually a place of anonymity, where its summertime denizens can get away from their daily lives and be fully open.

So far, so good. The only thing that jumped out at him was the word *denizens*—not the usual vocabulary for a tabloid. The writer saved the lead for the second paragraph:

> Rumor-plagued movie star Clive Morgan was recently spotted in town, in the company of an unidentified woman. But was that also him canoodling on the beach, with another unknown person—this time, a man? They say that anything goes in Provincetown, after all.

"They're very cagey," Derick said, looking up.

"Yes, she is."

"Who?"

"The writer. I've seen her byline before. Always tongue-in-cheek, hiding behind innuendo."

Derick scanned to the top of the page. He recognized the name, too. Sera Mathison. An anxious tremor ran through him as he remembered her saying how much she hated her tabloid work. But writing was writing, she said. It was all about who you knew.

"Don't worry," Clive said. "It'll blow over. It always does."

Derick put the magazine back on the table. "But do you want it to? Maybe this is your chance."

Clive shook his head. "I'm not going to do it on Sera Mathison's terms," he said. "If I come out, I'll be the one controlling the situation, not some cannibalistic reporter."

"I'm sorry," Derick said. He wasn't sure if he was apologizing or just expressing sympathy. He hadn't said a word to Sera about Clive, but the mere fact that he'd met her made him feel responsible. "Where's Jeremy?"

Clive gazed into his glass and murmured, "He's gone."

"With the lawyers, too?"

Clive sat back with an ironic smile. "No. Great minds think alike, Derick. Jeremy agrees with you. He thinks I should use this as my opportunity to throw caution and my career to the wind." His eyes grew dark, focused. "I don't agree. So he left."

"For good? He left you?"

Clive raised the glass in a solitary toast.

They were silent for a long moment. Finally, Clive broke the look with a sigh. "He blames Vyse, of course."

"For what?"

"For my reluctance to spill the beans, as they say."

Derick leaned forward. "Is that why? Is it Vyse that holds you back?"

"They've been so good to me, Derick." The magic of Clive's eyes was their tendency to appear different colors with the light. They were pale green at the moment, matching his sweater. The last time Derick had seen him, they were blue.

"What does that have to do with it?"

Clive threw his head back and focused on the ceiling. "When I first got to Hollywood, I was lost. I had no direction, no idea what I wanted to do with my career. I was stuck in those teen films. God knows they wouldn't last forever. I was already in my twenties by then. I needed to figure out who I was. Surely you can understand that."

Derick nodded.

"So a friend introduced me to Vyse. And I learned how to take control of my life. I stopped worrying about 'finding myself' and learned to make my own reality."

"I still don't understand. About the other."

"My love life?" Clive asked, turning toward him again. "Well, I learned to control that, too. Or at least put it in its place. If I was going to have the kind of career I wanted, I had to project a certain image. And that didn't include giving blowjobs on the beach." He scowled down at the magazine on the table between them.

"I'm very important to Vyse. They rely on me for publicity. If my reputation is damaged, they have a lot to lose."

Derick waited a minute and cleared his throat. His legs

were shaking slightly. "So did you really take control of your life, or did you give it to them?"

"You misunderstand," Clive said. "It's not that simple."

"Of course it is." He felt emboldened now. It was all so absurd. Someone had to point out that the emperor was naked. "Isn't it uncomfortable," he asked, "sharing your secrets with them? I mean, a person in your position. The tabloids must be a constant threat."

"They are," Clive admitted, "but Vyse would never tell them anything unless . . ."

"Unless what?"

"Let's get back to the book," Clive said. "Where were we last time?"

"I have no idea," Derick said. "It sounds like the book isn't going where we planned."

Clive got up and walked across the room. He gazed into the mirror over the fireplace and combed his hair with curled fingers. When he turned back, everything in place, his smile was once again opaque. Where earlier Derick had seen vulnerability, something resembling real emotion, he now saw only the white teeth of a movie star.

"Not right now," Clive said, "but maybe this whole foolishness with the article will help, in the long run. It's like a trial balloon. We have no idea what public opinion will be."

"But you won't have a chance to assess public opinion if you fight it right out of the gate."

Clive walked to the bar and poured Derick a drink. "Let's see what happens," he said, placing the glass in his hand. "Worst-case scenario, we have a typical Hollywood story. It'll still be better than Monica Montgomery's." He laughed. "I tell you what. Let's take a break, just long enough for all this to blow over. I'll call you when we're ready to get back to it. Deal?"

They sat in silence, sipping their drinks. Derick was no aficionado of Scotch, but this one glided down silkily, leaving just enough of a subtle burn to bring his throat to life.

❖

Lucy had a fondness for downtown bars, the seedier the better. More than once, she had dragged him into places where he'd been afraid to touch the cocktail glasses, never mind the toilet. But tonight, he freely let her choose.

By the time he arrived, Lucy and Brad had already commandeered a couch in the back. They were sipping Manhattans and laughing raucously.

"What's so funny?" he said, relishing the fact that they hadn't seen him approach. He hoped the drinks were cheap, because the place didn't waste much money on lightbulbs.

"Darling brother!" Lucy cried. She rose from her seat, in the process spilling no more than a drop of her drink. Lucy was always careful about such things. "Never waste," she'd warned him on more than one occasion. "That's alcohol abuse."

She gave him a half-hug, one arm extended to keep the drink safe. "We were getting worried."

"About me? I can find my way around the Bowery."

"I don't know," she said. "I'm never sure you can survive below 57th Street."

"Very funny."

"Your lover's already here," she said. She nodded toward the back. "He's in the little boys' room."

"My lover?"

Brad shook his head, retaining his comfortable seat on the couch. "Such an eighties term," he said. "What's appropriate these days—*partner? significant other?*"

"*Husband?*" Lucy said hopefully.

"I'm still working on *boyfriend*," Derick retorted.

"What are we talking about?" Jared sidled up beside him and kissed his cheek.

"Terminology," Brad said.

Derick raised a hand to ward him off. "What are you drinking?"

"Don't know yet," Jared said. "I just got here a few minutes before you."

"Come with me." Derick headed for the bar.

Jared followed. "What's up, hon?" He patted Derick's shoulder.

Derick flinched, and Jared's hand fell away. "Sorry," he said, "you startled me."

Jared smiled uncomfortably, and Derick realized his mistake. He had reacted instinctively. This might not have been a gay bar, but it was still New York, and a hip spot, at that. They were safe here. His head knew that, at least.

"How was your day?" he asked, determined to put the moment behind him.

"Fine," Jared said, "but it looks like you can't say the same."

"What makes you think that?" Derick feigned a smile. "I'm fine." He signaled the bartender, a bearish guy in a red T-shirt. If not for the backward baseball cap, he would have fit in in Hell's Kitchen. "Two Manhattans."

He took a breath, watching the bartender reach for the whiskey. "I'm sorry," he said. "You're right, I have had a rough day."

"What happened?"

The bartender scooped ice into the glasses to cool them down and began aggressively working the cocktail shaker.

"Doesn't matter," Derick said. "Tonight I want to live in the moment."

The crowd was surprisingly sparse. Drink in hand, Derick took a seat in the rough Naugahyde armchair, Jared on the edge of the couch so that he and Brad bracketed Lucy.

"Where's Chris tonight?"

"He has a date," Lucy said.

Brad pursed his lips dramatically. "He's *nella Cucina* for the evening."

Derick laughed. "More likely, *Cucina* is *nella* him."

"What are you guys talking about?" Jared asked with a confused laugh.

"Angelo Cucina," Brad said with an exaggerated accent. *"Molto bello."*

*"Molto uomo,"* Derick added.

Lucy leaned forward. "You boys need to cut him some slack. I think it's great that he's seeing someone. The whole Brian thing did a number on him."

It was an apt moment to change the subject. "I had a dream about you the other night," Derick told Lucy.

"Me?"

"Yes. You killed me."

"Again?" She sighed dramatically and shook her head. "What did I do this time?"

Derick described the dream in detail—the stab wounds, the blood. Beside him, Jared cringed.

"Boy," Lucy said when he was done, "you're really terrified, aren't you?"

"It was a nightmare," Derick said, dangling his cocktail, trying to make light of it. "You had a knife."

"No, not the dream. Not me. You're terrified of your feminine side."

"My what? That's preposterous." He took a long sip of his drink.

"What's preposterous? That you're afraid of your feminine side, or that you *have* one?"

"It was just a dream, Lucy. I thought you'd find it amusing."

The oracle of the Upper East Side joined in from the corner. "She's right, you know."

"What?"

The glow from a red lampshade cut a swath across Brad's face. "It's called the anima—the feminine aspect of the unconscious—and what better vehicle to represent it than your own sister? You're afraid it will destroy you. That dream is classic. I had a client once who dreamt that a man in black was hunting him down with a gun."

"Anima?" Lucy asked.

"No. Animus. He was afraid to express his masculine side,

concerned that if he asserted himself everything would fall apart. I told him to get a black suit, head-to-toe ebony, just like the scary character in the dream. It worked. He felt much better after that, and learned to be in charge of his own life." Brad paused dramatically. "So, given my success with him, Derick," he said, "I think we should get you in a dress, *toute de suite.*"

Lucy burst out laughing.

"Very funny," Derick said. He tried to brush it off, but now Lucy was bent over herself, hysterical. "What is the matter with you?"

She fought for breath and came up, a hand against her chest, a look of determined self-control in her eyes. "I'm just trying to picture it. You in a dress."

"I have plenty you could borrow," Jared said with a wink. That just got Lucy started up all over again.

Even Brad was laughing before long. They were like the chorus in a musical farce, a gaggle of clowns in another nightmare. "I'm not a drag queen!" Derick shouted.

"What's wrong with drag queens?" Brad said. Despite the laughter, he was still holding his staid position in the corner.

Swiftly, Derick turned toward Jared, whose expression was less offended than puzzled. "I didn't mean that. It's just . . . not me. You know that."

"Of course we know that," said Lucy. "It was a joke, Derick. It's funny specifically because it's so hard to imagine."

"Exactly." Jared, tipping his glass, extended his pinky with an exaggerated wag. "If somebody had told *me* to wear a dress, it wouldn't be the least bit amusing."

"Yes," Lucy offered, "but if we told you to sing Andrew Lloyd Webber, it would be a *scream.*"

Derick couldn't stop thinking about Clive, wondering about the role Vyse played in his life. He was in the tabloids, and he turned to his church for damage control.

He had drunk too much, but he couldn't sleep when they settled into bed. The quiet in the room made him oddly uncomfortable. It was always too easy to talk in the dark, too easy to fill the blackness with the revelation of things that couldn't be seen.

Instead, he curled onto his side, head burrowed just under Jared's shoulder, and asked another question. "Were you religious growing up?"

Jared took a deep breath, Derick's head riding his chest like an inflating balloon. "Oh yes." He paused. "Let me correct that. I was raised religious, but it never really sank in."

"What happened?"

"My parents are evangelical. Literal. You know, God on a mountaintop carving the commandments, sending locusts to Pharaoh, impregnating virgins, cloning himself and then committing suicide for the greater good."

"Did you believe any of it?"

"I loved the stories. All that drama. That's probably where I got the acting bug. For some reason, I had a real thing for Mary Magdalene." He laughed. "But it didn't take long for me to realize it was all smoke and mirrors. And hate. A lot of hate." He stroked Derick's arm with the tips of his fingers. "When I was a kid, I remember watching the news. There was a story about AIDS. I think maybe it was when Reagan used the word for the first time, so how many thousands of people were dead already? Anyway, my father just got this look on his face. They were showing people marching in the streets, screaming for the government to do something. And my father was just livid. 'It's God's punishment,' he said. 'They deserve everything they get.'"

"Did you understand what he was talking about? *Who* he was talking about?"

"Oh, yeah. I had no idea what it meant to be gay, but I knew I was. You know how that is, how you just know even when you have no idea what it's about?"

Derick curled his legs and pressed in closer.

"So my father," Jared went on, "my father was telling me

that I deserved whatever it was that was happening to those people on television. I deserved to be a pariah. I deserved to die an agonizing death and then go to hell, because the suffering of AIDS wasn't enough."

"But he wasn't really talking about you."

"No," Jared said, "he was warning me. And a few years later, when the feelings started, that's when I really got scared. Hell, my parents thought masturbation was a sin if you were thinking about *girls* when you did it. So I was in deep shit."

Derick felt a tear sliding down his cheek, but Jared's voice was firm. There wasn't a shade of weakness or fear. "And I couldn't exactly pass," he said. "I wasn't one of those stealth homosexuals. I couldn't pretend to like sports or not be afraid of spiders. I couldn't hide my enthusiasm when the Academy Awards came on. I was a stereotypical sissy, and my parents just had to deal with it. They turned a blind eye as much as they could. And dragged me to church. I couldn't hide my gayness, so it was my atheism that I kept in the closet. That really would have pissed them off."

"Sounds like a nightmare."

"It was, for a while. But once I accepted that Jesus Christ was *not* my personal savior"—for the first time, Jared's accent was full-on Tennessee—"the gay thing got easier. I realized their hatred of homosexuality was based on this fantasy world they lived in, this nonsense they called a religion. So how could I take any of it seriously? How could I doubt myself when all the criticism of me was coming from idiots who believed that voices sprang out of bushes and dead people rolled stones away from their own tombs?"

"How did you survive?"

"By ignoring it. Oh, we had a few arguments now and then. You would not have enjoyed being in my house the day I decided to challenge my father about evolution. The worst of it, though, was a few years before, when I didn't know enough not to ask questions. I just kept asking 'why'—why did God do this, why did God do that, why does the Bible say one thing here and another thing there. My father lost patience one night and took out his belt." Jared paused again. Derick held him closer.

"As he lashed it toward me, I grabbed it. I gripped it as tightly as I could, and I turned to face him. To this day, I can feel the fire in my cheeks when I looked at him, the anger. His face froze. Like he was staring at the Medusa. I frightened him. He knew he couldn't control me. Maybe he thought I was possessed. Anyway, he never touched me again."

"That's horrifying," Derick said. "It makes my own child-hood sound like a Norman Rockwell painting."

"Now *that's* frightening."

They both laughed, the tension finally relieved. "So what did you do? How did you manage?"

"Mostly, I just lay low and waited. And when my senior year came along, every school I applied to was in New York. I ran out of that town as fast as I could."

"Have you been back?"

"Christmas," he said. "My brother's wedding. Needless to say, my parents have never visited me here."

"And they don't know . . ."

Jared laughed. "They think drag is something you do to a cigarette."

Derick pulled himself up and kissed Jared. Jared's face looked so calm and smooth, perched in the pillow like an egg in a nest. Derick smiled, lay back down and faced away. Jared held him until he fell asleep.

# CHAPTER 17

## The Other Half

Jared knew next to nothing about sports, but he did understand why teams tended to win more when playing at home. Being on your own turf was much more comfortable. He could imagine a football player knowing each divot in the field and precisely which section of the stands the moon would rise over.

In all this time, Derick still hadn't seen Jared's place. He seemed so comfortable on the Upper West Side, and Jared had been in no hurry to squeeze him into his own cramped space in Chelsea. So it was late December, snow threatening in the sky, before he invited him to dinner.

"It's beautiful," Derick said, settling his coat on the back of the sofa. He lifted his chin and took in the room, like a periscope getting the lay of the sea.

"Are you kidding? It's so tiny, everything's completely jammed together. I keep wanting to change it up, but there's never time."

The kitchen was separated from the living room by a white counter. Jared scooted behind it and pulled a bottle from the fridge. "White wine?"

Derick nodded. "Really," he said, "you have excellent taste. Not that I know much about that sort of thing."

Jared pulled the cork from a half-empty bottle and began to pour. "What do you mean?"

"You've been to my place," Derick said. "I won't be approached by *Architectural Digest* for a photo shoot anytime soon. Basically I just buy each thing as I need it, and half my furniture's from garage sales. Your apartment seems more . . . deliberate."

"I suppose so. But it's not as if I designed it all in one fell swoop. I guess I just have an eye for coordinating pieces."

"I'm all thumbs with that sort of thing," Derick went on, reaching for the glass. "I'm lucky if my belt matches my shoes." He made a show of glancing down to check, eliciting a chuckle from Jared. "Chris says I should turn in my gay card."

"Not to worry," Jared said, winking. He led Derick back into the living room.

"You know what I mean," Derick said. "There's the whole cultural thing. I'm not sure I've ever really fit into it all."

"Nobody is," he replied. "I think that's the point. You know how gay men are. Or some of us, anyway. We were all rejected as kids, so the first thing we do when we grow up is invent cliques of our own, just so we can feel superior by shutting somebody else out."

"That's awfully cynical."

"I'm generalizing. But how else do you explain the A-gays? I mean, really, how many spa treatments does one man need? And how many circuit parties can you attend before you lose all sense of reality?"

"Isn't losing all sense of reality the point of circuit parties?"

Jared saw the red flags of gender issues masking something deeper, the way Derick seemed to hold a piece of himself always separate from the world, but he couldn't get past the dark eyes. Derick's eyes hinted at something he hesitated to show, a gentleness he might not have even realized he possessed.

Watching Derick in public, even among friends, Jared sensed him encased in armor, with only the eyes suggesting any vulnerability. But when they were watching TV on the couch or holding each other in bed, with the lights out and the world comfortably at bay, Derick's air of bravado fell.

As they undressed for bed that night, he saw the loosening in Derick's limbs, the way the weight of armor lifted from his body as soon as he lay on the mattress. Derick kept his eyes mostly closed during sex, but the full, delicate smile on his lips brightened his features and took the worry from his face. He might have been weightless, his every movement fluid and sure.

"Tell me about your last boyfriend," Derick said into the darkness, as they lay quietly, his head on Jared's chest.

Jared sighed melodramatically. "I'm not sure I can remember back that far."

Derick laughed and reached a fist back to punch him half-heartedly.

"Carl was a nice enough guy," Jared said. "We just weren't right for each other."

"Why? How could you tell?"

A corner of the ceiling was in complete shadow, not even a sliver of moonlight reaching it. "We were at different stages of life. We wanted different things." He stroked Derick's side gently, the spot where his belly curved out, the hair soft, untrammeled. "What about *your* last boyfriend? What was he like?"

Derick's head lolled back. "My last serious boyfriend was quite a while ago—a couple of years, I guess. He was great."

"So what happened?"

"He got a job in California. It was a good opportunity, so he took it."

"Just like that? How long had you been together?"

"A little over a year. But it was fine. There wasn't any drama around it."

"Still," Jared said, "after all that time . . ."

"I understood. He did what he had to do."

Jared watched the darkness take over the ceiling, moving from the corner toward the center. "So what have you been doing since? Have you dated much?"

"A little. There have been a couple of guys since then, never longer than a month or two." Derick paused. "I didn't want to rush into anything."

Jared felt the lightness in his belly grow. "So you're not ready for another one?"

Derick fidgeted. "I didn't mean that," he said. He quickly rolled over and looked into Jared's eyes. "I didn't mean that at all." He kissed Jared softly.

"Good. Because I may have to take you up on that."

And the red flags gave way to a white one. Surrender.

Xander was fond of parties. He seemed to live for them, as if he could trust himself to come alive only when galloping through his tiny living room to refill glasses. He was relatively shy most of the time, often coming off as standoffish, even judgmental, but Jared knew better. They had known each other for so long. So he'd jumped at the chance to bring Derick to Xander's New Year's Eve party. He wanted Derick to see the real Xander.

When Derick arrived at Jared's, he was wearing a stylish black shirt tucked into stonewashed jeans. "Will this do?" he asked, gesturing at his outfit, all the way down to the slip-on black boots.

"Everyone will be totally jealous," Jared said. "I may have to fit you with a leash."

Derick blushed.

"To keep people from stealing you away, I mean." Jared grabbed a jacket off the rack by the door, and they headed out.

Xander lived a few blocks north, on the edge of Hell's Kitchen. Most of Jared's friends lived within a ten-block radius. He was slightly embarrassed by the provincial nature of his social circle. But it was unavoidable. People with similar interests and sensibilities naturally picked the same neighborhoods. He had nothing against the Bronx, but in his daily life, he wasn't likely to run into anyone who lived there.

Xander's apartment was nearly full when they arrived, but not so crushed that they couldn't mingle at will. Jared took Derick's hand and guided him easily through the crowd. Most of the faces were familiar but nameless. He smiled at the most recognizable and, as usual, was surprised by the com-

plete strangers who proffered him inexplicable smiles of
their own.

Cyrus was the first to grab him. "Darling!" he cried, coming in for the traditional European buss. Cyrus belonged to
the three-kiss school: left, right, left. He seemed convinced
the final one sealed the deal, despite its assault on symmetry.

"And who's the eye candy?"

"This is Derick," Jared said, surprised to find himself
squeezing Derick's hand tightly. Or was Derick squeezing *his*?

"Derick." Cyrus held out a hand. "*Enchanté.*"

Jared noted the look of relief that passed over Derick's
face when he realized he would be spared the kisses.

"So," Cyrus said, turning back to Jared, "where have you
been keeping yourself these days? We hardly ever see you."

"I've been busy with work," he said. "And stuff."

Cyrus smiled mischievously and took another look at
Derick. "Yes," he said, "so I see."

Jared turned toward Derick and attempted a reassuring
smile. But suddenly he felt hands around his waist and a
breathy voice whispering in his ear. "When is Bernadette
coming out to play again?"

Jared turned to find Daniel and a string of others facing
him. He felt as if he'd been away for a long time, like this was
a reunion of sorts. And once again he was caught up in the
whirlwind.

"Sister," Daniel said, grabbing both of Jared's hands,
"you're looking good!"

"She always looks good," said Cyrus. "Girl's got great genes."

Jared glanced back at Derick, whose expression had suddenly gone flat.

Cyrus noticed as well. And Cyrus was not shy. "What's
wrong, Derick?" His lips were sealed, his head tilted in an
exaggerated look of faux concern.

"Nothing," Derick said haltingly. "Just getting used to the
lingo."

"Oh, that." Cyrus grew wide-eyed. "When us girls get together, it can be a little much for newbies."

Jared put a hand on Derick's shoulder. "Cyrus is my drag mother, actually."

"Drag mother?"

Cyrus got that mischievous look in his eye. "I taught her everything she knows. And I invented her flawless makeup."

Derick wore the polite smile of a tourist who can't understand a word being slung around him. Jared reached for his hand and tried to change the subject. "Derick's a writer," he said.

"Oh." Cyrus scrutinized him more carefully now, his eyes reading a combination of interest and suspicion. "What do you write?"

"He's working on a novel," Jared said quickly.

"Oh, honey," Cyrus sighed, "you are welcome to my life story. It would sell millions!" And he was off. Cyrus had never mastered the difference between conversation and monologue.

Several minutes later, Jared realized he'd lost his grip on Derick's hand. He spun through the circle gathered around him, but Derick was nowhere to be seen. He must have found his way to another corner of the room, perhaps in search of a drink.

The point of coming to the party had been to introduce Derick to his friends, to show him a piece of his world. Jared felt like a parent losing a child in a crowded department store. His task had been to look out for Derick, and he had fallen down on the job.

He pushed his way through the crowd, brushing hands against various shoulders to find the periphery. Xander's parties were an occasion for overlapping circles one would assume should never overlap—the theater crowd, the Chelsea boy crowd, the dull office crowd, the straight-laced and the straight mingling with the uninhibited and the gay.

There were two drinks tables, in opposite corners of the room. Xander was presiding over one, chatting with cocktail in hand. As he moved closer, Jared saw his companion was Derick.

"Eagerton?" Xander was saying. "I've never heard of it."

"No surprise there," Derick said. "It's pretty new, poor stepchild among writers' retreats."

Jared slid in between them. "It was impressive enough to snag Graham Whitcomb," he said, taking Derick's hand. It was cold, as if he'd only recently switched his drink to the other.

"Obviously," Derick said, "they signed him up before the awards started pouring in. I'm sure they couldn't afford him now." He darted his eyes off to the side. "And to be perfectly honest, he's kind of a dick."

Xander pursed his lips. Xander with his lips pursed was notorious. It was the same expression he wore at gallery openings when he decided that the art was complete bullshit, or when Sarah Palin's smug twang screeched out of a TV set.

But there was nothing to fear this time. In a second, he was laughing. "Oh well," he said at last. "Another idol smashed to bits."

It was nearly midnight. Xander ran over to turn up the volume on the widescreen TV. A few blocks away, a million people were hovering in the cold with wool coats and no room to fall down, all eyes on an iceberg of Swarovski crystals.

In the more commodious accommodations of Xander's apartment, couples found each other quickly—those who had come together and those who had just met, everyone positioning to start the year with a lucky kiss. Jared caressed the small of Derick's back as the countdown began.

Noisemakers were hurriedly passed around, along with bottles of bubbly to make sure everyone's glass was full before the big moment. And then, as one minute, one second, passed into another with nothing to show for it but an inordinate cacophony of raised voices and screeching car horns, Derick turned his face toward Jared's and kissed him. They kissed from one year into the next, as though sealing something.

Xander returned with a bottle of champagne and refilled their glasses. "So," he said, "I just heard congratulations are in order. Why didn't you tell me?"

Jared felt the wine rushing to his head without even taking a sip. "Tell you what?"

"Ken back there just told me some big agent was at your show last week and wants to sign you up. I guess Tai Chita Rivera did the trick."

Derick turned with a start.

"Oh." Jared shook his head. "Nothing's final yet. I don't like to get my hopes up, so I keep things like that to myself. Until they're real, you know."

"Well," Xander said, "I don't want to jinx anything, so . . . Mumm's the word." He toasted with the bottle.

They waited until 1:00 to take their leave, hoping the crowd from Times Square had dispersed a bit. Even though the walk home was short, Jared didn't want to be caught in the middle of that insanity.

He stopped at the bottom of the staircase. Derick, several steps ahead, sensed his absence and turned around. "So," Jared said, "I didn't want to tell Xander this, not before you. There's more to the story."

"What story?"

"I signed a contract." He was suddenly aware of the cold; his feet were tingling. "I've never said it out loud before but . . . this is big." He began to laugh nervously. "My agent's getting me booked all across town, *out* of town. He's talking about cruise ships, god knows what."

Derick's face looked frozen suddenly. "Well," he said, stumbling, "that's what you want, isn't it?"

"I think so. Yeah."

"Then, good for you."

"Are you okay with it?"

"With what?"

Jared put on his best stage smile. "Dating a full-time drag queen."

The streetlight was bright, but a branch cast a shadow over the lower half of Derick's face. Above it, his eyes looked soft. He stared at Jared for a long moment, breathing quite steadily, consciously, as if he were trying to see if he could tell what Jared was talking about, if looking more closely would show him who Jared was.

Derick took his hand and waded into the intersection. They were already across the street before Jared realized he hadn't answered the question.

# CHAPTER 18

## Vyse and Consent

The New York branch of the Vyse Foundation was housed in a converted church on the West Side, on a nondescript street tucked away from the bustle of its midtown neighbors. The building had been completely gutted, but the façade still bore the filigreed traces of its origins.

It seemed an odd location, given the membership Derick imagined. He envisioned one town car after another pulling up at the entrance, unloading the denizens of far trendier neighborhoods who were slumming for an hour or two.

He stood across the street for a few minutes and watched. He didn't see any cars, just an occasional pedestrian strolling down the street before turning abruptly into the courtyard and up the short flight of steps. Derick waited as five or six people went in. No one arrived in pairs or with kids in tow, like church. He didn't recognize anyone. In fact, most of them didn't even seem particularly well off. They were dressed nicely, but no five-thousand-dollar suits or gaudy jewelry. If they had money, this was evidently not a place to flaunt it.

He crossed the street and affected a nonchalant expression as he stepped into the courtyard. The building had been beautifully restored, the white stone gleaming above the grass. A series of hedges ringed the courtyard, with a single tree in the center he had to walk around to reach the door.

The door opened smoothly, a burst of warm air from inside fighting the morning chill. He stepped inside and was immediately impressed by the quiet. He imagined the deafening sound when the building had been a real church, the cavernous lobby filled with the dirge-like echoes of an organ.

It had seemed too easy, he thought, just opening the door and entering this mysterious world. Surely, it couldn't be that easy.

"Good morning." He turned to find a bright young blonde at his side, clipboard in hand. "Welcome to the Foundation." Her smile was huge, as if someone were pulling the corners of her lips back with string.

"Good morning."

"How can I help you today?"

Derick fumbled. He hadn't rehearsed a speech, created a persona. He just wanted to see what was going on. "I . . . I don't really know." He gave her a crooked smile. That usually worked.

"I understand," she said brightly. She probably got a lot of befuddled people at the door, he thought. "New here? Why don't I show you around?"

This was too good to be true. He imagined her taking him into the inner sanctum and spilling all the secrets.

Instead, she led him toward the far corner, to a long table covered in brochures and several teetering piles of books. "What do you know about the Foundation?" she asked, grabbing a flyer without breaking eye contact.

"Not very much," he said. "I just . . . well, a friend said it might be helpful."

"Oh, wonderful. Word of mouth is the best thing, don't you think? When someone you trust introduces you to something." She unfolded the brochure and placed it in his hand. "Who's your friend? I know almost everyone who comes here."

"He's not from New York, actually. He lives in Washington, belongs to the Seattle . . ." He stumbled for the right word: *parish? club? diocese?*

Her hair was short to begin with, but pulled back and held in place with a scrunchie, it barely moved as she nodded. "I see. Well, as you probably know, Vyse has touched people all over the world. We have thousands of members now from as far away as Japan, South Africa, Scandinavia. We have campuses all over."

"Campuses?"

She laughed. "I know, it sounds like a college, doesn't it? Of course, education is the backbone of the movement, giving people the tools to improve their lives."

As she spoke, he looked around the room. The walls were decorated with posters of natural spectacles, each with a pithy caption in bold letters at the bottom. A churning waterfall, a rainbow arcing over it and into the surrounding trees: COURAGE. Pink rocks under a mottled sky somewhere in the Painted Desert: RESPONSIBILITY. Sunlight dappling through a thick forest: FOCUS. A butterfly dragging its new body out of a chrysalis: TRANSFORMATION.

"I'm Bethany, by the way." She extended a hand.

"Fred." He turned his attention back to the room.

They had retained the stained glass windows. Sunlight fell now in parallel streams of color against the white walls. Looking up, Derick noted the roseate ceiling, covered in gold leaf. The design overall was elegant but never ostentatious. Rather like his hostess, who wore a simple suit jacket and skirt, no jewelry, just the barest hint of makeup. And that smile.

"So, Fred," she said, "aside from your friend, what brings you here today?"

He needed to learn to think faster on his feet. "I've just always been curious. I mean, nothing else seems to work for me, you know? I was raised Catholic."

She nodded.

"I couldn't relate to that after a while. I tried meditation, too. Yoga." She kept nodding like a dashboard Chihuahua. "Even psychotherapy."

"Well," she said, "it's good that you've been exploring. But I think Vyse can offer you something more substantial."

"Can it?"

"It worked for me."

He imagined it had. Bethany looked quite together and

comfortable in her own skin. He was always impressed by people who were comfortable in their own skin.

This wasn't at all what he'd expected. He'd been afraid that he'd be strapped to a chair by now with electrodes glued to his head, stealing his thoughts. But instead, he was standing calmly next to a charming, beautiful young woman who seemed to have the best intentions. She believed in what she was telling him. Like a nun, he thought. He'd never thought of nuns as nefarious. Delusional, perhaps, but not nefarious. Why should she be any different?

She pointed out a large room in the back, long rows of chairs facing an elevated platform, and explained that there were weekly lectures there, mostly delivered by Vyse senior staff.

"Motivational speeches," she said, "that sort of thing. The majority of our education efforts take place in smaller groups." She led him down a narrow hallway with dark paneling and gestured toward the smaller conference rooms opening off either side.

At the end of the hall, she stopped abruptly. Her eyes took on the sympathetic, pleading look his therapist had used from time to time. Bethany opened a door onto a small, square office and led him inside. She gestured for him to sit in the guest chair, then pulled the other out from behind the desk and repositioned it on the side, so they had nothing between them. She sat, clipboard in lap.

"So," she said, "tell me about yourself. Where are you from?"

"New York," he said. "All my life."

She chuckled demurely. "I don't meet many natives. Everyone seems to be from somewhere else." She tapped a manicured nail against the clipboard. "And what do you do?"

"I'm a teacher," he said, "at a private school on the Upper East Side." He couldn't risk telling her what he really did, so appropriating Chris's life seemed a viable alternative.

They continued like that for a few minutes, Derick piecing together a composite identity, true enough so he could keep track of which parts were lies. And then her expression changed again.

She leaned toward him, eyes narrowed, features harsher. "And what do you want from life?" she asked softly. "If you could change anything, what would it be?"

"I suppose I could stand to be more confident," he said. It had just come out, the first uncalculated sentence of the day. It surprised him. He made a mental note to watch out for abrupt responses.

"In what way?"

"Professionally, for the most part."

"You don't like teaching."

"It's not that," he said. "Exactly. I just . . . wish I'd had the courage to explore my dreams more."

Bethany nodded, chin scrunched to project understanding. "What's held you back?"

It had always taken him a while to get used to a therapist. He'd never wanted to spill his guts too soon, before he was sure he was sitting across from someone he could really work with. And all the evidence pointed to Bethany not being that person. But something about her drew the words out, or perhaps it was just the room's warm wood, the coziness, a faint scent of lavender. He caught them before they reached his lips, but he still heard them in his head. He knew exactly how he would answer her questions if he felt safe, if he weren't just on a fishing expedition.

*I wasn't raised to be confident*, he heard echoing in his head. *I was raised to be cautious.*

"I don't know," he told her. The sentence felt false, bouncing off the wall behind her.

"Would you like to find out?"

"How?"

She scooted toward the back of the desk and opened a drawer. Another brochure, this one fatter, the cover designed in autumnal colors, maroon print in the familiar all-caps font of the posters: FINDING YOUR WAY, FINDING **THE** WAY. She placed it before him and, looking at it upside down, began to flip through the pages.

"This gives you some detail on how the Vyse method

works, what it's done for others, and describes the classes we have here, as well as individual work you can do." She turned to the back. "And here are some worksheets. Questions to ask yourself, to decide what it is you really need, so we can figure out how best to help."

She closed the book and pushed it gently toward him. Then she leaned back in her seat, her smile once again broad and unthreatening. "Take it home, see what you think, and let us know."

"Thank you."

Now she held out the clipboard. "Give me your contact information and I'll check in with you in a day or so."

He hesitated. This was not going to work at all. "I don't know," he said.

"Why not? I promise I won't push you to do anything you don't want."

"I just..."

Bethany's smile grew thinner. "I understand," she said. "You hate getting those annoying telemarketing calls, right? Don't we all. But I assure you, we're not selling anything here. We're just offering you ... yourself, to put it simply. If you think you're important enough, if you believe you deserve to be happy, fulfilled." She ducked her head. "You do believe that, don't you, Fred?"

Silence usually worked with his clients. He'd gotten Debbie Kirkendall to open up about her teenage eating disorder that way.

"We've helped a lot of people, Fred. People just like you. All sorts of people." Eyes focused on him, burrowing into him, she launched into a series of stories, illustrations of her point, all following what became a familiar formula: a person whose life was off course comes to the Foundation and learns to confront his demons, take responsibility for his life, and find unexpected success. The Princeton graduate who saw his classmates climbing corporate ladders right and left, achieving fame and fortune, while he was stuck behind the bar at Starbucks, wasting his education and not understanding why. The woman who'd defined herself as a mother who, at middle age, found herself lost in an empty nest with grown children who never called and showed no gratitude for her sacrifice. The man who made millions on Wall Street and woke up one morning to realize he had no sense of purpose, and never had. All of these people had come to Vyse at the lowest point in their lives. And all of them were now fulfilled, successful both financially and personally, happy to be alive. They had taken control of their lives. They had taken responsibility for their own happiness.

"Wouldn't you like to live like that, Fred? Wouldn't you like to know how that feels?"

He decided to play along, for now. "Yes," he said, "I would."

Bethany's shoulders relaxed, the stiff jacket draping more easily on her arms. "Good," she said. "I'm glad."

"I'm not sure I'm like the people you described, though. I think my life is okay. It could be better, but I'm not miserable. I'm not turning to drugs or anything."

"Of course not. But you're not fulfilled, are you?" Bethany tapped the brochure again.

He'd bought enough time to come up with an out. He took her pen and filled out the information on her form: *Frederick Whitcomb*, with a phone number just two digits off from his own.

That seemed to satisfy her. In a couple of days, a complete stranger would be getting a call from a saccharine-toned young woman, and his day would be made.

She led him back to the lobby. Clutching the brochure to his side, he thanked her and tried to match her smile.

"By the way," he said, almost as an afterthought, "I just wanted to clarify something. I've heard that Vyse . . . well, I wanted to make sure there would be no problem. I'm gay."

Bethany arched her eyebrows slightly. His college girlfriend had displayed that same look when he came out to her a year after graduation, a look that said, *Yes, and what else is new?*

"We can talk about that," Bethany said.

"Talk?"

She bundled him toward the door. "Are you happy?"

"With being gay? Of course."

She gave him the head tilt again.

"Is it a problem? I've heard . . ."

"Never mind what you've heard, Fred. You've probably heard a lot of stories about Vyse that aren't true."

"Well, do you have any gay members?"

Her smile narrowed. "A lot of people like you come to us, Fred. And we don't turn anyone away."

Finally, he thought, it was getting interesting.

But then the door opened and changed everything. A blast of cold air barreled toward them, along with a familiar figure—a short, middle-aged woman with tight red curls and an even tighter smile. They made eye contact for the briefest moment, before Derick clutched the brochure to his chest and zoomed past her, out through the courtyard and up the street.

It was too late, of course. Greta had recognized him instantly.

He read through the brochure on the subway. The basic precepts of the "program" seemed one part Ayn Rand, two parts New Age spirituality, and a lot of what Derick's father would call common sense. He began to wonder if the scam was less evil than boring: Vyse made a lot of money by offering platitudes about personal responsibility.

No matter what had happened in the past, the brochure counseled, you are responsible for what you do next. Vyse left no room for excuses. In fact, it was the idea of victimhood that came in for the greatest criticism. "People can hurt you," he read, "rob you of material goods, insult you, but they can't make you a victim. Only you can do that. Victimhood is a state of mind."

The worst sin, the text implied, was wallowing. Always, Vyse's emphasis was on the force of will. "There is nothing binding you to the past, other than your own laziness. The present is all there is, all there ever is. Be what you want to be *now*."

Derick could see the attraction of such a simple argument, despite his inherent skepticism of simple arguments.

❖

"What were you thinking?"

The fedora was tilted over his forehead, casting a shadow on Clive's face. The gray cashmere scarf wrapped around his neck completed the frame. Winter provided more opportunities for disguise.

"I *wasn't* thinking," Derick admitted. A sudden gust of cold wind blasted its way through the trees, and he wished he'd worn a hat himself.

It was like an emergency field trip, or a scene from one of Clive's movies. In the morning, Clive had texted him. He needed to talk to Derick in private. Derick read between the lines and realized trouble must have been brewing with Greta. He had suggested meeting at a café, but Clive had insisted on a walk instead. When you want privacy, there's no better choice than Central Park.

Clive stopped on the path and turned toward the pond, the barren trees in the distance. "Greta was apoplectic," he said. "She thinks you're investigating Vyse now."

"I was."

"Why?" Clive's cheeks were pink from the cold.

"Because it's important to you. I'm writing a book about you."

"No, Derick. *We're* writing a book about me. And if I don't want Vyse dragged into it, they won't be. You're not talking to anyone else, are you?"

"Like who?"

"I don't know. My ex-wife, maybe?"

"No." He laughed the suggestion off, but it suddenly seemed like not a bad idea. "I just wanted to understand Vyse better."

"What's to understand? It's an organization that has helped me out from time to time. It's given me some perspective on life and helped me focus my career."

"How?"

"That's not relevant."

"I think it is."

"Well, your thoughts don't matter."

He'd never seen this side of Clive before. Even in his movies, he seldom looked so angry. Derick chose silence over apology.

Finally, Clive's features softened. "I'm sorry," he said. "Of course I appreciate your thoughts. I just meant that I need you to accept my decision. Vyse is a boundary you can't cross. They're absolutely adamant about controlling their public image. They've had terrible experiences with the press in the past, surely you know that."

Derick stood by Clive's side, forming fists in the depth of his coat pockets. "Ironically, I didn't see much worth writing about. The precepts seem pretty innocuous to me." He was fumbling for the right words. "What troubled me was the pressure. It was like a used car shop. It made me wonder what was really under the hood."

"I'm sorry," Clive said. "But any group can be like that, people enthusiastic about what they've discovered, wanting to share it, put it in the best possible light."

"Like bridge clubs? Tennis tournaments?"

"No." His face looked pinched, trapped between the hat and the scarf.

"More like religions. Or cults."

Clive turned his gaze back to Derick. "I'm not going to argue that with you."

They started walking west along the gravel path. Patches of snow were scattered here and there, left over from last night's dusting. "Everyone has secrets," Clive said.

A young woman in a ponytail and a running suit jogged past. Clive ducked his head to avoid being recognized.

"But we can't let them rule our lives, can we?"

The path curled around the pond and then, suddenly, opened into a wider expanse of the park. Clive stopped, as though paralyzed by the sudden exposure. Derick imagined what it was like to step from the dark comfort of the wings onto a brightly lit stage.

"So what are we going to do?" Derick said. "About the book."

"I don't know," Clive said. "I think the Provincetown story is going to go away, but we'll see."

"Go away?"

Clive squinted at him. "My lawyers are taking care of it," he said firmly. End of discussion.

"What do you want me to do?"

"Nothing," he said, "for now. Just leave it to me." And then, as though someone had called his cue, Clive's expression abruptly changed. Smiling almost innocently, he led Derick back through the trees. "Leave it all to me."

# CHAPTER 19

## Lying with Chris

T hree days?!" Chris yelled into his mobile phone. He set his overnight bag down outside Derick's door and knocked. "What am I supposed to do for three days?"

Derick pulled open the door. Chris gave him a cursory glance and strode into the living room, bag in hand, phone still pressed against his ear. He dropped the bag on the floor and stretched out on the couch. "All right," he said. "Just let me know how it goes."

"How what goes?" Derick asked. "What's up?" He closed the door and sat on the edge of the love seat, facing Chris's feet.

"Ants," Chris announced.

"Ants?"

"Everywhere," he said. "I've been invaded, like Poland by the Nazis. Same little helmets. Everything but the bayonets and the barbed wire." He lay back on the sofa for a moment, enjoying the image. He would have to find a way to use it in his book.

"That's terrible!" Derick said. "So what are they doing about it?"

"They're going to 'let me know.'" Chris gazed up at the ceiling. "I tell you, man," he said, "it's always something. This city'll kill you if you let it."

"They're ants, Chris. They won't kill you."

"No," Chris replied, "but the stress will."

"What stress?"

"Angelo. That boy is a caution."

"You're still seeing him?"

Chris sighed and threw an arm behind his head. "Don't act so surprised. Only a few dates, actually, but I swear, I'm worn out already. He's just so . . . Italian."

"But you're half-Italian yourself. Your mother—"

Chris threw him a pointed glance. "I was in my mother for nine months. My mother was never in *me*."

"Oh." Derick pulled away and sat back in his chair.

Chris had learned long ago that the best way to shut him up was to go graphic. "Don't worry," he said, "it won't last much longer."

"Why not?" Derick was clearly doing his best to cover his relief with feigned disappointment.

Chris shook his head. "It sounds callous," he said, hesitating.

"That never stopped you before."

"Angelo has served his purpose. A little romance. A lot of sex. And Brian is now completely out of my system."

"Congratulations!"

"Thanks. And thanks for suffering through the death spiral with me."

"My pleasure." Well trained, Derick immediately changed the subject. "Jared took me to a New Year's Eve party one of his friends was throwing. Quite the crowd."

"Drag queens? Did you choke on the fumes of Chanel No. 5?"

"Only a few," Derick said, "at least that I could tell. Nobody was in drag. But they were all artsy and pretentious."

"Derick, *we're* artsy and pretentious."

"Not like them."

Chris loved watching him squirm his way out of hypocrisy. "Look, hon," he said, "as your best friend, I consider it my duty to tell you when you're full of shit."

"What are you talking about?"

"What am I talking about?" Chris had to stifle a laugh. They had started out talking about him and suddenly Derick had managed to make it all about himself. He couldn't help remembering Graham in class one day decrying the same thing. Point of view, he said, must remain consistent—

preferably throughout the entire book, but at the very least within a scene.

"I'm talking about you, Melville, and your artistic integrity. How many arguments have we had because I write fun little romps and you fancy yourself so 'literary'? You're as pretentious as the rest of them."

Derick smiled, taking in Chris's regal pose on the sofa, ankles hovering over the arm. "Look, if Jackie Collins said she was writing literary fiction, *that* would be pretentious. I'm just . . ." He burst out laughing. "I'm just a pretentious little shit."

"Finally!" Chris screeched. "Something we can agree on."

"So," Derick said, "about the ants."

"Yes!" Chris's eyes widened in horror. "The last thing I need at a time like this."

Derick gestured toward Chris's overnight bag, bulging on the floor beside the sofa. "You're welcome to stay here if you need to, while they're fumigating."

"Thanks," Chris said matter-of-factly. "You're a doll."

*How could there have been any question?* Derick thought. The bag was already packed—like the gun in the first act of a Chekhov play.

"So what are you doing today?" Chris said, pulling himself up into a sitting position.

"I need to work." Derick gestured toward his laptop, closed and lifeless on the desk, an unopened clamshell.

"Fine," Chris said, pulling his own laptop out of his bag. "I'll join you. Then I'll take you out to dinner." He flipped open the computer and turned it on. The machine began to whir. "And dancing."

"Dancing? I'm not sure I'm up for shaking my booty."

"Yes, you are," Chris said. "You could use the exercise."

Dutifully, Derick made his way to the desk and opened the laptop. He marveled at the irony. For once, Chris was actually encouraging him to work rather than tempting him away from it. Derick's comment about needing to work had simply been an excuse not to be drawn into another of Chris's days of self-indulgence.

His desk faced the window, the narrow silence of 73rd Street. The sky was gray. The sky had been gray for weeks now, as if the sun was in hibernation. Maybe, he thought, he was just suffering from seasonal affective disorder. Everyone else had a clinical name for the human condition—fibromyalgia, chronic fatigue, restless leg syndrome—why shouldn't he?

It took only a click of the mouse to open the novel file, but still he hesitated. He hadn't touched it in months, too distracted by Clive's drama, not to mention his own. All he could see were Graham's red marks on the page, eviscerating his work. Clive's life was an easy subject by comparison, even with the lies.

He opened the file, entered a page break at the bottom, hoping to coax a new chapter out of the keys, but his fingers wouldn't move. The blank screen seemed to be accusing him, like a child pouting from lack of attention.

On the couch, Chris was immersed in his own work. "Let's have a drink," Derick said.

Chris's head darted up. "I thought you'd never ask. What's on tap?"

"I have some mint," he said. "I think mojitos are in order."

"Perfect!"

Derick dashed into the kitchen and pulled a bag of mint out of the fridge. It had been in there for at least a week, so several leaves had turned brown. He picked out a bunch of good ones and marched back to the living room, mint and glasses in tow.

As Derick muddled the mint, Chris paced the room. "They say cockroaches will outlive us in a nuclear war," he whined, "but you can bet your ass it's ants that will drive us crazy enough to push the button in the first place."

"Maybe they're in cahoots with Al-Qaeda," Derick said with a smirk.

Accepting his drink, Chris looked at him with a glint in his eye, and Derick suddenly felt amused by the things that usually annoyed him—Chris's sarcastic edge, his affected narcissism. Not that the narcissism wasn't real—clearly, Chris spent an above average amount of time thinking solely about himself—but he was aware of it. He knew its attractive possibilities, the way a comedian can make an entire career out of a big nose. He used it at once to draw people in and protect himself from getting too close.

They toasted and sipped, slivers of crushed mint floating through the drinks.

Derick's phone, crammed into his jeans pocket, vibrated. He squeezed it out of his pocket and into the light. Jared. He pressed the red button to send the call to voicemail.

"Who was that?"

"No one," Derick said. He looked up, into Chris's eyes. "Jared."

"When did Jared become no one?"

Derick shook his head nervously. "I didn't mean that. I just don't feel like talking right now. This is *our* evening." He hoped the smile and the sentiment would drive away more questions.

Chris gave him a none-of-my-business shrug. "So where shall we go?" he asked.

"You choose," Derick said. The straw was clogged with mint. He tapped it against the bottom of the glass and stirred it around.

The sky had turned a deeper shade of gray by the time they made their way out to dinner. They ate quickly. It wasn't a particularly nice restaurant, just one of the regular spots where they went when they were in a hurry. And Chris clearly was in a hurry. All he wanted to do was dance. It was his way of pushing thought aside, and Derick was easily won over to gyrating on the dance floor, all body, no mind.

They made their way to one of Chris's favorite spots—a warehouse just a block from the Hudson, behind an unmarked door. In the daylight, Derick suspected he wouldn't be able to find it, but at night you could hear the music a block away and just follow the human breadcrumbs—youngish people in semi-punk outfits, smoking European cigarettes outside, waiting to get back in, waiting for their drugs to take effect.

He had always been self-conscious about his dancing. He'd taken a class once in ballroom—waltz, foxtrot, even, in a deluded moment, tango—but he'd never gotten the hang of it. His brain could remember most of what was poured into it, but his body memory was more challenged.

He felt much more comfortable in places like this, where the music was little more than a pulse in the air and the bodies were so close together that no one could really see what anyone else was doing.

And, of course, it was nearly impossible to talk amid the music. Derick was grateful for that, too. It gave him a chance to spend some time with Chris without words—to just watch him dance, with that joyful look on his face.

The lights flashing around them cast purple and blue shadows over Chris's forehead. He reached into his shirt pocket. "Here," he mouthed, holding out a small pill—round, faintly green.

It had been ages since Derick had taken Ecstasy, or anything else besides alcohol for that matter. He hesitated for a moment, as he always did with drugs, wondering where it had come from and whether the source could be trusted. A drug, he thought, was like sex: in the moment of taking it, you were actually trusting not just the person who gave it to you, but a whole chain of others—the seller, the maker, the guy who manufactured the scale the components got measured with. But there were no prophylactics to protect you on this score. Some things just had to be done on faith.

He popped the pill in and threw his head back to swallow. Chris passed him a small bottle of water, which he'd tucked in the side pocket of his cargo pants.

He waited for the moment, but as always, it wasn't until the feeling had been with him for several minutes that he recognized it. The sensation of peace, belonging, sheer joy built slowly, so that by the time he was aware that anything was different, he was already fully under its spell. The people dancing around him—men, women, gay, straight; these days, it was impossible to tell any of those categories with complete certainty—moved in complex patterns, patterns he hadn't noticed before, when he'd been looking with just his eyes. Everything seemed to have slowed down, the spins and swirls languid, effortless. Everyone moved together now like random bits of DNA floating in a single cell.

It didn't seem to matter anymore that, only halfway through their thirties, he and Chris were among the older people in the crowd. They were surrounded by babies, he thought, noting the pacifiers clamped between the sealed lips of his fellow dancers, a horde of twenty-somethings. The pacifiers protected their teeth from the grinding that was a common side effect of Ecstasy. He hadn't done it often enough to notice. All he ever noticed was this—the lightness in his head, the warmth rushing through his entire body, the heightened sensations. The music rumbled through his feet, up his legs, into his belly. The music itself made his limbs move. The music was the dance. He was just its vehicle, like a player piano automatically spinning through a tune.

On the way in, he had noticed several kids wearing white gloves strewn with multicolored Christmas lights, waving their fingers in the air. He had thought it was just another affectation, the latest in rave wear. But now, now that the Ecstasy was coursing through him, he understood. A tall Asian boy beside him waved electric fingers directly in front of his dance partner's face, and the girl—long straight hair bobbing around her—stared, mesmerized by the show. The lights were forming colored parabolas in the air, figure-8s, Mobius strips. Yellow, red, blue, green all merging, a rainbow of pulses hypnotizing her, hypnotizing Derick. He found himself drifting away from Chris, focusing instead on the lights. The boy pulled one hand out of the orbit of the other, extending the show to encompass Derick as well as the girl. Behind the light, Derick could barely see him—the shadow of a face, eerily lit by his own exhibition, a magician weaving a spell, bringing them both willingly, with craving, into his power.

A pair of hands gently caressed his shoulders, and he felt someone's hips tenderly grinding against his. It might have been Chris, it might have been anyone. He didn't turn around to see. It didn't matter. It was all light and feeling and music, and the sensation of hundreds of bodies sharing a single space—together and apart, whole and separate, at once yearning and having. He danced. He just danced.

By the time they left the club, he was on his way down from the high. But the streetlights still shimmered a deeper orange against the night sky, the cool air felt like a thousand tongues caressing his face. Away from the music at last, he was practically deaf to the sounds of the world, but he was grateful for the muffled almost-silence as his legs, drained from apparent hours of dancing, trod through the Jell-O evening to carry him home.

They collapsed together onto Derick's bed and pulled the covers up around them.

"That was fun," Chris whispered.

The hearing was coming back, too. "Yes," Derick replied. "I'd forgotten how cool it can be. Just to be so totally in your body." As they spooned, he could visualize the double-S their bodies made, back tight against chest, knees in knees, curled at a 45-degree angle. They were one, just starting to become two—a cell dividing to make life.

"So why didn't you answer the phone?" Chris asked the darkness.

"What phone?"

Chris's lips were against his ear. "Jared," he said.

"Jared."

He was alert enough now to remember nights like this years ago, when their friendship was new and the judgments rare, when he could tell Chris anything, when he felt safe.

"Do you think drugs alter the way you feel, or do they just reveal the truth of how you feel?"

"It depends on the drug, I suppose," Chris said. "What are you feeling?"

He cherished the invisibility of the darkness. "It's too much," he said. His skin was tingling now, like the kid's electric fingers, short-circuiting.

"What is?"

"The way he makes me feel. Jared."

"How does he make you feel?"

He craved it. He hated it. "I don't know. I've never felt it like this before."

"Do you love him?"

"Words," Derick said. "Let's not label things with words."

"We're writers, darling." Chris chuckled lightly.

The truth, he realized, was that he didn't know how to live without words. If he couldn't label something, he didn't know what it was. Words were his way of understanding the world—signs along the road, telling him which way to turn. Without words, how would he know where he was, let alone where he was going? But sometimes—like now—words just got in the way.

"You love him," Chris said.

"No." What was love? What language was that? "Did you love Brian?" he asked.

"Of course. Brian broke my heart."

"They do that, don't they?" He felt a smile curl onto his face. "Are you sure it wasn't you?" he said.

"What?"

"Did you break Brian's heart?"

Chris's sigh warmed the back of Derick's neck. "I suppose I did," he said. "I wish I'd been stronger. I wish I'd been able to give him what he needed."

"What was that?"

"Me, I guess. Me without all the crap."

"You're awfully wise tonight," Derick said with a giggle.

"I'm cold. When I'm cold, I get pensive."

"I like you when you're pensive." Derick squeezed Chris's hand against his chest.

"You've been in love before," Chris said.

"Have I? I'm not so sure." The images sprang up now—Garrett, Peter, one or two others he'd dated longer than three months: did he love them? "I was happy," he said. "I had fun for a while." His head sank deeper into the pillow. "But nobody ever broke my heart."

"Never?"

"How would I know?" he asked.

That chuckle again. "You'd know."

"So maybe *Jared* will break my heart. Maybe that's how I'll know I love him."

"Does he scare you?"

Now it was Derick's turn to laugh. "Like the shark in *Jaws*," he said. "Like terrorism."

"Why?"

"He wants so much," Derick said. "He wants to suck the life out of me, I think. I can't do it. I can't be what he wants me to be."

"What do you think he wants you to be?"

"His."

"If it bothers you so much," Chris said, "then you already are."

The night closed in around them. Derick settled into the dark and the stillness. His body was growing warm at last, safe on its own.

# CHAPTER 20

## Lying with Jared

When the phone rang, he assumed he was dreaming. All night he'd had a series of elaborate, fantastic dreams, imagery carved from ancient myths and modern nightmares. In one dream, he was being chased down a long corridor by a slithery, angry dragon who barked sulfur that burned his heels. In another, he was lying beside a still lake, under the shade of a willow: the most peaceful sight imaginable, until an earthquake rent the ground beneath him.

He was actually grateful to be woken up. But his mouth felt like it had just been to the taxidermist.

"Hello?" Still lying down, he glanced across the room, feeling the need to confirm these unfamiliar surroundings were home.

"Did I wake you?"

Derick turned back to the nightstand, the alarm clock blaring 11:11 in blue. He'd always thought it lucky when he happened to look at just the moment when all the numbers were aligned. The symmetry gave him hope.

He was awake enough at least to recognize Jared's voice. "No," he mumbled. "I was just getting up."

"I'm sorry," Jared said. "I'll call back later."

"No. No, I'm fine. Let's talk now. How are you?"

"I'm okay, Derick. Are you all right? You sound kind of—"

"It's nothing," he replied quickly. "Just a little sore throat, but I'm fighting it off successfully." That wasn't all. His head was pounding, too, and he was still exhausted. What time had he gone to bed? And what on earth had he done last night?

"That's good," Jared said. "You need to take care of yourself."

Derick took advantage of the long pause in the conversation to pull himself up and grab a swallow of water from the glass beside the bed.

"Listen," Jared continued, "I've been thinking, and . . ." His voice trailed off.

"Yes?" Derick let his head fall against the wall, resting on the picture behind the bed. For years now, he'd been meaning to lift the poster just six inches, so his head would rest against the cool wall rather than threaten the stability of a huge frame filled with fragile and deadly glass.

"Sorry," Jared said, "I just wanted to see if everything was okay. Between us."

"Of course it is," he said. "Why? What's wrong?"

"You've just been so moody. Ever since New Year's, really. I thought . . ."

"No, no," Derick said. "I'm sorry. I know, I've been distracted. There's a lot going on these days. I know it's not fair to you."

"I understand that, Derick. It's not about being fair to me. It's about being fair to yourself."

He closed his eyes at the threat of cliché.

"Your heart's not in this," Jared said. His tone was flat, rehearsed.

"In what?"

"Us. I think we should stop."

"Stop?"

The floor squeaked, drawing his attention toward the doorway. Chris was standing there in jeans and a sweatshirt, a steaming mug in each hand. And instantly, Derick remembered. The dancing, the Ecstasy. And they had talked all night. They had talked about Jared.

"It's not working, Derick. We both know that. I think you want something I don't have."

Chris raised an eyebrow solicitously and laid a purple mug on the nightstand.

Derick picked it up and took a sip. Through the steam, he saw Chris backing out of the room.

"You don't know what I want, Jared."

"No," Jared said quickly, his tone harsher now. "That's precisely the point, Derick. I have no idea what you want. You won't tell me."

"What am I supposed to say?"

"I don't know. *You're* the writer."

It was so easy to find words to describe other people's actions, thoughts, motivations. But he might as well have been mute with Jared.

"It's this job," he said. "The memoir."

"The job you can't talk about."

"Yeah. Anyway, it's been really difficult. I'm beginning to feel . . . compromised."

"What do you mean?"

What *did* he mean? He should have been used to it. He'd been asked to lie before. Every book he'd ever written had been full of lies.

"You're right," he said at last. "I . . . I can't do this. The truth, Jared, is I don't know how." He studied the coffee, the ripples on the surface settling as he laid the mug back down.

Jared sighed into his ear. "Nobody knows how," he said softly. "You just do it. You figure it out."

"But our worlds are so different. Your friends, I just don't fit in with them." He remembered how he'd flinched when Cyrus moved toward him, how that screeching voice had made him shiver.

"You're not dating my friends." His pause was so long Derick feared the connection had been lost. "Is there something else bothering you?"

It was stupid. He knew it was stupid. He couldn't even say it. It shouldn't have mattered.

"Is it the drag?"

He didn't have to say it.

"Derick?"

"You should do whatever makes you happy," he said at last. "And you're so good at it. You really are."

Another long pause. "Seriously? You can't date a man who occasionally wears a dress."

"No, that's not it at all."

"It sounds like it." Jared sighed, and Derick could almost feel the air swirling through the phone. "Look, Derick, everyone pretends now and then. I put on makeup. You put words in other people's mouths. Sometimes to be yourself, you have to be someone else first."

"It's not like that. Jared—"

"Look," said Jared, in yet another tone—matter-of-fact now, reassuring, "I don't know how to fix this. Maybe nothing needs fixing. Whatever happens, we'll be fine. Let's not make more of it than we have to."

He had never known what Jared wanted, either. He'd never known what any of them had wanted.

"Take care of that sore throat," Jared said.

"I will. And you—"

"Good-bye, Derick."

He placed the phone beside the mug and, eyes closed, massaged his temples. If he'd had energy, he thought, they'd still be talking. If every word in the language hadn't escaped him, he might have known what to say.

"Jared?" Chris was in the doorway again.

"Yes." Derick blew out a puff of air. "You like irony, don't you? He broke up with me."

"On the phone?"

"Apparently I'm very hard to reach."

"Well," Chris said, "at least you took the call this morning. That's more than you did last night."

"Don't rub it in," he said. "And besides, if I'd had my wits about me, I wouldn't have picked up now. I was in no condition for that conversation."

"Who ever is?"

"I just feel like I let him down."

"This morning?"

Derick threw his head back against the wall, the jittery picture frame. "From the beginning," he said.

"So what do you want to do about it?"

Derick shut his eyes. "I don't know."

"Then don't do anything," Chris said.

"If I don't do anything, I lose him." He looked back at Chris, hoping for an answer.

"Haven't you already?"

"I don't know."

"You can't lose something," Chris said gently, "unless you want it. Do you want it?"

"I don't know."

Chris sipped his coffee. As he adjusted the mug back down, he said quite calmly, "No, then."

## CHAPTER 21

## Lying with Dr. Beane

The Billy-Bobs would be in the city by the end of the week. For the time being, they'd arranged for corporate housing, Bill said, temporary but comfortable.

They didn't need the apartment. But it was the principle of the thing that bothered Derick. He'd never been much for principles, but this one he couldn't let go of.

"Have you given any more thought to the apartment?" he said. They were in the kitchen, cleaning up after lunch.

"What, dear?" Mrs. Sweetwater closed the dishwasher and reached for a towel.

"The apartment. Downstairs. My friends will be arriving soon, and I'd love for them to see it."

"Oh, yes," she said, wiping down the counter, "your friends. I remember."

"Well?"

She shook her head. "I told you, Derick. I can't."

The place had a hold on her, even though she probably hadn't seen it since his father cleaned it out. *Maybe that was why*, he thought. *The place is haunted.* You'd think that would be reason enough to get rid of it. With the Billy-Bobs redecorating, the apartment would soon be unrecognizable. His mother could go downstairs for tea or to collect the rent and never have to picture what she had seen that day. She could sit in the Billy-Bobs' living room on a new sofa, and the leather couch where she had seen Dolores Detweiler's head bobbing up and down would never cross her mind.

"Will you at least think about it?" he prodded. "I wouldn't ask if I didn't believe it would be good for everyone."

"Yes, dear," she said, finally returning her gaze to her son, "I'll think about it."

From Derick's point of view, the only surprising thing about Dolores Detweiler was that his mother had been surprised. Derick had never met Mrs. Detweiler, of course, but he didn't have to. He didn't have to know anything about her, in fact. He had seen it coming.

They had never fought, his parents. Not to any appreciable degree, at least. The Sweetwaters were economical. Stella specialized in the perfectly aimed passive-aggressive barb that destroyed all defenses. Derick had learned over the years that his parents were never more furious with each other than when they were saying nothing at all. Throughout the last few years of their marriage, they had never been more polite.

For now, he thought, the best choice was to change the subject. "Have you seen Lucy?" he said, pouring a cup of coffee. His mother always had a pot on, but it never seemed to empty. Derick had come to think of the coffee as another *objet d'art*, just something she liked to have around.

"If you want to call it that," she replied. "She shows up now and then for twenty minutes and calls it a visit."

So much for that line of discussion. He poured an inch of cream into his cup—sitting on the burner all day tended to make the coffee unpalatably strong—and gazed out the window.

"Are you still seeing . . . what was his name?" his mother asked.

The sun was reflecting off a glass building up the block. "Jared," he said.

"Yes, Jared. Well, are you? Seeing him."

"Not really."

"'Not really.' Such an interesting response. Whenever I dare to ask *her* the same thing, Lucy's always quite clear about it: 'No, Mother.' As if I'm stupid for asking the question.

That girl is never going to get married, you know. Of course, I can't exactly recommend the institution, myself."

A few sips of coffee were enough. He could already feel it staining his teeth.

Outside, he ambled down the stairs and peered into the window of the lower apartment. He could just make out the fireplace on the far side of the sitting room, a bookcase with a few volumes leaning haphazardly against one another. It had all the makings of a cozy cave, a refuge just a closed door away from the noisy world. He refused to see it go to waste.

Exercise usually helped. When bad feelings threatened, he would go to the gym and work them out. Some days, it took just a few minutes on the Stairmaster to do the trick. On others, like today, only the treadmill would do.

The belt rolled beneath him, his body floating above it for a nanosecond before one foot or the other came pounding down, snapping against the rubber. It always felt as if he were in danger of racing directly through the window. If a brownout were to suddenly stop the belt, he would go hurtling backward, crashing into the girl behind him, who was lost in repetitive movements on the thigh machine.

He was staring straight ahead, trying to zone out, when Brad's voice arched over the treadmill to his right. "Hi there," he said, draping his towel over the bar and getting the belt started.

"Brad. I can't remember the last time I saw you here."

"I don't like to overdo it," Brad said, patting his round belly. "Don't want the boys in Chelsea to feel threatened."

They made small talk for a minute as Brad's power walk gradually turned into a run to match Derick's seven-mile-per-hour pace. By that point, their collective breath was too short for words.

It was all about longevity. The longer he ran, the more his thoughts splintered, dissolved into the air around him. It reminded him of the way other people talked about meditation. Derick had never been able to sit still long enough, cross-legged like a yogi, chanting some meaningless word, concentrating on not concentrating. On the treadmill, he could just focus on his feet. The thoughts went away more naturally there. Everything went away.

He forgot about Jared, about Clive, his mother, the black hole that was his career. *Just put one foot in front of the other*, he thought, *and run away from it all*.

"I don't know about you," Brad said at last, "but I'm exhausted. I'm not as young as I used to be." He slowed his belt down to a crawl and let it carry him backward before stepping forward again and shutting it off.

Derick shut his machine down as well, suddenly aware of the thick sweat rolling down from his temples. "I think I've had enough, too," he said softly. "Care for a shvitz?"

"You took the words right out of my mouth," Brad said. Derick led him downstairs to the locker room.

Their lockers were in opposite corners. Derick had to search for a minute to find his. He had bought a green combination lock because he thought it would stand out from the carbon-copy silver ones, but the color had worn away in patches, so it hardly made a difference anymore. He rolled through the combination and popped it open quickly.

He dropped his clothes to the floor in a wet pile and scooped them into a plastic bag before wrapping the towel around himself. Not far away, another man, still wearing his underwear, draped himself in his own towel, and then shimmied his way out of the briefs, which he quickly swept off the floor.

As they headed into the steam room, Brad whispered, "Straight boys, so modest. Little do they know I'm a chest man."

Brad's words echoed off the tile of the room as they entered, startling the lone inhabitant, a thin, middle-aged man in the far corner, who suddenly looked up with a combination of surprise and expectation. The white tile was slick from condensed steam. Derick climbed to the upper bench, the towel still wrapped around his waist.

"Mind if I get some steam going?" Brad said.

The man scrunched up his chin in an expression of indifference and emphasized it by shaking his head. Brad opened his water bottle and poured out a cupful over the sensor on the wall. Then he nonchalantly removed his towel and laid it out on the tile beside Derick. He sat upon it, legs folded under him.

A knocking echoed through the room, followed by the hiss of steam emerging from the bottom of the side wall. Instantly, the temperature climbed. Before the steam had fully taken over, the other man tightened his towel around himself and left.

Derick sat back against the wet tile and lifted his eyes into the steam. "I needed this," he said softly.

"What's up?"

"I just came from visiting my mother."

"That'll do it," Brad snarled knowingly.

"She has this wonderful townhouse just off Riverside, and the downstairs apartment has been empty for two years."

"Why?"

"It was my father's office. It was also the scene of the crime."

"What crime?"

"He was having an affair with one of his clients."

"In the office?"

Derick nodded. "Right downstairs from where my mother was washing his dirty socks."

"What happened?"

"She threw him out. And his office. And the place has been unoccupied ever since, when it could be generating an income." He paused, relishing the heat. "I want her to rent the place out to our friends from Indiana."

"The Billy-Bobs? Are they in town already?"

"Soon. They have a corporate hotel for now. But my mother's place would be perfect for them. You know how hard it is to find a decent apartment in New York. I wanted to spare them the trouble."

"Sweet gesture, Derick. But why does it mean so much to you? Why do you have to fix it?"

"I don't have to fix it. But they're a nice couple, and they deserve something nice. And besides, it would kill two birds with one stone. My mother would get the rent, and she'd finally be able to put the whole affair thing to rest. Right now, the place is just a dusty shrine to my father's indiscretion."

"Maybe that's the point."

Derick shook his head. "Maybe."

The steam was already beginning to die down. He could feel it condensing on his skin. He untied his towel, got up from the bench, and gave the sensor another drenching.

"What about you?" Brad said. "What's going on in Derick's world?"

"Same old, same old." He listened for the distant rumbling, which grew more raucous as the steam pushed its way through the pipes. "The writing is at a standstill."

"I heard you broke up with Jared."

Derick pulled his towel off the top bench and laid it out along the lower one, beneath Brad. He stretched out upon it, his head just beyond Brad's feet. "Yes," he said, looking up into the billowing steam.

"Why?"

Such a simple question. Such a simple syllable. "I guess we wanted different things."

"I see." Brad was just a disembodied voice at this point, floating behind his head.

"We have different interests," he went on, "different temperaments." It was the first thing that came to mind. Like the opening line of a story—no second-guessing, he had learned long ago. Just go with what comes.

The steam hid everything. There was only white in the room. When he imagined being blind, he saw an immense blackness. But it might just as well have been white.

"Do you love him?"

The steam was opening his pores, the skin tingling from his neck down to his feet.

First thing that came to mind. "Yes." He breathed in the steam, the warmth tickling his nostrils. "But is that enough?"

"What do you expect?"

"I expect to be certain. I just don't feel certain."

Brad laughed softly and quickly cut himself off. "I'm sorry. But really, Derick, what on earth makes you think love has anything to do with certainty?"

"Lots of people have that," he countered. "They know. Instantly. And they never question."

"Who have you been talking to?"

"I know a lot of couples like that."

"You know a lot of liars."

He focused on the whiteness and imagined for a moment nothing was behind it. This hollow, vaporous glow was all there was.

"What about the Billy-Bobs?"

"What about them? If their relationship appears simple to you, it means either you're not seeing the whole picture, or they're idiots."

"What?"

"Some people are just idiots, Derick. They're blessed, actually. The world doesn't touch them. They can be happy with anyone. And if they find each other, well, that's heaven on earth."

"They're not idiots."

"No." There was a sternness in the voice now, the Wizard before the curtain opened. "And neither are you."

"I should have talked to you a long time ago. Therapists have all the answers."

Brad laughed. "Oh no. We just know the right questions." He took a long pause before going on. "People are complicated, Derick. Our desires are constantly evolving. And desire is a hell of a lot more interesting than fulfillment. So as soon as we get what we want, we find ourselves wanting something else. We look at what we've attained and start to see flaws. 'Ooh, that's not what I signed up for; look, it has a chip in it; it doesn't work as smoothly as it should; it's not so pretty up close.' And we convince ourselves something better is out there. It's always *out there*."

"What is?"

"Whatever we think will make us happy. Because as long as we can convince ourselves it's *out there*, we never have to look *in here*."

"So Jared could be anyone, is that what you're telling me? I shouldn't bother expecting anything else?"

"Not exactly. Jared is what you have. And you were drawn to him for a reason."

"He's cute. He's funny. I can't make a relationship out of that."

"Really?"

He wasn't being fair. "No, of course there's more. He's smart, he's very kind. And he's strong."

"All lovely characteristics. But how does he make you feel?"

"What do you mean?"

"Derick, when you're lying in bed together, when the conversation is over, when the sex is over, when the lights are out, how do you feel just having him beside you?"

The steam was breaking up again, revealing the pale blue tile on the ceiling, the grout a hazy gray. Off to the side, a light bulb shone dimly, trapped in a protective cage.

"Alive," he said. He wasn't even sure that Brad could hear him. The word might simply have been swallowed by the steam.

He lay in silence. For all he knew, Brad was no longer there, behind him in the steam.

"Does it ever get boring," he asked into the emptiness, "listening to other people's problems?"

"Not really," Brad said. Disembodied, his voice seemed deeper. "I know I joke about that, but hearing my clients actually helps me, in an odd way. It reassures me intimacy is possible after all, if you just learn to get through the crap."

"And how do you do that?" Derick said. "Get through the crap."

"It starts with trust." Brad's voice was soft, soothing as a prayer. "I think we all know what the crap is, but we're terrified of letting go of it. You know the cliché about building walls to protect yourself. Well, it's more than that. We get so damn used to the walls, we start to think they're necessary. We believe the ceiling will cave in without them. What I try to do is convince people the protective power of the walls is an illusion. Safety comes in knocking them down. And if the ceiling does cave in, maybe they'll get a skylight and more sun."

"I can barely recognize the walls sometimes," Derick said. The steam was sinking into his skin. His muscles all felt weak, in hibernation. "They just seem natural, like they've always been there. Like they're supposed to be there. They make life easier."

"But how much of life are they actually separating you from?"

He couldn't answer. He preferred silence now. He wanted to feel nothing, for his heart to be as deaf as his ears. He wanted the moisture, sweat, steam, and endless heat to be absorbed into his skin and fill what was empty. He had to keep the ceiling over his head. He wasn't ready for a skylight.

## Chapter 22

## A Match Made in Hollywood

Maybe the thing that scared him most about fiction was the freedom. In a novel, he could put anything down on the page. Each time he settled on a plot turn, a character's hair color, or where he went to school, he would find himself questioning it, discovering a reason to change it. Gwendolyn was a natural blonde for fifty pages, until suddenly he realized she had been dying her hair all along. And in the course of a single paragraph, Roger could go from an insurance executive on Sixth Avenue to a public defender in Brooklyn. Until he rethought it all again. Writing was a puzzle whose pieces got rearranged constantly, forming a different picture each time. On good days, that is, it was a puzzle. On bad days, it was just . . .

"A muddle," he said aloud, realizing with a jolt he'd been running the vacuum over the same square of carpet for the past five minutes. It wasn't a word he used much, but it was perfect just now. He was in a muddle. He had made a muddle of everything.

The carpet was clean enough for now, or at least that one square of it. He needed something else, something more substantial than housework and puff pieces. He grabbed his coat and headed downtown to his agent's office.

He'd been avoiding Larry for months. Soon after he returned from Provincetown, he'd gotten a call from him. Larry had the perfect project lined up, a personal investment guide from a muckety-muck on Wall Street. "Your father's in the business, right?" he said. "And your sister, too? You have the inside scoop. This should be a slam-dunk."

Derick had begged off. He told Larry that Provincetown had been a revelation, that it had reinvigorated his desire to write fiction. He needed a few months, he said, to work on his novel. Once that was behind him, he'd be happy to entertain offers.

Larry hadn't gotten where he was by letting authors push him around, but he and Derick had worked together for a while, so he was willing to cut him some slack. "Call me when you're ready to make some serious money," he said, "because that ain't gonna happen with some 'novel.'"

The time had come, but money had nothing to do with it.

Larry worked out of a narrow office on Bleecker Street, behind a mottled glass door with his name in chipped paint. His secretary, Wilma, worked only a couple of days a week, so there was little formality to any visit.

Still, Derick always knocked. The glass rattled against his knuckles.

"Come on in!" Larry called in a bellowing voice. If the agenting thing didn't work out, he'd told Derick once, he could always become a conductor at Grand Central. Nobody would miss the train after his rendition of "All aboard!"

"Hi, Larry." Derick closed the door behind him and stood before the desk.

"Well, well, well, he comes up for air at last." Larry rolled his chair away from the desk and looked up at him. His belly had grown rounder, the suspenders he insisted on wearing every day stretched to capacity. "So how's the Great American Novel?"

"It's good," Derick said. "Percolating."

"Percolating," Larry echoed. "I like that. Is that the title?"

"No. No, it doesn't have a title yet."

"Good," Larry said, "cuz that one sucks."

Derick had always fantasized meeting with his agent in a room lined with books, a room that smelled as musty as the stacks of his college library. Larry's office, by contrast, was spartan. An ancient dictionary and the latest edition of *Literary Marketplace* lay lonely on one shelf, and a few manuscripts were scattered here and there, jagged pages wrapped loosely in rubber bands.

"Have a seat, Shakespeare." Larry gestured to the guest chair, which was currently occupied by a stack of manila folders. Derick picked them up and looked around for a place to put them. Larry cleared a spot on the corner of his desk.

"So, you ready to do some real work?"

"Maybe," Derick said. "It depends." The chair gave with his weight. He had to lean forward to avoid tipping over.

"On what?" Larry asked. "How hungry you are?"

Derick smiled nervously. "I'd just rather do something other than a memoir, you know."

"What's wrong with memoir? It's the hottest genre out there. Unless you can do a gluten-free cookbook. How people eat that shit is beyond me. Somebody needs to find a way to make a decent cookie without flour."

Needless to say, Larry specialized in a particular niche of publishing, and fiction was not part of it. Fiction, Larry believed, was dead. His prescience is yet to be confirmed.

"So how'd that finance book go? Did you find someone to do it?"

"Oh yeah, that's well under way. It's gonna be hot, Derick. You missed a good thing there."

"Sorry about that. The novel just . . . really . . . I had to do it."

"So what's it about? Is it a mystery? A love story?"

"Yes."

"Which? Mystery? Love story? What?"

"Both. Kind of." Derick suddenly realized he could be talking about either his novel or Clive's autobiography. Both were mysteries to him, at least.

"Good," Larry said, "because those are the only kind of fiction that sells. You want a referral? I know some people who could help."

"Thanks," Derick said. "Maybe later, when it's more polished. I'm letting it sit right now."

"Gotcha. So you want something to fill the time, right?"

"Depends."

"Yeah, yeah, June Allyson, I know." He laughed. "Is that before your time? June Allyson? Depends?"

"No," Derick said, smiling dutifully. "I get it."

Larry pushed his glasses higher up his nose and turned to the computer. "Okay," he said, "something came in just yesterday. I think you're gonna love it." He peered at the screen and jiggled the mouse in frustration. "Friggin' thing," he said, picking it up and shaking. He slammed the mouse back onto the desk and rolled it around. "Here we go."

The bookcase to Derick's left was dedicated to the volumes Larry had agented, in no particular order. He scanned the shelves, looking for his own titles. Debbie Kirkendall's was face out on the third shelf. As if Larry had known he was coming, Derick thought. Debbie smiled broadly on the cover, her head tilted to one side, hair falling to create a backdrop for her name printed along the bottom.

"Got it," Larry said. "You're gonna love this, I'm telling you. You know Frank Jones, that TV doctor? The show's called *Frank Talk*—get it?"

Derick got it. "No, I've never seen it."

"Oh, he's great. Very approachable. Anyway, he wants to write—for baby boomers, basically—*The Idiot's Guide to Aging.* He wants to let people know what to expect. You know, hormones dropping, bones cracking, whatever. This generation thinks they're invincible. He wants to set them straight. Think of it as *What to Expect When You're Falling Apart.*" Larry guffawed. He was the only person Derick knew for whom that verb was appropriate.

"Sounds . . . interesting."

He got the classic Larry gesture—arms open, head tilted, one eyebrow arched—the look that said he'd be a fool not to take it. Derick remembered that look from when the Kirkendall book was proposed. His greatest success so far, for what that was worth.

"I'll think about it," Derick said.

"Good," Larry said. "I'll hold it for you. You know you're my favorite client, but if I don't get this thing ironed out by next week, I'll lose Dr. Frank. So let me know in a couple of days, okay?"

Derick couldn't get downstairs fast enough.

Outside, the cold wind blasted his skin and sent trash on a circuitous ride through the gutter. Despite the cold, it was the sunniest day in weeks, and the streets were alive with people hoping for the death of winter. They bustled along the streets, all shiny smiling faces, eyes aglow, tongues wagging in friendly chatter. Winter was on its way out, and the world would soon come back to life.

He ducked into the nearest Starbucks, though a bar might have been a more appropriate choice after Larry. It was a little quieter there, most of the tables taken by singles, laptops gaping, earbuds shutting out the world. Derick lingered by the counter, took his time adding sugar to his latte.

He was moving toward the door when a familiar voice stopped him. "Don't tell me," Jeremy said, craning his neck to gaze at Derick's cup. "Did they spell it right?"

Derick laughed and turned the cup to show him.

"Sam?" Jeremy cried. "Is that your Starbucks name now?"

"It works. Like a charm."

Jeremy laughed. "Great. I should try it myself."

"No," Derick said. "It won't work if everyone does it. Get your own fake name."

"I'll give it a shot," Jeremy said, swooping into line. "Are you busy? Can you stick around for a bit?"

"Sure."

Jeremy smiled and waited his turn.

"So, what's up?" Derick said as they left the café together a few minutes later. Ironically, the street seemed less crowded, less noisy, with company. "I'm sorry about you and Clive."

"Yes," Jeremy said. "That's old news at this point."

"You're doing okay, though?"

"Yes, I'm fine. Everyone moves on."

"What do you mean?"

"You haven't heard?"

"I guess I haven't."

Jeremy stopped at the corner, despite the walk signal. "Clive's getting married."

"What? To whom?"

"I guess it hasn't quite hit the media yet," Jeremy said. "It will soon enough. Hell, that's what it's intended for."

"What are you talking about?"

"It's a match made in heaven. Hollywood heaven."

"Who?"

"Debbie Kirkendall."

The drink began to burn his hand. He'd forgotten to get a cardboard sleeve. "Clive is marrying Debbie?"

"Film at eleven."

"But I didn't even realize they knew each other."

"That's hardly necessary. She passed the test, that's what counts." Jeremy started across the street.

"What test?" Derick said, lagging behind.

"Vyse," Jeremy said. "She's been approved."

"They have to approve who he marries?"

"They have to approve everything."

They were approaching Sheridan Square now, and Jeremy led him onto the island, where a stand of trees drowned out the ambient voices.

"I still had hopes he was going to come out," Derick said. "He led me to believe he was going to come out."

Jeremy laughed. "I'm sorry, but if Clive were as good an actor in his movies as he is in so-called real life, he'd have an Oscar by now."

"So what happened?"

"That tabloid piece was the last straw," Jeremy said. "Even though you couldn't be sure it was Clive in the photo, the mere existence of it was enough to put the fear of God into people. Or the fear of Howard Vyse."

He sat on the bench, and Derick took a spot beside him. "Vyse got even more nervous than usual. Everybody did. Clive has been single for too long, and every once in a while my picture would end up in the tabloids, too. I was never naked, just the mysterious 'friend' of Clive Morgan, that sort of thing. So they arranged the perfect solution. God knows Debbie's career needs a boost, so it was win-win, as they say. It was all kind of provisional when he told me. She was still being vetted, I guess. But it's a done deal now. The mail-order bride is on her way."

"I'm so sorry."

Jeremy laughed. "Don't be," he said. "This enables me to really put it all behind me. I feel free."

"Really?"

"Clearly you've never been in love with a movie star," Jeremy said. "They're very seductive."

"I'm sure."

"Clive Morgan can turn on the charm when he wants to. And make promises like nobody's business." He waved a hand in the air, taking in the neighborhood. "But in the end, it's all about his career. That will always come first. He has millions of people who love him. What's one more or less?"

The doorman at Clive's building recognized him, though he hadn't been there in several weeks. Not waiting for him to call upstairs, Derick slid past when the elevator door opened. A well-dressed elderly woman exited, her face disguised behind wide-framed sunglasses. Derick quickly took her place and pressed the *close* button before hitting Clive's floor.

Upstairs, he had visions of security guards chasing him down the hall. He rang the bell but didn't wait for an answer before rapping on the door.

After what seemed like several minutes, the door finally creaked open and Greta was standing before him, her face as expressionless as ever.

"I need to speak to Clive," he said breathlessly.

"Mr. Morgan is unavailable at the moment," she said. "If you had waited, the doorman could have told you that."

"I need to speak to him."

"I'm sorry, Mr. Sweetwater. That is impossible." Her accent seemed thicker suddenly, the *w*s slithering into *v*s, the *th* a Teutonic *z*.

He had a sudden vision of *Dawn Comes Early*, the film he had watched with Jared the night of their first New York date. At this point, he was supposed to push the door open and run through the apartment calling Clive's name. Preferably with gun drawn.

"It's all right, Greta."

Or this scenario, he thought, as Clive appeared behind her shoulder. Less the espionage plot than the melodrama.

Slowly, Greta backed away. "I don't think this is a good idea," she said to Clive.

"It's all right. I'm sure Mr. Sweetwater will only be a minute."

"You lied to me," Derick said as Greta shut the door behind him. "You lied about everything."

"Derick, please, calm down." Clive led him toward the study. "Greta, could you give us a minute, please?"

Greta was wringing her hands. "Mr. Morgan, I really don't—"

"It's all right, Greta," Clive said, nearly pushing Derick through the doorway, "I assure you." He slammed the door, and the sound echoed briefly in the tiny room, the way the softest cough would reverberate terrifyingly in a cave.

They faced each other for a moment, no more than six feet apart, eye to eye, before Clive finally broke the gaze and turned toward the bar. "What are you so upset about?" he asked among the clinking of glassware.

"I heard about Debbie," Derick said. "You're marrying Debbie Kirkendall."

Turning back, Clive handed him a drink, whiskey not quite covering the ice cubes. When Derick ignored it, Clive laid the glass on the table and took a seat.

Derick remained standing. "Was this a setup from the beginning? You knew that I'd ghosted Debbie's book. Is that why you chose me for yours?"

"No, Derick," Clive said, cradling his glass, "I'm afraid that was a coincidence."

"I don't believe in coincidences."

"Nevertheless, occasionally they do occur. The truth is that I read your book because . . . well, someone was urging me to meet Debbie. And I wanted to know as much about her as possible."

"It goes back that far? This arranged marriage of yours."

"Derick, you don't understand. Now please, sit."

The familiar chair felt strangely uncomfortable, constricting. Once again, he looked across the table at Clive. Too bad the recorder wasn't sitting between them this time.

"I admired the book. And when I met Debbie, I asked her about it. She was quite modest and freely admitted she hadn't written it herself. She told me about you. She was very complimentary of your talents." Clive paused for a sip of whiskey. His eyes met Derick's over the lip of the glass. "So when we met in Provincetown, I was perhaps as surprised as you. I felt like I was meeting a celebrity, too."

"But you led me to believe that the book would be your coming-out story. And all the while, you were . . . what, interviewing a potential wife?"

"We live in different worlds, Derick."

"I suppose we do. In my world, people are honest about who they are."

Clive threw his head back and laughed. "Really, Derick. Do tell."

"What does that mean?"

"You think it's easy being so open, whether in my life or yours or anyone else's? The whole world is full of people pretending. That's how I earn my living. When audiences come to my films, they're imagining themselves living the lives they see on the screen. And when they read the tabloids, they imagine living the life I call real. Everyone wants to be a *star.*" He spat the word out like poison.

"Was it Vyse?"

Clive put the glass down and folded his arms. "In old Hollywood, it would have been the studios. You have no idea how many 'arranged marriages' there were then."

"You tried it once before," Derick said, "with Alison."

"Yes. But I've been single for quite a while now. And I'm sure you appreciate the rumor mill. Particularly after their latest attack." Clive cast his eyes down toward the Oriental rug. "The more I got to know you, once we'd started working together, the more impressed I was. You were so enthusiastic about the book," he said, "so reassuring that it was the right thing to do, tell the world my truth. And I saw something else. The way you talked about your new boyfriend."

"Did I talk to you about Jared?"

"Only a word here and there. When I asked what you were up to in the evening and you said you were going to dinner or a movie, your whole face lit up, Derick. I saw what love was doing to you, the comfort it gave you, the sense of joy. It seemed to free you. Love has never done that for me, because I've always kept it behind closed doors."

"I thought the book was going to change that."

Clive smiled wistfully, and their eyes finally met again. "So did I. That was my intention. Really, it was. I wanted what you had." The late afternoon sun cast a golden beam onto the bookshelves behind Clive's head, cutting a diagonal swath across the spines. "But in the end, I couldn't do it. You see, Derick, that's *not* who I am. I don't have that courage."

Their meeting ended as it had begun, with a long-held silence, words spent or proven futile. Finally, Clive rose from his chair and led Derick to the door. They passed by a Nicoletti sketch he had admired on his first visit, a charcoal study for the oil portrait that hung in the living room. Behind Clive's head, Derick caught his own reflection in the glass, his soft, blank expression.

Greta was waiting anxiously in the next room. She squinted at him, as though she could read his thoughts with sheer effort.

"Good-bye, Derick," Clive said. Holding the door open, he paused for a moment, and something flickered across his face—a struggle between personality and character.

The scene ended with the familiar click of the deadbolt echoing in the empty hallway. It could have been a movie. Maybe, he thought, it all had been.

On the way downstairs, he texted Larry. Dr. Frank would have to write his own book. Derick was out of the business.

## Chapter 23

### Twenty-three

He wandered through the park alone for a while until the sky turned from white to gray. As the sun faded, the entire landscape turned into an Ansel Adams print, black branches like sharp fingers grasping at an empty sky.

Home at last, he kicked off his wet shoes at the door and headed for his desk. He needed to do something different, something that had nothing to do with Clive Morgan.

The novel had left off in mid-sentence.

```
He had only wanted to protect her.
Gwendolyn needed protecting. She clung to
his arm when they crossed the street,
looked away when strangers approached.
The world and all its stimuli were too
much for her to bear at times; it pained
her just to look at it. She needed him to
field it all for her, to absorb some of
the energy and be her white knight, her
protector. If the pain clung to him in-
stead, he was a man. He could bear it.
That was the price he paid for love.
There was
```

*There was what?* Derick asked himself. He wondered why he'd stopped just there, why he'd run out of steam at precisely that point. He had no idea what he'd been thinking.

The cursor flashed. Derick rose from his chair, poured himself a whiskey, and stared at the screen. He paced and poured another whiskey. He watched a few minutes of TV, stared out the window, paced, and poured another.

"Writer's block?"

He heard the voice in his head, like one of those sudden eruptions from his conscience warning whenever he was about to make a misstep. Only this time the voice had a very upper-crust British accent.

"It's a dreadful feeling. I had it for years once, couldn't write a word."

He might have been in a movie, one of those horror films that even Clive never deigned to make, where the protagonist sits in a dark room and is suddenly confronted by god knows what mysterious shadows. Derick had seen enough of those movies to know this was the moment he should turn around in his chair and check out every corner of the apartment just in case.

Nothing, of course. The room was free of ghosts. He couldn't be so sure about his head, but this was not the time to sift through that rubble.

He started. Anything was better than nothing. Even if he just randomly hit keys, putting gibberish onto the screen, it would get some flow. He might even trick himself into writing something decent.

> There was an odd pleasure in it, taking the hits for her, being battered by the world he protected her from. He built her a castle, a sandstone fortress in the middle of the richest city in the world, and carved a moat around it that only he could cross. Gwendolyn was safe, and he could be the world for her.

A floorboard creaked behind him, and he felt an unseen shadow cross his back. Fixated on the screen and still a little anxious about the voice he'd imagined, he didn't bother turning around this time. He heard a throat clearing before the faltering voice resumed from somewhere in the room.

"Oh dear," it said, masculine but disturbingly high-pitched, "that doesn't sound like you at all. Have you been talking to Eleanor Lavish?"

Slowly, Derick craned his neck toward the window seat. An elderly man sat before him, shoulders hunched inside a heavy black greatcoat, hands folded in his lap. He was smiling sadly beneath a thick, graying mustache.

"Have I taught you nothing?" he asked, shaking his head subtly. His face was dominated by a wide, hawk-like nose that obscured the midpoint of his mustache. A series of deep wrinkles creased his temples, radiating from the outer edge of either eye. It was the face that had peered back at Derick from the covers of his favorite books—*Howards End* and *A Passage to India*. This was absurd. Too much whiskey, no doubt.

"I'd say you're in quite a muddle, my young friend." Despite the words, the old man's voice was surprisingly soothing. "*He could be the world for her*? Surely you're not serious. Is this a parody you're writing?"

"No," Derick said, his frightened voice shaking its way through the syllable. "It's supposed to be . . . well, I don't know what it's supposed to be."

"That's evident. Now, what would you *like* it to be?"

The question was so probing, Derick hardly had time to balk at its being posed by a hallucination. "Well," he said, "I'd like it to make sense."

"You'd like what to make sense?"

"Their story."

"Be precise, my boy. We're only talking about your desire, not the final result. In your fantasy, you can have whatever you want. For heaven's sake, you have *me* in the room at the moment—doesn't that prove my point?"

You can't argue with an idol, Derick decided, even if he is imaginary. "I want it to be a sympathetic satire. I mean, the circumstances can be heightened, even a bit absurd, but I want the reader to sympathize with the characters, see them as real people."

"Marvelous!" Forster said, clapping his hands. "And quite a challenge, I might add. How do you propose to meet it?"

"Shouldn't I be asking you that?"

"No, no, my boy. I can't write it for you. That wouldn't work at all. My voice is a hundred years past its time! They wouldn't care if I were Shakespeare, I'd be laughed off the page. No, no, no, you must do it yourself, in your own way. I'll just provide a little . . . inspiration."

"So a clue, maybe?" Derick looked beseechingly at the apparition.

"All right. First of all, does the phrase 'show not tell' mean anything to you?" Forster gestured a dimpled chin toward the computer screen.

"I'm telling too much?"

"My dear boy, you are telling it *all*. You must learn to respect the reader's intelligence. Of course, I know today's readers aren't as intelligent as mine were, but we can't give in to that now, can we? Where would the world be if everyone could understand everything? There wouldn't be a great deal worth understanding, now would there?"

"I suppose not."

Forster nodded happily, his eyes shut in gentle satisfaction. Derick turned back to the computer. He entered a string of returns until he got to a blank screen.

> She clung to his arm as they crossed the street. Even with her full weight leaning upon him, he felt light. Gwendolyn hadn't gained a pound after all these years—two children and a life of leisure. They dodged the crowd on Fifth Avenue, Gwendolyn never looking up to see the onslaught. Roger steered them like a tugboat in the harbor. It was his job just to get through.

He had never spent so much time on a single paragraph. Stamping the last period, he clicked *save* and sat back once again in his chair. He could feel the old man's heavy breath just behind his ear as he leaned forward to read over Derick's shoulder.

"Much better," Forster said. "You see how we learn so much about Roger now simply through his attitudes, his ability to observe? It's in the moment, not his ruminations. Anyone can ruminate, for heaven's sake. You want your characters to *live!* So much better than all that . . . what was it, white knights and damsels in distress? Oh, dear." Reflected in the flickering monitor, he creaked back to his full height, taller than Derick had always imagined. "Yes, this is much better. Now I'm actually interested."

"Thank you," Derick said.

"What happens next?"

"He leaves her."

"After all that? My, things have certainly changed since my day." Forster folded his hands before his chest, locking his long fingers and drawing taut the loose, mottled skin. "Why does he leave her?"

"I don't know," Derick said. He stared at the screen, Forster's reflection minuscule in the corner. "He gets tired, I guess."

"This isn't just a story, is it, Freddy?"

Derick turned around and gazed into the old man's face. He looked so real, as if he were actually standing in the room, a real man covered in a greatcoat and not just a convenient ghost.

"Don't just restate the facts," Forster said, his voice fallen to a whisper. "Don't be limited by what actually happened in the world. This is a novel. Novels aren't about facts. They're about truth. What you are obliged to show me here is the *truth* of these people's lives." He stopped in front of the cold fireplace, his shadowed body framed by matching sets of brass pokers.

"I'm not sure I know it."

Forster shook his head slowly. "My dear boy, you know everything about it. It's the same truth for all of us. It's only a mystery if you're not observant. And most people are blissfully unobservant. But *you* are a writer. It's your job to see on their behalf." And suddenly, despite the darkness, the old man's eyes actually twinkled—if anything about this unreal moment could be termed *actual*. Derick felt the reluctance, his own disbelief, spilling away. Forster could as easily have been talking about himself. Whether he was actually standing in the room, giving a writing lesson forty years after his own death, was a question of fact. Truth was an entirely different matter. Derick cast him a grateful smile and turned back to his work.

He wrote quickly, not editing as he went, but simply letting the story tell him where it was going. The words formed themselves upon the screen, one letter at a time, typos multiplying as his fingers occasionally rushed to get through a flickering idea. In the corner of the screen, he could still see Forster's figure, standing in the back of the room, smiling like Mona Lisa, another muse certain of her task.

He awoke at the keyboard, his head resting on the desk. He jostled the mouse as he sat up, and the dancing cube on the screen flew away into the darkness, replaced by a white page dense with type. Still groggy, he glanced at the corner of the monitor for the time. It was 4:13. He had been asleep for a couple of hours, at least.

He barely remembered writing the words before him on the screen, pages of a scene that had somehow spilled out of him in the night. Squinting, he read over the last few paragraphs, and it began to come back to him. Roger and Gwendolyn were arguing. He saw real emotion on the page now, not the weighted silence of before, characters and author alike afraid to say what needed to be said.

> She wanted to be swept away. That what she called it, a line she'd heard in

a movie she could no longer remember. "I want to be swept away," she said.

"Swept away?" Roger repeated. "What the hell are you talking about? You wouldn't know passion if it bit you in the ass."

"Oh, but you know all about it," she said. "You've swept away quite a few in your time, haven't you?"

"Gwendolyn, please. Have another martini." He poured several shots of gin into the shaker.

"I know about Ellen," she said. "I know all about her."

It still needed tinkering with the dialogue and more physical description, but it was definitely better than where he'd started. Somewhere between the lines, perhaps, it was beginning to click.

He backed up the file onto a flash drive and closed Word. Enough fiction for one night. Before bed he needed a dose of real life.

He went to the *Times* website first, to see what he was missing back in the real world. Terrorist attacks in the Middle East, bickering at City Hall. He surfed for less disturbing stuff—horoscopes, porn—then headed to the bathroom to brush his teeth.

The curtains were billowing slightly when he returned to the living room. Forster stepped forward from the fireplace, as though he'd been hiding in the shadows all along.

He moved slowly toward the computer, the monitor lighting up his face, revealing the depth of ninety years' worth of experience.

"Ah, what a contraption. If I'd had one of these . . ."

"Yes?"

The old man looked up from the screen, smiling brightly. His teeth were yellow, but surprisingly straight. "I never would have used it," he admitted. Behind him, a bare-chested stranger smiled on the screen. "Too impersonal, somehow."

"Some people like that."

"So it would seem."

Derick smiled.

"That's what I came back to talk to you about."

"What?"

Forster cocked his head toward the desk. "Go back to the computer and find your story."

"Okay." It wasn't worth asking anymore if he was dreaming. It was safer just to go with it. Sitting at the desk again, he pulled Roger and Gwendolyn back onto the screen and scrolled toward the end.

"Let's see," Forster said, peering over his shoulder. His coat smelled damp, mildewy. But then again, he had been wearing it for forty years. "We've gotten rid of the purple prose." He took the mouse in his hand and scrolled for a moment, nodding in satisfaction. "We've gotten rid of the sentimentality." He stood to his full height again, smiling broadly. "Now there's only one thing left to get rid of."

"What?"

"Gwendolyn."

Derick smiled and scratched his chin. "I *was* concerned about that name," he murmured.

"No, no, no," Forster tittered, "not just the name. Although I imagine one would be hard-pressed to find a twenty-first century American woman named Gwendolyn. No, my boy, you must get rid of the *character*."

"The character? But she's the entire story."

"Precisely." Forster hissed out the word and sealed his lips in self-satisfaction. It was like the end of a lecture, or a psychiatrist's reaction to the patient's expected revelation about childhood abuse.

"I don't understand."

"Frederick, Frederick, Frederick." Forster smiled again. "Do you know that one of my favorite characters was named Frederick?"

"*A Room with a View,*" Derick said. "It was my mother's favorite book. That's where Lucy and I got our names."

"Yes, of course. Your mother's a wiser woman than you give her credit for." He paused. "But now, imagine what would have happened if I had written that book about Frederick instead of his sister."

"What do you mean?"

"Don't you think he might have been a somewhat better match for George?"

"I never thought about it."

Forster's eyes grew misty. "I did," he said quietly. "I thought about it quite a lot."

"But didn't you tell that story eventually? You wrote *Maurice.* And all those short stories."

"Ah, yes. Opus posthumous. In which the hero either dies a violent death or retreats into the nebula with his illiterate boyfriend."

"But that was beautiful."

Forster sighed. "Oh, Frederick. It isn't beautiful, it's pathetic. In my day, the only choice for happiness was to escape the world. To lose everything for love. And yes, I believed it was worth it. But did you notice? I never took my own advice."

"What are you saying?"

"You, my boy, have no excuse. Your characters don't have to hide who they are, and you don't have to hide behind them. There is only one way for you to write your book—the honest way. *You* are Gwendolyn."

"But it's not my story."

"Not the details, perhaps. But you understand what she's feeling. You know the desire to be swept away. You understand Roger, too. They're both you. In truth, it has to be your story. Or there is no story to be told."

This was all too much for one night. Suddenly, Derick understood why Ebenezer Scrooge had finally given in.

"Now," Forster said, hovering closer once more. "Let's try again, shall we? Do it for me."

Derick placed his hands on the keys, the gentle ridges on the *f* and the *j* helping him keep his place, and closed his eyes. He waited a moment, breathed, and typed.

It all began, he wrote, with the room.

# Chapter 24

## Fate

It was his place. It seemed like a waste of money, actually—paying admission to the museum and heading straight for the one spot he'd already practically memorized, ignoring two millennia of art history. But he didn't come there for the paintings on the walls. On days like this, he came merely to contemplate the past.

The sun shone brightly through the wall of windows facing the park, illuminating the nearly orange sandstone of the Temple of Dendur. He never ceased to be amazed by the enormity of the room. The temple took up less than a quarter of the space, as if it weren't the monument itself that was important, but the atmosphere it created. The energy needed room to spread. It needed this great space, whose height and breadth dwarfed everything, even in this overstuffed city.

The hardy visitors who came to the museum for anything other than the Rembrandts meandered through in a hush, acknowledging the sacredness of the space. Their whispers bounced off the high ceiling and broad walls in a meditative *Om*. Derick sat on the long bench on the Fifth Avenue side and gazed at the reconstructed temple. He thought sometimes that if he stared long enough, the meaning of the hieroglyphs lining its walls would become miraculously clear, the indecipherable figures finally revealing themselves as elements of the language they once were.

But the unknowability was somehow satisfying. He had made a habit of coming there when things in his life were just as inscrutable as the writing on the temple walls, when nothing made sense as he knew it.

He had misread everything lately. Nothing was as it seemed anymore. But all he knew for sure was that the illusions were illusions. He still had no idea what lay beneath.

Gazing at the temple, he tried to still the theories bouncing their way through his muddled mind. He spent too much time searching for connections between things, explanations of human behavior. His imagination had constructed an entire way of life for Clive, another for Jared. Another, perhaps, for himself. He no longer had to doubt his gift for fiction.

A small group of children were laughing loudly beside the temple. He turned his attention in their direction, hoping to give a parent the evil eye. Almost immediately, the children scurried away and into the next exhibit hall. In their place he saw a familiar gray-bearded head bowed to examine the stones at the base of the temple. Derick rose from his seat and joined him.

"How are you, Bob?"

Bob turned with a start and pulled Derick into a tight embrace. "I'm great," he said, drawing away but still firmly gripping Derick's arm.

"Where's Bill?"

Bob was still beaming. "He's upstairs, lost somewhere in the Renaissance." He finally released Derick, whose arm throbbed for a moment longer. "I've never been much into that representational stuff," Bob went on. "I like my art a little wackier."

"Wackier?"

"There isn't a lot here for me," he said. "That's how I got through it so quickly. I'm more into abstract expressionism, the Impressionists when I'm feeling generous. I'll drag him to MoMA later."

"Wow," Derick said. "I—"

Bob smiled. "You didn't peg me for an art snob, did you?"

Derick laughed. "Uh, no."

"I am so excited to be in New York," Bob said. "I'll probably *live* in places like this."

"I'm glad," Derick said. "You seemed so ambivalent before."

Bob smiled knowingly. "Imagining it was one thing," he said. "Living here is another."

"Speaking of living ..." Derick led him toward the temple's entrance, where a clump of people were waiting to step inside. "I'm still working on my mother."

"Who isn't?" Bob said with a laugh. "No worries, though. The hotel's fine. And Bill's office has us fixed up with a realtor. We'll have a place of our own in no time."

"But her place is perfect for you. I know you'd love it."

"As long as I have a place to hang my hat," Bob said, "I'm fine." He winked, bearded cheek lifting in a familiar way. Derick's father winked like that, usually a sign for cutting off a conversation, sealing a deal. But Bob did it with a smile that felt genuine. With Bob, it was an opening instead.

"How's married life treating you?" Derick said as they moved closer to the doorway.

"It's great."

"Does it feel different?"

"Not really. We've been together for so long, the marriage license was really just a formality."

A chilly draft greeted them as they entered the temple. It was dimmer inside, just enough to encourage a reverent silence. The space fit only a few people at a time. They moved slowly, silently, in an orderly line. There really wasn't much to see. It wasn't about seeing for Derick. The feeling the old stones conjured up was more important for him.

"Well," Bob said as they emerged back into the brightness, "that was interesting."

"This is my favorite place in the city," Derick confessed as they retraced their steps down to the modern tile of the larger room. The space seemed suddenly full of echoing whispers.

"Why is that?"

"The quiet, I guess, the sense of history. Even though we're obviously surrounded by the twenty-first century, in an odd way it's like we've been transported to antiquity."

"A simpler time?"

"I don't know about that. But certainly more focused. They may not have known as much or had as many options, but I think life was pretty clear for them. They had certainty."

Bob stopped beside the window, his face framed by the expanse of the park. "Isn't it the lack of certainty that makes people create gods and temples to them?"

"I suppose so. In that sense, I guess we haven't changed all that much." Derick laughed, shaking his head. "When I was a kid, my parents would drag me to St. Patrick's now and then, just to look around. Our regular church was on the Upper West Side. I think they brought me to the cathedral to impress upon me that there was something bigger than me out there."

"Did you need reminding?" Bob asked. "Were you an arrogant little boy?"

"Yes, I suppose I was. But comparing me to people who put their faith in an imaginary cast of characters with wings on their backs didn't help any."

"What do you put *your* faith in?"

"Good question," Derick said. "Art, maybe?"

Bob's gaze didn't alter. His pale eyes were open, waiting. No winks.

"What about you?"

Bob smiled again, more broadly now. He looked off at some indistinct spot in the room, as if he could see something there, something no one else could. "It sounds like a cliché," he confessed after a long pause.

"What?"

He turned back to Derick, his eyes darker suddenly, as though they'd acquired depth. "Love."

Derick felt his lips curling into that familiar smile, the condescending one he turned on at parties when someone said something stupid or absurd.

He caught himself and instead of just nodding politely, said, "How do you do that? How do you allow yourself to depend on something so undependable?"

"That's just it, Derick. That's why they call it faith."

"But with all the things you can control in life," Derick said, "why grant so much power to something you can't? I think it's safer to just depend on myself."

Now it was Bob's turn to smile. "And you think you can control yourself?"

"Certainly more than I can control anyone else."

"But why does it need to have anything to do with control? How about surrender?"

"Surrender? That sounds like defeat."

"Oh, no," Bob said softly. His lower lip curled under his teeth and gently glided its way free. "No, quite the opposite."

"Now you're talking in riddles."

He was relieved to see Bill striding across the hall, speeding past the still milling crowd. He passed directly by the temple without even turning his head, as if he hadn't noticed its imposing presence.

"Derick!" he cried. With one arm settling across Bob's shoulders, he reached out a hand to Derick. "Fancy meeting you here, as they say."

"Yes," Derick said. "It must be fate."

Bill chuckled. "I see you've been talking to this one," he said, squeezing Bob against him. "He's the one who believes in that nonsense."

"It's not nonsense," Bob said, pulling away with a laugh.

"Of course it is," Bill insisted. "Derick, what do you do for a living?"

"You know that," Bob said.

"I know, I know, but I'm trying to make a point." He leaned toward Derick. "Well?"

"I'm a writer."

"Precisely. You're an artist." He gestured around the room. "And Bob and I happen to love art. So why shouldn't we all find ourselves in a museum, let alone the greatest one in America?"

"But he's not a visual artist," Bob said. "He's a writer."

Bill shrugged. "Six of one . . ."

They left the museum together, emerging into sharp sun-light. Hundreds of people gathered about the steps of the building, moving in every direction, huddled in clumps here and there, chatting, smoking, eating lunch. Derick had to wend his way down, looking for openings, Bill and Bob following close behind before the clusters of people reshaped and cut off their path.

Derick led them into the park, where the trees provided a mild cushion from the noise and the light.

"So how is Jared?" Bob said.

Derick stopped on the pavement and painted on a nonchalant grin. "I don't know, actually. We—we're not together anymore."

"What happened?" Bill angled his head, a gesture that suggested more professorial curiosity than sentiment.

"It just wasn't working out."

"The hump," Bob said, lifting his eyebrows toward Bill.

"The what?"

"The hump," Bill repeated. "You didn't get over the hump."

"No," Derick said, "I guess we didn't. Why do you—"

"You gotta get over the hump," Bill said.

"Yeah, you do." Bob nodded almost violently.

"What are you talking about?"

"You know," Bob said, "that moment when his beautiful eyes are suddenly bloodshot."

"The first time he farts in bed." Bill playfully squeezed Bob's arm.

"When he says something stupid in front of your friends."

"The moment," Bill said, "when you first realize you can live without him."

"Because one more minute," Bob added, "and you won't be able to."

The park was full of joggers, cyclists, romantic couples strolling. And still it felt quiet. The voices of strangers barely carried. He wished they would. He wished he could eavesdrop on someone else's conversation instead.

"So," Derick finally said, "when you do get over the hump, then what? Does it get easy?"

"Easier."

"Look," Bill said, moving closer. "It's always difficult. There are always things to learn about each other. And yourself. That's what it's all about, really. A relationship teaches you who you are."

"I know who I am," Derick said. He could feel his ears getting red.

"So did I," Bill said. "I mean, I thought I did." He looked into the branches of a tree as if he were gazing at a memory. "I thought I knew everything."

"So, what, you're happier knowing you don't know anything?"

"Kind of."

"Jared and I just have very different temperaments."

"And that's a bad thing?"

"It's fine. He can be who he is. I don't want to change him."

"But you want him to change."

"No."

"You think Bob and I are just alike, don't you?"

"You seem to have a lot in common."

Bob laughed and rolled his eyes. "Not in the beginning, we didn't."

"Really?"

Bill sighed. "Derick, do you believe in love at first sight?"

"No, not really."

"Do you believe in Mr. Right?"

"I don't know."

"But you'll know him when you see him, right?"

"I hope so."

Bill shook his head. "Not a chance."

Lucy would have none of it. "Enough is enough," she told Derick. "A person can wallow in self-pity only so long."

And with that, she hung up the phone and took a cab to the Upper West Side, bearing a bouquet of roses and a bottle of pinot noir. Their mother had never been able to resist a good Burgundy. When the bottle was empty and Lucy's voice almost as dry as the wine, it was all settled. The Billy-Bobs could move in as soon as they liked.

"What exactly did you say to her?" Derick said when they met up later that night.

Lucy leaned across the table, breasts hovering over her cosmo, and said quite plainly, "I told her she was acting like Grandma."

"Why didn't I think of that?" Derick said, knocking his temple playfully with an open palm.

"Because I'm the one with emotional intelligence." She lifted her glass with both hands, as though accepting a trophy.

That wasn't far from the truth, Derick reflected. Particularly if you defined emotional intelligence as a complete unwillingness to take shit from anybody. Lucy had been his role model since childhood, although his admiration had always been expressed mostly through avoidance. Whenever he found himself poised on a fence of indecision or tempted to do something that was probably not in his best interest, Lucy was the last person he wanted to see.

But he couldn't avoid her now. She was too excited after her conquest of their mother's depressed castle. She needed to celebrate, and for some reason, her favorite venue for celebration was a gay bar. He didn't mind that part. Derick was always up for a drink, particularly when surrounded by beautiful men. What he dreaded was that Lucy was on a roll now. At times like this, no one was safe from the bullshit detector.

She was barely done with the first drink when she hit her next target. "So where's Jared?" she said. She glanced around the room, as though expecting him to come bounding in at any minute and drape his lithe arms around Derick's neck.

"Do you want another?" Derick pointed at her cocktail.

"I'm not that much of a lush, Freddy. I'll finish this one first. Now answer the question."

"What question?"

"Where's Jared?"

Derick fought a chuckle. He tended to laugh when he was lying. And Lucy knew it.

"You broke up with him," she said flatly.

"Well . . ." And then the look he couldn't defeat—lips pursed, one eyebrow raised so that it grazed her bangs. She had recently switched to bangs. "Yes," he said finally. He felt like he should be hanging his head in shame.

"What were you thinking?"

"Not you too."

"Yes, me, too. Freddy, what am I going to do with you?"

"Nothing, Lucy. Except maybe accept the fact that I know who I am. And by the way, my name is Derick."

"No, hon," she said, tossing her head to one side, "you'll always be Freddy to me."

"Freddy is a little boy's name."

"Well," she said, finally lifting her glass again, "stop acting like one, and I might consider the change."

"That's the whole problem," he said. "No one's ever allowed to change in this family. Whatever role you were cast in thirty years ago, that's where you're stuck."

"Hey, it worked for Carol Channing. She played Dolly Levi in her seventies."

"I don't want to be Freddy Sweetwater in my dotage."

"You could do worse," Lucy said. "You could be Freddy Sweetwater and alone."

"Maybe that's how I want it," he said. "Except the Freddy part, of course."

"You want to grow old alone."

"Why not? Or to be more precise, why pretend otherwise? Doesn't everyone end up alone, anyway? Why pretend Prince Charming is out there for either one of us? Even if he does show up, it won't last. We'll both still be old maids feeding too many cats and dying in front of the television."

"Speak for yourself, you old bag." Lucy burst out laughing and had to place her drink back down lest she spill it all over the table.

And that was the end of it. The laughter broke the tension, and at that point, the conversation shifted. No more discussion of Jared, no more dirty looks. They talked instead about the usual minutiae that they never tired of—her best friend's endless diet attempts, the paucity of decent drama on Broadway, recent celebrity sightings.

Finally, Lucy relented and let him head to the bar to fetch a second round. There was no question what to order: Lucy was on a cosmo kick these days and would accept no other drink.

On the way back, he walked as carefully as possible, his eyes rolling up and down from the drinks in his hands to the people he had to make his way through. He hadn't had to concentrate this hard since the SATs.

He was nearly at the table when he spotted a familiar blond head not six feet away. He stopped abruptly and was jostled by the person behind him, the pink drinks splashing stickily onto his hands. His whole body tightened up, less to protect the alcohol than his own psyche. He prayed the blond head wouldn't turn around, and somewhere deeper inside, he felt himself craving that it would.

It did. And the face was completely unfamiliar. He breathed again, relieved. Relieved and disappointed.

"What took you so long?" Lucy said as he settled the glasses messily on the table. "And why do I get only half a drink?"

"Okay," he said, sitting, "both questions have the same answer. Look at this place!" He wiped his hands with a cocktail napkin. "Cosmos," he said. "Who are you, Carrie Bradshaw?"

"Who put cayenne in *your* Massengill, sweetheart?"

He laughed. "You really are a gay man in drag," he said. "You know that, right?"

"You've always had a soft spot for drag queens." She pursed her lips again.

"Thanks for doing what you did tonight," he said. "The Billy-Bobs will appreciate it."

"Why was it so important to you?"

"I don't really know. I just like them. I mean, they're not like anyone else I've ever met. They're not your typical New York sophisticates, they're more like Z-Gays than A-Gays. But maybe that's it. They're real somehow." He laughed and gestured at the room. "They'd probably hate this place. No flannel."

"It's funny," she said, "how you can sometimes connect so easily with people you'd never seek out. Being thrown together is a strange opportunity for bonding. It makes life seem like an Irwin Allen movie."

"But life *is* an Irwin Allen movie, haven't you heard?"

"So who do you like more," she asked, "Bill or Bob? Assuming you can tell them apart."

"A while ago I would have said Bill without hesitation. But I got a vibe from Bob when I ran into them at the museum. He's an old soul."

"That sounds nice."

"It is. I mean, both of them are free of pretension. And they don't wear their gayness on their sleeves. They're men who just happen to be gay."

"You like that, dontcha?"

"Yeah," he said. "This shit gets old."

"This shit," Lucy said, gesturing around the room, "is real, too."

"Says the lone woman in the joint."

"You know, Freddy, sometimes I think I'm gayer than you are."

She pulled her chair closer and held her glass from the top, fingers splayed around the rim. "What did he do to you?"

"Who?"

"Dad."

"Nothing. What are you talking about?"

Now it was her turn to sigh. "Honey, you've spent your life trying to please him. But he's really okay with you as you are, don't you know that?"

"I don't know what you're talking about, Lucy. I know who I am. I told you that already."

"I know who you are, too, bro. But I think sometimes you wish you were someone else."

"Who?"

"You can be happy, you know," she said softly. He was amazed he could hear her over the crowd, but the ambient noise had become merely a low-grade murmur.

"I *am* happy."

"This is me, Freddy."

"Don't call me that."

"It's who you are, Freddy."

"I am who I *say* I am, Luce. *I* get to decide that."

She shook her head gently. "No," she said. "That's exactly the point. Nobody gets to decide that."

He gazed into his drink, the lemon twist floating precariously in the pink alcohol. For a second, he thought he could see his reflection on the surface, but when he lifted the glass, the image rippled into nothing.

# Chapter 25

## Clive's End

Time passed, the one thing you can't stop, even when you're standing still. Months passed, long enough for the earth to shift on its axis a bit, for spring showers to give way to summer heat, time enough for a dusty hovel to be reborn as a beautiful home.

The place was unrecognizable. The white walls had been repainted in vibrant maroon in the living room and lavender in the hall. The bath, just visible from the foyer, had been papered over with a gilded paisley design. The cold, angular furniture Derick remembered had been replaced by dark colonial pieces, all curved wood and pale upholstery.

Stella Sweetwater prided herself on being *au courant* in all things. But once she reached that certain age at which a woman's wardrobe freezes, ceding the dynamics of fashion to a younger generation, her home became her only canvas. Her style of hair and dress might now be forever limited to the classic wavy chignon, the perfectly tailored cardigan and pencil skirt, but the apartment freely changed with the times.

So this was not her thing at all.

She squeezed Derick's arm as soon as they strolled in. He was afraid she might faint. "Are you okay?" he whispered, leaning in.

She greeted his gaze with a mischievous grin, eyes alight. "I love it," she said. In a cartoon, she would have been portrayed as a panther licking its chops.

"Really?"

"Yes," she said, her eyes suddenly drawn to a Mucha print that nearly covered an entire wall of the foyer.

Derick got it in a flash. Her reaction had nothing to do with the Billy-Bob's particular design choices. It was as if someone had stepped into her past and drenched it in lime, the memories disintegrating instantly, covered by a radically different present.

"Welcome!" Bob said, striding up with flutes of sparkling wine. "I'm so glad you could come."

"Wouldn't miss it," Stella said as they both took glasses. "It's so nice of you to arrange this little gathering tonight."

"Well," Bob said, "we just had to give the place a proper debut. We love it, you know."

And suddenly Bill was there, the two of them side by side, like matching salt and pepper shakers. "Would you like a tour?"

Stella's voice arched over her son's muffled *maybe later*. "Absolutely! I can't wait to see what you've done to the place."

Bill took her arm and led her through the living room. "Have some hors d'oeuvres," Bob said to Derick, gesturing toward a table set up in the next room.

This smaller space, Derick remembered, had been his father's inner office. In place of the floor-to-ceiling bookcases and the marble-topped desk that had once dominated the room was a side table loaded down with finger food, and a love seat aimed directly at a wide-screen TV.

"The place looks wonderful," Derick said, spreading a slab of Brie onto a Triscuit.

"Thanks," Bob said. "Really, I can't thank you enough for arranging this. That corporate hotel was so cold. But this place feels like home."

"I'm glad. It looks very lived in already."

Bob laughed. "Oh, that's just because the furniture's so damn old. We've had it for years. We thought about getting new stuff, but there's something comforting about having it all here, at least for now."

Chris and Brad approached from the foyer, the lower half of Chris's face obscured by the leaves of a plant he was carrying.

"Happy housewarming!" he said, awkwardly depositing the plant into Bob's hands.

"Thank you! It's lovely." Bob made a show of turning the plant around to find the prettiest angle and set it on the table, away from the hors d'oeuvres.

"I went for something more traditional," said Brad, holding aloft a bottle of wine.

"Oh well, we may need to break into this before the night is over," Bob said, barely glancing at the label.

They all settled themselves in with drinks and commandeered a corner of the living room. A dozen or so other guests were collected in pockets throughout the space.

"Who are all these people?" Chris said. "You guys sure make friends quickly."

"Mostly Bill's work colleagues," Bob said. "I haven't even met them all myself yet."

"Have you changed your mind about New York?" Brad said.

Bob's eyes lit up. "Oh yes, I love it! I've been to a different museum each week since I got here."

"Well, that's something."

"So," Bob said, moving in closer, "what do you guys think about our old friend Clive?"

He was looking straight at Derick, who mumbled awkwardly, "What about him?"

"Oh my god, haven't you heard? It was on *E!* last night."

Brad scowled. "Sorry, I missed the Kardashians this week."

"Wait, it's in the paper, too." He scurried away and began riffling through a stack of magazines on a side table in the foyer.

"Another tabloid?" Chris said when Bob returned, clutching a magazine against his chest like a teenager trying to hide his porn.

"Look."

It wasn't a tabloid. It was the latest *Vanity Fair,* hot off the

presses. On the cover was a collage of celebrity photos—
Felipe de Vega, Lauren King, a handful of others, and at the
center, Clive Morgan. The headline read, *Vyse Foundation:
Hollywood's Walk-in Closet.*

"Oh my god!" Chris cried, quickly flipping through the
pages.

"The quasi-religious Vyse Foundation," he read aloud,
"has been the center of controversy for years, with allega-
tions of brainwashing, tax evasion, and embezzlement
surrounding its practices. We can now add blackmail to the
list. An extensive investigation reveals that Vyse maintains
its power by threatening to expose the sexual secrets of a
number of Hollywood stars."

"I told you they were up to no good," Brad intoned.

"That poor bastard," Chris said, shaking his head. "He's ruined now."

"Ruined, my ass," said Brad. "I have no sympathy for any
of them. How many millions does he make on each movie? He
could afford to come out of the closet."

"What if he never works again?"

Brad snarled. "Then he never works again."

"No wonder he makes all those shitty action films," Chris
said. "Blackmail's expensive."

"It's just hard to believe," said Bob. "A church blackmailing
its members. I mean, it's the twenty-first century, not the
Spanish Inquisition."

"Where have you been, honey?" Chris said. "The twenty-
first century is nothing if not insane with religious nuts. Ar-
mageddon and all, they're just waiting for the bomb to drop
and Jesus Himself to show up in a new dress."

As if on cue, their eyes were drawn to the front door.

Lucy had a way of entering a room. While her mother
made a point of gliding in, commanding attention merely by
quietly expecting it, Lucy relied on noise—the voice arched
over the murmur of the room, the heels snapping loudly on
the floorboards, the bracelets jangling on her forearms.
There was no missing her.

She rushed up now and stood at Chris's side, gazing over his elbow at the article. "Well, that's old news," she said.

"What do you mean?"

"Is there one person listed there who hasn't had gay rumors swirling about him or her for years?"

"Well," Derick said, "rumors aren't truth."

Lucy snorted. "Really? They don't spring up from nowhere, you know."

"Still, people do have a right to their privacy, don't they?"

"Oh, please." She waved a hand dismissively in the air, her bracelets ringing like castanets. "I saw Morgan on TV tonight, denying everything."

"Seriously?" Chris said.

"Oh yeah. It was like watching Larry Craig all over again. 'I am not a gay man.' And there was Debbie Kirkendall, standing beside him with a lascivious look on her face as if he'd just made her come three times in a row."

"Maybe he's bisexual," Bob offered.

"Yeah," said Lucy, "and I'm a tricycle." She grabbed the magazine away from Chris and started flipping through it. She gave up interest quickly and rather cavalierly passed it back.

"So how is everyone?" she asked. "I see you're all moved in. The place looks fabulous. You could never tell that my philandering father had his trysts in this very spot."

"Lucy!" Derick raised a cautionary finger to his lips. "Mother's in the next room," he whispered.

"Yeah, well, she knows all about it." Lucy was already bent over the table, scoping out the cheese.

"Champagne?" Bob asked jovially.

"Absolutely!" Lucy cried. "You don't think I can get through this evening sober, do you?"

"What are you worried about?" Derick said as Bob hurried away in pursuit of another bottle of bubbly. "Why do you need a drink so badly?"

"Nothing," she mumbled through a mouthful of cheese. "But you know me—never turn down champagne."

"Well," Chris said, waving his own flute dismissively, "don't get your hopes up."

By the time Bob got back with a glass of for her, Lucy had filled a tiny plate with cheese and crackers. "Fabulous!" she cried, snatching the flute. "You're an angel, Bill, an absolute angel."

"That's Bob," Derick said, pasting a delicate smile on his lips.

"Of course," Lucy said. "Please forgive me. I just always think of you boys in the same breath. Like Romeo and Juliet, or Antony and Cleopatra."

The bull in the china shop had struck again, but she was the most amusing bull Derick had ever known. This was what he loved most about Lucy. "So you often mistake Antony for Cleopatra, do you?"

"In some productions. The West Village, especially."

In a few minutes, the family was reunited, Stella emerging into the room still on Bill's arm. "Lucy. You look lovely this evening."

"Why, thanks, Mom." She swayed in place to show off the soft draping of her skirt. All dark chiffon and lace, with an excess of layering. Derick half-expected her to break into a chorus of "Rhiannon."

Chris and Brad joined them in the corner, Chris's nose still buried in the magazine.

"For heaven's sake," Derick said, "can you give that thing up?" He pulled it from Chris's hands.

A familiar name in bold print at the bottom of the page caught his eye. *Story by Sera Mathison.*

"Oh god."

"What is it?" Lucy said.

"She scooped me."

"Who? What?"

"I know the writer. She also did the piece about Clive on the beach in Provincetown. I met her at the workshop."

"Was she working on this then?"

"She must have been," Derick said. "She said her dream was to be in *Vanity Fair*."

"Well, she certainly achieved that," Brad said with a hearty laugh. "Now what is this about scooping you?"

Derick sighed. Apparently, it was a night for truth telling. "So, you all know I've been working on something. Another faux biography."

"Yes," Chris said, "the mysterious memoir du jour. What's that got to do with it?"

"Oh no," Lucy said suddenly.

Chris peered at her for a moment before his eyes opened wide. "Oh no."

"Oh yes," Derick said. "Yes, indeed."

Mrs. Sweetwater frowned. "Will somebody please tell me what's going on?"

"Apparently," Brad said, "your son is writing a book about Clive Morgan."

"*Was*," Derick corrected. "I quit months ago. Over this, actually."

"Over what?"

"I knew it all," he said. "I knew about Vyse. I even met Clive's boyfriend."

"Seriously?" Lucy said. "The guy on the beach?"

"No. I have no idea who the guy on the beach was."

"So what happened? With the book?"

"It's a long story. I encouraged him to come out in the book. He said he wanted to. That was what he told me back in Provincetown, anyway, when he first approached me. He said he wanted to tell the truth."

"I can't believe you kept this to yourself for so long," Lucy said. "I mean, I'd be dying to spill!"

"That's why I could never be a ghostwriter," Chris said. "I can't keep my mouth shut. Gossip is just too tempting."

They were all laughing now, all except Derick. He felt surrounded by waves of schadenfreude.

"What's wrong?" Lucy said.

Derick's head was pounding. The room began to blur. "He couldn't be honest."

"What?"

"He couldn't be honest about who he is, and look what it's done to him."

"If you ask me," Brad said, "the Clives of the world deserve this. Deception always leads to a bad end."

Across the room, Bob had taken a seat on the sofa, in more or less the same spot where Derick's father's desk had once stood. As a child, Derick had loved playing under that desk, a shadowy space that smelled of wood. In his imagination, it became a stage, where he could enact anything he could dream of. He had been playing there one Saturday when his father unexpectedly came in with work to do. Derick tried to be quiet, but when his father sat at the desk, all bets were off. Shuffling aside to avoid his father's feet, Derick tumbled through the front opening.

"What are you doing under there?" his father yelled. His tone, in Derick's memory, seemed composed as much of surprise as annoyance. He stood up and peered over the desk. Derick's dolls were laid out on the floor—three G.I. Joes and the Barbie he had stolen from Lucy's room. She had so many, she never seemed to notice when one went missing.

"What is that, Derick?" his father boomed.

"What?" Derick swept the dolls behind him, but the secret was out. His father emerged from behind the desk and picked Barbie up by her auburn hair.

"This," he said. "You can't play with this. Give it back to your sister."

"But I—" He wanted to say he needed it. He put on little plays with his G.I. Joes. And there were very few plays you could stage without a female character. But instinctively, he knew that putting on plays with dolls intended only for battle was no better than squeezing Barbie into those gooey plastic heels. He took the doll from his father's hand and, head bowed, went back upstairs. He left the G.I. Joes on the floor but took the shame with him.

Now, almost thirty years later, he remembered every curve of the doll's body—the mechanical click under the soft skin as he bent her legs into place, the eyelashes painted on her face beneath faint blue shadow. That day, he had tucked the doll back on a shelf in Lucy's room and vowed never to touch any of her toys again. It wasn't until just before college, when she was packing them all up to give to charity, that she told him she'd known all along. Lucy had always known everything before he did.

"What are you looking at?" she asked now, smiling.

"Them," he said. He gestured toward the sofa. Bill had come up behind Bob and was gently stroking the back of his head.

"They're sweet."

"Yes." There was a flow, a lack of self-consciousness in Bill's touch. Touching Bob like that came so naturally to him, no matter who was looking, no matter what they might think.

"What's going to happen to Clive Morgan now?" Chris said loudly. "I wonder if he'll be in any more of those blow-'em-ups."

"One can only hope," Brad said.

"It shouldn't matter," Bob added, leaning into Bill's caress.

"But it will," Bill said.

Stella sighed. "And you people wonder why I'm not interested in all this Hollywood stuff. Too much melodrama." She folded herself into the armchair, which sat in the same spot where her husband's office sofa had once been, the sofa where she'd found him cavorting with Mrs. Detweiler. She seemed to have completely forgotten.

Derick carried the magazine back to the foyer, happy to never see it again. A haphazard pile of newspapers sat on the table, as if this spot were a remnant of his father's waiting room. At the top of the stack, he found a local gay rag, upside down. On the back, in a corner of the page, was an ad for a drag show at the Stonewall Inn—*Broadway Divas on Parade.* A grotesquely masculine Patti LuPone peered bug-eyed off the page, an angelic Kristen Chenoweth behind her, and just off to the side, a regal Bernadette.

He stared for a moment. Even in black and white, he could see the intensity of those eyes. The eyes were what stood out, not the springy curls that framed the face, not the smear of rouge that shaped the cheek, not the sparkle of rhinestones on the dress. Those were eyes that had seen past his own veneer, the face he turned to the world. Those eyes had seen him as he was.

"Derick, are you okay?"

Lucy was at his side again. Her hand settled softly on his arm, waking him from what felt like a trance, waking him from all of it.

"I have to go," he said.

"Where?" She dipped her head toward the table. "Oh," she said, surprise turning into excitement in her voice.

He moved to the door.

"I'll go with you," she said. Her cry caught the others' attention, and by the time Derick pulled open the door, Chris and Brad were right behind. They followed him as he raced up the stairs to the street.

"Where are we going?" Chris said, breathing hard as they hurried down the street.

But once again, Derick wasn't talking.

He flagged down a cab on Broadway, and the four of them squeezed in, Brad in the front seat to accommodate his long legs. "Sheridan Square," Derick barked to the driver.

"What are we doing?" Chris said.

"This is so romantic!" Lucy cried.

Brad just turned toward him and smiled.

"What's so romantic?" Chris persisted.

Lucy rolled her eyes. "You jumped into the cab with us and you have no idea what's going on?"

"No," Chris said. "I just got caught up in the excitement."

"Story of his life," Brad murmured and turned back toward the windshield.

The streets passed by in an electric jumble, lights and vehicles speeding in every direction. After a minute, Derick lost track of the conversation around him.

When the cab stopped on Christopher Street, Brad paid the driver, and they all spilled onto the sidewalk. The red neon sign glowed, coloring Lucy's face as she led Derick toward the door, under the red brick arch. A lifetime in New York, and he hadn't set foot in this building, where it had all begun.

As they entered, the show was just ending. The packed audience was on their feet, swaying, all eyes on the stage, where their diva was belting out "Move On" from *Sunday in the Park with George*. Derick smiled. His favorite song, his favorite show. But he had the sense that he hadn't really understood it until this moment.

The stage went black with a sudden crescendo, and when the lights came back up, she was gone. Derick pushed his way forward, the others following in a touchless conga line. Behind the stage, he drew back the purple curtain. A burly man at the side blocked his way.

"I need to see Jared," Derick said.

"Everybody needs to see Jared."

"No, really, I—he knows me. We—" He rose onto his toes to peer into the distance.

"Hold on, buddy, hold on."

And suddenly, over the guy's shoulder, he saw the familiar mane of red curls moving forward. "It's okay, Lenny."

Lenny slowly stepped aside.

"Fancy meeting you here," Jared said. Although he hadn't removed a stitch of clothing or wiped away any makeup, Derick could still see Jared clearly in the face that greeted him.

He fumbled for words, as writers often do, when they're words that count. "I tried emailing you, calling, but when you didn't respond, I—"

"I was on a cruise," Jared said. "The cell reception's not very good in the middle of the ocean." He dug one long red fingernail against the underside of another. "I got the messages. I've just been so busy since I got back. And confused . . ."

Lucy brushed up against Derick, but he was still staring into Jared's eyes.

"Hi, Jared," she said breathlessly.

Jared smiled. "Hi."

"I was an idiot," Derick said abruptly.

"Yes," Jared said, still smiling. "You were."

"I'm not anymore."

"He's not," said Lucy.

Jared laughed. "She really loves you, doesn't she?"

Derick continued to ignore her. "I'm sorry, Jared." A sudden lightness in his gut rose to his throat, like a bubble of air in water, seeking its own. "There's so much I didn't understand, about you, about us." He ran out of words. He just looked into Jared's eyes now. That was all he could do.

Jared's head bowed slightly, as if to break the gaze. When he looked up again, it was at an angle, his eyes peering through heavily adorned lashes, glitter that couldn't hide the blue.

Jared leaned in and pressed his lips against Derick's. Derick fell against him, the trim, muscular body hard beneath the soft silk of the dress.

When he drew away, Jared began to chuckle. "You're a mess," he said, wiping a long-nailed thumb across Derick's lips. He held it up for scrutiny: jungle red.

# CHAPTER 26

## Ever and Ever

One of Clive's romantic comedies would have ended right there, with the hero realizing the error of his ways and rushing through traffic, jumping over potholes, and dodging baby strollers to confess his sins. And the heroine would forgive him without taking the time to remove her makeup.

In real life, it's never quite that easy. Jared welcomed Derick's apology. In fact, they stayed up half the night talking about it. At first, he blamed the stress he had felt about Clive and the book, stress he'd been unable to discuss with anyone. But in the end, he admitted, it had nothing to do with Clive. As Brad had told him, we all have our own closets, and we're each responsible for cleaning them out.

It was a lesson Clive hadn't learned quickly enough. He and Vyse put the PR machine into overdrive after the *Vanity Fair* article, issuing denials right and left. And when *Charity* bombed at the box office, the consensus was that it had nothing to do with the scandal. His fan base had turned against him not because he was gay, but because he had denied it so vehemently for so long. Clive Morgan was ashamed of the wrong thing.

Jared understood. Jared dealt with false images every day, but consciously. He knew, with every dab of powder, every stroke of lipstick, that he was constructing something for other people to believe in. He never fell for it himself.

But if anybody has patience, he said, it's a man who has to spend an hour just to get his eyebrows right for a show.

So they worked at it together. Epiphanies don't change everything. They just give you the impetus to change things on your own.

❖

The window was cold to the touch. Derick pressed a finger against the glass, his skin a darkening pink among the snowflakes dancing on the other side. The sky met the ocean as competing shades of gray, the palette growing whiter as the sand gave way to sidewalk and the virtually untrammeled Commercial Street.

Behind him, the printer purred, spilling out pages. A compact thing not much bigger than a box of Cling Wrap, it had been a present from Jared. It wouldn't have occurred to Derick to print out anything here, on vacation. He would have kept it all on the laptop until he got home, but Jared insisted. "I hate scrolling," he'd said, slipping the printer into Derick's bag as they packed. "I want the feel of real paper in my hands."

And now he was pulling the pages out one by one, barely letting them kiss the tabletop.

"Well?" Derick asked, turning away from the storm to watch.

Jared held one hand blindly beside the printer to catch the next sheet of paper. In the other, he held a stack of loose pages and was poring over the top one, reading intensely.

"Sshhh," he said, "I'm just getting to the good part."

"There's a good part?"

Jared looked up with an exasperated smile. "It's all good," he said. "But this part's better."

Derick dutifully turned back to the window. He'd been up late, writing in the glow of the laptop as Jared slept. Something in the night had inspired him—the silence, perhaps, the stars winking over the bay. He'd come here to write, a year and a half ago. It seemed the appropriate place to finish what he'd started. That, too, was Jared's idea.

Of course, there wasn't much else to do in Provincetown in winter. The hubbub of the summer was long gone, along with virtually everyone but the locals. They'd had no trouble getting a room at the inn. To be specific, they'd had no trouble getting this particular room, the one he'd shared with Chris that summer. Derick remembered liking the view.

The view was different now, but only because everything outside was covered in snow. With the color and the noise washed away, the city was, surprisingly, even more beautiful. Provincetown wore winter well.

The printer sputtered, the last page now out and in Jared's eager hand.

"Come here," Derick whispered.

"I'm busy." Jared scooped the final sheet onto the bottom of his pile, still reading.

"It can't be that good," Derick said.

"Shut up."

Derick laughed. He'd killed Gwendolyn long ago, or at least transformed her. She was now called Geoffrey. One thing they had in common was an insistence that everyone use their full names. No diminutive Gwen or Geoff for these two.

Once he'd settled in, the book had come quickly. He could sit at the computer for hours, spilling it out. He'd wake up in the middle of the night with an idea and scratch notes onto the pad he left by the bed. Geoffrey and Roger became real to him after a while. When he wrote their first break-up scene late one night, he wept. He shut off the computer, crawled into bed, and wept. As if he'd just killed something real.

He was constantly surprised by how real it felt, far more alive than his other work. He might have told true stories before—reproducing the chronology of some stranger's life—but only now, in fiction, was he telling the truth.

He smiled and looked out the window again. The snow was beginning to taper off. He could make out shapes more clearly now, the gables on the building across the street, the stop sign on the corner. Even the horizon was becoming sharper, the line between sea and sky.

And then, abruptly, as if he'd been there all along, Derick spotted an old man in a familiar overcoat standing idly on the sidewalk. He seemed to be looking up, looking right at him, winking. But as suddenly as Derick noticed him, the old man turned and shuffled away. Derick craned his neck to follow him as long as he could, but in a moment the old man vanished, absorbed back into the snow.

"I'm getting stir-crazy," he said. "Why don't you finish it later? We should go for a walk or something."

"I'm almost done," Jared said. "And it's still snowing."

Jared slinked onto the window seat beside him, his nose still buried in the pages flopping around in his hand. In the past six months, Derick had memorized his face, watching Jared sleep so he could count the freckles behind his ear, measure the curve of his chin, the elegant swoop of his neck. He leaned forward now and kissed that neck.

"Stop!" Jared said with a laugh. "I'm trying to read."

"I'll help you," Derick said, moving his head up beside Jared's ear. "They live happily ever after."

As he pulled away, Jared peered at him over the top of the page. "I know that much," he said and returned to his reading.

# ACKNOWLEDGMENTS

For their cogent insight and advice on early drafts, I would like to thank my San Francisco brotherhood of writers: Patrick Letellier, James Van Buskirk, Andrew Ramer, and Erik Gleiberman. I am also indebted to the wonderful Jerry Wheeler, who has been a great support over the years and whose guidance helped make this book a better one.

The incomparable Dot brought my vision to life with beautiful cover photography. Immense thanks also go to my editor, Louis Flint Ceci, whose wisdom and eye for detail have been invaluable assets, and whose faith in my work has been deeply encouraging.

Finally, I must acknowledge the brilliant E. M. Forster (Morgan to his friends), whose work I fell in love with at first read many years ago. While he has never visited me in quite the way he appears to Derick in these pages, he has always been an inspiration in both my work and my life.

## About the Author

Lewis DeSimone is the author of two previous novels, *Chemistry* and *The Heart's History*. His work has appeared in *Chelsea Station, Christopher Street, The James White Review, Glitterwolf, Jonathan,* and the anthologies *Second Person Queer; I Like It Like That: True Tales of Gay Male Desire; Best Gay Romance 2014; My Diva: 65 Gay Men on the Women Who Inspire Them; The Other Man*; and, from Beautiful Dreamer Press, *Not Just Another Pretty Face*. He lives in San Francisco, where he is working on his next novel. For more information, please visit www.lewisdesimone.com.

CPSIA information can be obtained
at www.ICGtesting.com
Printed in the USA
BVOW03s2200291017
498934BV00001BA/23/P